Tarubadur Tales

-

Folklore, Fairy Tales and Legends from North Africa and Ancient Egypt

Compiled & Edited by Clive Gilson

Tales from the World's Firesides

Book 4 in Part 3 of the series: Africa

Tarubadur Tales,

edited by Clive Gilson, Solitude, Bath, UK

www.clivegilson.com

First published as an eBook in 2021

2nd edition © 2021 Clive Gilson

3rd edition © 2023 Clive Gilson

Printed by IngramSpark

ISBN: 978-1-915081-01-8

I have edited Clive Gilson's books for over a decade now – he's prolific and can turn his hand to many genres - poetry, short fiction, contemporary novels, folklore and science fiction – and the common theme is that none of them ever fails to take my breath away. There's something in each story that is either memorably poignant, hauntingly unnerving or sidesplittingly funny.

Lorna Howarth, *The Write Factor*

Tales From The World's Firesides is a grand project. I've collected thousands of traditional texts as part of other projects, and while many of the original texts are available through channels like Project Gutenberg, some of the narratives can be hard to read for modern audiences, and so the Fireside project was born. Put simply, I collect, collate and adapt traditional tales from around the world and publish them as a modern archive.

This is the fourth book in *Part 3 – Africa*, following on from the titles in *Parts 1* and *2* covering a host of nations and regions across Europe and North America.

I'm not laying any claim to insight or specialist knowledge, but these collections are born out of my love of story-telling and I hope that you'll share my affection for traditional tales, myths and legends.

Images by Open Clipart Vectors and DIY Team from Pixabay

Contents

ORIGINAL FICTION BY CLIVE GILSON

- Songs of Bliss
- Out of the Walled Garden
- The Mechanic's Curse
- The Insomniac Booth
- A Solitude of Stars

AS EDITOR – *FIRESIDE TALES* – *Part 1, Europe*

- Tales From the Land of Dragons
- Tales From the Land of The Brave
- Tales From the Land of Saints And Scholars
- Tales From the Land of Hope And Glory
- Tales From Lands of Snow and Ice
- Tales From the Viking Isles
- Tales From the Forest Lands
- Tales From the Old Norse
- More Tales About Saints and Scholars
- More Tales About Hope and Glory
- More Tales About Snow and Ice
- Tales From the Land of Rabbits
- Tales Told by Bulls and Wolves
- Tales of Fire and Bronze
- Tales From the Land of the Strigoi
- Tales Told by the Wind Mother
- Tales from Gallia
- Tales from Germania

EDITOR – *FIRESIDE TALES – Part 2, North America*

- Okaraxta - Tales from The Great Plains
- Tibik-Kìzis – Tales from The Great Lakes & Canada
- Jóhonaa'éí –Tales from America's Southwest
- Qugaaĝiŝ - First Nation Tales from Alaska & The Arctic
- Karahkwa - First Nation Tales from America's Eastern States
- Pot-Likker - Folklore, Fairy Tales, and Settler Stories from America

EDITOR – *FIRESIDE TALES – Part 3, Africa*

- Arokin Tales – Folklore & Fairy Tales from West Africa
- Hadithi Tales – Folklore & Fairy Tales from East Africa
- Inkathaso Tales – Folklore & Fairy Tales from Southern Africa
- Tarubadur Tales – Folklore & Fairy Tales from North Africa
- Elephant And Frog – Folklore from Central Africa

Preface

I've been collecting and telling stories for a couple of decades now, having had several of my own works published in recent years. My particular focus is on short story writing in the realms of magical realities and science fiction fantasies.

I've always drawn heavily on traditional folk and fairy tales, and in so doing have amassed a collection of many thousands of these tales from around the world. It has been one of my long-standing ambitions to gather these stories together and to create a library of tales that tell the stories of places and peoples from the four corners of our world.

One of the main motivations for me in undertaking the project is to collect and tell stories that otherwise might be lost or, at best forgotten. Given that a lot of my sources are from early collectors, particularly covering works produced in the late eighteenth century, throughout the nineteenth century, and in the early years of the twentieth century, I do make every effort to adapt stories for a modern reader. Early collectors had a different world view to many of us today, and often expressed views about race and gender, for example, that we find difficult to reconcile in the early years of the twenty-first century. I try, although with varying degrees of success, to update these stories with sensitivity while trying to stay as true to the original spirit of each story as I can.

I also want to assure readers that I try hard not to comment on or appropriate originating cultures. It is almost certainly true that the early collectors of these tales, with their then prevalent world views, have made assumptions about the originating cultures that have given us these tales. I hope that you'll accept my mission to preserve these tales, however and wherever I find them, as just that. I have, therefore, made sure that every story has a full attribution, covering both the original collector / writer and the collection title that this version has been adapted from, as well as having notes about publishers and other relevant and, I hope, interesting source data. Wherever possible I have added a cultural or indigenous attribution as well, although for some of the tiles, the country-based theme is obvious.

Tarubadur Tales includes a range of stories that originate in Northern Africa and ancient Egypt. The Sahara runs from east to west across the widest part of Africa, a vast desert dividing the continent into two main regions. North Africa consists of the Mediterranean coast from Morocco to Egypt and includes the valley of the Nile River as far south as Ethiopia. With strong ties to the Mediterranean and Arab worlds, North Africans felt the influence of Christianity by the A.D. 300S, and in the 700s, much of the area came under the influence of Islam.

The people of the Maghreb and the Sahara speak various dialects of Berber and Arabic and almost exclusively follow Islam. The Arabic and Berber groups of languages are distantly related, both being members of the Afro-Asiatic family. The Sahara dialects are generally considered to be notably more conservative than those of coastal cities. Over the years, Berber peoples have been influenced by other cultures with which they came in contact: Nubians, Greeks, Phoenicians, Egyptians, Romans, Vandals, Arabs, and lately Europeans. The cultures of the Maghreb and the Sahara, therefore, combine elements from indigenous Berber, Arab and neighbouring parts of Africa and beyond. In the Sahara, the distinction between sedentary oasis inhabitants and nomadic Bedouin and Tuareg is particularly marked.

The diverse peoples of the Sahara are usually categorized along ethno-linguistic lines. In the Maghreb, where Arab and Berber identities are often integrated, these lines can be blurred. Some Berber-speaking North Africans may identify as "Arab" depending on the social and political circumstances, although substantial numbers of Berbers, or Imazighen have retained a distinct cultural identity which in recent times has been expressed as a clear ethnic identification with Berber history and language. Arabic-speaking Northwest Africans, regardless of ethnic background, often identify with Arab history and culture and may share a common vision with other Arabs. This, however, may or may not exclude pride in and identification with Berber or other parts of their heritage.

The Nile Valley through northern Sudan traces its origins to the ancient civilizations of Egypt and Kush. The Egyptians over the centuries have shifted their language from Egyptian to modern Egyptian Arabic, while retaining a sense of national identity that has historically set them apart from other people in the region. Most Egyptians are Sunni Muslim and a significant minority adheres to Coptic Christianity. In Nubia, straddling Egypt and Sudan, a significant population retains the ancient Nubian language but has adopted Islam. The northern part of the Sudan is home to a largely Arab Muslim population, but further down the Nile Valley you find the largely non-Muslim Nilotic and Nuba peoples.

As you will, no doubt, appreciate, this rich melange of migrations and contacts has profoundly influenced storytelling among the varied cultural, ethnic and religious groups across North Africa. There is the usual mix of magic and animism and a strong sense of duty and morality, even if those senses are a little different to some of the cultural norms of the early twenty-first century. There is also the usual mix of force and brutality in folklore and fairy tales, themes that we have seen writ large across all of the books in the *Fireside* series.

One thing that I have taken the liberty of changing in general terms is the more overt racism and social and political supremacist influences inherent in nineteenth century presentation, particularly amongst European collectors. I have not altered the core of any story, but have mostly adapted certain characters to remove obvious biases.

That said, and as ever, selecting and adapting these tales has been both a joy and a labour, but always a labour of love.

Clive,

Bath, 2023

Part I – General North African Tales

Djokhrane And The Jays

This story has been edited and adapted from Moorish Literature, a collection work from sources such as Adolphe Hanoteau's Poésies Populaires de la Khabylie du Jurgura of 1867, Émile Masqueray's Observations grammaticales sur la grammaire Touareg et textes de la Tourahog des Tailog, and René Basset's L'insurrection Algerienne, de 1871 dans les chansons populaires Khabyles Lourain of 1892. This version was taken from the English translation introduced by René Basset and published by the University of France and the Académie D'Alger, published in 1901.

The ancestor of the grandfather of Mahomet Amokrane was named Djokhrane. He was a Roman of old times, who lived at T'kout at the period of the Romans. One of his countrymen rose against them, and they fought. This Roman had the advantage, until a bird of the kind called jays came to the assistance of Djokhrane, and pecked the Roman in the eyes until the enemy was defeated and Djokhrane was saved.

From that time forth he remained a friend to Djokhrane. The latter said to his children, "As long as you live, never eat this bird. If you meet anyone who brings one of these birds to eat, buy it and set it free."

To this day when anyone brings a jay to one of his descendants, he buys it for silver and gives it liberty. This story is true, and is not a lie.

Mohammed With The Magic Finger

This story has been edited and adapted from Andrew Lang's Red Book of Heroes, originally published by Longmans, Green And Company, London And New York, in 1909. The original story was included in Märchen und Gedichte aus der Stadt Tripolis by Hans Stumme.

Once upon a time, there lived a woman who had a son and a daughter. One morning she said to them, "I have heard of a town where there is no such thing as death, let us go and dwell there." So she broke up her house, and went away with her son and daughter.

When she reached the city, the first thing she did was to look about and see if there was any churchyard, and when she found none, she exclaimed, "This is a delightful spot. We will stay here for ever."

By-and-by, her son grew to be a man, and he took for a wife a girl who had been born in the town. But after a little while he grew restless, and went away on his travels, leaving his mother, his wife, and his sister behind him.

He had not been gone many weeks when one evening his mother said, "I am not well, my head aches dreadfully."

"What did you say?" inquired her daughter-in-law.

"My head feels ready to split," replied the old woman.

The daughter-in-law asked no more questions, but left the house, and went in haste to some butchers in the next street.

"I have got a woman to sell, what will you give me for her?" said she.

The butchers answered that they must see the woman first, and they all returned together.

Then the butchers took the woman and told her they must kill her.

"But why?" she asked.

"Because," they said, "it is always our custom that when persons are ill and complain of their head they should be killed at once. It is a much better way than leaving them to die a natural death."

"Very well," replied the woman. "But leave, I pray you, my lungs and my liver untouched, till my son comes back. Then give both to him."

But the men took them out at once, and gave them to the daughter-in-law, saying, "Put away these things till your husband returns." And the daughter-in-law took them, and hid them in a secret place.

When the old woman's daughter, who had been in the woods, heard that her mother had been killed while she was out, she was filled with fright, and ran away as fast as she could. At last she reached a lonely spot far from the town, where she thought she was safe, and sat down on a stone, and wept bitterly. As she was sitting, sobbing, a man passed by.

"What is the matter, little girl? Answer me! I will be your friend."

"Ah, sir, they have killed my mother, my brother is far away, and I have nobody."

"Will you come with me?" asked the man.

"Thankfully," said she, and he led her down, down, under the earth, till they reached a great city. Then he married her, and in course of time she had a son. And the baby was known throughout the city as 'Mohammed with the magic finger,' because, whenever he stuck out his little finger, he was able to see anything that was happening for as far as two days' distance.

By-and-by, as the boy was growing bigger, his uncle returned from his long journey, and went straight to his wife.

"Where are my mother and sister?" he asked but his wife answered, "Have something to eat first, and then I will tell you."

But he replied, "How can I eat till I know what has become of them?"

Then she fetched, from the upper chamber, a box full of money, which she laid before him, saying, "That is the price of your mother. She sold well."

"What do you mean?" he gasped.

"O, your mother complained one day that her head was aching, so I got in two butchers and they agreed to take her. However, I have got her lungs and liver hidden, till you came back, in a safe place."

"And my sister?"

"Well, while the people were chopping up your mother she ran away, and I heard no more of her."

"Give me my mother's liver and lungs," said the young man. And she gave them to him. Then he put them in his pocket, and went away, saying, "I can stay no longer in this horrible town. I go to seek my sister."

Now, one day, the little boy stretched out his finger and said to his mother, "My uncle is coming!"

"Where is he?" she asked.

"He is still two days' journey off, looking for us, but he will soon be here." And in two days, as the boy had foretold, the uncle had found the hole in the earth, and arrived at the gate of the city. All his money was spent, and not knowing where his sister lived, he began to beg of all the people he saw.

"Here comes my uncle," called out the little boy.

"Where?" asked his mother.

"Here at the house door," and the woman ran out and embraced him, and wept over him. When they could both speak, he said, "My sister, were you by when they killed my mother?"

"I was absent when they slew her," replied she, "and as I could do nothing, I ran away. But you, my brother, how did you get here?"

"By chance," he said, "after I had wandered far, but I did not know I should find you!"

"My little boy told me you were coming," she explained, "when you were yet two days distant. He alone of all men has that great gift."

But she did not tell him that her husband could change himself into a serpent, a dog, or a monster, whenever he pleased. He was a very rich man, and possessed large herds of camels, goats, sheep, cattle, horses and asses - all the best of their kind. And the next morning, the sister said, "Dear brother, go and watch our sheep, and when you are thirsty, drink their milk!"

"Very well," answered he, and he went.

Soon after, she said again, "Dear brother, go and watch our goats."

"But why? I like tending sheep better!"

"O, it is much nicer to be a goatherd," she said, so he took the goats out.

When he was gone, she said to her husband, "You must kill my brother, for I cannot have him living here with me."

"But, my dear, why should I? He has done me no harm."

"I wish you to kill him," she answered, "or if not I will leave."

"O, all right, then," said he. "Tomorrow I will change myself into a serpent, and hide myself in the date barrel, and when he comes to fetch dates I will sting him in the hand."

"That will do very well," said she.

When the sun was up next day, she called to her brother, "Go and mind the goats."

"Yes, of course," he replied but the little boy called out, "Uncle, I want to come with you."

"Delighted," said the uncle, and they started together.

After they had got out of sight of the house the boy said to him, "Dear uncle, my father is going to kill you. He has changed himself into a serpent, and has hidden himself in the date barrel. My mother has told him to do it."

"And what am I to do?" asked the uncle.

"I will tell you. When we bring the goats back to the house, and my mother says to you, "I am sure you must be hungry, get a few dates out of the cask, and just say to me, 'I am not feeling very well, Mohammed, you go and get them for me.'"

So, when they reached the house the sister came out to meet them, saying, "Dear brother, you must certainly be hungry. Go and get a few dates."

But he answered, "I am not feeling very well. Mohammed, you go and get them for me."

"Of course I will," replied the little boy, and ran at once to the cask.

"No, no," his mother called after him, "come here directly! Let your uncle fetch them himself!"

But the boy would not listen, and crying out to her "I would rather get them," thrust his hand into the date cask.

Instead of the fruit, it struck against something cold and slimy, and he whispered softly, "Keep still. It is I, your son!"

Then he picked up his dates and went away to his uncle.

"Here they are, dear uncle. Eat as many as you want."

And his uncle ate them.

When he saw that the uncle did not mean to come near the cask, the serpent crawled out and regained his proper shape.

"I am thankful I did not kill him," he said to his wife, "for, after all, he is my brother-in-law, and it would have been a great sin!"

"Either you kill him or I leave you," said she.

"Well, well!" sighed the man, "Tomorrow I will do it."

The woman let that night go by without doing anything further, but at daybreak she said to her brother, "Get up, brother, it is time to take the goats to pasture!"

"All right," cried he.

"I will come with you, uncle," called out the little boy.

"Yes, come along," replied he.

But the mother ran up, saying, "The child must not go out in this cold or he will be ill," to which he only answered, "Nonsense! I am going, so it is no use your talking! I am going! I am! I am!"

"Then go!" she said.

And so they started, driving the goats in front of them.

When they reached the pasture the boy said to his uncle, "Dear uncle, this night my father means to kill you. While we are away he will creep into your room and hide in the straw. Directly we get home my mother will say to you, 'Take that straw and give it to the sheep,' and, if you do, he will bite you."

"Then what am I to do?" asked the man.

"O, do not be afraid, dear uncle! I will kill my father myself."

"All right," replied the uncle.

As they drove the goats back towards the house, the sister cried, "Be quick, dear brother, go and get me some straw for the sheep."

"Let me go," said the boy.

"You are not big enough, your uncle will get it," replied she.

"We will both get it," answered the boy. "Come, uncle, let us go and fetch that straw!"

"All right," replied the uncle, and they went to the door of the room.

"It seems very dark," said the boy, "I must go and get a light," and when he came back with one, he set fire to the straw, and the serpent was burnt.

Then the mother broke into sobs and tears. "O, you wretched boy! What have you done? Your father was in that straw, and you have killed him!"

"Now, how was I to know that my father was lying in that straw, instead of in the kitchen?" said the boy.

But his mother only wept the more, and sobbed out, "From this day you have no father. you must do without him as best you can!"

"Why did you marry a serpent?" asked the boy. "I thought he was a man! How did he learn those odd tricks?"

As the sun rose, she woke her brother, and said, "Go and take the goats to pasture!"

"I will come too," said the little boy.

"Go then!" said his mother, and they went together.

On the way the boy began, "Dear uncle, this night my mother means to kill both of us, by poisoning us with the bones of the serpent, which she will grind to powder and sprinkle in our food."

"And what are we to do?" asked the uncle.

"I will kill her, dear uncle. I do not want either a father or a mother like that!"

When they came home in the evening they saw the woman preparing supper, and secretly scattering the powdered bones of the serpent on one side of the dish. On the other, where she meant to eat herself, there was no poison.

And the boy whispered to his uncle, "Dear uncle, be sure you eat from the same side of the dish as I do!"

"All right," said the uncle.

So they all three sat down to the table, but before they helped themselves the boy said, "I am thirsty, mother, will you get me some milk?"

"Very well," said she, "but you had better begin your supper."

And when she came back with the milk they were both eating busily.

"Sit down and have something too," said the boy, and she sat down and helped herself from the dish, but at the very first moment she sank dead upon the ground.

"She has got what she meant for us," observed the boy, "and now we will sell all the sheep and cattle."

So the sheep and cattle were sold, and the uncle and nephew took the money and went to see the world.

For ten days they travelled through the desert, and then they came to a place where the road parted in two.

"Uncle!" said the boy.

"Well, what is it?" replied he.

"You see these two roads? You must take one, and I the other, for the time has come when we must part."

But the uncle cried, "No, no, my boy, we will keep together always."

"Alas! that cannot be," said the boy, "so tell me which way you will go."

"I will go to the west," said the uncle.

"One word before I leave you," continued the boy. "Beware of any man who has red hair and blue eyes. Take no service under him."

"All right," replied the uncle, and they parted.

For three days the man wandered on without any food, till he was very hungry. Then, when he was almost fainting, a stranger met him and said, "Will you work for me?"

"By contract?" asked the man.

"Yes, by contract," replied the stranger, "and whichever of us breaks it, shall have a strip of skin taken from his body."

"All right," replied the man, "what shall I have to do?"

"Every day you must take the sheep out to pasture, and carry my old mother on your shoulders, taking great care her feet shall never touch the ground. And, besides that, you must catch, every evening, seven singing birds for my seven sons."

"That is easily done," said the man.

Then they went back together, and the stranger said, "Here are your sheep, and now stoop down, and let my mother climb on your back."

"Very good," answered Mohammed's uncle.

The new shepherd did as he was told, and returned in the evening with the old woman on his back, and the seven singing birds in his pocket, which he gave to the seven boys, when they came to meet him. So the days passed, each one exactly like the other.

At last, one night, he began to weep, and cried, "O, what have I done, that I should have to perform such hateful tasks?"

And his nephew Mohammed saw him from afar, and thought to himself, "My uncle is in trouble - I must go and help him," and the next morning he went to his master and said, "Dear master, I must go to my uncle, and I wish to send him here instead of myself, while I serve under his master. And that you may know it is he and no other man, I will give him my staff, and put my mantle on him."

"All right," said the master.

Mohammed set out on his journey, and in two days he arrived at the place where his uncle was standing with the old woman on his back trying to catch the birds as they flew past. And Mohammed touched him on the arm, and spoke, "Dear uncle, did I not warn you never to take service under any blue-eyed red-haired man!

"But what could I do?" asked the uncle. "I was hungry, and he passed, and we signed a contract."

"Give the contract to me!" said the young man.

"Here it is," replied the uncle, holding it out.

"Now," continued Mohammed, "let the old woman get down from your back."

"O no, I mustn't do that!" cried he.

But the nephew paid no attention, and went on talking, "Do not worry yourself about the future. I see my way out of it all. And, first, you must take my stick and my mantle, and leave this place. After two days' journey, straight before you, you will come to some tents which are inhabited by shepherds. Go in there, and wait."

"All right!" answered the uncle.

Then Mohammed with the Magic Finger picked up a stick and struck the old woman with it, saying, "Get down, and look after the sheep, I want to go to sleep."

"O, certainly!" replied she.

So Mohammed lay down comfortably under a tree and slept till evening. Towards sunset he woke up and said to the old woman, "Where are the singing birds which you have got to catch?"

"You never told me anything about that," replied she.

"O, didn't I?" he answered. "Well, it is part of your business, and if you don't do it, I shall just kill you."

"Of course I will catch them!" cried she in a hurry, and ran about the bushes after the birds, till thorns pierced her foot, and she shrieked from pain and exclaimed, "O dear, how unlucky I am, and how abominably this man is treating me!" However, at last she managed to catch the seven birds, and brought them to Mohammed, saying, "Here they are!"

"Then now we will go back to the house," said he.

When they had gone some way he turned to her sharply and said, "Be quick and drive the sheep home, for I do not know where their fold is." And she drove them before her. By-and-by the young man spoke again, saying, "Look here, old hag. If you say anything to your son about my having struck you, or about my not being the old shepherd, I'll kill you!"

"O, no, of course I won't say anything!"

When they got back, the son said to his mother, "That is a good shepherd I've got, isn't he?"

"O, a splendid shepherd!" answered she. "Why, look how fat the sheep are, and how much milk they give!"

"Yes, indeed!" replied the son, as he rose to get supper for his mother and the shepherd.

In the time of Mohammed's uncle, the shepherd had had nothing to eat but the scraps left by the old woman, but the new shepherd was not going to be content with that.

"You will not touch the food till I have had as much as I want," whispered he.

"Very good!" replied she. And when he had had enough, he said, "Now, eat!"

But she wept, and cried, "That was not written in your contract. You were only to have what I left!"

"If you say a word more, I will kill you!" said he.

The next day he took the old woman on his back, and drove the sheep in front of him till he was some distance from the house, when he let her fall, and said, "Quick! Go and mind the sheep!"

Then he took a ram, and killed it. He lit a fire and broiled some of its flesh, and called to the old woman, "Come and eat with me," and she came. But instead of letting her eat quietly, he took a large lump of the meat and rammed it down her throat with his crook, so that she died. And when he saw she was dead, he said, "That is what you have got for tormenting my uncle!"

He left her lying where she was, while he went after the singing birds. It took him a long time to catch them but at length he had the whole seven hidden in the pockets of his tunic, and then he threw the old woman's body into some bushes, and drove the sheep before him, back to their fold. And when they drew near the house the seven boys came to meet him, and he gave a bird to each.

"Why are you weeping?" asked the boys, as they took their birds.

"Because your grandmother is dead!"

And they ran and told their father. Then the man came up and said to Mohammed, "What was the matter? How did she die?"

And Mohammed answered, "I was tending the sheep when she said to me, "Kill me that ram, I am hungry." So I killed it, and gave her the meat. But she had no teeth, and it choked her."

"But why did you kill the ram, instead of one of the sheep?" asked the man.

"What was I to do?" said Mohammed. "I had to obey orders!"

"Well, I must see to her burial!" said the man, and the next morning Mohammed drove out the sheep as usual, thinking to himself, "Thank goodness I've got rid of the old woman! Now for the boys!"

All day long he looked after the sheep, and towards evening he began to dig some little holes in the ground, out of which he took six scorpions. These he put in his pockets, together with one bird which he caught. After this he drove his flock home.

When he approached the house the boys came out to meet him as before, saying, "Give me my bird!" He put a scorpion into the hand of each, and it stung him, and he died. But to the youngest only he gave a bird.

As soon as he saw the boys lying dead on the ground, Mohammed lifted up his voice and cried loudly, "Help, help! The children are dead!"

And the people came running fast, saying, "What has happened? How have they died?"

And Mohammed answered, "It was your own fault! The boys had been accustomed to birds, and in this bitter cold their fingers grew stiff, and could hold nothing, so that the birds flew away, and their spirits flew with them. Only the youngest, who managed to keep tight hold of his bird, is still alive."

And the father groaned, and said, "I have borne enough! Bring no more birds, lest I lose the youngest also!"

"All right," said Mohammed.

As he was driving the sheep out to grass he said to his master, "Out there is a splendid pasture, and I will keep the sheep there for two or, perhaps, three days, so do not be surprised at our absence."

"Very good!" said the man, and Mohammed started. For two days he drove them on and on, till he reached his uncle, and said to him, "Dear uncle, take these sheep and look after them. I have killed the old woman and the boys, and the flock I have brought to you!"

Then Mohammed returned to his master, and on the way he took a stone and beat his own head with it till it bled, and bound his hands tight, and began to scream. The master came running and asked, "What is the matter?"

And Mohammed answered, "While the sheep were grazing, robbers came and drove them away, and because I tried to prevent them, they struck me on the head and bound my hands. See how bloody I am!"

"What shall we do?" said the master, "Are the animals far off?"

"So far that you are not likely ever to see them again," replied Mohammed. "This is the fourth day since the robbers came down. How should you be able to overtake them?"

"Then go and herd the cows!" said the man.

"All right!" replied Mohammed, and for two days he went. But on the third day he drove the cows to his uncle, first cutting off their tails. Only one cow he left behind him.

"Take these cows, dear uncle," said he. "I am going to teach that man a lesson."

"Well, I suppose you know your own business best," said the uncle. "And certainly he almost worried me to death."

So Mohammed returned to his master, carrying the cows' tails tied up in a bundle on his back. When he came to the sea-shore, he stuck all the tails in the sand, and went and buried the one cow, whose tail he had not cut off, up to her neck, leaving the tail projecting. After he had got everything ready, he began to shriek and scream as before, till his master and all the other servants came running to see what the matter was.

"What in the world has happened?" they cried

"The sea has swallowed up the cows," said Mohammed, "and nothing remains but their tails. But if you are quick and pull hard, perhaps you may get them out again!"

The master ordered each man instantly to take hold of a tail, but at the first pull they nearly tumbled backwards, and the tails were left in their hands.

"Stop," cried Mohammed, "you are doing it all wrong. you have just pulled off their tails, and the cows have sunk to the bottom of the sea."

"See if you can do it any better," said they, and Mohammed ran to the cow which he had buried in the rough grass, and took hold of her tail and dragged the animal out at once.

"There! That is the way to do it!" said he, "I told you that you knew nothing about it!"

The men slunk away, much ashamed of themselves but the master came up to Mohammed. "Get you gone!" he said, "there is nothing more for you to do! You have killed my mother, you have slain my children, you have stolen my sheep, you have drowned my cows. I have now no work to give you."

"First give me the strip of your skin which belongs to me of right, as you have broken your contract!"

"That a judge shall decide," said the master. "We will go before him."

"Yes, we will," replied Mohammed. And they went before the judge.

"What is your case?" asked the judge of the master.

"My lord," said the man, bowing low, "my shepherd here has robbed me of everything. He has killed my children and my old mother, he has stolen my sheep, and he has drowned my cows in the sea."

The shepherd answered, "He must pay me what he owes me, and then I will go."

"Yes, that is the law," said the judge.

"Very well," returned the master, "let him reckon up how long he has been in my service."

"That won't do," replied Mohammed, "I want my strip of skin, as we agreed in the contract."

Seeing there was no help for it, the master cut a bit of skin, and gave it to Mohammed, who went off at once to his uncle.

"Now we are rich, dear uncle," cried he. "We will sell our cows and sheep and go to a new country. This one is no longer the place for us."

The animals were soon sold, and the two comrades started on their travels. That night they reached some Bedouin tents, where they had supper with the Arabs. Before they lay down to sleep, Mohammed called the owner of the tent aside. "Your greyhound will eat my strip of leather," he said to the Arab.

"No, do not fear."

"But supposing he does?"

"Well, then, I will give him to you in exchange," replied the Arab.

Mohammed waited till everyone was fast asleep, then he rose softly, and tearing the bit of skin in pieces, threw it down before the greyhound, setting up wild shrieks as he did so.

"O, master, said I not well that your dog would eat my thong?"

"Be quiet, don't make such a noise, and you shall have the dog."

So Mohammed put a leash round his neck, and led him away.

In the evening they arrived at the tents of some more Bedouin, and asked for shelter. After supper Mohammed said to the owner of the tent, "Your ram will kill my greyhound."

"O, no, he won't."

"And supposing he does?"

"Then you can take him in exchange."

So in the night Mohammed killed the greyhound, and laid his body across the horns of the ram. Then he set up shrieks and yells, till he roused the Arab, who said, "Take the ram and go away."

Mohammed did not need to be told twice, and at sunset he reached another Bedouin encampment. He was received kindly, as usual, and after supper he said to his host, "Your daughter will kill my ram."

"Be silent, she will do nothing of the sort. My daughter does not need to steal meat, she has some every day."

"Very well, I will go to sleep, but if anything happens to my ram I will call out."

"If my daughter touches anything belonging to my guest I will kill her," said the Arab, and went to his bed.

When everybody was asleep, Mohammed got up, killed the ram, and took out his liver, which he broiled on the fire. He placed a piece of it in the girl's hands, and laid some more on her night-dress while she slept and knew nothing about it. After this he began to cry out loudly.

"What is the matter? Be silent at once!" called the Arab.

"How can I be silent, when my ram, which I loved like a child, has been slain by your daughter?"

"But my daughter is asleep," said the Arab.

"Well, go and see if she has not some of the flesh about her."

"If she has, you may take her in exchange for the ram," and as they found the flesh exactly as Mohammed had foretold, the Arab gave his daughter a good beating, and then told her to get out of sight, for she was now the property of this stranger.

They wandered in the desert till, at nightfall, they came to another Bedouin encampment, where they were hospitably bidden to enter. Before lying down to sleep, Mohammed said to the owner of the tent, "Your mare will kill my wife."

"Certainly not."

"And if she does?"

"Then you shall take the mare in exchange."

When everyone was asleep, Mohammed said softly to his wife, "Maiden, I have got such a clever plan! I am going to bring in the mare and put it at your feet, and I will cut you, just a few little flesh wounds, so that you may be covered with blood, and everybody will suppose you to be dead. But remember that you must not make a sound, or we shall both be lost."

This was done, and then Mohammed wept and wailed louder than ever.

The Arab hastened to the spot and cried, "O, cease making that terrible noise! Take the mare and go, and carry off the dead girl with you. She can lie quite easily across the mare's back."

Then Mohammed and his uncle picked up the girl, and, placing her on the mare's back, led it away, being very careful to walk one on each side, so that she might not slip down and hurt herself. After the Arab tents could be seen no longer, the girl sat up on the saddle and looked about her, and as they were all hungry they tied up the mare, and took out some dates to eat.

When they had finished, Mohammed said to his uncle, "Dear uncle, the maiden shall be your wife. I give her to you. But the money we got from the sheep and cows we will divide between us. you shall have two-thirds and I will have one, for you will have a wife, but I never mean to marry. And now, go in peace, for never more will you see me. The bond of bread and salt is at an end between us."

So they wept, and fell on each other's necks, and asked forgiveness for any wrongs in the past. Then they parted and went their ways.

The Ogre And The Beautiful Woman

This story has been edited and adapted from Moorish Literature, a collection work from sources such as Adolphe Hanoteau's Poésies Populaires de la Khabylie du Jurgura of 1867, Émile Masqueray's Observations grammaticales sur la grammaire Touareg et textes de la Tourahog des Tailog, and René Basset's L'insurrection Algerienne, de 1871 dans les chansons populaires Khabyles Lourain of 1892. This version was taken from the English translation introduced by René Basset and published by the University of France and the Académie D'Alger, published in 1901.

Some hunters set out with their camels. When they came to the hunting-ground they loosed their camels to let them graze, and hunted until the setting of the sun, and then came back to their camp. One day while one of them was going along he saw the marks of an ogre, each one three feet wide, and began to follow them. He proceeded and found the place where the ogre had lately made his lair. He returned and said to his companions, "I've found the traces of an ogre. Come, let us seek him."

"No," they answered, "we will not go to seek him, because we are not stronger than he is."

"Grant me fourteen days," said the huntsman. "If I return, you shall see. If not, take back my camel with the game."

The next day he set out and began to follow the traces of the ogre. He walked for four days, when he discovered a cave, into which he entered. Within he found a beautiful woman, who said to him, "What brings you here, where you will be devoured by this ogre?"

"But you," answered the hunter, "what is your story and how did the ogre bring you here?"

"Three days ago he stole me," she replied. "I was betrothed to the son of my uncle, then the ogre took me. I have stayed in the cavern. He often brings me food. I stay here, and he does not kill me."

"Where does he enter," asked the hunter, "when he comes back here?"

"This is the way," she answered.

The hunter went into the middle of the cave, loaded his gun, and waited. At sunset the ogre arrived. The hunter took aim and fired, hitting the ogre between the eyes as he was sitting down. Approaching him he saw that he had brought with him two men to cook and eat them. In the morning he employed the day in collecting the ogre's hidden silver, took what he could, and set out on the return. On the fourteenth day he arrived at the place where he had left his comrades, and found them there.

"Leave the game you have secured and return with me to the cave," he said to them.

When they arrived they took all the arms and clothing, loaded it upon their camels, and set out to return to their village. Halfway home they fought to see which one should marry the woman. The powder spoke between them. Our man killed four, and took the woman home and married her.

Samba The Coward

This story has been edited and adapted from Andrew Lang's Red Book of Heroes, originally published by Longmans, Green And Company, London And New York, in 1909. The original story was included in Contes Soudainais by Charles Monteil, published in 1905.

In the great country far away south, through which flows the river Nile, there lived a king who had an only child called Samba.

Now, from the time that Samba could walk he showed signs of being afraid of everything, and as he grew bigger he became more and more frightened. At first his father's friends made light of it, and said to each other, "It is strange to see a boy of our race running into a hut at the trumpeting of an elephant, and trembling with fear if a lion cub half his size comes near him, but, after all, he is only a baby, and when he is older he will be as brave as the rest."

"Yes, he is only a baby," answered the king who overheard them, "it will be all right by-and-by." But, somehow, he sighed as he said it, and the men looked at him and made no reply.

The years passed away, and Samba had become a tall and strong youth. He was good-natured and pleasant, and was liked by all, and if during his father's hunting parties he was seldom to be seen in any place of danger, he was too great a favourite for much to be said.

"When the king holds the feast and declares him to be his heir, he will cease to be a child," murmured the rest of the people, as they had done before, and on the day of the ceremony their hearts beat gladly, and they cried to each other, "It is Samba, Samba, whose chin is above the heads of other men, who will defend us against the tribes of the robbers!"

Not many weeks after, the dwellers in the village awoke to find that during the night their herds had been driven away, and their herdsmen carried off into slavery by their enemies. Now was the time for Samba to show the brave spirit that had come to him with his manhood, and to ride forth at the head of the warriors of his race. But Samba could nowhere be found, and a party of the avengers went on their way without him.

It was many days later before he came back, with his head held high, and a tale of a lion which he had tracked to its lair and killed, at the risk of his own life. A little while earlier and his people would have welcomed his story, and believed it all, but now it was too late.

"Samba the Coward," cried a voice from the crowd, and the name stuck to him, even the very children shouted it at him, and his father did not spare him. At length he could bear it no longer, and made up his mind to leave his own land for another where peace had reigned since the memory of man. So, early next morning, he slipped out to the king's stables, and choosing the quietest horse he could find, he rode away northwards.

Never as long as he lived did Samba forget the terrors of that journey. He could hardly sleep at night for dread of the wild beasts that might be lurking behind every rock or bush, while, by day, the distant roar of a lion would cause him to start so violently, that he almost fell from his horse. A dozen times he was on the point of turning back, and it was not the terror of the mocking words and scornful laughs that kept him from doing so, but the terror lest he should be forced to take part in their wars. Therefore he held on, and deeply thankful he felt when the walls of a city, larger than he had ever dreamed of, rose before him.

Drawing himself up to his full height, he rode proudly through the gate and past the palace, where, as was her custom, the princess was sitting on the terrace roof, watching the bustle in the street below.

"That is a gallant figure," thought she, as Samba, mounted on his big black horse, steered his way skilfully among the crowds, and, beckoning to a slave, she ordered him to go and meet the stranger, and ask him who he was and where he came from.

"O, princess, he is the son of a king, and heir to a country which lies near the Great River," answered the slave, when he had returned from questioning Samba. And the princess on hearing this news summoned her father, and told him that if she was not allowed to wed the stranger she would die unmarried.

Like many other fathers, the king could refuse his daughter nothing, and besides, she had rejected so many suitors already that he was quite alarmed lest no man should be good enough for her. Therefore, after a talk with Samba, who charmed him by his good humour and pleasant ways, he gave his consent, and three days later the wedding feast was celebrated with the utmost splendour.

The princess was very proud of her tall handsome husband, and for some time she was quite content that he should pass the days with her under the palm trees, telling her the stories that she loved, or amusing her with tales of the manners and customs of his country, which were so different to those of her own. But, by-and-by, this was not enough, for she wanted other people to be proud of him too, and one day she said, "I really almost wish that those Moorish thieves from the north would come on one of their robbing expeditions. I should love so to see you ride out at the head of our men, to chase them home again. Ah, how happy I should be when the city rang with your noble deeds!"

She looked lovingly at him as she spoke, but, to her surprise, his face grew dark, and he answered hastily, "Never speak to me again of the Moors or of war. It was to escape from them that I fled from my own land, and at the first word of invasion I should leave you for ever."

"How funny you are," cried she, breaking into a laugh. "The idea of anyone as big as you being afraid of a Moor! But still, you mustn't say those things to anyone except me, or they might think you were in earnest."

Not very long after this, when the people of the city were holding a great feast outside the walls of the town, a body of Moors, who had been in hiding for days, drove off all the sheep and goats which were peacefully feeding on the slopes of a hill. Directly the loss was discovered, which was not for some hours, the king gave orders that the war drum should be beaten, and the warriors assembled in the great square before the palace, trembling with fury at the insult which had been put upon them. Loud were the cries for instant vengeance, and for Samba, son-in-law of the king, to lead them to battle. But shout as they might, Samba never came.

And where was he? No further than in a cool, dark cellar of the palace, crouching among huge earthenware pots of grain. With a rush of pain at her heart, there his wife found him, and she tried with all her strength to kindle in him a sense of shame, but in vain. Even the thought of the future danger he might run from the contempt of his subjects was as nothing when compared with the risks of the present.

"Take off your tunic of mail," said the princess at last, and her voice was so stern and cold that none would have known it. "Give it to me, and hand me besides your helmet, your sword and your spear."

And with many fearful glances to right and to left, Samba stripped off the armour inlaid with gold, the property of the king's son-in-law. Silently his wife took, one by one, the pieces from him, and fastened them on her with firm hands, never even glancing at the tall form of her husband who had slunk back to his corner. When she had fastened the last buckle, and lowered her vizor, she went out, and mounting Samba's horse, gave the signal to the warriors to follow.

Now, although the princess was much shorter than her husband, she was a tall woman, and the horse which she rode was likewise higher than the rest, so that when the men caught sight of the gold-inlaid suit of chain armour, they did not doubt that Samba was taking his rightful place, and cheered him loudly. The princess bowed in answer to their greeting, but kept her vizor down, and touching her horse with the spur, she galloped at the head of her troops to charge the enemy. The Moors, who had not expected to be so quickly pursued, had scarcely time to form themselves into battle array, and were speedily put to flight. Then the little troop of horsemen returned to the city, where all sung the praises of Samba their leader.

The instant they reached the palace the princess flung her reins to a groom, and disappeared up a side staircase, by which she could, unseen, enter her own rooms. Here she found Samba lying idly on a heap of mats, but he raised his head uneasily as the door opened and looked at his wife, not feeling sure how she might act towards him. However, he need not have been afraid of harsh words, for she merely unbuttoned her armour as fast as possible, and bade him put it on with all speed. Samba obeyed, not daring to ask any questions, and when he had finished the princess told him to follow her, and led him on to the flat roof of the house, below which a crowd had gathered, cheering lustily.

"Samba, the king's son-in-law! Samba, the bravest of the brave! Where is he? Let him show himself!"

And when Samba did show himself the shouts and applause became louder than ever.

"See how modest he is! He leaves the glory to others!" cried they.

And Samba only smiled and waved his hand, and said nothing.

Out of all the mass of people assembled there to do honour to Samba, one alone there was who did not shout and praise with the rest. This was the princess's youngest brother, whose sharp eyes had noted certain things during the fight which recalled his sister much more than they did her husband. Under promise of secrecy, he told his suspicions to the other princes, but only got laughed at, and was bidden to carry his dreams elsewhere.

"Well, well," answered the boy, "we shall see who is right, but the next time we give battle to the Moors I will take care to place a private mark on our commander."

In spite of their defeat, not many days after the Moors sent a fresh body of troops to steal some cattle, and again Samba's wife dressed herself in her husband's armour, and rode out at the head of the avenging column. This time the combat was fiercer than before, and in the thick of it her youngest brother drew near, and gave his sister a slight wound on the leg. At the moment she paid no heed to the pain, which, indeed, she scarcely felt, but when the enemy had been put to flight and the little band returned to the palace, faintness suddenly overtook her, and she could hardly stagger up the staircase to her own apartments.

"I am wounded," she cried, sinking down on the mats where he had been lying, "but do not be anxious, it is really nothing. You have only got to wound yourself slightly in the same spot and no one will guess that it was I and not you who were fighting."

"What!" cried Samba, his eyes nearly starting from his head in surprise and terror. "Can you possibly imagine that I should agree to anything so useless and painful? Why, I might as well have gone to fight myself!"

"Ah, I ought to have known better, indeed," answered the princess, in a voice that seemed to come from a long way off, but, quick as thought, the moment Samba turned his back she pierced one of his bare legs with a spear.

He gave a loud scream and staggered backwards, from astonishment, much more than from pain. But before he could speak his wife had left the room and had gone to seek the medicine man of the palace.

"My husband has been wounded," said she, when she had found him, "come and tend him with speed, for he is faint from loss of blood."

And she took care that more than one person heard her words, so that all that day the people pressed up to the gate of the palace, asking for news of their brave champion.

"You see," observed the king's eldest sons, who had visited the room where Samba lay groaning, "you see, O wise young brother, that we were right and you were wrong about Samba, and that he really did go into the battle."

But the boy answered nothing, and only shook his head doubtfully.

It was only two days later that the Moors appeared for the third time, and though the herds had been tethered in a new and safer place, they were promptly carried off as before. "For," said the Moors to each other, "the tribe will never think of our coming back so soon when they have beaten us so badly."

When the drum sounded to assemble all the fighting men, the princess rose and sought her husband.

"Samba," cried she, "my wound is worse than I thought. I can scarcely walk, and could not mount my horse without help. For today, then, I cannot do your work, so you must go instead of me."

"What nonsense," exclaimed Samba, "I never heard of such a thing. Why, I might be wounded, or even killed! You have three brothers. The king can choose one of them."

"They are all too young," replied his wife. "The men would not obey them. But if, indeed, you will not go, at least you can help me harness my horse."

And to this Samba, who was always ready to do anything he was asked when there was no danger about it, agreed readily. So the horse was quickly harnessed, and when it was done the princess said, "Now ride the horse to the place of meeting outside the gates, and I will join you by a shorter way, and will change places with you."

Samba, who loved riding in times of peace, mounted as she had told him, and when he was safe in the saddle, his wife dealt the horse a sharp cut with her whip, and he dashed off through the town and through the ranks of the warriors who were waiting for him. Instantly the whole place was in motion. Samba tried to check his steed, but he might as well have sought to stop the wind, and it seemed no more than a few minutes before they were grappling hand to hand with the Moors.

Then a miracle happened. Samba the coward, the skulker, the terrified, no sooner found himself pressed hard, unable to escape, than something sprang into life within him, and he fought with all his might. And when a man of his size and strength begins to fight he generally fights well.

That day the victory was really owing to Samba, and the shouts of the people were louder than ever. When he returned, bearing with him the sword of the Moorish chief, the old king pressed him in his arms and said, "O, my son, how can I ever show you how grateful I am for this splendid service?"

But Samba, who was good and loyal when fear did not possess him, answered straightly, "My father, it is to your daughter and not to me to whom thanks are due, for it is she who has turned the coward that I was into a brave man."

The False Vizier

This story has been edited and adapted from Moorish Literature, a collection work from sources such as Adolphe Hanoteau's Poésies Populaires de la Khabylie du Jurgura of 1867, Émile Masqueray's Observations grammaticales sur la grammaire Touareg et textes de la Tourahog des Tailog, and René Basset's L'insurrection Algerienne, de 1871 dans les chansons populaires Khabyles Lourain of 1892. This version was taken from the English translation introduced by René Basset and published by the University of France and the Académie D'Alger, published in 1901.

A king had a wife who said to him, "I would like to go and visit my father."

"Very well," said he. "Wait today, and tomorrow you shall go with my vizier."

The next day they set out, taking the children with them, and an escort lest they should be attacked on the way. They stopped at sunset, and passed the night on the road. The vizier said to the guards, "Watch that we be not taken, if the robbers should come to seize us."

They guarded the tent.

The vizier then asked the King's wife to marry him, and killed one of her sons because she refused. The next day they set out again. The next night he again asked the King's wife to marry him, threatening to kill a second child should she refuse. She did refuse, so he killed the second son. The next morning they set out, and when they stopped at night again he asked the King's wife to marry him.

"I'll kill you if you refuse."

She asked for delay, and time to say her prayers. She prayed to God, the Master of all worlds, and said, "O God, save me from the vizier."

The Master of the worlds heard her prayer. He gave her the wings of a bird, and she flew up in the sky. At dawn she alighted in a great city, and met a man upon the roadside. She said, "By the face of God, give me your raiment and I'll give you mine."

"Take it, and may God honour you," he said.

Then she was handsome. This city had no king. The members of the council said, "This creature is handsome. We'll make him our king." The cannon spoke in his honour and the drums beat.

When she flew up into the sky, the vizier said to the guards, "You will be my witnesses that she has gone to the sky, so that when I shall see the King he cannot say, 'Where is she?'"

But when the vizier told this story, the King said, "I shall go to seek my wife. you have lied. you shall accompany me."

They set out, and went from village to village. They inquired, and said, "Has a woman been found here recently? We have lost her."

And the village people said, "We have not found her."

They went then to another village and inquired. At this village the Sultan's wife recognized them, called her servant, and said to him, "Go, bring to me this man."

She said to the King, "Why have you come here?"

He said, "I have lost my wife."

She answered, "Stay here, and pass the night. We will give you a dinner and will question you."

When the sun had set she said to the servant, "Go, bring the dinner, that the guests may eat." When they had eaten she said to the King, "Tell me your story."

He answered, "My story is long. My wife went away in the company of a trusted vizier. He returned and said, 'By God, your wife has gone to heaven.'

"I replied, 'No, you have lied. I'll go and look for her.'"

She said to him, "I am your wife."

"How came you here?" he asked.

She replied, "After having started, your vizier came to me and asked me to marry him or he would kill my son, 'Kill him,' I said, and he killed them both."

Addressing the vizier, she said, "And your story? Let us hear it."

"I will return in a moment," said the vizier, for he feared her. But the King cut off his head.

The next day he assembled the village council, and his wife said, "Forgive me and let me go, for I am a woman."

The Adventures Of The Jackal's Eldest Son

This story has been edited and adapted from Andrew Lang's Red Book of Heroes, originally published by Longmans, Green And Company, London And New York, in 1909. The original story was included in Nouveaux Contes Berbères by René Basset.

Now, though the jackal was dead, he had left two sons behind him, every whit as cunning and tricksy as their father. The elder of the two was a fine handsome creature, who had a pleasant manner and made many friends. The animal he saw most of was a hyena, and one day, when they were taking a walk together, they picked up a beautiful green cloak, which had evidently been dropped by someone riding across the plain on a camel. Of course each wanted to have it, and they almost quarrelled over the matter, but at length it was settled that the hyena should wear the cloak by day and the jackal by night.

After a little while, however, the jackal became discontented with this arrangement, declaring that none of his friends, who were quite different from those of the hyena, could see the splendour of the mantle, and that it was only fair that he should sometimes be allowed to wear it by day. To this the hyena would by no means consent, and they were on the eve of a quarrel when the hyena proposed that they should ask the lion to judge between them. The jackal agreed to this, and the hyena wrapped the cloak about him, and they both trotted off to the lion's den.

The jackal, who was fond of talking, at once told the story, and when it was finished the lion turned to the hyena and asked if it was true.

"Quite true, your majesty," answered the hyena.

"Then lay the cloak on the ground at my feet," said the lion, "and I will give my judgment." So the mantle was spread upon the red earth, the hyena and the jackal standing on each side of it.

There was silence for a few moments, and then the lion sat up, looking very great and wise.

"My judgment is that the garment shall belong wholly to whoever first rings the bell of the nearest mosque at dawn tomorrow. Now go, for much business awaits me!"

All that night the hyena sat up, fearing lest the jackal should reach the bell before him, for the mosque was close at hand. With the first streak of dawn he bounded away to the bell, just as the jackal, who had slept soundly all night, was rising to his feet.

"Good luck to you," cried the jackal. And throwing the cloak over his back he darted away across the plain, and was seen no more by his friend the hyena.

After running several miles the jackal thought he was safe from pursuit, and seeing a lion and another hyena talking together, he strolled up to join them.

"Good morning," he said, "may I ask what is the matter? You seem very serious about something."

"Pray sit down," answered the lion. "We were wondering in which direction we should go to find the best dinner. The hyena wishes to go to the forest, and I to the mountains. What do you say?"

"Well, as I was sauntering over the plain, just now, I noticed a flock of sheep grazing, and some of them had wandered into a little valley quite out of sight of the shepherd. If you keep among the rocks you will never be observed. But perhaps you will allow me to go with you and show you the way?"

"You are really very kind," answered the lion. And they crept steadily along till at length they reached the mouth of the valley where a ram, a sheep and a lamb were feeding on the rich grass, unconscious of their danger.

"How shall we divide them?" asked the lion in a whisper to the hyena.

"O, it is easily done," replied the hyena. "The lamb for me, the sheep for the jackal, and the ram for the lion."

"So I am to have that lean creature, which is nothing but horns, am I?" cried the lion in a rage. "I will teach you to divide things in that manner!" And he gave the hyena two great blows, which stretched him dead in a moment. Then he turned to the jackal and said, "How would you divide them?"

"Quite differently from the hyena," replied the jackal. "You will breakfast off the lamb, you will dine off the sheep, and you will sup off the ram."

"Dear me, how clever you are! Who taught you such wisdom?" exclaimed the lion, looking at him admiringly.

"The fate of the hyena," answered the jackal, laughing, and running off at his best speed, for he saw two men armed with spears coming close behind the lion!

The jackal continued to run till at last he could run no longer. He flung himself under a tree, panting for breath, when he heard a rustle amongst the grass, and his father's old friend the hedgehog appeared before him.

"O, is it you?" asked the little creature, "How strange that we should meet so far from home!"

"I have just had a narrow escape of my life," gasped the jackal, "and I need some sleep. After that we must think of something to do to amuse ourselves." And he lay down again and slept soundly for a couple of hours.

"Now I am ready," said he. "Have you anything to propose?"

"In a valley beyond those trees," answered the hedgehog, "there is a small farmhouse where the best butter in the world is made. I know their ways, and in an hour's time the farmer's wife will be off to milk the cows, which she keeps at some distance. We could easily get in at the window of the shed where she keeps the butter, and I will watch, lest someone should come unexpectedly, while you have a good meal. Then you shall watch, and I will eat."

"That sounds a good plan," replied the jackal, and they set off together.

But when they reached the farmhouse the jackal said to the hedgehog, "Go in and fetch the pots of butter and I will hide them in a safe place."

"O no," cried the hedgehog, "I really couldn't. They would find out directly! And, besides, it is so different just eating a little now and then."

"Do as I bid you at once," said the jackal, looking at the hedgehog so sternly that the little fellow dared say no more, and soon rolled the jars to the window where the jackal lifted them out one by one.

When they were all in a row before him he gave a sudden start.

"Run for your life," he whispered to his companion, "I see the woman coming over the hill!"

And the hedgehog, his heart beating, set off as fast as he could. The jackal remained where he was, shaking with laughter, for the woman was not in sight at all, and he had only sent the hedgehog away because he did not want him to know where the jars of butter were buried. But every day he stole out to their hiding-place and had a delicious feast.

At length, one morning, the hedgehog suddenly said, "You never told me what you did with those jars?"

"O, I hid them safely till the farm people should have forgotten all about them," replied the jackal. "But as they are still searching for them we must wait a little longer, and then I'll bring them home, and we will share them between us."

So the hedgehog waited and waited, but every time he asked if there was no chance of getting jars of butter the jackal put him off with some excuse. After a while the hedgehog became suspicious, and said, "I should like to know where you have hidden them. Tonight, when it is quite dark, you shall show me the place."

"I really can't tell you," answered the jackal. "You talk so much that you would be sure to confide the secret to somebody, and then we should have had our trouble for nothing, besides running the risk of our necks being broken by the farmer. I can see that he is getting disheartened, and very soon he will give up the search. Have patience just a little longer."

The hedgehop said no more, and pretended to be satisfied, but when some days had gone by he woke the jackal, who was sleeping soundly after a hunt which had lasted several hours.

"I have just had notice," remarked the hedgehog, shaking him, "that my family wish to have a banquet tomorrow, and they have invited you to it. Will you come?"

"Certainly," answered the jackal, "with pleasure. But as I have to go out in the morning you can meet me on the road."

"That will do very well," replied the hedgehog. And the jackal went to sleep again, for he was obliged to be up early.

Punctual to the moment the hedgehog arrived at the place appointed for their meeting, and as the jackal was not there he sat down and waited for him.

"Ah, there you are!" he cried, when the dusky yellow form at last turned the corner. "I had nearly given you up! Indeed, I almost wish you had not come, for I hardly know where I shall hide you."

"Why should you hide me anywhere?" asked the jackal. "What is the matter with you?"

"Well, so many of the guests have brought their dogs and mules with them, that I fear it may hardly be safe for you to go amongst them. No, don't run off that way," he added quickly, "because there is another troop that are coming over the hill. Lie down here, and I will throw these sacks over you, and keep still for your life, whatever happens."

And what did happen was, that when the jackal was lying covered up, under a little hill, the hedgehog set a great stone rolling, which crushed him to death.

47

The Soufi And The Targui

This story has been edited and adapted from Moorish Literature, a collection work from sources such as Adolphe Hanoteau's Poésies Populaires de la Khabylie du Jurgura of 1867, Émile Masqueray's Observations grammaticales sur la grammaire Touareg et textes de la Tourahog des Tailog, and René Basset's L'insurrection Algerienne, de 1871 dans les chansons populaires Khabyles Lourain of 1892. This version was taken from the English translation introduced by René Basset and published by the University of France and the Académie D'Alger, published in 1901.

Two Souafa were brothers. Separating one day one said to the other, "O my brother, let us marry your son with my daughter."

So the young cousins were married, and the young man's father gave them a separate house. It happened that a man among the Touareg heard tell of her as a remarkable woman. He mounted his swiftest camel, ten years old, and went to her house. Arrived near her residence, he found some shepherds.

"Who are you?" he said.

"We are Souafa."

He confided in one of them, and said to him, "By the face of the Master of the worlds, O favourite of fair women, man of remarkable appearance, tell me if the lady so and so, daughter of so and so, is here."

"She is here."

"Well, if you have the sentiments of most men, I desire you to bring her here, I want to see her."

"I will do what you ask. If she'll come, I'll bring her. If not, I will return and tell you."

He set out, and, arriving at the house of the lady, he saw some people, and said "Good-evening" to them.

"Come dine with us," they said to him.

"I have but just now eaten and am not hungry." He pretended to amuse himself with them to shorten the night, in reality to put to sleep their vigilance. These people went away to amuse themselves while he met the lady.

"A man sends me to you," he said, "a Targui, who wants to marry you. He is as handsome as you are, his eyes are fine, his nose is fine, his mouth is fine."

"Well, I will marry him."

She went to him and married him, and they set out on a camel together. When the first husband returned, he found that she had gone. He said to himself, "She is at my father's or perhaps my uncle's."

When day dawned he said to his sister, "Go see if she is in your father's house or your uncle's."

She went, and did not find her there. He went out to look for her, and perceived the camel's traces. Then he saddled his own camel. The women came out and said, "Stay! Do not go. We will give you our own daughters to marry."

"No," he replied, "I want to find my wife."

He went out, and he followed the tracks of the camel, here, here, here, until the sun went down. He spent the night upon the trail. His camel was a runner of five years. When the sun rose he started and followed the trail again.

About four o'clock he arrived at an encampment of the Touareg, and found some shepherds with their flocks. He confided in one of these men, and said to him, "A word, brave man, brother of beautiful women, I would say a word to you which you will not repeat."

"Speak."

"Did a woman arrive at this place night before last?"

"She did."

"Have you the sentiments of a man of heart?"

"Truly."

"I desire to talk to her."

"I will take you to her. Go, hide your camel. Tie him up. Change your clothing. you will not then be recognized among the sheep. Bring your sabre and come. You shall walk as the sheep walk."

"I will walk toward you, taking the appearance of a sheep, so as not to be perceived."

"The wedding-festival is set for tonight, and everybody will be out of their houses. When I arrive at this lady's tent I will strike a stake with my stick. Where I shall strike, that is where she lives."

He waited and concealed himself among the flocks, and the women came out to milk. He looked among the groups of tents. He found his wife and bade her come with him.

"I will not go with you, but if you are hungry, I will give you food."

"You'll come with me or I will kill you!"

She went with him. He found his camel, unfastened him, donned his ordinary clothing, took his wife upon the camel's back with him, and departed. The day dawned. She said, "O, you who are the son of my paternal uncle, I am thirsty." Now she planned a treachery.

He said to her, "Is there any water here?"

"The day the Targui took me off we found some in that pass."

They arrived at the well.

"Go down into the well," said the Soufi.

"I'm only a woman. I'm afraid. Go down yourself."

He went down. He drew the water. She drank. He drew more water for the camel, which also drank. Then she poured the water on the ground.

"Why does you turn out the water?"

"I did not turn it out. Your camel drank it."

And nevertheless she cast her glances backwards and saw a column of dust in the distance. The Targui was coming. The woman said, "Now I have trapped him for you."

"Brava!" he cried, and addressing the Soufi he said, "Draw me some water that I may drink."

He drew the water, and the Targui drank. The woman said to him, "Kill him in the well. He is a good shot. You are not stronger than he is."

"No," he answered, "I do not want to soil a well of the tribes. I'll make him come up."

The Soufi came up till his shoulders appeared. They seized him, hoisted and bound him, and tied his feet together. Then they seized and killed his camel.

"Bring wood," said the Targui to the woman, "we'll roast some meat."

She brought him some wood. He cooked the meat and ate it, while she roasted pieces of fat till they dripped upon her cousin.

"Don't do that," said the Targui.

She said, "He drew his sword on me, crying, 'Come with me or I will kill you.'"

"In that case do as you like."

She dropped the grease upon his breast, face, and neck until his skin was burnt. While she was doing this, the Targui felt sleep coming upon him, and said to the woman, "Watch over him, lest he should slip out of our hands."

While he slept the Soufi spoke, "Word of goodness, O excellent woman, bend over me that I may kiss your mouth or else your cheek."

She said, "God make your tent empty. You'll die soon, and you think of kisses?"

"Truly I am going to die, and I die for you. I love you more than the whole world. Let me kiss you once. I'll have a moment of joy, and then I'll die."

She bent over him, and he kissed her.

She said, "What do you want?"

"That you shall untie me."

She untied him.

He said to her, "Keep silent. Do not speak a word." Then he unfastened the shackles that bound his feet, put on his cloak, took his gun, drew out the old charge and loaded it anew. He examined the flint-lock and saw that it worked well. Then he said to the woman, "Lift up the Targui."

The latter awoke and cried, "Why did you not kill me in my sleep?"

"Because you did not kill me when I was in the well. Get up. Stand down there, while I stand here."

The Targui obeyed, and said to the Soufi, "Fire first."

"No, I'll let you fire first."

The woman spoke, "Strike, strike, O Targui, you are not as strong as the Soufi."

The Targui rose, fired, and now the woman gave voice to a long "You…you."

It struck the *chechias* that flew above his head. At his turn the Soufi prepared himself and said, "Stand up straight now, as I did for you." He fired, and hit him on the forehead. His enemy dead, he flew at him and cut his throat. He then went to the camel, cut some meat, and said to the woman, "Go, find me some wood, I want to cook and eat."

"I will not go," she said. He approached, threatening her, and made her go. She got up then and brought him some wood. He cooked the meat and ate his fill. He thought then of killing the woman, but he feared that the people of his tribe would say, "You did not bring her back." So he took her on the camel and started homeward. His cousins were pasturing their flocks on a hill. When he had nearly arrived a dust arose. He drew near, and they saw that it was he. His brother spoke, "What have they done to you?"

He answered, "The daughter of my uncle did all this."

Then they killed the woman and cut her flesh in strips and threw it on a jujube-tree. And the jackals and birds of prey came and passed the whole day eating it, until there was none left.

The Prince And The Three Fates

This story has been edited and adapted from Andrew Lang's All Sorts of Stories, originally published by Longmans, Green And Company, London And New York, in 1911. The original story was included in Les Contes Populaires de l'Egypte Ancienne.

Once upon a time a little boy was born to a king who ruled over a great country called Egypt, through which ran a wide river. The king was nearly beside himself with joy, for he had always longed for a son to inherit his crown, and he sent messages to beg all the most powerful fairies to come and see this wonderful baby. In an hour or two, so many were gathered round the cradle, that the child seemed in danger of being smothered, but the king, who was watching the fairies eagerly, was disturbed to see them looking grave. "Is there anything the matter?" he asked anxiously.

The fairies looked at him, and all shook their heads at once.

"He is a beautiful boy, and it is a great pity, but what IS to happen WILL happen," said they. "It is written in the books of fate that he must die, either by a crocodile, or a serpent, or by a dog. If we could save him we would, but that is beyond our power."

And so saying they vanished.

For a time the king stood where he was, horror-stricken at what he had heard but, being of a hopeful nature, he began at once to invent plans to save the prince from the dreadful doom that awaited him. He instantly sent for his master builder, and bade him construct a strong castle on the top of a mountain, which should be fitted with the most precious things from the king's own palace, and every kind of toy a child could wish to play with. And, besides, he gave the strictest orders that a guard should walk round the castle night and day.

For four or five years the baby lived in the castle alone with his nurses, taking his airings on the broad terraces, which were surrounded by walls, with a moat beneath them, and only a drawbridge to connect them with the outer world.

One day, when the prince was old enough to run quite fast by himself, he looked from the terrace across the moat, and saw a little soft fluffy ball of a dog jumping and playing on the other side. Now, of course, all dogs had been kept from him for fear that the fairies' prophecy should come true, and he had never even beheld one before. So he turned to the page who was walking behind him, and said, "What is that funny little thing which is running so fast over there?"

"That is a dog, prince," answered the page.

"Well, bring me one like it, and we will see which can run the faster." And he watched the dog till it had disappeared round the corner.

The page was much puzzled to know what to do. He had strict orders to refuse the prince nothing, yet he remembered the prophecy, and felt that this was a serious matter. At last he thought he had better tell the king the whole story, and let him decide the question.

"O, get him a dog if he wants one," said the king, "he will only cry his heart out if he does not have it." So a puppy was found, exactly like the other, for they might have been twins, and perhaps they were.

Years went by, and the boy and the dog played together till the boy grew tall and strong. The time came at last when he sent a message to his father, saying, "Why do you keep me shut up here, doing nothing? I know all about the prophecy that was made at my birth, but I would far rather be killed at once than live an idle, useless life here. So give me arms, and let me go, I pray you, me and my dog too."

And again the king listened to his wishes, and he and his dog were carried in a ship to the other side of the river, which was so broad here it might almost have been the sea. A black horse was waiting for him, tied to a tree, and he mounted and rode away wherever his fancy took him, the dog always at his heels. Never was any prince so happy as he, and he rode and rode till at length he came to a king's palace.

The king who lived in it did not care about looking after his country, and seeing that his people lived cheerful and contented lives. He spent his whole time in making riddles, and inventing plans which he had much better have let alone. At the period when the young prince reached the kingdom he had just completed a wonderful house for his only child, a daughter. It had seventy windows, each seventy feet from the ground, and he had sent the royal herald round the borders of the neighbouring kingdoms to proclaim that whoever could climb up the walls to the window of the princess should win her for his wife.

The fame of the princess's beauty had spread far and wide, and there was no lack of princes who wished to try their fortune. Very funny the palace must have looked each morning, with the dabs of different colour on the white marble as the princes were climbing up the walls. But though some managed to get further than others, nobody was anywhere near the top.

They had already been spending several days in this manner when the young prince arrived, and as he was pleasant to look upon, and civil to talk to, they welcomed him to the house, which had been given to them, and saw that his bath was properly perfumed after his long journey.

"Where do you come from?" they said at last. "And whose son are you?"

But the young prince had reasons for keeping his own secret, and he answered, "My father was master of the horse to the king of my country, and after my mother died he married another wife. At first all went well, but as soon as she had babies of her own she hated me, and I fled, lest she should do me harm."

The hearts of the other young men were touched as soon as they heard this story, and they did everything they could think of to make him forget his past sorrows.

"What are you doing here?" said the youth, one day.

"We spend our whole time climbing up the walls of the palace, trying to reach the windows of the princess," answered the young men, "but, as yet, no one has reached within ten feet of them."

"O, let me try too," cried the prince, "but tomorrow I will wait and see what you do before I begin.

So the next day he stood where he could watch the young men go up, and he noted the places on the wall that seemed most difficult, and made up his mind that when his turn came he would go up some other way.

Day after day he was to be seen watching the wooers, till, one morning, he felt that he knew the plan of the walls by heart, and took his place by the side of the others. Thanks to what he had learned from the failure of the rest, he managed to grasp one little rough projection after another, till at last, to the envy of his friends, he stood on the sill of the princess's window. Looking up from below, they saw a white hand stretched forth to draw him in.

Then one of the young men ran straight to the king's palace, and said, "The wall has been climbed, and the prize is won!"

"By whom?" cried the king, starting up from his throne, "which of the princes may I claim as my son-in-law?"

"The youth who succeeded in climbing to the princess's window is not a prince at all," answered the young man. "He is the son of the master of the horse to the great king who dwells across the river, and he fled from his own country to escape from the hatred of his stepmother."

At this news the king was very angry, for it had never entered his head that anyone BUT a prince would seek to woo his daughter.

"Let him go back to the land where he came," he shouted in wrath. "Does he expect me to give my daughter to an exile?" And he began to smash the drinking vessels in his fury, indeed, he quite frightened the young man, who ran hastily home to his friends, and told the youth what the king had said.

Now the princess, who was leaning from her window, heard his words and bade the messenger go back to the king her father and tell him that she had sworn a vow never to eat or drink again if the youth was taken from her. The king was angrier than ever when he received this message, and ordered his guards to go at once to the palace and put the successful wooer to death, but the princess threw herself between him and his murderers.

"Lay a finger on him, and I shall be dead before sunset," said she, and as they saw that she meant it, they left the palace, and carried the tale to her father.

By this time the king's anger was dying away, and he began to consider what his people would think of him if he broke the promise he had publicly given. So he ordered the princess to be brought before him, and the young man also, and when they entered the throne room he was so pleased with the noble air of the victor that his wrath quite melted away, and he ran to him and embraced him.

"Tell me who you are?" he asked, when he had recovered himself a little, "for I will never believe that you have not royal blood in your veins."

But the prince still had his reasons for being silent, and only told the same story. However, the king had taken such a fancy to the youth that he said no more, and the marriage took place the following day, and great herds of cattle and a large estate were given to the young couple.

After a little while the prince said to his wife, "My life is in the hands of three creatures - a crocodile, a serpent, and a dog."

"Ah, how rash you are!" cried the princess, throwing her arms round his neck. "If you know that, how can you have that horrid beast about you? I will give orders to have him killed at once."

But the prince would not listen to her.

"Kill my dear little dog, who had been my playfellow since he was a puppy?" exclaimed he. "O, never would I allow that."

And all that the princess could get from him was that he would always wear a sword, and have somebody with him when he left the palace.

When the prince and princess had been married a few months, the prince heard that his stepmother was dead, and his father was old and ill, and longing to have his eldest son by his side again. The young man could not remain deaf to such a message, and he took a tender farewell of his wife, and set out on his journey home. It was a long way, and he was forced to rest often on the road, and so it happened that, one night, when he was sleeping in a city on the banks of the great river, a huge crocodile came silently up and made its way along a passage to the prince's room. Fortunately one of his guards woke up as it was trying to steal past them, and shut the crocodile up in a large hall, where a giant watched over it, never leaving the spot except during the night, when the crocodile slept. And this went on for more than a month.

Now, when the prince found that he was not likely to leave his father's kingdom again, he sent for his wife, and bade the messenger tell her that he would await her coming in the town on the banks of the great river. This was the reason why he delayed his journey so long, and narrowly escaped being eaten by the crocodile. During the weeks that followed the prince amused himself as best he could, though he counted the minutes to the arrival of the princess, and when she did come, he at once prepared to start for the court.

That very night, however, while he was asleep, the princess noticed something strange in one of the corners of the room. It was a dark patch, and seemed, as she looked, to grow longer and longer, and to be moving slowly towards the cushions on which the prince was lying. She shrank in terror, but, slight as was the noise, the thing heard it, and raised its head to listen. Then she saw it was the long flat head of a serpent, and the recollection of the prophecy rushed into her mind. Without waking her husband, she glided out of bed, and taking up a heavy bowl of milk which stood on a table, laid it on the floor in the path of the serpent - for she knew that no serpent in the world can resist milk. She held her breath as the snake drew near, and watched it throw up its head again as if it was smelling something nice, while its forky tongue darted out greedily. At length its eyes fell upon the milk, and in an instant it was lapping it so fast that it was a wonder the creature did not choke, for it never took its head from the bowl as long as a drop was left in it. After that it dropped on the ground and slept heavily. This was what the princess had been waiting for, and catching up her husband's sword, she severed the snake's head from its body.

The morning after this adventure the prince and princess set out for the king's palace, but found when they reached it, that he was already dead. They gave him a magnificent burial, and then the prince had to examine the new laws which had been made in his absence, and do a great deal of business besides, till he grew quite ill from fatigue, and was obliged to go away to one of his palaces on the banks of the river, in order to rest. Here he soon got better, and began to hunt, and to shoot wild duck with his bow, and wherever he went, his dog, now grown very old, went with him.

One morning the prince and his dog were out as usual, and in chasing their game they drew near the bank of the river. The prince was running at full speed after his dog when he almost fell over something that looked like a log of wood, which was lying in his path. To his surprise a voice spoke to him, and he saw that the thing which he had taken for a branch was really a crocodile.

"You cannot escape from me," it was saying, when he had gathered his senses again. "I am your fate, and wherever you go, and whatever you do, you will always find me before you. There is only one means of shaking off my power. If you can dig a pit in the dry sand which will remain full of water, my spell will be broken. If not death will come to you speedily. I give you this one chance. Now go."

The young man walked sadly away, and when he reached the palace he shut himself into his room, and for the rest of the day refused to see anyone, not even his wife. At sunset, however, as no sound could be heard through the door, the princess grew quite frightened, and made such a noise that the prince was forced to draw back the bolt and let her come in.

"How pale you look," she cried, "has anything hurt you? Tell me, I pray you, what is the matter, for perhaps I can help!"

So the prince told her the whole story, and of the impossible task given him by the crocodile.

"How can a sand hole remain full of water?" asked he. "Of course, it will all run through. The crocodile called it a "chance", but he might as well have dragged me into the river at once. He said truly that I cannot escape him."

"O, if that is all," cried the princess, "I can set you free myself, for my fairy godmother taught me to know the use of plants and in the desert not far from here there grows a little four-leaved herb which will keep the water in the pit for a whole year. I will go in search of it at dawn, and you can begin to dig the hole as soon as you like.

To comfort her husband, the princess had spoken lightly and gaily, but she knew very well she had no light task before her. Still, she was full of courage and energy, and determined that, one way or another, her husband should be saved.

It was still starlight when she left the palace on a snow-white donkey, and rode away from the river straight to the west. For some time she could see nothing before her but a flat waste of sand, which became hotter and hotter as the sun rose higher and higher. Then a dreadful thirst seized her and the donkey, but there was no stream to quench it, and if there had been she would hardly have had time to stop, for she still had far to go, and must be back before evening, or else the crocodile might declare that the prince had not fulfilled his conditions. So she spoke cheering words to her donkey, who brayed in reply, and the two pushed steadily on.

O, how glad they both were when they caught sight of a tall rock in the distance. They forgot that they were thirsty, and that the sun was hot, and the ground seemed to fly under their feet, till the donkey stopped of its own accord in the cool shadow. But though the donkey might rest the princess could not, for the plant, as she knew, grew on the very top of the rock, and a wide chasm ran round the foot of it. Luckily she had brought a rope with her, and making a noose at one end, she flung it across with all her might. The first time it slid back slowly into the ditch, and she had to draw it up, and throw it again, but at length the noose caught on something, the princess could not see what, and had to trust her whole weight to this little bridge, which might snap and let her fall deep down among the rocks. And in that case her death was as certain as that of the prince.

But nothing so dreadful happened. The princess got safely to the other side, and then became the worst part of her task. As fast as she put her foot on a ledge of the rock the stone broke away from under her, and left her in the same place as before. Meanwhile the hours were passing, and it was nearly noon.

The heart of the poor princess was filled with despair, but she would not give up the struggle. She looked round till she saw a small stone above her which seemed rather stronger than the rest, and by only poising her foot lightly on those that lay between, she managed by a great effort to reach it. In this way, with torn and bleeding hands, she gained the top, but here such a violent wind was blowing that she was almost blinded with dust, and was obliged to throw herself on the ground, and feel about after the precious herb.

For a few terrible moments she thought that the rock was bare, and that her journey had been to no purpose. Feel where she would, there was nothing but grit and stones, when, suddenly, her fingers touched something soft in a crevice. It was a plant, that was clear, but was it the right one? See she could not, for the wind was blowing more fiercely than ever, so she lay where she was and counted the leaves. One, two, three - yes! yes! there were four! And plucking a leaf she held it safe in her hand while she turned, almost stunned by the wind, to go down the rock.

When once she was safely over the side all became still in a moment, and she slid down the rock so fast that it was only a wonder that she did not land in the chasm. However, by good luck, she stopped quite close to her rope bridge and was soon across it. The donkey brayed joyfully at the sight of her, and set off home at his best speed, never seeming to know that the earth under his feet was nearly as hot as the sun above him.

On the bank of the great river he halted, and the princess rushed up to where the prince was standing by the pit he had dug in the dry sand, with a huge water pot beside it. A little way off the crocodile lay blinking in the sun, with his sharp teeth and whity-yellow jaws wide open.

At a signal from the princess the prince poured the water in the hole, and the moment it reached the brim the princess flung in the four-leaved plant. Would the charm work, or would the water trickle away slowly through the sand, and the prince fall a victim to that horrible monster? For half an hour they stood with their eyes rooted to the spot, but the hole remained as full as at the beginning, with the little green leaf floating on the top. Then the prince turned with a shout of triumph, and the crocodile sulkily plunged into the river.

The prince had escape for ever the second of his three fates!

He stood there looking after the crocodile, and rejoicing that he was free, when he was startled by a wild duck which flew past them, seeking shelter among the rushes that bordered the edge of the stream. In another instant his dog dashed by in hot pursuit, and knocked heavily against his master's legs. The prince staggered, lost his balance and fell backwards into the river, where the mud and the rushes caught him and held him fast. He shrieked for help to his wife, who came running, and luckily brought her rope with her. The poor old dog was drowned, but the prince was pulled to shore.

"My wife," he said, "has been stronger than my fate."

Ahmed El Hilalieu And El Redah

This story has been edited and adapted from Moorish Literature, a collection work from sources such as Adolphe Hanoteau's Poésies Populaires de la Khabylie du Jurgura of 1867, Émile Masqueray's Observations grammaticales sur la grammaire Touareg et textes de la Tourahog des Tailog, and René Basset's L'insurrection Algerienne, de 1871 dans les chansons populaires Khabyles Lourain of 1892. This version was taken from the English translation introduced by René Basset and published by the University of France and the Académie D'Alger, published in 1901.

Ahmed el Hilalieu was not loved by people in general. His enemies went and found an old sorceress, and spoke to her as follows, "O sorceress, we want you to drive this man out of our country. Ask what you will, we will give it to you!"

She said to them, "May God gladden your faces. Call aloud. Our man will come out and I will see him."

They obeyed her, crying out that a camel had escaped. Straightway Ahmed went to find his father, and told him of his intention of going to join in the search. He started forth mounted on his courser, and on the way met some people, who told him, "It is nothing."

He made a half turn, not forgetting to water his horse, and met at the fountain the sorceress, who was drawing water.

"Let me pass," he said to her, "and take your buckskin out of my way."

"You may pass," she answered. He started his horse, which stepped on the buckskin and tore it.

"You who are so brave with a poor woman," she said, "would you be able to bring back Redah Oum Zaid?"

"By the religion of Him whom I adore, you shall show me where this Redah lives or I'll cut off your head."

"Know, then, that she lives far from here, and that there is between her and you no less than forty days' journey."

Ahmed went home, and took as provisions for the journey forty dates of the deglet-nour variety, putting them into his pocket. He mounted his steed and departed.

He went on and on without stopping, until he came to the country of the sand. The charger threw his feet forward and buried himself in the sand up to his breast, but soon stopped, conquered and worn out by fatigue. Ahmed el Hilalieu then addressed him:

"My good grey horse, of noble mien, the sand,

The cruel sand would eat your very eyes.

The air no longer your loud whinnies bears,

No strength is left you in your head or heart.

The prairies of Khafour I'll give to you,

With Nouna's eyes I'll quench your thirst, by God

A mule's whole pack of barley shall you have

That Ben Haddjouna shall bring here for you."

In his turn the steed spoke and said, "Dismount, unfasten the breast-strap, and tighten the girth, for some women are coming to show themselves to us in this country."

Ahmed unfastened the breast-strap, then remounted and departed. While he proceeded he saw before him the encampment of a tribe, and perceived a horseman coming, mounted on a white mare, engaged in herding camels.

"Blessings upon you!" cried Ahmed. "You behind the camels!"

The horseman kept silence, and would not return his salutations.

"Greetings to you," cried Ahmed again, "you who are in the middle of the camels."

The same obstinate silence.

"Greetings to you, you who are before the camels."

The horseman still was silent.

Ahmed then said, "Greetings to you, you who own the white mare."

"Greetings to you!" replied the horseman.

"How comes it that you would not answer my greetings for so long?"

The horseman answered, "You cried to me, 'Greetings to you, you who are behind the camels,' Now, behind them are their tails. Then you said, 'Greetings to you, you who are in the middle of the camels,' In the middle of them are their bellies. you said, again, 'Greetings to you, you who are before the camels.' Before them are their heads. you said, 'Greetings to you, O master of the white mare,' And then I answered to you, 'Greetings to you also,'"

Ahmed el Hilalieu asked of the shepherd, "What is your name?"

"I am called Chira."

"Well, Chira, tell me where Redah lives. Is it at the city of the stones or in the garden of the palms?"

"Redah dwells in the city. Her father is the Sultan. Seven kings have fought for her, and one of them has refreshed his heart. He is named Chalau. Go, seek the large house. you will be with Redah when I see you again."

Ahmed set out, and soon met the wife of the shepherd, who came before him and said, "Enter, be welcome, and may good luck attend you!"

She tied his horse, gave him a drink, and went to find dates for Ahmed. She took care to count them before serving him with them. He took out a pit, closed the date again, put them all together, and put down the pit. He ate nothing, and he said to the woman, "Take away these dates, for I have eaten my fill."

She looked, took up the tray, counted the dates again, and perceived that none of them has been eaten. Nevertheless, there was a pit, and not a date missing. She cried out, "Alas! My heart for love of this young man is void of life as is this date of pit."

Then she heaved a sigh and her soul flew away.

Ahmed remained there as if in a dream until the shepherd came back. "Your wife is dead," he said to him, "and if you wish, I'll give you her weight in gold and silver."

But the shepherd answered, "I, too, am the son of a sultan. I have come to pay this woman a visit and desire to see her. Calm yourself. I will take neither your gold nor silver. This is the road to follow. Go, till you arrive at the castle where she is."

Ahmed started, and when he arrived at the castle, he stood up in his stirrups and threw the shadow of his spear upon the window.

Redah, addressing her servant, said to her, "See now what casts that shadow. Is it a cloud, or an Arab's spear?"

The servant went to see, came back to her mistress, and said to her, "It is a horseman, such as I have never seen the like of before in all my life."

"Return," said Redah, "and ask him who he is."

Redah then went to see, and said:

"O horseman, who does come before our eyes,

Why do you seek your death? Tell me upon

Your honour true, what is your origin?"

He answered:

"O, I am Ahmed el Hilalieu called. Well known

'Mongst all the tribes of daughters of Hilal.

I bear in hand a spear that loves to kill,

Whoever attacks me counts on flight and dies."

She then said to him:

"You are Ahmed el Hilalieu? Never prowls

A noble bird about the Zeriba;

The generous falcon turns not near the nests,

O madman! Why take so much care

About a tree that bears not any dates?"

He too answered:

"I will demand of our great Lord of all

To give us rain to cover all the land

With pasturage and flowers. And we shall eat

Of every sort of fruit that grows on earth."

Redah then sang:

"We women are like silk. And only those

Who are true merchants know to handle us."

Ahmed el Hilalieu then sang:

"I've those worth more than you amid the girls

Of Hilal, clad in daintiest of silk

Of richest dye, O Redah, O fifth rite."

And, turning his horse's head, he went away. But she recalled him:

"I am an orange, them the gardener;

I am a palm and you cut my fruit;

I am a beast and you slaughter me.

I am - upon your honour - O grey steed,

Turn back your head. For we are friends henceforth."

She said to her servant, "Go and open wide the door that he may come."

The servant admitted him, and tied up his horse. On the third day he saw the servant laughing. "Why do you laugh, woman?"

"You have not said your prayers for three days."

The Story Of Dschemil And Dschemila

This story has been edited and adapted from Andrew Lang's Strange Story Book, originally published by Longmans, Green And Company, London And New York, in 1913. The original story was included in Märchen und Gedichte aus der Stadt Tripolis.

There was once a man whose name was Dschemil, and he had a cousin who was called Dschemila. They had been betrothed by their parents when they were children, and now Dschemil thought that the time had come for them to be married, and he went two or three days' journey, to the nearest big town, to buy furniture for the new house.

While he was away, Dschemila and her friends set off to the neighbouring woods to pick up sticks, and as she gathered them she found an iron mortar lying on the ground. She placed it on her bundle of sticks, but the mortar would not stay still, and whenever she raised the bundle to put it on her shoulders it slipped off sideways. At length she saw the only way to carry the mortar was to tie it in the very middle of her bundle, and had just unfastened her sticks, when she heard her companions' voices.

"Dschemila, what are you doing? It is almost dark, and if you mean to come with us you must be quick!"

But Dschemila only replied, "You had better go back without me, for I am not going to leave my mortar behind, if I stay here till midnight."

"Do as you like," said the girls, and started on their walk home.

The night soon fell, and at the last ray of light the mortar suddenly became an ogre, who threw Dschemila on his back, and carried her off into a desert place, distant a whole month's journey from her native town. Here he shut her into a castle, and told her not to fear, as her life was safe. Then he went back to his wife, leaving Dschemila weeping over the fate that she had brought upon herself.

Meanwhile the other girls had reached home, and Dschemila's mother came out to look for her daughter. "What have you done with her?" she asked anxiously.

"We had to leave her in the wood," they replied, "for she had picked up an iron mortar, and could not manage to carry it."

So the old woman set off at once for the forest, calling to her daughter as she hurried along.

"Do go home," cried the townspeople, as they heard her, "we will go and look for your daughter, you are only a woman, and it is a task that needs strong men."

But she answered, "Yes, go, but I will go with you! Perhaps it will be only her corpse that we shall find after all. She has most likely been stung by asps, or eaten by wild beasts."

The men, seeing her heart was bent on it, said no more, but told one of the girls she must come with them, and show them the place where they had left Dschemila. They found the bundle of wood lying where she had dropped it, but the maiden was nowhere to be seen.

"Dschemila! Dschemila!" cried they, but nobody answered.

"If we make a fire, perhaps she will see it," said one of the men. And they lit a fire, and then went, one this way, and one that, through the forest, to look for her, whispering to each other that if she had been killed by a lion they would be sure to find some trace of it, or if she had fallen asleep, the sound of their voices would wake her, or if a snake had bitten her, they would at least come on her corpse.

All night they searched, and when morning broke and they knew no more than before what had become of the maiden, they grew weary, and said to the mother, "It is no use. Let us go home, nothing has happened to your daughter, except that she has run away with a man."

"Yes, I will come," answered she, "but I must first look in the river. Perhaps someone has thrown her in there." But the maiden was not in the river.

For four days the father and mother waited and watched for their child to come back, then they gave up hope, and said to each other, "What is to be done? What are we to say to the man to whom Dschemila is betrothed? Let us kill a goat, and bury its head in the grave, and when the man returns we must tell him Dschemila is dead."

Very soon the bridegroom came back, bringing with him carpets and soft cushions for the house of his bride. And as he entered the town Dschemila's father met him, saying, "Greeting to you. She is dead."

At these words the young man broke into loud cries, and it was some time before he could speak. Then he turned to one of the crowd who had gathered round him, and asked, "Where have they buried her?"

"Come to the churchyard with me," answered he, and the young man went with him, carrying with him some of the beautiful things he had brought. These he laid on the grass and then began to weep afresh. All day he stayed, and at nightfall he gathered up his stuffs and carried them to his own house. But when the day dawned he took them in his arms and returned to the grave, where he remained as long as it was light, playing softly on his flute. And this he did daily for six months.

One morning, a man who was wandering through the desert, having lost his way, came upon a lonely castle. The sun was very hot, and the man was very tired, so he said to himself, "I will rest a little in the shadow of this castle." He stretched himself out comfortably, and was almost asleep, when he heard a voice calling to him softly, "Are you a ghost or a man?"

He looked up, and saw a girl leaning out of a window, and he answered, "I am a man, and a better one, too, than your father or your grandfather."

"May all good luck be with you," said she, "but what has brought you into this land of ogres and horrors?"

"Does an ogre really live in this castle?" asked he.

"Certainly he does," replied the girl, "and as night is not far off he will be here soon. So, dear friend, depart quickly, lest he return and snap you up for supper."

"But I am so thirsty!" said the man. "Be kind, and give me some drink, or else I shall die! Surely, even in this desert there must be some spring?"

"Well, I have noticed that whenever the ogre brings back water he always comes from that side, so if you follow the same direction perhaps you may find some."

The man jumped up at once and was about to start, when the maiden spoke again, "Tell me, where are you going?"

"Why do you want to know?"

"I have an errand for you, but tell me first whether you go east or west."

"I travel to Damascus."

"Then do this for me. As you pass through our village, ask for a man called Dschemil, and say to him, 'Dschemila greets you, from the castle, which lies far away, and is rocked by the wind. In my grave lies only a goat. So take heart.'"

And the man promised, and went his way, till he came to a spring of water. And he drank a great draught and then lay on the bank and slept quietly. When he woke he said to himself, "The maiden did a good deed when she told me where to find water. A few hours more, and I should have been dead. So I will do her bidding, and seek out her native town and the man for whom the message was given."

For a whole month he travelled, till at last he reached the town where Dschemil dwelt, and as luck would have it, there was the young man sitting before his door with his beard unshaven and his shaggy hair hanging over his eyes.

"Welcome, stranger," said Dschemil, as the man stopped. "Where have you come from?"

"I come from the west, and go towards the east," he answered.

"Well, stop with us awhile, and rest and eat!" said Dschemil. And the man entered, and food was set before him, and he sat down with the father of the maiden and her brothers, and Dschemil. Only Dschemil himself was absent, squatting on the threshold.

"Why do you not eat too?" asked the stranger. But one of the young men whispered hastily, "Leave him alone. Take no notice! It is only at night that he ever eats."

So the stranger went on silently with his food. Suddenly one of Dschemil's brothers called out and said, "Dschemil, bring us some water!"

The stranger remembered his message and said, "Is there a man here named Dschemil? I lost my way in the desert, and came to a castle, and a maiden looked out of the window and..."

"Be quiet," they cried, fearing that Dschemil might hear. But Dschemil had heard, and came forward and said, "What did you see? Tell me truly, or I will cut off your head this instant!"

"My lord," replied the stranger, "as I was wandering, hot and tired, through the desert, I saw near me a great castle, and I said aloud, 'I will rest a little in its shadow.' And a maiden looked out of a window and said, 'Are you a ghost or a man?' And I answered, 'I am a man, and a better one, too, than your father or your grandfather.' And I was thirsty and asked for water, but she had none to give me, and I felt like to die. Then she told me that the ogre, in whose castle she dwelt, brought in water always from the same side, and that if I too went that way most likely I should come to it. But before I started she begged me to go to her native town, and if I met a man called Dschemil I was to say to him, 'Dschemila greets you, from the castle which lies far away, and is rocked by the wind. In my grave lies only a goat. So take heart.'"

Then Dschemil turned to his family and said, "Is this true? Is Dschemila not dead at all, but simply stolen from her home?"

"No, no," replied they, "his story is a pack of lies. Dschemila is really dead. Everybody knows it."

"That I shall see for myself," said Dschemil, and, snatching up a spade, hastened off to the grave where the goat's head lay buried.

And they answered, "Then hear what really happened. When you were away, she went with the other maidens to the forest to gather wood. And there she found an iron mortar, which she wished to bring home, but she could not carry it, neither would she leave it. So the maidens returned without her, and as night was come, we all set out to look for her, but found nothing. And we said, 'The bridegroom will be here tomorrow, and when he learns that she is lost, he will set out to seek her, and we shall lose him too. Let us kill a goat, and bury it in her grave, and tell him she is dead.' Now you know, so do as you will. Only, if you go to seek her, take with you this man with whom she has spoken that he may show you the way."

"Yes, that is the best plan," replied Dschemil, "so give me food, and hand me my sword, and we will set out directly."

But the stranger answered, "I am not going to waste a whole month in leading you to the castle! If it were only a day or two's journey I would not mind, but a month - no!"

"Come with me then for three days," said Dschemil, "and put me in the right road, and I will reward you richly."

"Very well," replied the stranger, "so let it be."

For three days they travelled from sunrise to sunset, then the stranger said, "Dschemil?"

"Yes," replied he.

"Go straight on till you reach a spring, then go on a little farther, and soon you will see the castle standing before you."

"So I will," said Dschemil.

"Farewell, then," said the stranger, and turned back the way he had come.

It was six and twenty days before Dschemil caught sight of a green spot rising out of the sandy desert, and knew that the spring was near at last. He hastened his steps, and soon was kneeling by its side, drinking thirstily of the bubbling water. Then he lay down on the cool grass, and began to think. "If the man was right, the castle must be somewhere about. I had better sleep here tonight, and tomorrow I shall be able to see where it is."

So he slept long and peacefully. When he awoke the sun was high, and he jumped up and washed his face and hands in the spring, before going on his journey. He had not walked far, when the castle suddenly appeared before him, though a moment before not a trace of it could be seen.

"How am I to get in?" he thought. "I dare not knock, lest the ogre should hear me. Perhaps it would be best for me to climb up the wall, and wait to see what will happen."

So he did, and after sitting on the top for about an hour, a window above him opened, and a voice said, "Dschemil!" He looked up, and at the sight of Dschemila, whom he had so long believed to be dead, he began to weep.

"Dear cousin," she whispered, "what has brought you here?"

"My grief at losing you."

"Oh! Go away at once. If the ogre comes back he will kill you."

"I swear by your head, queen of my heart, that I have not found you only to lose you again! If I must die, well, I must!"

"O, what can I do for you?"

"Anything you like!"

"If I let you down a cord, can you make it fast under your arms, and climb up?"

"Of course I can," said he.

So Dschemila lowered the cord, and Dschemil tied it round him, and climbed up to her window. Then they embraced each other tenderly, and burst into tears of joy.

"But what shall I do when the ogre returns?" asked she.

"Trust to me," he said.

Now there was a chest in the room, where Dschemila kept her clothes. And she made Dschemil get into it, and lie at the bottom, and told him to keep very still.

He was only hidden just in time, for the lid was hardly closed when the ogre's heavy tread was heard on the stairs. He flung open the door, bringing men's flesh for himself and lamb's flesh for the maiden. "I smell the smell of a man!" he thundered. "What is he doing here?"

"How could anyone have come to this desert place?" asked the girl, and burst into tears.

"Do not cry," said the ogre. "Perhaps a raven has dropped some scraps from his claws."

"Ah, yes, I was forgetting," answered she. "One did drop some bones about."

"Well, burn them to powder," replied the ogre, "so that I may swallow it."

So the maiden took some bones and burned them, and gave them to the ogre, saying, "Here is the powder, swallow it."

And when he had swallowed the powder the ogre stretched himself out and went to sleep.

In a little while the man's flesh, which the maiden was cooking for the ogre's supper, called out and said:

"Hist! Hist!

A man lies in the kist!"

And the lamb's flesh answered:

"He is your brother,

And cousin of the other."

The ogre moved sleepily, and asked, "What did the meat say, Dschemila?"

"Only that I must be sure to add salt."

"Well, add salt."

"Yes, I have done so," said she.

The ogre was soon sound asleep again when the man's flesh called out a second time:

"Hist! Hist!
A man lies in the kist!"

And the lamb's flesh answered:

"He is your brother,
And cousin of the other."

"What did it say, Dschemila?" asked the ogre.

"Only that I must add pepper."

"Well, add pepper."

"Yes, I have done so," said she.

The ogre had had a long day's hunting, and could not keep himself awake. In a moment his eyes were tight shut, and then the man's flesh called out for the third time:

"Hist! Hist

A man lies in the kist,"

And the lamb's flesh answered:

"He is your brother,

And cousin of the other."

"What did it say, Dschemila?" asked the ogre.

"Only that it was ready, and that I had better take it off the fire."

"Then if it is ready, bring it to me, and I will eat it."

So she brought it to him, and while he was eating she supped off the lamb's flesh herself, and managed to put some aside for her cousin.

When the ogre had finished, and had washed his hands, he said to Dschemila, "Make my bed, for I am tired."

So she made his bed, and put a nice soft pillow for his head, and tucked him up.

"Father," she said suddenly.

"Well, what is it?"

"Dear father, if you are really asleep, why are your eyes always open?"

"Why do you ask that, Dschemila? Do you want to deal treacherously with me?"

"No, of course not, father. How could I, and what would be the use of it?"

"Well, why do you want to know?"

"Because last night I woke up and saw the whole place shining in a red light, which frightened me."

"That happens when I am fast asleep."

"And what is the good of the pin you always keep here so carefully?"

"If I throw that pin in front of me, it turns into an iron mountain."

"And this darning needle?"

"That becomes a sea."

"And this hatchet?"

"That becomes a thorn hedge, which no one can pass through. But why do you ask all these questions? I am sure you have something in your head."

"O, I just wanted to know, and how could anyone find me out here?" and she began to cry.

"O, don't cry, I was only in fun," said the ogre.

He was soon asleep again, and a yellow light shone through the castle.

"Come quick!" called Dschemil from the chest, "we must fly now while the ogre is asleep."

"Not yet," she said, "there is a yellow light shining. I don't think he is asleep."

So they waited for an hour. Then Dschemil whispered again, "Wake up! There is no time to lose!"

"Let me see if he is asleep," said she, and she peeped in, and saw a red light shining. Then she stole back to her cousin, and asked, "But how are we to get out?"

"Get the rope, and I will let you down."

So she fetched the rope, the hatchet, and the pin and the needles, and said, "Take them, and put them in the pocket of your cloak, and be sure not to lose them."

Dschemil put them carefully in his pocket, and tied the rope round her, and let her down over the wall.

"Are you safe?" he asked.

"Yes, quite."

"Then untie the rope, so that I may draw it up."

And Dschemila did as she was told, and in a few minutes he stood beside her.

Now all this time the ogre was asleep, and had heard nothing. Then his dog came to him and said, "O, sleeper, are you having pleasant dreams? Dschemila has forsaken you and run away."

The ogre got out of bed, gave the dog a kick, then went back again, and slept till morning.

When it grew light, he rose, and called, "Dschemila! Dschemila!" but he only heard the echo of his own voice! Then he dressed himself quickly, buckled on his sword and whistled to his dog, and followed the road which he knew the fugitives must have taken.

"Cousin," said Dschemila suddenly, and turning round as she spoke.

"What is it?" answered he.

"The ogre is coming after us. I saw him."

"But where is he? I don't see him."

"Over there. He only looks about as tall as a needle."

Then they both began to run as fast as they could, while the ogre and his dog kept drawing always nearer. A few more steps, and he would have been by their side, when Dschemila threw the darning needle behind her. In a moment it became an iron mountain between them and their enemy.

"We will break it down, my dog and I," cried the ogre in a rage, and they dashed at the mountain till they had forced a path through, and came ever nearer and nearer.

"Cousin!" said Dschemila suddenly.

"What is it?"

"The ogre is coming after us with his dog."

"You go on in front then," answered he, and they both ran on as fast as they could, while the ogre and the dog drew always nearer and nearer.

"They are close upon us!" cried the maiden, glancing behind, "you must throw the hatchet."

So Dschemil took the hatchet from his cloak and threw it behind him, and a dense thicket of thorns sprang up round them, which the ogre and his dog could not pass through.

"I will get through it somehow, if I burrow underground," cried he, and very soon he and the dog were on the other side.

"Cousin," said Dschemila, "they are close to us now."

"Go on in front, and fear nothing," replied Dschemil.

So she ran on a little way, and then stopped.

"He is only a few yards away now," she said, and Dschemil flung the darning needle on the ground, and it turned into a lake.

"I will drink, and my dog shall drink, till it is dry," shrieked the ogre, and the dog drank so much that it burst and died. But the ogre did not stop for that, and soon the whole lake was nearly dry. Then he exclaimed, "Dschemila, let your head become a donkey's head, and your hair fur!"

But when it was done, Dschemil looked at her in horror, and said, "She is really a donkey, and not a woman at all!"

And he left her, and went home.

For two days poor Dschemila wandered about alone, weeping bitterly. When her cousin drew near his native town, he began to think over his conduct, and to feel ashamed of himself.

"Perhaps by this time she has changed back to her proper shape," he said to himself, "I will go and see!"

So he made all the haste he could, and at last he saw her seated on a rock, trying to keep off the wolves, who longed to have her for dinner. He drove them off and said, "Get up, dear cousin, you have had a narrow escape."

Dschemila stood up and answered, "Bravo, my friend. you persuaded me to fly with you, and then left me helplessly to my fate."

"Shall I tell you the truth?" asked he.

"Tell it."

"I thought you were a witch, and I was afraid of you."

"Did you not see me before my transformation? and did you not watch it happen under your very eyes, when the ogre bewitched me?"

"What shall I do?" said Dschemil. "If I take you into the town, everyone will laugh, and say, "Is that a new kind of toy you have got? It has hands like a woman, feet like a woman, the body of a woman, but its head is the head of an ass, and its hair is fur.""

"Well, what do you mean to do with me?" asked Dschemila. "Better take me home to my mother by night, and tell no one anything about it."

"So I will," said he.

They waited where they were till it was nearly dark, then Dschemil brought his cousin home.

"Is that Dschemil?" asked the mother when he knocked softly.

"Yes, it is."

"And have you found her?"

"Yes, and I have brought her to you."

"O, where is she? Let me see her!" cried the mother.

"Here, behind me," answered Dschemil.

But when the poor woman caught sight of her daughter, she shrieked, and exclaimed, "Are you making fun of me? When did I ever give birth to an ass?"

"Hush!" said Dschemil, "it is not necessary to let the whole world know! And if you look at her body, you will see two scars on it."

"Mother," sobbed Dschemila, "do you really not know your own daughter?"

"Yes, of course I know her."

"What are her two scars then?"

"On her thigh is a scar from the bite of a dog, and on her breast is the mark of a burn, where she pulled a lamp over her when she was little."

"Then look at me, and see if I am not your daughter," said Dschemila, throwing off her clothes and showing her two scars.

And at the sight her mother embraced her, weeping.

"Dear daughter," she cried, "what evil fate has befallen you?"

"It was the ogre who carried me off first, and then bewitched me," answered Dschemila.

"But what is to be done with you?" asked her mother.

"Hide me away, and tell no one anything about me. And you, dear cousin, say nothing to the neighbours, and if they should put questions, you can make answer that I have not yet been found."

"So I will," replied he.

Then he and her mother took her upstairs and hid her in a cupboard, where she stayed for a whole month, only going out to walk when all the world was asleep.

Meanwhile Dschemil had returned to his own home, where his father and mother, his brothers and neighbours, greeted him joyfully.

"When did you come back?" said they, "and have you found Dschemila?"

"No, I searched the whole world after her, and could hear nothing of her."

"Did you part company with the man who started with you?"

"Yes, after three days he got so weak and useless he could not go on. It must be a month by now since he reached home again. I went on and visited every castle, and looked in every house. But there were no signs of her, and so I gave it up."

And they answered him, "We told you before that it was no good. An ogre or an ogress must have snapped her up, and how can you expect to find her?"

"I loved her too much to be still," he said.

But his friends did not understand, and soon they spoke to him again about it.

"We will seek for a wife for you. There are plenty of girls prettier than Dschemila."

"I dare say, but I don't want them."

"But what will you do with all the cushions and carpets, and beautiful things you bought for your house?"

"They can stay in the chests."

"But the moths will eat them! For a few weeks, it is of no consequence, but after a year or two they will be quite useless."

"And if they have to lie there ten years I will have Dschemila, and her only, for my wife. For a month, or even two months, I will rest here quietly. Then I will go and seek her afresh."

"O, you are quite mad! Is she the only maiden in the world? There are plenty of others better worth having than she is."

"If there are I have not seen them! And why do you make all this fuss? Every man knows his own business best."

"Why, it is you who are making all the fuss yourself."

But Dschemil turned and went into the house, for he did not want to quarrel.

Three months later a traveller, who was journeying across the desert, came to the castle, and laid himself down under the wall to rest.

In the evening the ogre saw him there and said to him, "What are you doing here? Have you anything to sell?"

"I have only some clothes," answered the traveller, who was in mortal terror of the ogre.

"O, don't be afraid of me," said the ogre, laughing. "I shall not eat you. Indeed, I mean to go a bit of the way with you myself."

"I am ready, gracious sir," replied the traveller, rising to his feet.

"Well, go straight on till you reach a town, and in that town you will find a maiden called Dschemila and a young man called Dschemil. Take this mirror and this comb with you, and say to Dschemila, 'Your father, the ogre, greets you, and begs you to look at your face in this mirror, and it will appear as it was before, and to comb your hair with this comb, and it will be as it was formerly.' If you do not carry out my orders, I will eat you the next time we meet."

"O, I will obey you punctually," cried the traveller.

After thirty days the traveller entered the gate of the town, and sat down in the first street he came to, hungry, thirsty, and very tired.

Quite by chance, Dschemil happened to pass by, and seeing a man sitting there, full in the glare of the sun, he stopped, and said, "Get up at once, or you will have a sunstroke if you sit in such a place."

"Ah, good sir," replied the traveller, "for a whole month I have been travelling, and I am too tired to move."

"Which way did you come?" asked Dschemil.

"From out there," answered the traveller pointing behind him.

"And you have been travelling for a month, you say? Well, did you see anything remarkable?"

"Yes, good sir, I saw a castle, and lay down to rest under its shadow. And an ogre woke me, and told me to come to this town, where I should find a young man called Dschemil, and a girl called Dschemila."

"My name is Dschemil. What does the ogre want with me?"

"He gave me some presents for Dschemila. How can I see her?"

"Come with me, and you shall give them into her own hands."

So the two went together to the house of Dschemil's uncle, and Dschemil led the traveller into his aunt's room.

"Aunt!" he cried, "this man who is with me has come from the ogre, and has brought with him, as presents, a mirror and a comb which the ogre has sent her."

"But it may be only some wicked trick on the part of the ogre," said she.

"O, I don't think so," answered the young man, "give her the things."

Then the maiden was called, and she came out of her hiding place, and went up to the traveller, saying, "Where have you come from?"

"From your father the ogre."

"And what errand did he send you on?"

"He told me I was to give you this mirror and this comb, and to say, 'Look in this mirror, and comb your hair with this comb, and both will become as they were formerly.'"

And Dschemila took the mirror and looked into it, and combed her hair with the comb, and she no longer had an ass's head, but the face of a beautiful maiden.

Great was the joy of both mother and cousin at this wonderful sight, and the news that Dschemila had returned soon spread, and the neighbours came flocking in with greetings.

"When did you come back?"

"My cousin brought me."

"Why, he told us he could not find you!"

"O, I did that on purpose," answered Dschemil. "I did not want everyone to know."

Then he turned to his father and his mother, his brothers and his sisters-in-law, and said, "We must set to work at once, for the wedding will be today."

A beautiful litter was prepared to carry the bride to her new home, but she shrank back, saying, "I am afraid, lest the ogre should carry me off again."

"How can the ogre get at you when we are all here?" they said. "There are two thousands of us all told, and every man has his sword."

"He will manage it somehow," answered Dschemila, "he is a powerful king!"

"She is right," said an old man. "Take away the litter, and let her go on foot if she is afraid."

"But it is absurd!" exclaimed the rest. "How can the ogre get hold of her?"

"I will not go," said Dschemila again. "You do not know that monster as I do."

And while they were disputing the bridegroom arrived.

"Let her alone. She shall stay in her father's house. After all, I can live here, and the wedding feast shall be made ready."

And so they were married at last, and died without having had a single quarrel.

The Turtle, The Frog, And The Serpent

This story has been edited and adapted from Moorish Literature, a collection work from sources such as Adolphe Hanoteau's Poésies Populaires de la Khabylie du Jurgura of 1867, Émile Masqueray's Observations grammaticales sur la grammaire Touareg et textes de la Tourahog des Tailog, and René Basset's L'insurrection Algerienne, de 1871 dans les chansons populaires Khabyles Lourain of 1892. This version was taken from the English translation introduced by René Basset and published by the University of France and the Académie D'Alger, published in 1901. This is a Berber tale.

Once upon a time the turtle married a frog. One day they quarrelled. The frog escaped and withdrew into a hole. The turtle was troubled and stood in front of his door very much worried. In those days the animals spoke. The griffin came by that way and said, "What is the matter with you? you look worried this morning."

"Nothing ails me," answered the turtle, "except that the frog has left me."

The griffin replied, "I'll bring her back."

"You will do me a great favour."

The griffin took up his journey and arrived at the hole of the frog. He scratched at the door. The frog heard him and asked, "Who dares to rap at the door of a king's daughter?"

"It is I, the griffin, son of a griffin, who lets no carrion escape him."

"Get out of here, among your corpses. I, a daughter of the King, will not go with you."

He departed immediately.

The next day the vulture came along by the turtle and found it worrying before its door, and asked what the trouble was. It answered, "The frog has gone away."

"I'll bring her back," said the vulture.

"You will do me a great favour."

The vulture started, and reaching the frog's house began to beat its wings.

The frog said, "Who comes to the east to make a noise at the house of the daughter of kings, and will not let her sleep at her ease?"

"It is I, the vulture, son of a vulture, who steals chicks from under her mother."

The frog replied, "Get away from here, father of the dunghill. you are not the one to conduct the daughter of a king."

The vulture was angry and went away much disturbed. He returned to the turtle and said, "The frog refuses to come back with me. Seek someone else who can enter her hole and make her come out. Then I will bring her back even if she won't walk."

The turtle went to seek the serpent, and when he had found him he began to weep.

"I'm the one to make her come out," said the serpent. He quickly went before the hole of the frog and scratched at the door.

"What is the name of this other one?" asked the frog.

"It is I, the serpent, son of the serpent. Come out or I'll enter."

"Wait awhile until I put on my best clothes, gird my girdle, rub my lips with nut-shells, and put some *koheul* in my eyes. Then I will go with you."

"Hurry up," said the serpent. Then he waited a little while. Finally he got angry, entered her house, and swallowed her. Ever since that time the serpent has been at war with the frog. Whenever he sees one he chases her and eats her.

The Story Of Halfman

This story has been edited and adapted from Andrew Lang's Strange Story Book, originally published by Longmans, Green And Company, London And New York, in 1913. The original story was included in Märchen und Gedichte aus der Stadt Tripolis by Hans Stumme.

In a certain town there lived a judge who was married but had no children. One day he was standing lost in thought before his house, when an old man passed by.

"What is the matter, sir, said he, "you look troubled?"

"O, leave me alone, my good man!"

"But what is it?" persisted the other.

"Well, I am successful in my profession and a person of importance, but I care nothing for it all, as I have no children."

Then the old man said, "Here are twelve apples. If your wife eats them, she will have twelve sons."

The judge thanked him joyfully as he took the apples, and went to seek his wife. "Eat these apples at once," he cried, "and you will have twelve sons."

So she sat down and ate eleven of them, but just as she was in the middle of the twelfth her sister came in, and she gave her the half that was left.

The eleven sons came into the world, strong and handsome boys, but when the twelfth was born, there was only half of him. By-and-by they all grew into men, and one day they told their father it was high time he found wives for them.

"I have a brother," he answered, "who lives away in the East, and he has twelve daughters, go and marry them." So the twelve sons saddled their horses and rode for twelve days, till they met an old woman.

"Good greeting to you, young men!" said she, "we have waited long for you, your uncle and me. The girls have become women, and are sought, in marriage by many, but I knew you would come one day, and I have kept them for you. Follow me into my house."

And the twelve brothers followed her gladly, and their father's brother stood at the door, and gave them meat and drink. But at night, when everyone was asleep, Halfman crept softly to his brothers, and said to them, "Listen, all of you! This man is no uncle of ours, but an ogre."

"Nonsense, of course he is our uncle," answered they.

"Well, this very night you will see!" said Halfman. And he did not go to bed, but hid himself and watched.

Now in a little while he saw the wife of the ogre steal into the room on tiptoe and spread a red cloth over the brothers and then go and cover her daughters with a white cloth. After that she lay down and was soon snoring loudly. When Halfman was quite sure she was sound asleep, he took the red cloth from his brothers and put it on the girls, and laid their white cloth over his brothers. Next he drew their scarlet caps from their heads and exchanged them for the veils which the ogre's daughters were wearing. This was hardly done when he heard steps coming along the floor, so he hid himself quickly in the folds of a curtain. There was only half of him!

The ogress came slowly and gently along, stretching out her hands before her, so that she might not fall against anything unawares, for she had only a tiny lantern slung at her waist, which did not give much light. And when she reached the place where the sisters were lying, she stooped down and held a corner of the cloth up to the lantern. Yes! It certainly was red! Still, to make sure that there was no mistake, she passed her hands lightly over their heads, and felt the caps that covered them. Then she was quite certain the brothers lay sleeping before her, and began to kill them one by one. And Halfman whispered to his brothers, "Get up and run for your lives, for the ogress is killing her daughters." The brothers needed no second bidding, and in a moment were out of the house.

By this time the ogress had slain all her daughters but one, who awoke suddenly and saw what had happened. "Mother, what are you doing?" cried she. "Do you know that you have killed my sisters?"

"O, woe is me!" wailed the ogress. "Halfman has outwitted me after all!" And she turned to wreak vengeance on him, but he and his brothers were far away.

They rode all day till they got to the town where their real uncle lived, and inquired the way to his house.

"Why have you been so long in coming?" asked he when they had found him.

"O, dear uncle, we were very nearly not coming at all!" replied they. "We fell in with an ogress who took us home and would have killed us if it had not been for Halfman. He knew what was in her mind and saved us, and here we are. Now give us each a daughter to wife, and let us return where we came."

"Take them!" said the uncle. "The eldest for the eldest, the second for the second, and so on to the youngest."

But the wife of Halfman was the prettiest of them all, and the other brothers were jealous and said to each other, "What, is he who is only half a man to get the best? Let us put him to death and give his wife to our eldest brother!" And they waited for a chance.

After they had all ridden, in company with their brides, for some distance, they arrived at a brook, and one of them asked, "Now, who will go and fetch water from the brook?"

"Halfman is the youngest," said the elder brother, "he must go."

So Halfman got down and filled a skin with water, and they drew it up by a rope and drank. When they had done drinking, Halfman, who was standing in the middle of the stream, called out, "Throw me the rope and draw me up, for I cannot get out alone." And the brothers threw him a rope to draw him up the steep bank, but when he was half-way up they cut the rope, and he fell back into the stream. Then the brothers rode away as fast as they could, with his bride.

Halfman sank down under the water from the force of the fall, but before he touched the bottom a fish came and said to him, "Fear nothing, Halfman, I will help you." And the fish guided him to a shallow place, so that he scrambled out. On the way it said to him, "Do you understand what your brothers, whom you saved from death, have done to you?"

"Yes, but what am I to do?" asked Halfman.

"Take one of my scales," said the fish, "and when you find yourself in danger, throw it in the fire. Then I will appear before you."

"Thank you," said Halfman, and went his way, while the fish swam back to its home.

The country was strange to Halfman, and he wandered about without knowing where he was going, till he suddenly found the ogress standing before him. "Ah, Halfman, have I got you at last? you killed my daughters and helped your brothers to escape. What do you think I shall do with you?"

"Whatever you like!" said Halfman.

"Come into my house, then," said the ogress, and he followed her.

"Look here!" she called to her husband, "I have got hold of Halfman. I am going to roast him, so be quick and make up the fire!"

So the ogre brought wood, and heaped it up till the flames roared up the chimney. Then he turned to his wife and said, "It is all ready, let us put him on!"

"What is the hurry, my good ogre?" asked Halfman. "You have me in your power, and I cannot escape. I am so thin now, I shall hardly make one mouthful. Better fatten me up, for you will enjoy me much more."

"That is a very sensible remark," replied the ogre. "but what fattens you quickest?"

"Butter, meat, and red wine," answered Halfman.

"Very good, we will lock you into this room, and here you shall stay till you are ready for eating."

So Halfman was locked into the room, and the ogre and his wife brought him his food. At the end of three months he said to his gaolers, "Now I have got quite fat, take me out, and kill me."

"Get out, then!" said the ogre.

"But," went on Halfman, "you and your wife had better go to invite your friends to the feast, and your daughter can stay in the house and look after me!"

"Yes, that is a good idea," answered they.

"You had better bring the wood in here," continued Halfman, "and I will split it up small, so that there may be no delay in cooking me."

So the ogress gave Halfman a pile of wood and an axe, and then set out with her husband, leaving Halfman and her daughter busy in the house.

After he had chopped for a little while he called to the girl, "Come and help me, or else I shan't have it all ready when your mother gets back."

"All right," said she, and held a billet of wood for him to chop.

But he raised his axe and cut off her head, and ran away like the wind. By-and-by the ogre and his wife returned and found their daughter lying without her head, and they began to cry and sob, saying, "This is Halfman's work, why did we listen to him?" But Halfman was far away.

When he escaped from the house he ran on straight before him for some time, looking for a safe shelter, as he knew that the ogre's legs were much longer than his, and that it was his only chance. At last he saw an iron tower which he climbed up. Soon the ogre appeared, looking right and left lest his prey should be sheltering behind a rock or tree, but he did not know Halfman was so near till he heard his voice calling, "Come up! Come up! You will find me here!"

"But how can I come up?" said the ogre, "I see no door, and I could not possibly climb that tower."

"O, there is no door," replied Halfman.

"Then how did you climb up?"

"A fish carried me on his back."

"And what am I to do?"

"You must go and fetch all your relations, and tell them to bring plenty of sticks, then you must light a fire, and let it burn till the tower becomes red hot. After that you can easily throw it down."

"Very good," said the ogre, and he went round to every relation he had, and told them to collect wood and bring it to the tower where Halfman was. The men did as they were ordered, and soon the tower was glowing like coral, but when they flung themselves against it to overthrow it, they caught themselves on fire and were burnt to death. And overhead sat Halfman, laughing heartily. But the ogre's wife was still alive, for she had taken no part in kindling the fire.

"O," she shrieked with rage, "you have killed my daughters and my husband, and all the men belonging to me, how can I get at you to avenge myself?"

"O, that is easy enough," said Halfman. "I will let down a rope, and if you tie it tightly round you, I will draw it up."

"All right," returned the ogress, fastening the rope which Halfman let down. "Now pull me up."

"Are you sure it is secure?"

"Yes, quite sure."

"Don't be afraid."

"O, I am not afraid at all!"

So Halfman slowly drew her up, and when she was near the top he let go the rope, and she fell down and broke her neck. Then Halfman heaved a great sigh and said, "That was hard work. The rope has hurt my hands badly, but now I am rid of her for ever."

So Halfman came down from the tower, and went on, till he got to a desert place, and as he was very tired, he lay down to sleep. While it was still dark, an ogress passed by, and she woke him and said, "Halfman, tomorrow your brother is to marry your wife."

"O, how can I stop it?" asked he. "Will you help me?"

"Yes, I will," replied the ogress.

"Thank you, thank you!" cried Halfman, kissing her on the forehead. "My wife is dearer to me than anything else in the world, and it is not my brother's fault that I am not dead long ago."

"Very well, I will rid you of him," said the ogress, "but only on one condition. If a boy is born to you, you must give him to me!"

"O, anything," answered Halfman, "as long as you deliver me from my brother, and get me my wife."

"Mount on my back, then, and in a quarter of an hour we shall be there."

The ogress was as good as her word, and in a few minutes they arrived at the outskirts of the town where Halfman and his brothers lived. Here she left him, while she went into the town itself, and found the wedding guests just leaving the brother's house. Unnoticed by anyone, the ogress crept into a curtain, changing herself into a scorpion, and when the brother was going to get into bed, she stung him behind the ear, so that he fell dead where he stood. Then she returned to Halfman and told him to go and claim his bride. He jumped up hastily from his seat, and took the road to his father's house. As he drew near he heard sounds of weeping and lamentations, and he said to a man he met, "What is the matter?"

"The judge's eldest son was married yesterday, and died suddenly before night."

"Well," thought Halfman, "my conscience is clear anyway, for it is quite plain he coveted my wife, and that is why he tried to drown me."

He went at once to his father's room, and found him sitting in tears on the floor. "Dear father," said Halfman, "are you not glad to see me? You weep for my brother, but I am your son too, and he stole my bride from me and tried to drown me in the brook. If he is dead, I at least am alive."

"No, no, he was better than you!" moaned the father.

"Why, dear father?"

"He told me you had behaved very ill," said he.

"Well, call my brothers," answered Halfman, "as I have a story to tell them." So the father called them all into his presence. Then Halfman began, "After we were twelve days" journey from home, we met an ogress, who gave us greeting and said, 'Why have you been so long coming? The daughters of your uncle have waited for you in vain,' and she bade us follow her to the house, saying, 'Now there need be no more delay. You can marry your cousins as soon as you please, and take them with you to your own home.' But I warned my brothers that the man was not our uncle, but an ogre.

"When we lay down to sleep, she spread a red cloth over us, and covered her daughters with a white one, but I changed the cloths, and when the ogress came back in the middle of the night, and looked at the cloths, she mistook her own daughters for my brothers, and killed them one by one, all but the youngest. Then I woke my brothers, and we all stole softly from the house, and we rode like the wind to our real uncle.

"And when he saw us, he bade us welcome, and married us to his twelve daughters, the eldest to the eldest, and so on to me, whose bride was the youngest of all and also the prettiest. And my brothers were filled with envy, and left me to drown in a brook, but I was saved by a fish who showed me how to get out. Now, you are a judge! Who did well, and who did evil - I or my brothers?"

"Is this story true?" said the father, turning to his sons.

"It is true, my father," answered they. "It is even as Halfman has said, and the girl belongs to him."

Then the judge embraced Halfman and said to him, "You have done well, my son. Take your bride, and may you both live long and happily together!"

At the end of the year Halfman's wife had a son, and not long after she came one day hastily into the room, and found her husband weeping. "What is the matter?" she asked.

"The matter?" said he.

"Yes, why are you weeping?"

"Because," replied Halfman, "the baby is not really ours, but belongs to an ogress."

"Are you mad?" cried the wife. "What do you mean by talking like that?"

"I promised," said Halfman, "when she undertook to kill my brother and to give you to me, that the first son we had should be hers."

"And will she take him from us now?" said the poor woman.

"No, not quite yet," replied Halfman, "when he is bigger."

"And is she to have all our children?" asked she.

"No, only this one," returned Halfman.

Day by day the boy grew bigger, and one day as he was playing in the street with the other children, the ogress came by. "Go to your father," she said, "and repeat this speech to him, 'I want my forfeit, when am I to have it?'"

"All right," replied the child, but when he went home forgot all about it. The next day the ogress came again, and asked the boy what answer the father had given. "I forgot all about it," said he.

"Well, put this ring on your finger, and then you won't forget."

"Very well," replied the boy, and went home.

The next morning, as he was at breakfast, his mother said to him, "Child, where did you get that ring?"

"A woman gave it to me yesterday, and she told me, father, to tell you that she wanted her forfeit, and when was she to have it?"

Then his father burst into tears and said, "If she comes again you must say to her that your parents bid her take her forfeit at once, and depart."

At this they both began to weep afresh, and his mother kissed him, and put on his new clothes and said, "If the woman bids you to follow her, you must go," but the boy did not heed her grief. He was so pleased with his new clothes. And when he went out, he said to his play-fellows, "Look how smart I am. I am going away with my aunt to foreign lands."

At that moment the ogress came up and asked him, "Did you give my message to your father and mother?"

"Yes, dear aunt, I did."

"And what did they say?"

"Take it away at once!"

So she took him.

But when dinner-time came, and the boy did not return, his father and mother knew that he would never come back, and they sat down and wept all day. At last Halfman rose up and said to his wife, "Be comforted, we will wait a year, and then I will go to the ogress and see the boy, and how he is cared for."

"Yes, that will be the best," said she.

The year passed away and then Halfman saddled his horse, and rode to the place where the ogress had found him sleeping. She was not there, but not knowing what to do next, he got off his horse and waited. About midnight she suddenly stood before him.

"Halfman, why did you come here?" said she.

"I have a question I want to ask you."

"Well, ask it, but I know quite well what it is. Your wife wishes you to ask whether I shall carry off your second son as I did the first."

"Yes, that is it," replied Halfman. Then he seized her hand and said, "O, let me see my son, and how he looks, and what he is doing."

The ogress was silent, but stuck her staff hard in the earth, and the earth opened, and the boy appeared and said, "Dear father, have you come too?" And his father clasped him in his arms, and began to cry. But the boy struggled to be free, saying "Dear father, put me down. I have got a new mother, who is better than the old one, and a new father, who is better than you."

Then his father sat him down and said, "Go in peace, my boy, but listen first to me. Tell your father the ogre and your mother the ogress, that never more shall they have any children of mine."

"All right," replied the boy, and called "Mother!"

"What is it?"

"You are never to take away any more of my father and mother's children!"

"Now that I have got you, I don't want any more," answered she.

Then the boy turned to his father and said, "Go in peace, dear father, and give my mother greeting and tell her not to be anxious anymore, for she can keep all her children."

And Halfman mounted his horse and rode home, and told his wife all he had seen, and the message sent by Mohammed, Mohammed the son of Halfman, the son of the judge.

The Hedgehog, The Jackal, And The Lion

This story has been edited and adapted from Moorish Literature, a collection work from sources such as Adolphe Hanoteau's Poésies Populaires de la Khabylie du Jurgura of 1867, Émile Masqueray's Observations grammaticales sur la grammaire Touareg et textes de la Tourahog des Tailog, and René Basset's L'insurrection Algerienne, de 1871 dans les chansons populaires Khabyles Lourain of 1892. This version was taken from the English translation introduced by René Basset and published by the University of France and the Académie D'Alger, published in 1901. This is a Berber tale.

Once upon a time the jackal went in search of the hedgehog and said to it, "Come along. I know a garden of onions. We will fill our bellies."

"How many tricks have you?" asked the hedgehog.

"I have a hundred and one."

"And I," said the other, "have one and a half."

They entered the garden and ate a good deal. The hedgehog ate a little and then went to see if he could get out of the entrance or not. When he had eaten enough so that he could just barely slip out, he stopped eating. As for the jackal, he never stopped eating until he was swollen very much.

As these things were going on, the owner of the garden arrived. The hedgehog saw him and said to his companion, "Escape! The master is coming."

He himself took flight. But in spite of his exhortations the jackal couldn't get through the opening. "It is impossible," he said.

"Where are those one hundred and one tricks? They don't serve you now."

"May God have mercy on your parents, my uncle, lend me your half a trick."

"Lie down on the ground," answered the hedgehog. "Play dead, shut your mouth, stretch out your paws as if you were dead, until the master of the garden shall see it and cast you into the street, and then you can run away."

On that the hedgehog departed. The jackal lay down as he had told him until the owner of the garden came with his son and saw him lying as if dead. The child said to his father, "Here is a dead jackal. He filled his belly with onions until he died."

Said the man, "Go, drag him outside."

"Yes," said the child, and he took him and stuck a thorn into him.

"Hold on, enough!" said the jackal. "They play with reeds, but this is not sport."

The child ran to his father and said, "The jackal cried out, 'A reed! a reed!'"

The father went and looked at the animal, which feigned death. "Why do you tell me that it still lives?"

"It surely does."

"Come away and leave that carrion."

The child stuck another thorn into the jackal, which cried, "What, again?" The child went to his father. "He has just said, 'What, again?'"

"Come now," said the man, and he sent away his son. The latter took the jackal by the motionless tail and cast him into the street. Immediately the animal jumped up and started to run away. The child threw his slippers after him. The jackal took them, put them on, and departed.

On the way he met the lion, who said, "What is that footwear, my dear?"

"You don't know, my uncle? I am a shoemaker. My father, my uncle, my mother, my brother, my sister, and the little girl who was born at our house last night are all shoemakers."

"Won't you make me a pair of shoes?" replied the lion.

"I will make you a pair. Bring me two fat camels. I will skin them and make you some good shoes."

The lion went away and brought the two fat camels. "They are thin," said the jackal. "Go change them for others."

He brought two thin ones.

"They are fat," said the jackal. He skinned them, cut some thorns from a palm-tree, rolled the leather around the lion's paws and fastened it there with the thorns.

"Ouch!" screamed the lion.

"He who wants to look finely ought not to say, 'Ouch.'"

"Enough, my dear."

"My uncle, I will give you the rest of the slippers and boots."

He covered the lion's skin with the leather and stuck in the thorns. When he reached the knees, "Enough, my dear," said the lion. "What kind of shoes are those?"

"Keep still, my uncle, these are slippers, boots, breeches, and clothes."

When he came to the girdle the lion said, "What kind of shoes are those?"

"My uncle, they are slippers, boots, breeches, and clothing."

In this way he reached the lion's neck. "Stay here," he said, "until the leather dries. When the sun rises look it in the face. When the moon rises, too, look it in the face."

"It is good," said the lion, and the jackal went away.

The lion remained and did as his companion had told him. But his feet began to swell, the leather became hard, and he could not get up. When the jackal came back he asked him, "How are you, my uncle?"

"How am I? Wretch, son of a wretch, you have deceived me. Go, go. I will recommend you to my children."

The jackal came near and the lion seized him by the tail. The jackal fled, leaving his tail in the lion's mouth.

"Now," said the lion, "you have no tail. When my feet get well I will catch you and eat you up."

The jackal called his cousins and said to them, "Let us go and fill our bellies with onions in a garden that I know."

They went with him. Arriving he tied their tails to the branches of a young palm-tree, and twisted them well.

"Who has tied our tails like this?" they asked.

"No one will come before you have filled your bellies. If you see the master of the garden approach, struggle and fly. you see that I, too, am bound as you are." But he had tied an onion-stalk on himself.

When the owner of the garden arrived, the jackals saw him coming. They struggled, their tails were all torn out, and stayed behind with the branches to which they were fastened. When the jackal saw the man, he cut the onion stem and escaped the first of all.

As for the lion, when his feet were cured, he went to take a walk and met his friend the jackal. He seized him and said, "Now I've got you, son of a wretch."

The other answered, "What have I done, my uncle?"

"You stuck thorns in my flesh. You said to me, 'I will make you some shoes.' Now what shall I do to you?"

"It was not I," said the jackal.

"It was you, and the proof is that you have your tail cut off."

"But all my cousins are without tails, like me."

"You lie, joker."

"Let me call them and you will see."

"Call them."

At his call the jackals ran up, all without tails.

"Which of you is a shoemaker?" asked the lion.

"All of us," they answered.

He said to them, "I am going to bring you some red pepper. you shall eat it, and the one who says, 'Ouch!' that will be the one I'm looking for."

"Go and get it."

He brought them some red pepper, and they were going to eat it when the first jackal made a noise with his shoes, but he said to the lion, "My uncle, I did not say, 'Ouch!'"

The lion sent them away, and they went about their business.

The Stolen Woman

This story has been edited and adapted from Moorish Literature, a collection work from sources such as Adolphe Hanoteau's Poésies Populaires de la Khabylie du Jurgura of 1867, Émile Masqueray's Observations grammaticales sur la grammaire Touareg et textes de la Tourahog des Tailog, and René Basset's L'insurrection Algerienne, de 1871 dans les chansons populaires Khabyles Lourain of 1892. This version was taken from the English translation introduced by René Basset and published by the University of France and the Académie D'Alger, published in 1901. This is a Berber tale.

It is said that a man of the Onlad Draabad married his cousin, whom he loved greatly. He possessed a single slave and some camels. Fearing lest someone should carry off his wife on account of her beauty, he resolved to take her to a place where no one should see her. He started, therefore, with his slave, his camels, and his wife, and proceeded night and day until he arrived at the shore of the great salt sea, knowing that nobody would come there.

One day when he had gone out to see his camels and his slave, leaving his wife alone in the tent, she saw a ship that had just then arrived. It had been sent by a sultan of a far country, to seek in the islands of the salt sea a more beautiful wife for him than the women of his land. The woman in the tent, seeing that the ship would not come first to her, went out of the tent.

The people said to her, "Come on board in order to see the whole ship."

She went aboard. Finding her to be just the one for whom they were seeking, they seized her and took her to their Sultan. On his return, the husband, not finding his wife, realized that she had been stolen. He went to find the son of Keij, the Christian. Between them there existed a friendship. The son of Keij said to him, "Bring a ship and seven men, whose guide I will be on the sea. They need not go astray nor be frightened. The city is three or four months' journey from here."

They set sail in a ship to find the city. Arriving, they cast their anchor near the city, which was at the top of a high mountain. Their chief went ashore and saw a fire lighted by someone. He went in that direction. It was an old woman, to whom he told his story. She gave him news of his wife. They agreed to keep silence between themselves. Then the old woman added, "In this place there are two birds that devour people. At their side are two lions like to them, and two men. All of these keep guard over your wife."

He bought a sheep, which he killed. Then he went to the two birds and threw them a part of it. While they were quarrelling over it he passed by them and came near to the two lions, to which he did the same. Approaching the two men, he found them asleep. He went as far as the place where his wife was in prison, and attracted her attention by scratching her foot. He was disguised and said to her, "I have sought you to tell you something." He took her by the hand. They both went out, and he swore that if she made the slightest noise he would kill her. He also asked her which was the swiftest boat for the journey. She pointed out the best boat there, and they embarked in it. There were some stones on board, and when he threw one at a ship it was crushed from stem to stern, and all on board perished.

He went to find the son of Keij. While they were at sea a marine monster swallowed them and the ship on which they were sailing. The chief took some pitch and had it boiled in a kettle. The monster cast up the ship on the shore of the sea. They continued their journey, proceeding by the seashore.

One day they came to a deserted city. They desired to take what it contained of riches, silver, and gold. All of a sudden the image of an armed man appeared to them. They could not resist or kill him at first, but finally they destroyed him and took all the riches of the houses.

When they finally reached Keij he said to them, "I want only the ship."

So the other man took the treasures and returned home with his wife.

The Story Of The Sham Prince, Or The Ambitious Tailor

This story has been edited and adapted from Andrew Lang's Strange Story Book, originally published by Longmans, Green And Company, London And New York, in 1913. The original story was included in Contes Berbères.

Once upon a time there lived a respectable young tailor called Labakan, who worked for a clever master in Alexandria. No one could call Labakan either stupid or lazy, for he could work extremely well and quickly when he chose, but there was something not altogether right about him. Sometimes he would stitch away as fast as if he had a red-hot needle and a burning thread, and at other times he would sit lost in thought, and with such a queer look about him that his fellow-workmen used to say, "Labakan has got on his aristocratic face today."

On Fridays he would put on his fine robe which he had bought with the money he had managed to save up, and go to the mosque. As he came back, after prayers, if he met any friend who said "Good-day," or "How are you, friend Labakan?" he would wave his hand graciously or nod in a condescending way, and if his master happened to say to him, as he sometimes did, "Really,

Labakan, you look like a prince," he was delighted, and would answer, "Have you noticed it too?" or "Well, so I have long thought."

Things went on like this for some time, and the master put up with Labakan's absurdities because he was, on the whole, a good fellow and a clever workman.

One day, the sultan's brother happened to be passing through Alexandria, and wanted to have one of his state robes altered, so he sent for the master tailor, who handed the robe over to Labakan as his best workman.

In the evening, when everyone had left the workshop and gone home, a great longing drove Labakan back to the place where the royal robe hung. He stood a long time gazing at it, admiring the rich material and the splendid embroidery in it. At last he could hold out no longer. He felt he must try it on, and it fitted as though it had been made for him.

"Am not I as good a prince as any other?" he asked himself, as he proudly paced up and down the room. "Has not the master often said that I seemed born to be a prince?"

It seemed to him that he must be the son of some unknown monarch, and at last he determined to set out at once and travel in search of his proper rank.

He felt as if the splendid robe had been sent him by some kind fairy, and he took care not to neglect such a precious gift. He collected all his savings, and, concealed by the darkness of the night, he passed through the gates of Alexandria.

The new prince excited a good deal of curiosity wherever he went, for his splendid robe and majestic manner did not seem quite suitable to a person travelling on foot. If anyone asked questions, he only replied with an important air of mystery that he had his own reasons for not riding. However, he soon found out that walking made him ridiculous, so at last he bought a quiet, steady old horse, which he managed to get cheap.

One day, as he was ambling along upon his horse, Murva, a horseman overtook him and asked leave to join him, so that they might both beguile the journey with pleasant talk. The newcomer was a bright, cheerful, good-looking young man, who soon plunged into conversation and asked many questions. He told Labakan that his own name was Omar, that he was a nephew of Elfi Bey, and was travelling in order to carry out a command given him by his uncle on his death bed. Labakan was not quite so open in his confidences, but hinted that he too was of noble birth and was travelling for pleasure.

The two young men took a fancy to each other and rode on together. On the second day of their journey Labakan questioned Omar as to the orders he had to carry out, and to his surprise heard this tale.

Elfi Bey, Pacha of Cairo, had brought up Omar from his earliest childhood, and the boy had never known his parents. On his deathbed Elfi Bey called Omar to him, and then told him that he was not his nephew, but the son of a great king, who, having been warned of coming dangers by his astrologers, had sent the young prince away and made a vow not to see him till his twenty-second birthday.

Elfi Bey did not tell Omar his father's name, but expressly desired him to be at a great pillar four days' journey east of Alexandria on the fourth day of the coming month, on which day he would be twenty-two years old. Here he would meet some men, to whom he was to hand a dagger which Elfi Bey gave him, and to say, "Here am I for whom you seek."

If they answered, "Praised be the Prophet who has preserved you," he was to follow them, and they would take him to his father.

Labakan was greatly surprised and interested by this story, but after hearing it he could not help looking on Prince Omar with envious eyes, angry that his friend should have the position he himself longed so much for. He began to make comparisons between the prince and himself, and was obliged to confess that he was a fine-looking young man with very good manners and a pleasant expression. At the same time, he felt sure that had he been in the prince's place any royal father might have been glad to own him.

These thoughts haunted him all day, and he dreamt them all night. He woke very early, and as he saw Omar sleeping quietly, with a happy smile on his face, a wish arose in his mind to take by force or by cunning the things which an unkind fate had denied him.

The dagger which was to act as a passport was sticking in Omar's girdle. Labakan drew it gently out, and hesitated for a moment whether or not to plunge it into the heart of the sleeping prince. However, he shrank from the idea of murder, so he contented himself with placing the dagger in his own belt, and, saddling Omar's swift horse for himself, was many miles away before the prince woke up to realise his losses.

For two days Labakan rode on steadily, fearing lest, after all, Omar might reach the meeting place before him. At the end of the second day he saw the great pillar at a distance. It stood on a little hill in the middle of a plain, and could be seen a very long way off.

Labakan's heart beat fast at the sight. Though he had had some time in which to think over the part he meant to play his conscience made him rather uneasy. However, the thought that he must certainly have been born to be a king supported him, and he bravely rode on.

The neighbourhood was quite bare and desert, and it was a good thing that the new prince had brought food for some time with him, as two days were still wanting till the appointed time.

Towards the middle of the next day he saw a long procession of horses and camels coming towards him. It halted at the bottom of the hill, and some splendid tents were pitched. Everything looked like the escort of some great man. Labakan made a shrewd guess that all these people had come here on his account, but he checked his impatience, knowing that only on the fourth day could his wishes be fulfilled.

The first rays of the rising sun woke the happy tailor. As he began to saddle his horse and prepare to ride to the pillar, he could not help having some remorseful thoughts of the trick he had played and the blighted hopes of the real prince. But the die was cast, and his vanity whispered that he was as fine looking a young man as the proudest king might wish his son to be, and that, moreover, what had happened had happened.

With these thoughts he summoned up all his courage sprang on his horse, and in less than a quarter of an hour was at the foot of the hill. Here he dismounted, tied the horse to a bush, and, drawing out Prince Omar's dagger climbed up the hill.

At the foot of the pillar stood six men round a tall and stately person. His superb robe of cloth of gold was girt round him by a white cashmere shawl, and his white, richly jewelled turban showed that he was a man of wealth and high rank. Labakan went straight up to him, and, bending low, handed him the dagger, saying, "Here am I whom you seek."

"Praised be the Prophet who has preserved you," replied the old man with tears of joy. "Embrace me, my dear son Omar!"

The proud tailor was deeply moved by these solemn words, and with mingled shame and joy sank into the old king's arms.

But his happiness was not long unclouded. As he raised his head he saw a horseman who seemed trying to urge a tired or unwilling horse across the plain.

Only too soon Labakan recognised his own old horse, Murva, and the real Prince Omar, but having once told a lie he made up his mind not to own his deceit.

At last the horseman reached the foot of the hill. Here he flung himself from the saddle and hurried up to the pillar.

"Stop!" he cried. "Whoever you may be, do not let a disgraceful impostor take you in. My name is Omar, and let no one attempt to rob me of it."

This turn of affairs threw the standers-by into great surprise. The old king in particular seemed much moved as he looked from one face to the other. At last Labakan spoke with forced calmness, "Most gracious lord and father, do not let yourself be deceived by this man. As far as I know, he is a half-crazy tailor's apprentice from Alexandria, called Labakan, who really deserves more pity than anger."

These words infuriated the prince. Foaming with rage, he tried to press towards Labakan, but the attendants threw themselves upon him and held him fast, whilst the king said, "Truly, my dear son, the poor fellow is quite mad. Let him be bound and placed on a dromedary. Perhaps we may be able to get some help for him."

The prince's first rage was over, and with tears he cried to the king, "My heart tells me that you are my father, and in my mother's name I entreat you to hear me."

"Oh! Heaven forbid!" was the reply. "He is talking nonsense again. How can the poor man have got such notions into his head?"

With these words the king took Labakan's arm to support him down the hill. They both mounted richly caparisoned horses and rode across the plain at the head of their followers.

The unlucky prince was tied hand and foot, and fastened on a dromedary, a guard riding on either side and keeping a sharp look-out on him.

The old king was Sached, Sultan of the Wachabites. For many years he had had no children, but at length the son he had so long wished for was born. But the sooth-sayers and magicians whom he consulted as to the child's future all said that until he was twenty-two years old he stood in danger of being injured by an enemy. So, to make all safe, the sultan had confided the prince to his trusty friend Elfi Bey, and deprived himself of the happiness of seeing him for twenty-two years. All this the sultan told Labakan, and was much pleased by his appearance and dignified manner.

When they reached their own country they were received with every sign of joy, for the news of the prince's safe return had spread like wildfire, and every town and village was decorated, whilst the inhabitants thronged to greet them with cries of joy and thankfulness. All this filled Labakan's proud heart with rapture, whilst the unfortunate Omar followed in silent rage and despair.

At length they arrived in the capital, where the public rejoicings were grander and more brilliant than anywhere else. The queen awaited them in the great hall of the palace, surrounded by her entire court. It was getting dark, and hundreds of coloured hanging lamps were lit to turn night into day.

The brightest hung round the throne on which the queen sat, and which stood above four steps of pure gold inlaid with great amethysts. The four greatest nobles in the kingdom held a canopy of crimson silk over the queen, and the Sheik of Medina fanned her with a peacock-feather fan.

In this state she awaited her husband and her son. She, too, had not seen Omar since his birth, but so many dreams had shown her what he would look like that she felt she would know him among a thousand.

And now the sound of trumpets and drums and of shouts and cheers outside announced the long looked for moment. The doors flew open, and between rows of low-bending courtiers and servants the king approached the throne, leading his pretended son by the hand.

"Here," said he, "is he for whom you have been longing so many years."

But the queen interrupted him, "That is not my son!" she cried. "That is not the face the Prophet has shown me in my dreams!"

Just as the king was about to reason with her, the door was thrown violently open, and Prince Omar rushed in, followed by his keepers, whom he had managed to get away from. He flung himself down before the throne, panting out, "Here will I die, kill me at once, cruel father, for I cannot bear this shame any longer."

Everyone pressed round the unhappy man, and the guards were about to seize him, when the queen, who at first was dumb with surprise, sprang up from her throne.

"Hold!" cried she. "This and no other is the right one, this is the one whom my eyes have never yet seen, but whom my heart recognises."

The guards had stepped back, but the king called to them in a furious voice to secure the madman.

"It is I who must judge," he said in tones of command, "and this matter cannot be decided by women's dreams, but by certain unmistakable signs." He pointed at Labakan. "This one is my son, for it was he who brought me the dagger from my friend Elfi Bey."

"He stole it from me," shrieked Omar, "he betrayed my unsuspicious confidence."

But the king would not listen to his son's voice, for he had always been accustomed to depend on his own judgment. He let the unhappy Omar be dragged from the hall, whilst he himself retired with Labakan to his own rooms, full of anger with the queen his wife, in spite of their many years of happy life together.

The queen, on her side, was plunged into grief, for she felt certain that an impostor had won her husband's heart and taken the place of her real son.

When the first shock was over she began to think how she could manage to convince the king of his mistake. Of course it would be a difficult matter, as the man who declared he was Omar had produced the dagger as a token, besides talking of all sorts of things which happened when he was a child. She called her oldest and wisest ladies about her and asked their advice, but none of them had any to give. At last one very clever old woman said, "Did not the young man who brought the dagger call him whom your majesty believes to be your son Labakan, and say he was a crazy tailor?"

"Yes," replied the queen, "but what of that?"

"Might it not be," said the old lady, "that the impostor has called your real son by his own name? If this should be the case, I know of a capital way to find out the truth."

And she whispered some words to the queen, who seemed much pleased, and went off at once to see the king.

Now the queen was a very wise woman, so she pretended to think she might have made a mistake, and only begged to be allowed to put a test to the two young men to prove which was the real prince.

The king, who was feeling much ashamed of the rage he had been in with his dear wife, consented at once, and she said, "No doubt others would make them ride or shoot, or something of that sort, but everyone learns these things. I wish to set them a task which requires sharp wits and clever hands, and I want them to try which of them can best make a kaftan and pair of trousers."

The king laughed. "No, no, that will never do. Do you suppose my son would compete with that crazy tailor as to which could make the best clothes? O, dear, no, that won't do at all."

But the queen claimed his promise, and as he was a man of his word the king gave in at last. He went to his son and begged that he would humour his mother, who had set her heart on his making a kaftan.

The worthy Labakan laughed to himself. "If that is all she wants," thought he, "her majesty will soon be pleased to own me."

Two rooms were prepared, with pieces of material, scissors, needles and threads, and each young man was shut up in one of them. The king felt rather curious as to what sort of garment his son would make, and the queen, too, was very anxious as to the result of her experiment.

On the third day they sent for the two young men and their work. Labakan came first and spread out his kaftan before the eyes of the astonished king. "See, father," he said, "see, my honoured mother, if this is not a masterpiece of work. I'll bet the court tailor himself cannot do better."

The queen smiled and turned to Omar, "And what have you done, my son?"

Impatiently he threw the stuff and scissors down on the floor. "I have been taught how to manage a horse, to draw a sword, and to throw a lance some sixty paces, but I never learnt to sew, and such a thing would have been thought beneath the notice of the pupil of Elfi Bey, the ruler of Cairo."

"Ah, true son of your father," cried the queen, "if only I might embrace you and call you son! Forgive me, my lord and husband," she added, turning to the king, "for trying to find out the truth in this way. Do you not see yourself now which is the prince and which the tailor? Certainly this kaftan is a very fine one, but I should like to know what master taught this young man how to make clothes."

The king sat deep in thought, looking now at his wife and now at Labakan, who was doing his best to hide his vexation at his own stupidity. At last the king said, "Even this trial does not satisfy me, but happily I know of a sure way to discover whether or not I have been deceived."

He ordered his swiftest horse to be saddled, mounted, and rode off alone into a forest at some little distance. Here lived a kindly fairy called Adolzaide, who had often helped the kings of his race with her good advice, and to her he took himself.

In the middle of the forest was a wide open space surrounded by great cedar trees, and this was supposed to be the fairy's favourite spot. When the king reached this place he dismounted, tied his horse to the tree, and standing in the middle of the open place said, "If it is true that you have helped my ancestors in their time of need, do not despise their descendant, but give me counsel, for that of men has failed me."

He had hardly finished speaking when one of the cedar trees opened, and a veiled figure all dressed in white stepped from it. "I know your errand, King Sached," she said. "It is an honest one, and I will give you my help. Take these two little boxes and let the two men who claim to be your son choose between them. I know that the real prince will make no mistake."

She then handed him two little boxes made of ivory set with gold and pearls. On the lid of each, which the king vainly tried to open, was an inscription in diamonds. On one stood the words 'Honour and Glory,' and on the other 'Wealth and Happiness.'

"It would be a hard choice," thought the king as he rode home.

He lost no time in sending for the queen and for all his court, and when all were assembled he made a sign, and Labakan was led in. With a proud air he walked up to the throne, and kneeling down, asked, "What does my lord and father command?"

The king replied, "My son, doubts have been thrown on your claim to that name. One of these boxes contains the proofs of your birth. Choose for yourself. No doubt you will choose right."

He then pointed to the ivory boxes, which were placed on two little tables near the throne. Labakan rose and looked at the boxes. He thought for some minutes, and then said, "My honoured father, what can be better than the happiness of being your son, and what nobler than the riches of your love. I choose the box with the words 'Wealth and Happiness.'"

"We shall see presently if you have chosen the right one. For the present take a seat there beside the Pacha of Medina," replied the king.

Omar was next led in, looking sad and sorrowful. He threw himself down before the throne and asked what the king's pleasure was. The king pointed out the two boxes to him, and he rose and went to the tables. He carefully read the two mottoes and said, "The last few days have shown me how uncertain is happiness and how easily riches vanish away. Should I lose a crown by it I make my choice of 'Honour and Glory.'"

He laid his hand on the box as he spoke, but the king signed to him to wait, and ordered Labakan to come to the other table and lay his hand on the box he had chosen.

Then the king rose from his throne, and in solemn silence all present rose too, whilst he said, "Open the boxes, and may Allah show us the truth."

The boxes were opened with the greatest ease. In the one Omar had chosen to lay a little gold crown and sceptre on a velvet cushion. In Labakan's box was found a large needle with some thread!

The king told the two young men to bring him their boxes. They did so. He took the crown in his hand, and as he held it, it grew bigger and bigger, till it was as large as a real crown. He placed it on the head of his son Omar, kissed him on the forehead, and placed him on his right hand.

Then, turning to Labakan, he said, "There is an old proverb, 'The cobbler sticks to his last.' It seems as though you were to stick to your needle. You do not deserve any mercy, but I cannot be harsh on this day. I give you your life, but I advise you to leave this country as fast as you can."

Full of shame, the unlucky tailor could not answer. He flung himself down before Omar, and with tears in his eyes asked, "Can you forgive me, prince?"

"Go in peace," said Omar as he raised him.

"O, my true son!" cried the king as he clasped the prince in his arms, whilst all the pachas and emirs shouted, "Long live Prince Omar!"

In the midst of all the noise and rejoicing Labakan slipped off with his little box under his arm. He went to the stables, saddled his old horse, Murva, and rode out of the gate towards Alexandria. Nothing but the ivory box with its diamond motto was left to show him that the last few weeks had not been a dream.

When he reached Alexandria he rode up to his old master's door. When he entered the shop, his master came forward to ask what his pleasure was, but as soon as he saw who it was he called his workmen, and they all fell on Labakan with blows and angry words, till at last he fell, half fainting, on a heap of old clothes.

The master then scolded him soundly about the stolen robe, but in vain Labakan told him he had come to pay for it and offered three times its price. They only fell to beating him again, and at last pushed him out of the house more dead than alive.

He could do nothing but remount his horse and ride to an inn. Here he found a quiet place in which to rest his bruised and battered limbs and to think over his many misfortunes. He fell asleep fully determined to give up trying to be great, but to lead the life of an honest workman.

Next morning he set to work to fulfil his good resolutions. He sold his little box to a jeweller for a good price, bought a house and opened a workshop. Then he hung up a sign with, "Labakan, Tailor," over his door, and sat down to mend his own torn clothes with the very needle which had been in the ivory box.

After a while he was called away, and when he went back to his work he found a wonderful thing had happened! The needle was sewing away all by itself and making the neatest little stitches, such as Labakan had never been able to make even at his best.

Certainly even the smallest gift of a kind fairy is of great value, and this one had yet another advantage, for the thread never came to an end, however much the needle sewed.

Labakan soon got plenty of customers. He used to cut out the clothes, make the first stitch with the magic needle, and then leave it to do the rest. Before long the whole town went to him, for his work was both so good and so cheap. The only puzzle was how he could do so much, working all alone, and also why he worked with closed doors.

And so the promise on the ivory box of "Wealth and Happiness" came true for him, and when he heard of all the brave doings of Prince Omar, the pride and darling of his people and the terror of his enemies, Labakan thought to himself, "After all, I am better off as a tailor, for 'Honour and Glory' are very dangerous things."

The King, The Arab, And The Monster

This story has been edited and adapted from Moorish Literature, a collection work from sources such as Adolphe Hanoteau's Poésies Populaires de la Khabylie du Jurgura of 1867, Émile Masqueray's Observations grammaticales sur la grammaire Touareg et textes de la Tourahog des Tailog, and René Basset's L'insurrection Algerienne, de 1871 dans les chansons populaires Khabyles Lourain of 1892. This version was taken from the English translation introduced by René Basset and published by the University of France and the Académie D'Alger, published in 1901. This is a Berber tale.

In former times there was a king of the At Taberchant, whose city was situated at the foot of a mountain. An enormous beast came against them, entered the city, and devoured all the people. The beast established itself in the city and stayed there a century. One day it was hungry. It came out into the plain, found some Arabs with their tents, their sheep, their oxen, their mares, and their camels. The beast fell upon them in the night and ate them all up, leaving the earth all white with their bones. Then it went back to the city.

A single man escaped, thanks to his good mare. He arrived at a city of the At Taberchant and, starving, began to beg. The King said to him, "From where do you come into our country - you who invoke the lord of men? you don't know where you are. We are Jews. If you embrace our religion, we will give you food."

"Give me some food," said the Arab, "and I will give you some good advice."

The King took him to his house and gave him some supper, and then asked him what he had to say.

"An enormous monster has fallen upon us," said the Arab. "It ate up everybody. I will show you its city. It has two gates, one at the north and the other at the south."

"Tomorrow," said the King.

When he awoke the next day, they mounted horses and followed the way to the gate of the monster's city. They looked at it and went away.

"What shall we do?" said the King.

"Let us make a great trap the size of the entrance to the city, at the southern gate. At the northern gate we will place a forty-mule load of yellow sulphur. We will set it on fire, and then escape and see what will happen."

"Your advice is good," said the King.

They returned to the city of the Jews, ordered the smiths to make a big trap and commanded the citizens to furnish the sulphur. When all was ready, they loaded the mules, went to the monster's city, set the trap at the southern gate, and at the northern gate they placed the sulphur, which they set on fire, and then fled. The monster came out by the southern gate. Half of his body was caught in the trap that the two men had set. He was cut in two, filling the river with blood. The King and the Arab entered the city and found a considerable treasure, which they removed in eighty loads to the city of the Jews. When they had got back to the palace the King said to his companion, "Be my caliph. My fortune and your fortune shall be the same."

They sat down and had supper. The prince put some poison in the stew and turned it to the Arab. The latter observed what he had done and said, "Where did that bird come from?"

When the King of the Jews raised his head to look, the Arab turned the dish around, placing the poison side of it in front of the King. He did not perceive the trick, and died on the spot. The Arab went to the gate of the city and said to the inhabitants, "I am your King. you are in my power. He who will not accept my religion, I will cut off his head."

They all embraced Islamism and practised fasting and prayer.

The Three Treasures Of The Giants

This story has been edited and adapted from Andrew Lang's Strange Story Book, originally published by Longmans, Green And Company, London And New York, in 1913. The original story was included in Contes Berbères.

Long, long ago, there lived an old man and his wife who had three sons, the eldest was called Martin, the second Michael, while the third was named Jack.

One evening they were all seated round the table, eating their supper of bread and milk.

"Martin," said the old man suddenly, "I feel that I cannot live much longer. You, as the eldest, will inherit this hut but, if you value my blessing, be good to your mother and brothers."

"Certainly, father, how can you suppose I should do them wrong?" replied Martin indignantly, helping himself to all the best bits in the dish as he spoke. The old man saw nothing, but Michael looked on in surprise, and Jack was so astonished that he quite forgot to eat his own supper.

A little while after, the father fell ill, and sent for his sons, who were out hunting, to bid him farewell. After giving good advice to the two eldest, he turned to Jack.

"My boy," he said, "you have not got quite as much sense as other people, but if Heaven has deprived you of some of your wits, it was given you a kind heart. Always listen to what it says, and take heed to the words of your mother and brothers, as well as you are able!" So saying the old man sank back on his pillows and died.

The cries of grief uttered by Martin and Michael sounded through the house, but Jack remained by the bedside of his father, still and silent, as if he were dead also. At length he got up, and going into the garden, hid himself in some trees, and wept like a child, while his two brothers made ready for the funeral.

No sooner was the old man buried than Martin and Michael agreed that they would go into the world together to seek their fortunes, while Jack stayed at home with their mother. Jack would have liked nothing better than to sit and dream by the fire, but the mother, who was very old herself, declared that there was no work for him to do, and that he must seek it with his brothers.

So, one fine morning, all three set out. Martin and Michael carried two great bags full of food, but Jack carried nothing. This made his brothers very angry, for the day was hot and the bags were heavy, and about noon they sat down under a tree and began to eat. Jack was as hungry as they were, but he knew that it was no use asking for anything, and he threw himself under another tree, and wept bitterly.

"Another time perhaps you won't be so lazy, and will bring food for yourself," said Martin, but to his surprise Jack answered, "You are a nice pair! You talk of seeking your fortunes so as not to be a burden on our mother, and you begin by carrying off all the food she has in the house!"

This reply was so unexpected that for some moments neither of the brothers made any answer. Then they offered their brother some of their food, and when he had finished eating they went their way once more.

Towards evening they reached a small hut, and knocking at the door, asked if they might spend the night there. The man, who was a wood-cutter, invited them in and begged them to sit down to supper. Martin thanked him, but being very proud, explained that it was only shelter they wanted, as they had plenty of food with them, and he and Michael at once opened their bags and began to eat, while Jack hid himself in a corner. The wife, on seeing this, took pity on him, and called him to come and share their supper, which he gladly did, and very good he found it. At this, Martin regretted deeply that he had been so foolish as to refuse, for his bits of bread and cheese seemed very hard when he smelt the savoury soup his brother was enjoying.

"He shan't have such a chance again," thought he, and the next morning he insisted on plunging into a thick forest where they were likely to meet nobody.

For a long time they wandered here and there, for they had no path to guide them, but at last they came upon a wide clearing, in the midst of which stood a castle. Jack shouted with delight, but Martin, who was in a bad temper, said sharply, "We must have taken a wrong turning! Let us go back."

"Idiot!" replied Michael, who was hungry too, and, like many people when they are hungry, very cross also. "We set out to travel through the world, and what does it matter if we go to the right or to the left?" And, without another word, took the path to the castle, closely followed by Jack, and after a moment by Martin likewise.

The door of the castle stood open, and they entered a great hall, and looked about them. Not a creature was to be seen, and suddenly Martin - he did not know why - felt a little frightened. He would have left the castle at once, but stopped when Jack boldly walked up to a door in the wall and opened it. He could not for very shame be outdone by his younger brother, and passed behind him into another splendid hall, which was filled from floor to ceiling with great pieces of copper money.

The sight quite dazzled Martin and Michael, who emptied all the provisions that remained out of their bags, and heaped them up instead with handfuls of copper.

Scarcely had they done this when Jack threw open another door, and this time it led to a hall filled with silver. In an instant his brothers had turned their bags upside down, so that the copper money tumbled out on to the floor, and were shovelling in handfuls of the silver instead. They had hardly finished, when Jack opened yet a third door, and all three fell back in amazement, for this room as a mass of gold, so bright that their eyes grew sore as they looked at it. However, they soon recovered from their surprise, and quickly emptied their bags of silver, and filled them with gold instead.

When they would hold no more, Martin said, "We had better hurry off now lest somebody else should come, and we might not know what to do", and, followed by Michael, he hastily left the castle.

Jack lingered behind for a few minutes to put pieces of gold, silver, and copper into his pocket, and to eat the food that his brothers had thrown down in the first room. Then he went after them, and found them lying down to rest in the midst of a forest. It was near sunset, and Martin began to feel hungry, so, when Jack arrived, he bade him return to the castle and bring the bread and cheese that they had left there.

"It is hardly worth doing that," answered Jack, "for I picked up the pieces and ate them myself."

At this reply both brothers were beside themselves with anger, and fell upon the boy, beating him, and calling him names, till they were quite tired.

"Go where you like," cried Martin with a final kick, "but never come near us again." And poor Jack ran weeping into the woods.

The next morning his brothers went home, and bought a beautiful house, where they lived with their mother like great lords. Jack remained for some hours in hiding, thankful to be safe from his tormentors, but when no one came to trouble him, and his back did not ache so much, he began to think what he had better do. At length he made up his mind to go to the castle and take away as much money with him as would enable him to live in comfort for the rest of his life. This being decided, he sprang up, and set out along the path which led to the castle. As before, the door stood open, and he went on till he had reached the hall of gold, and there he took off his jacket and tied the sleeves together so that it might make a kind of bag. He then began to pour in the gold by handfuls, when, all at once, a noise like thunder shook the castle. This was followed by a voice, hoarse as that of a bull, which cried, "I smell the smell of a man." And two giants entered.

"So, little worm! It is you who steal our treasures!" exclaimed the biggest. "Well, we have got you now, and we will cook you for supper!"

But here the other giant drew him aside, and for a moment or two they whispered together. At length the first giant spoke, "To please my friend I will spare your life on condition that, for the future, you shall guard our treasures. If you are hungry take this little table and rap on it, saying, as you do so, 'The dinner of an emperor!' and you will get as much food as you want."

With a light heart Jack promised all that was asked of him, and for some days enjoyed himself mightily. He had everything he could wish for, and did nothing from morning till night, but by-and-by he began to get very tired of it all.

"Let the giants guard their treasures themselves," he said to himself at last. "I am going away. But I will leave all the gold and silver behind me, and will take nought but you, my good little table."

So, tucking the table under his arm, he started off for the forest, but he did not linger there long, and soon found himself in the fields on the other side. There he saw an old man, who begged Jack to give him something to eat.

"You could not have asked a better person," answered Jack cheerfully. And signing to him to sit down with him under a tree, he set the table in front of them, and struck it three times, crying, "The dinner of an emperor!" He had hardly uttered the words when fish and meat of all kinds appeared on it!

"That is a clever trick of yours," said the old man, when he had eaten as much as he wanted. "Give it to me in exchange for a treasure I have which is still better. Do you see this cornet? Well, you have only to tell it that you wish for an army, and you will have as many soldiers as you require."

Now, since he had been left to himself, Jack had grown ambitious, so, after a moment's hesitation, he took the cornet and gave the table in exchange. The old man bade him farewell, and set off down one path, while Jack chose another, and for a long time he was quite pleased with his new possession. Then, as he felt hungry, he wished for his table back again, as no house was in sight, and he wanted some supper badly. All at once he remembered his cornet, and a wicked thought entered his mind.

"Two hundred hussars, forward!" cried he. And the neighing of horses and the clanking of swords were heard close at hand. The officer who rode at their head approached Jack, and politely inquired what he wished them to do.

"A mile or two along that road," answered Jack, "you will find an old man carrying a table. Take the table from him and bring it to me."

The officer saluted and went back to his men, who started at a gallop to do Jack's bidding. In ten minutes they had returned, bearing the table with them.

"That is all, thank you," said Jack, and the soldiers disappeared inside the cornet.

O, what a good supper Jack had that night, quite forgetting that he owed it to a mean trick. The next day he breakfasted early, and then walked on towards the nearest town. On the way there he met another old man, who begged for something to eat.

"Certainly, you shall have something to eat," replied Jack. And, placing the table on the ground he cried. "The dinner of an emperor!" when all sorts of food dishes appeared.

At first the old man ate quite greedily, and said nothing but, after his hunger was satisfied, he turned to Jack and said, "That is a very clever trick of yours. Give the table to me and you shall have something still better."

"I don't believe that there is anything better," answered Jack.

"Yes, there is. Here is my bag, it will give you as many castles as you can possibly want."

Jack thought for a moment, then he replied, "Very well, I will exchange with you." And passing the table to the old man, he hung the bag over his arm.

Five minutes later he summoned five hundred lancers out of the cornet and bade them go after the old man and fetch back the table.

Now that by his cunning he had obtained possession of the three magic objects, he resolved to return to his native place. Smearing his face with dirt, and tearing his clothes so as to look like a beggar, he stopped the passers-by and, on pretence of seeking money or food, he questioned them about the village gossip. In this manner he learned that his brothers had become great men, much respected in all the country round. When he heard that, he lost no time in going to the door of their fine house and imploring them to give him food and shelter, but the only thing he got was hard words, and a command to beg elsewhere.

At length, however, at their mother's entreaty, he was told that he might pass the night in the stable. Here he waited until everybody in the house was sound asleep, when he drew his bag from under his cloak, and desired that a castle might appear in that place, and the cornet gave him soldiers to guard the castle, while the table furnished him with a good supper. In the morning, he caused it all to vanish, and when his brothers entered the stable they found him lying on the straw.

Jack remained here for many days, doing nothing, and - as far as anybody knew - eating nothing. This conduct puzzled his brothers greatly, and they put such constant questions to him, that at length he told them the secret of the table, and even gave a dinner to them, which far outdid any they had ever seen or heard of. But though they had solemnly promised to reveal nothing, somehow or other the tale leaked out, and before long reached the ears of the king himself. That very evening his chamberlain arrived at Jack's dwelling, with a request from the king that he might borrow the table for three days.

"Very well," answered Jack, "you can take it back with you. But tell his majesty that if he does not return it at the end of the three days I will make war upon him."

So the chamberlain carried away the table and took it straight to the king, telling him at the same time of Jack's threat, at which they both laughed till their sides ached.

Now the king was so delighted with the table, and the dinners it gave him, that when the three days were over he could not make up his mind to part with it. Instead, he sent for his carpenter, and bade him copy it exactly, and when it was done he told his chamberlain to return it to Jack with his best thanks. It happened to be dinner time, and Jack invited the chamberlain, who knew nothing of the trick, to stay and dine with him. The good man, who had eaten several excellent meals provided by the table in the last three days, accepted the invitation with pleasure, even though he was to dine in a stable, and sat down on the straw beside Jack.

"The dinner of an emperor!" cried Jack. But not even a morsel of cheese made its appearance.

"The dinner of an emperor!" shouted Jack in a voice of thunder.

Then the truth dawned on him, and, crushing the table between his hands, he turned to the chamberlain, who, bewildered and half-frightened, was wondering how to get away.

"Tell your false king that tomorrow I will destroy his castle as easily as I have broken this table."

The chamberlain hastened back to the palace, and gave the king Jack's message, at which he laughed more than before, and called all his courtiers to hear the story. But they were not quite so merry when they woke next morning and beheld ten thousand horsemen, and as many archers, surrounding the palace. The king saw it was useless to hold out, and he took the white flag of truce in one hand, and the real table in the other, and set out to look for Jack.

"I committed a crime," said he, "but I will do my best to make up for it. Here is your table, which I own with shame that I tried to steal, and you shall have besides, my daughter as your wife!"

There was no need to delay the marriage when the table was able to furnish the most splendid banquet that ever was seen, and after everyone had eaten and drunk as much as they wanted, Jack took his bag and commanded a castle filled with all sorts of treasures to arise in the park for himself and his bride.

At this proof of his power the king's heart died within him. "Your magic is greater than mine," he said, "and you are young and strong, while I am old and tired. Take, therefore, the sceptre from my hand, and my crown from my head, and rule my people better than I have done."

So at last Jack's ambition was satisfied. He could not hope to be more than king, and as long as he had his cornet to provide him with soldiers he was secure against his enemies. He never forgave his brothers for the way they had treated him, though he presented his mother with a beautiful castle, and everything she could possibly wish for. In the centre of his own palace was a treasure chamber, and in this chamber the table, the cornet, and the bag were kept as the most prized of all his possessions, and not a week passed without a visit from king Jack to make sure they were safe. He reigned long and well, and died a very old man, beloved by his people. But his good example was not followed by his sons and his grandsons. They grew so proud that they were ashamed to think that the founder of their race had once been a poor boy, and as they and all the world could not fail to remember it, as long as the table, the cornet, and the bag were shown in the treasure chamber, one king, more foolish than the rest, thrust them into a dark and damp cellar.

For some time the kingdom remained, though it became weaker and weaker every year that passed. Then, one day, a rumour reached the king that a large army was marching against him. Vaguely he recollected some tales he had heard about a magic cornet which could provide as many soldiers as would serve to conquer the earth, and which had been removed by his grandfather to a cellar. There he hastened that he might renew his power once more, and in that black and slimy spot he found the treasures indeed. But the table fell to pieces as he touched it. Of the cornet there remained only a few fragments of leather belts which the rats had gnawed, and in the bag there was nothing but broken bits of stone.

And the king bowed his head to the doom that awaited him, and in his heart cursed the ruin wrought by the pride and foolishness of himself and his forefathers.

The Lion, The Jackal, And The Man

This story has been edited and adapted from Moorish Literature, a collection work from sources such as Adolphe Hanoteau's Poésies Populaires de la Khabylie du Jurgura of 1867, Émile Masqueray's Observations grammaticales sur la grammaire Touareg et textes de la Tourahog des Tailog, and René Basset's L'insurrection Algerienne, de 1871 dans les chansons populaires Khabyles Lourain of 1892. This version was taken from the English translation introduced by René Basset and published by the University of France and the Académie D'Alger, published in 1901. This is a Berber tale.

In times past, when the animals spoke, there existed, they say, a labourer who owned a pair of oxen, with which he worked. It was his custom to start out with them early in the morning, and in the evening he returned with one ox. The next day he bought another and went to the fallow land, but the lion came and took one ox from him and left him only one. He was in despair, seeking someone to advise him, when he met the jackal and told him what had taken place between him and the lion.

The jackal demanded, "What will you give me if I deliver you from the lion?"

"Whatever you wish I will give it to you."

"Give me a fat lamb," answered the jackal. "You will follow my advice. Tomorrow when the lion comes, I will be there. I will arrive on that hill on the other side. you will bring your axe very well sharpened and when I say to you, 'What is that which I see with you now?' you must answer, 'It is an ass which I have taken with me to carry barley.' I will say to you, 'I am looking for the lion, and not for an ass,' Then he will ask you, 'Who is speaking to you?' Answer him, 'It is the nems!' He will say to you, 'Hide me, for I am afraid of him,' When I ask you, 'Who is that stretched there before you?' answer, 'It is a beaver,' I will say, 'Take your axe and strike, to know if it be not the lion,' you will take your axe and you will strike the lion hard between the eyes. Then I will continue, 'I have not heard very well. Strike him again once more until he shall really be dead,'"

The next day the lion came to him as before to eat an ox. When the jackal saw him he called his friend and said, "Who is that with you?"

"It is a beaver which is before me."

The jackal answered, "Where is the lion? I am looking for him."

"Who is talking to you?" asked the lion, of the labourer.

"The nems.'"

"Hide me," cried the lion, "for I fear him."

The labourer said to him, "Stretch yourself out before me, shut your eyes, and don't move."

The lion stretched out before him, shut his eyes, and held his breath.

The peasant said to the jackal, "I have not seen the lion pass today."

"What is that stretched before you?"

"It is a beaver."

"Take your axe," said the jackal, "and strike that beaver." The labourer obeyed and struck the lion violently between the eyes.

"Strike hard," said the jackal again, "I did not hear very well."

He struck him three or four times more, until he had killed him. Then he called the jackal, "See, I have killed him. Come, let me embrace you for your good advice. Tomorrow you must come here to get the lamb which I will give you."

They separated and each went his way. As for the peasant, the next day, as soon as dawn, he took a lamb, put it into a sack, tied it up, went into the court-yard and hung it up. Then while he went to get his oxen to till his fields, at that moment, his wife opened the sack, set the lamb free, and replaced it by a dog. The peasant took the sack and went to his work. He attached his oxen and set to work, till the arrival of the jackal.

The jackal said to him, "Where is that promise you made me?"

"It is in the sack. Open it and you'll find the lamb which I give you."

He followed his advice, opened the sack, and saw two eyes which shone more brightly than those of a lamb, and said to the labourer, "My friend, you have deceived me."

"How have I deceived you?" asked the other. "As for the lamb, I put him in the sack. Open it well. I do not lie."

The jackal followed his advice. He opened the sack and a dog jumped fiercely out. When the jackal saw the dog he ran away, but the dog caught him and ate him up.

Udea And Her Seven Brothers

This story has been edited and adapted from Andrew Lang's Strange Story Book, originally published by Longmans, Green And Company, London And New York, in 1913. The original story was included in Märchen und Gedichte aus der Stadt Tripolis by Hans Stumme.

Once upon a time there was a man and his wife who had seven boys. The children lived in the open air and grew big and strong, and the six eldest spent part of everyday hunting wild beasts. The youngest did not care so much about sport, and he often stayed with his mother.

One morning, however, as the whole seven were going out for a long expedition, they said to their aunt, "Dear aunt, if a baby sister comes into the world today, wave a white handkerchief, and we will return immediately, but if it is only a boy, just brandish a sickle, and we will go on with what we are doing."

Now the baby when it arrived really proved to be a girl, but as the aunt could not bear the boys, she thought it was a good opportunity to get rid of them. So she waved the sickle. And when the seven brothers saw the sign they said, "Now we have nothing to go back for," and plunged deeper into the desert.

The little girl soon grew to be a big girl, and she was called Udea by all of her friends, who had driven her seven brothers into strange lands."

One day, when she had been quarrelling with her playmates, the oldest among them said to her, "It is a pity you were born, as ever since, your brothers have been obliged to roam about the world."

Udea did not answer, but went home to her mother and asked her, "Have I really got brothers?"

"Yes," replied her mother, "seven of them. But they went away the day you were born, and I have never heard of them since."

Then the girl said, "I will go and look for them till I find them."

"My dear child," answered her mother, "it is fifteen years since they left, and no man has seen them. How will you know which way to go?"

"O, I will follow them, north and south, east and west, and though I may travel far, yet someday I will find them."

Then her mother said no more, but gave her a camel and some food, and a servant and his wife to take care of her, and she fastened a cowrie shell round the camel's neck for a charm, and bade her daughter go in peace.

During the first day the party journeyed on without any adventures, but the second morning the servant said to the girl, "Get down, and let my wife ride instead of you."

"Mother," cried Udea across the leagues.

"What is it?" asked her mother.

"Barka wants me to dismount from my camel."

"Leave her alone, Barka," commanded the mother, and Barka did not dare to persist.

But on the following day he said again to Udea, "Get down, and let my wife ride instead of you," and though Udea called to her mother she was too far away, and the mother never heard her. Then the servant seized her roughly and threw her on the ground, and said to his wife, "Climb up," and the wife climbed up, while the girl walked by the side. She had meant to ride all the way on her camel as her feet were bare and the stones cut them till the blood came. But she had to walk on till night, when they halted, and the next morning it was the same thing again. Weary and bleeding the poor girl began to cry, and implored the servant to let her ride, if only for a little. But he took no notice, except to bid her walk a little faster.

By-and-by they passed a caravan, and the servant stopped and asked the leader if they had come across seven young men, who were thought to be hunting somewhere about. And the man answered, "Go straight on, and by midday you will reach the castle where they live."

When he heard this, the servant melted some pitch in the sun, and smeared the girl with it, till she looked as dark skinned as he did. Next he bade his wife get down from the camel, and told Udea to mount, which she was thankful to do. So they arrived at her brothers' castle.

Leaving the camel kneeling at the entrance for Udea to dismount, the servant knocked loudly at the door, which was opened by the youngest brother, all the others being away hunting. He did not of course recognise Udea, but he knew the servant and his wife, and welcomed them gladly, adding, "But who does the other girl belong to?"

"O, that is your sister!" said they.

"My sister! But she is so dark skinned!"

"That may be, but she is your sister for all that."

The young man asked no more questions, but took them into the castle, and he himself waited outside till his brothers came home.

As soon as they were alone, the servant whispered to Udea, "If you dare to tell your brothers that I made you walk, or that I smeared you with pitch, I will kill you."

"O, I will be sure to say nothing," replied the girl, trembling, and at that moment the six elder brothers appeared in sight.

"I have some good news for you," said the youngest, hastening to meet them. "Our sister is here!"

"Nonsense," they answered. "We have no sister. You know the child that was born was a boy."

"But that was not true," replied he, "and here she is with the servant and his wife. Only - she too is dark," he added softly, but his brothers did not hear him, and pushed past joyfully.

"How are you, good old Barka?" they said to the servant, "and how comes it that we never knew that we had a sister till now?" And they greeted Udea warmly, while she shed tears of relief and gladness.

The next morning they all agreed that they would not go out hunting. And the eldest brother took Udea on his knee, and she combed his hair and talked to him of their home till the tears ran down his cheeks and dropped on her bare arm. And where the tears fell a white mark was made. Then the brother took a cloth and rubbed the place, and he saw that she was not dark skinned at all.

"Tell me, who painted you over like this?" cried he.

"I am afraid to tell you," sobbed the girl, "the servant will kill me."

"Afraid! And with seven brothers!"

"Well, I will tell you then," she answered. "Barka forced me to dismount from the camel and let his wife ride instead. And the stones cut my feet till they bled and I had to bind them. And after that, when we heard your castle was nearby, he took pitch and smeared my body with it."

Then the brother rushed in wrath from the room, and seizing his sword, cut off first the servant's head and then his wife's. He next brought in some warm water, and washed his sister all over, till her skin was fair and shining again.

"Ah, now we see that you are our sister!" they all said. "What fools the servant must have thought us, to believe for an instant that we could have a sister of the desert!" And all that day and the next they remained in the castle.

But on the third morning they said to their sister, "Dear sister, you must lock yourself into this castle, with only the cat for company. And be very careful never to eat anything which she does not eat too. You must be sure to give her a bit of everything. In seven days we shall be back again."

"All right," she answered, and locked herself into the castle with the cat.

On the eighth day the brothers came home. "How are you?" they asked. "You have not been anxious?"

"No, why should I be anxious? The gates were fast locked, and in the castle are seven doors, and the seventh is of iron. What is there to frighten me?"

"No one will try to hurt us," said the brothers, "for they fear us greatly. But for yourself, we implore you to do nothing without consulting the cat, who has grown up in the house, and take care never to neglect her advice."

"All right," replied Udea, "and whatever I eat she shall have half."

"Capital! And if ever you are in danger the cat will come and tell us - only elves and pigeons, which fly round your window, know where to find us."

"This is the first I have heard of the pigeons," said Udea. "Why did you not speak of them before?"

We always leave them food and water for seven days," replied the brothers.

"Ah," sighed the girl, "if I had only known, I would have given them fresh food and fresh water, for after seven days anything becomes bad. Would it not be better if I fed them every day?"

"Much better," said they, "and we shall feel any kindnesses you do towards the cat or the pigeons exactly as if they were shown to ourselves."

"Set your minds at ease," answered the girl, "I will treat them as if they were my brothers."

That night the brothers slept in the castle, but after breakfast next morning they buckled on their weapons and mounted their horses, and rode off to their hunting grounds, calling out to their sister, "Mind you let nobody in till we come back."

"Very well," cried she, and kept the doors carefully locked for seven days and on the eighth the brothers returned as before. Then, after spending one evening with her, they departed as soon as they had done breakfast.

Directly they were out of sight Udea began to clean the house, and among the dust she found a bean which she ate.

"What are you eating?" asked the cat.

"Nothing," said she.

"Open your mouth, and let me see." The girl did as she was told, and then the cat said, "Why did you not give me half?"

"I forgot," answered she, "but there are plenty of beans about, you can have as many as you like."

"No, that won't do. I want half of that particular bean."

"But how can I give it you? I tell you I have eaten it. I can roast you a hundred others."

"No, I want half of that one."

"Oh! Do as you like, only go away!" cried she.

So the cat ran straight to the kitchen fire, and spit on it and put it out, and when Udea came to cook the supper she had nothing to light it with. "Why did you put the fire out?" asked she.

"Just to show you how nicely you would be able to cook the supper. Didn't you tell me to do what I liked?"

The girl left the kitchen and climbed up on the roof of the castle and looked out. Far, far away, so far that she could hardly see it, was the glow of a fire. "I will go and fetch a burning coal from there and light my fire," thought she, and opened the door of the castle. When she reached the place where the fire was kindled, a hideous man-eater was crouching over it.

"Peace be with you, grandfather," said she.

"The same to you," replied the man-eater. "What brings you here, Udea?"

"I came to ask for a lump of burning coal, to light my fire with."

"Do you want a big lump or a little lump?"

"Why, what difference does it make?" said she.

"If you have a big lump you must give me a strip of your skin from your ear to your thumb, and if you have a little lump, you must give me a strip from your ear to your little finger."

Udea, who thought that one sounded as bad as the other, said she would take the big lump, and when the man-eater had cut the skin, she went home again. And as she hastened on a raven beheld the blood on the ground, and plastered it with earth, and stayed by her till she reached the castle. And as she entered the door he flew past, and she shrieked from fright, for up to that moment she had not seen him. In her terror she called after him. "May you get the same start as you have given me!"

"Why should you wish me harm," asked the raven pausing in his flight, "when I have done you a service?"

"What service have you done me?" said she.

"O, you shall soon see," replied the raven, and with his bill he scraped away all the earth he had smeared over the blood and then flew away.

In the night the man-eater got up, and followed the blood till he came to Udea's castle. He entered through the gate which she had left open, and went on till he reached the inside of the house. But here he was stopped by the seven doors, six of wood and one of iron, and all fast locked. And he called through them "O Udea, what did you see your grandfather doing?"

"I saw him spread silk under him, and silk over him, and lay himself down in a four-post bed."

When he heard that, the man-eater broke in one door, and laughed and went away.

And the second night he came back, and asked her again what she had seen her grandfather doing, and she answered him as before, and he broke in another door, and laughed and went away, and so each night till he reached the seventh door. Then the maiden wrote a letter to her brothers, and bound it round the neck of a pigeon, and said to it, "O, you pigeon that served my father and my grandfather, carry this letter to my brothers, and come back at once." And the pigeon flew away.

It flew and it flew and it flew till it found the brothers. The eldest unfastened the letter from the pigeon's neck, and read what his sister had written, "I am in a great strait, my brothers. If you do not rescue me tonight, tomorrow I shall be no longer living, for the man-eater has broken open six doors, and only the iron door is left. So haste, haste, post haste."

"Quick, quick, my brothers," cried he.

"What is the matter?" asked they.

"If we cannot reach our sister tonight, tomorrow she will be the prey of the man-eater."

And without more words they sprang on their horses, and rode like the wind.

The gate of the castle was thrown down, and they entered the court and called loudly to their sister. But the poor girl was so ill with fear and anxiety that she could not even speak. Then the brothers dismounted and passed through the six open doors, till they stood before the iron one, which was still shut. "Udea, open!" they cried, "it is only your brothers!" And she arose and unlocked the door, and throwing herself on the neck of the eldest burst into tears.

"Tell us what has happened," he said, "and how the man-eater traced you here."

"It is all the cat's fault," replied Udea. "She put out my fire so that I could not cook. All about a bean! I ate one and forgot to give her any of it."

"But we told you so particularly," said the eldest brother, "never to eat anything without sharing it with the cat."

"Yes, but I tell you I forgot," answered Udea.

"Does the man-eater come here every night?" asked the brothers.

"Every night," said Udea, "and he breaks one door in and then goes away."

Then all the brothers cried together, "We will dig a great hole, and fill it with burning wood, and spread a covering over the top, and when the man-eater arrives we will push him into it."

So they all set to work and prepared the great hole, and set fire to the wood, till it was reduced to a mass of glowing charcoal. And when the man-eater came, and called as usual, "Udea, what did you see your grandfather doing?" she answered, "I saw him pull off the ass's skin and devour the ass, and he fell in the fire, and the fire burned him up."

Then the man-eater was filled with rage, and he flung himself upon the iron door and burst it in. On the other side stood Udea's seven brothers, who said, "Come, rest yourself a little on this mat."

And the man-eater sat down, and he fell right into the burning pit which was under the mat, and they heaped on more wood, till nothing was left of him, not even a bone. But one of his finger-nails was blown away, and fell into an upper chamber where Udea was standing, and stuck under one of the nails of her own fingers. And she sank lifeless to the earth.

Meanwhile her brothers sat below waiting for her and wondering why she did not come. "What can have happened to her!" exclaimed the eldest brother. "Perhaps she has fallen into the fire, too."

So one of the others ran upstairs and found his sister stretched on the floor. "Udea! Udea!" he cried, but she did not move or reply. Then he saw that she was dead, and rushed down to his brothers in the courtyard and called out, "Come quickly, our sister is dead!"

In a moment they were all beside her and knew that it was true, and they made a bier and laid her on it, and placed her across a camel, and said to the camel, "Take her to her mother, but be careful not to halt by the way, and let no man capture you, and see you kneel down before no man, save him who shall say 'string' to you. But to him who says 'string,' then kneel."

So the camel started, and when it had accomplished half its journey it met three men, who ran after it in order to catch it but they could not. Then they cried "Stop!" but the camel only went the faster. The three men panted behind till one said to the others, "Wait a minute! The string of my sandal is broken!" The camel caught the word "string" and knelt down at once, and the men came up and found a dead girl lying on a bier, with a ring on her finger. And as one of the young men took hold of her hand to pull off the ring, he knocked out the man-eater's finger-nail, which had stuck there, and the maiden sat up and said, "Let him live who gave me life, and slay him who slew me!"

And when the camel heard the maiden speak, it turned and carried her back to her brothers.

Now the brothers were still seated in the court bewailing their sister, and their eyes were dim with weeping so that they could hardly see. And when the camel stood before them they said, "Perhaps it has brought back our sister!" and rose to give it a beating. But the camel knelt down and the girl dismounted, and they flung themselves on her neck and wept more than ever for gladness.

"Tell me," said the eldest, as soon as he could speak, "how it all came about, and what killed you."

"I was waiting in the upper chamber," said she, "and a nail of the man-eater's stuck under my nail, and I fell dead upon the ground. That is all I know."

"But who pulled out the nail?" asked he.

"A man took hold of my hand and tried to pull off my ring, and the nail jumped out and I was alive again. And when the camel heard me say "Let him live who gave me life, slay him who slew me!" it turned and brought me back to the castle. That is my story."

She was silent and the eldest brother spoke. "Will you listen to what I have to say, my brothers?"

And they replied, "How should we not hear you? Are you not our father as well as our brother?"

"Then this is my advice. Let us take our sister back to our father and mother, that we may see them once more before they die."

And the young men agreed, and they mounted their horses and placed their sister in a litter on the camel. So they set out.

At the end of five days" journey they reached the old home where their father and mother dwelt alone. And the heart of their father rejoiced, and he said to them, "Dear sons, why did you go away and leave your mother and me to weep for you night and day?"

"Dear father," answered the son, "let us rest a little now, and then I will tell you everything from the beginning."

"All right," replied the father, and waited patiently for three days.

And on the morning of the fourth day the eldest brother said, "Dear father, would you like to hear our adventures?"

"Certainly I should!"

"Well, it was our aunt who was the cause of our leaving home, for we agreed that if the baby was a sister she should wave a white handkerchief, and if it was a brother, she should brandish a sickle, for then there would be nothing to come back for, and we might wander far away. Now our aunt could not bear us, and hated us to live in the same house with her, so she brandished the sickle, and we went away. That is all our story."

Salomon And The Griffin

This story has been edited and adapted from Moorish Literature, a collection work from sources such as Adolphe Hanoteau's Poésies Populaires de la Khabylie du Jurgura of 1867, Émile Masqueray's Observations grammaticales sur la grammaire Touareg et textes de la Tourahog des Tailog, and René Basset's L'insurrection Algerienne, de 1871 dans les chansons populaires Khabyles Lourain of 1892. This version was taken from the English translation introduced by René Basset and published by the University of France and the Académie D'Alger, published in 1901. This is a Berber tale.

Our Lord Salomon was talking one day with the genii. He said to them, "There is born a girl at Dabersa and a boy at Djaberka. This boy and this girl shall meet."

The griffin said to the genii, "In spite of the will of the divine power, I shall never let them meet each other."

The son of the King of Djaberka came to Salomon's house, but hardly had he arrived when he fell ill. Then the griffin carried away the daughter of the King of Djaberka and put her upon a big tree at the shore of the sea. The wind impelled the prince, who had embarked. He said to his companions, "Put me ashore."

He went under the big tree and fell asleep. The young girl threw leaves at him. He opened his eyes, and she said to him, "Beside the griffin, I am alone here with my mother. Where do you come from?"

"From Djaberka."

"Why," she continued, "has God created any human beings except myself, my mother, and our Lord Salomon?"

He answered her, "God has created all kinds of human beings and countries."

"Go," she said, "bring a horse and kill it. Bring also some camphor to dry the skin, which you will hang on the top of the mast." The griffin came, and she began to cry, saying, "Why don't you conduct me to the house of our Lord Salomon?"

"Tomorrow I will take you."

She said to the son of the King, "Go hide inside the horse."

He hid there.

The next day the griffin took away the carcass of the horse, and the young girl departed also. When they arrived at the house of our Lord Salomon, the latter said to the griffin, "I told you that the young girl and the young man should be united."

Full of shame the griffin immediately fled and took refuge in an island.

The Wagtail And The Jackal

This story has been edited and adapted from The Talking Beasts by Kate Douglas Wiggin and Nora Archibald Smith, published in 1922.

At a time when the animals spoke, a Wagtail laid her eggs on the ground. The little ones grew up. A Jackal and a Fox came to them.

The Jackal said to the Fox, "Swear to me that the Wagtail owes me a pound of butter."

The Fox swore to it. The Bird began to weep. A Greyhound came to her and asked her what the matter was. She answered him, "The Fox has calumniated me."

"Well," said the Hound, "put me in this sack of skin."

She put him in the sack.

"Tie up the top well," said the Hound.

When the Jackal returned she said to him, "Come and measure out the butter."

The Jackal advanced and unfastened the sack. He saw the Hound, who stretched out his paws and said to the Fox, "I am ill. Come and measure, Fox."

The Fox approached.

The Hound seized him.

The Jackal said, "Remember your false testimony."

Adventure Of Sidi Mahomet

This story has been edited and adapted from Moorish Literature, a collection work from sources such as Adolphe Hanoteau's Poésies Populaires de la Khabylie du Jurgura of 1867, Émile Masqueray's Observations grammaticales sur la grammaire Touareg et textes de la Tourahog des Tailog, and René Basset's L'insurrection Algerienne, de 1871 dans les chansons populaires Khabyles Lourain of 1892. This version was taken from the English translation introduced by René Basset and published by the University of France and the Académie D'Alger, published in 1901. This is a Berber tale.

One day Mouley Mahomet summoned Sidi Adjille to come to Morocco, or he would put him in prison. The saint refused to go until the prince had sent him his chaplit and his "dalil" as pledges of safety. Then he started on the way and arrived at Morocco, where he neither ate nor drank until three days had passed.

The Sultan said to him, "What do you want at my palace? I will give it to you, whatever it may be."

Sidi Adjille answered, "I ask of you only one thing, that is, to fill with wheat the feed-bag of my mule."

The prince called the guardian, and said to him, "Fill the feed-bag of his mule." The guardian went and opened the door of the first granary and put wheat in the feed-bag until the first granary was entirely empty. He opened another granary, which was soon equally exhausted, then a third, and so on in this fashion until all the granaries of the King were emptied. Then he wanted to open the silos, but their guardian went and spoke to the Sultan, together with the guardian of the granaries.

"Lord," they said, "the royal granaries are all empty, and yet we have not been able to fill the feed-bag of the saint's mule."

The donkey-drivers came from Fas and from all countries, bringing wheat on mules and camels. The people asked them, "Why do you bring this wheat?"

"It is the wheat of Sidi Mahomet Adjille that we are taking."

The news came to the King, who said to the saint, "Why do you act so, now that the royal granaries are empty?" Then he called together the members of his council and wanted to have Sidi Mahomet's head cut off. "Go out," he said to him.

"Wait till I make my ablutions for prayer", answered the saint.

The people of the makhzen who surrounded him watched him among them, waiting until he had finished his ablutions, to take him to the council of the King and cut off his head. When Sidi Mahomet had finished washing, he lifted his eyes to heaven, got into the washing tub and vanished completely from sight. When the guardians saw that he was no longer there, they went vainly to continue the search at his house at Tagountaft.

The Haunted Garden

This story has been edited and adapted from Moorish Literature, a collection work from sources such as Adolphe Hanoteau's Poésies Populaires de la Khabylie du Jurgura of 1867, Émile Masqueray's Observations grammaticales sur la grammaire Touareg et textes de la Tourahog des Tailog, and René Basset's L'insurrection Algerienne, de 1871 dans les chansons populaires Khabyles Lourain of 1892. This version was taken from the English translation introduced by René Basset and published by the University of France and the Académie D'Alger, published in 1901. This is a Berber tale.

A man who possessed much money had two daughters. The son of the caliph of the King asked for one of them, and the son of the cadi asked for the other, but their father would not let them marry, although they desired it.

He had a garden near his house. When it was night, the young girls went there, the young men came to meet them, and they passed the night in conversation. One night their father saw them. The next morning he killed his daughters, buried them in his garden, and went on a pilgrimage.

That lasted so until one night the son of the cadi and the son of the caliph went to a young man who knew how to play on the flute and the rebab. "Come with us," they said to him, "into the garden of the man who will not give us his daughters in marriage. you shall play for us on your instruments."

They agreed to meet there that night. The musician went to the garden, but the two young men did not go. The musician remained and played his music alone. In the middle of the night two lamps appeared, and the two young girls came out of the ground under the lamps.

They said to the musician, "We are two sisters, daughters of the owner of the garden. Our father killed us and buried us here. You, you are our brother for this night. We will give you the money which our father has hidden in three pots. Dig here," they added.

He obeyed, found the three pots, took them away, and became rich, while the two girls returned to their graves.

The Wren

This story has been edited and adapted from The Talking Beasts by Kate Douglas Wiggin and Nora Archibald Smith, published in 1922.

A Wren had built its nest on the side of a road. When the eggs were hatched, a Camel passed that way. The little Wrens saw it and said to their father when he returned from the fields, "O papa, a gigantic animal passed by."

The Wren stretched out his foot. "As big as this, my children?"

"O papa, much bigger."

He stretched out his foot and his wing. "As big as this?"

"O papa, much bigger."

Finally he stretched out fully his feet and legs.

"As big as this then?"

"Much bigger."

"That is a lie. There is no animal bigger than I am."

"Well, wait," said the little ones, "and you will see."

The Camel came back while browsing the grass of the roadside.

The Wren stretched himself out near the nest. The Camel seized the bird, which passed through its teeth safe and sound.

"Truly," he said to them, "the Camel is a gigantic animal, but I am not ashamed of myself."

On the earth it generally happens that the vain are as if they did not exist, but sooner or later a rock falls and crushes them.

The Woman And The Fairy

This story has been edited and adapted from Moorish Literature, a collection work from sources such as Adolphe Hanoteau's Poésies Populaires de la Khabylie du Jurgura of 1867, Émile Masqueray's Observations grammaticales sur la grammaire Touareg et textes de la Tourahog des Tailog, and René Basset's L'insurrection Algerienne, de 1871 dans les chansons populaires Khabyles Lourain of 1892. This version was taken from the English translation introduced by René Basset and published by the University of France and the Académie D'Alger, published in 1901. This is a Berber tale.

A woman who was named Omm Halima went one day to the stream to wash at the old spring. Alone, in the middle of the day, she began her work, when a woman appeared to her and said, "Let us be friends, you and I, and let us make a promise. When you come to this spring, bring me some henna and perfumes. Cast them into the fountain which faces the qsar. I will come forth and I will give you money."

And so the wife of Ben Sernghown returned every day and found the other woman, who gave her pieces of money. Omm Khalifah was poor. When she "became friends" with the fairy she grew rich all of a sudden. The people were curious to know how she had so quickly acquired a fortune.

There was a rich man, the possessor of much property. He was called Mouley Ismail. They said to Omm Khalifah, "You are the mistress of Mouley Ismail, and he gives you pieces of money."

She answered, "Never have I been his mistress."

One day, when she went to the spring to bathe, the people followed her. The fairy came to meet her as usual, and gave her money. The people surprised them together. The fairy never came out of the fountain again.

Mule, Jackal, And Lion

This story has been edited and adapted from The Talking Beasts by Kate Douglas Wiggin and Nora Archibald Smith, published in 1922.

The Mule, the Jackal, and the Lion went in company.

"We will eat the one whose race is bad," they said to each other.

"Lion, who is your father?"

"My father is a lion, and my mother is a lioness."

"And you, Jackal, what is your father?"

"My father is a jackal, and my mother too."

"And you, Mule, what is your father?"

"My father is an ass, and my mother is a mare."

"Your race is bad. We will eat you."

Mule answered them, "I will consult an old man. If he says that my race is bad, you may devour me."

He went to a farrier, and said to him, "Shoe my hind feet, and make the nails stick out well."

He went back home. He called the Camel and showed him his feet, saying, "See what is written on this tablet."

"The writing is difficult to decipher," answered the Camel. "I do not understand it, for I only know three words - *outini, ouzatini, ouazakin.*"

He called the Lion, and said to him, "I do not understand these letters, I only know three words - *outini, ouzatini, ouazakin.*"

"Show it to me," said the Lion.

He approached. The Mule struck him between the eyes and stretched him out level.

He who goes with a knave is betrayed by him.

Hamed-Ben-Ceggad

This story has been edited and adapted from Moorish Literature, a collection work from sources such as Adolphe Hanoteau's Poésies Populaires de la Khabylie du Jurgura of 1867, Émile Masqueray's Observations grammaticales sur la grammaire Touareg et textes de la Tourahog des Tailog, and René Basset's L'insurrection Algerienne, de 1871 dans les chansons populaires Khabyles Lourain of 1892. This version was taken from the English translation introduced by René Basset and published by the University of France and the Académie D'Alger, published in 1901. This is a Berber tale.

There was in a city a man named Hamed-ben-Ceggad. He lived alone with his mother. He lived upon nothing but the chase. One day the inhabitants of the city said to the King, "Hamed-ben-Ceggad is getting the better of you."

He said to them, "Tell me why you talk thus to me, or I will cut off your heads."

"As he only eats the flesh of birds, he takes advantage of you for his food."

The King summoned Hamed and said to him, "You shall hunt for me, and I will supply your food and your mother's, too."

Every day Hamed brought game to the prince, and the prince grew very proud of him.

The inhabitants of the city were jealous of him, and went to the Sultan and said, "Hamed-ben-Ceggad is brave. He could bring you the tree of coral-wood and the palm-tree of the wild beasts."

The King said to him, "If you are not afraid, bring me the tree of coral-wood and the palm-tree of the wild beasts."

"It is well," said Hamed. And the next day he took away all the people of the city. When he came to the tree, he killed all the wild beasts, cut down the palm-tree, loaded it upon the shoulders of the people, and the Sultan built a house of coral-wood.

Seeing how he succeeded in everything, they said to the King, "Since he achieves all that he attempts, tell him to bring you the woman with the set of silver ornaments."

The prince repeated these words to Hamed, who said, "The task you give me is harsh, nevertheless I will bring her to you,"

He set out on the way, and came to a place where he found a man pasturing a flock of sheep, carrying a millstone hanging to his neck and playing the flute. Hamed said to him, "By the Lord, I cannot lift a small rock, and this man hangs a millstone to his neck."

The shepherd said, "You are Hamed-ben-Ceggad, who built the house of coral-wood?"

"Who told you?"

"A bird that flew into the sky." He added, "I will go with you."

"Come," said Hamed. The shepherd took the millstone from his neck, and the sheep were changed into stones.

On the way they met a naked man, who was rolling in the snow. They said to themselves, "The cold stings us, and yet that man rolls in the snow without the cold killing him."

The man said to them, "You are Hamed-ben-Ceggad, who built the house of coral-wood?"

"Who told you that?"

"A bird that passed flying in the sky told me. I will accompany you."

"Come," said Hamed.

After they had pursued their way some time, they met a man with long ears. "By the Lord," they said, "we have only small ears, and this man has immense ones."

"It is the Lord who created them thus, but if it pleases God I will accompany you, for you are Hamed-ben-Ceggad."

They arrived at the house of the woman with the silver ornaments, and Hamed said to the inhabitants, "Give us this woman, that we may take her away."

"Very well," said her brother, the ogre. They killed an ox, placed it upon a hurdle, which they lifted up and put down with the aid of ninety-nine men.

"Give us one of your men who can lift this hurdle."

He who wore millstones hanging from his neck said, "I can lift it."

When he had placed it on the ground, they served a couscous with this ox. The ogre said, "Eat all that we give you." They ate a little, and the man with the long ears hid the rest of the food.

The brother continued, "Give us one of you who will go to gather a branch of a tree that stands all alone on the top of a mountain two days' march in the snow."

The one who had rolled in the snow departed, and brought back the branch.

"There remains one more proof," said the ogre. "A partridge is flying in the sky. Let one of you strike it."

Hamed-ben-Ceggad killed it.

They gave him the woman, but before her departure her brother gave her a feather and said to her, "When anyone shall try to do anything to you against your will, cast this feather on the hearth and we will come to you."

People told the woman, "The old Sultan is going to marry you."

She replied, "An old man shall never marry me," and cast the feather into the fire. Her brother appeared, and killed all the inhabitants of the city, as well as the King, and gave the woman to Hamed-ben-Ceggad.

The Magic Napkin

This story has been edited and adapted from Moorish Literature, a collection work from sources such as Adolphe Hanoteau's Poésies Populaires de la Khabylie du Jurgura of 1867, Émile Masqueray's Observations grammaticales sur la grammaire Touareg et textes de la Tourahog des Tailog, and René Basset's L'insurrection Algerienne, de 1871 dans les chansons populaires Khabyles Lourain of 1892. This version was taken from the English translation introduced by René Basset and published by the University of France and the Académie D'Alger, published in 1901. This is a Berber tale.

A taleb made a proclamation in these terms, "Is there anyone who will sell himself for 100 mitquals?"

A man agreed to sell himself. The stranger took him to the cadi, who wrote out the bill of sale. He took the 100 mitquals and gave them to his mother and departed with the taleb. They went to a place where the latter began to repeat certain formulas. The earth opened and the man entered it. The other said to him, "Bring me the candlestick of reed and the box." He took this and came out keeping it in his pocket.

"Where is the box?" asked the taleb.

"I did not find it."

"By the Lord, let us go."

The taleb took him to the mountains, cast a stone at him, and went away. The man lay on the ground for three days. Then he came to himself, went back to his own country, and rented a house. He opened the box, found inside a silk napkin, which he opened, and in which he found seven folds. He unfolded one. Genii came around the chamber, and a young girl danced until the day dawned. The man stayed there all that day until night.

The King came out that night, and, hearing the noise of the dance, he knocked at the door, with his vizier. They received him with a red *h'aik*. The king amused himself until the day dawned. Then he went home with his vizier.

The latter sent for the man and said, "Give me the box which you have at home."

He brought it to the King, who said to him, "Give me the box which you have so that I may amuse myself with it, and I will marry you to my daughter."

The man obeyed and married the Sultan's daughter. The Sultan amused himself with the box, and after his death his son-in-law succeeded him.

The Child And The King Of The Genii

This story has been edited and adapted from Moorish Literature, a collection work from sources such as Adolphe Hanoteau's Poésies Populaires de la Khabylie du Jurgura of 1867, Émile Masqueray's Observations grammaticales sur la grammaire Touareg et textes de la Tourahog des Tailog, and René Basset's L'insurrection Algerienne, de 1871 dans les chansons populaires Khabyles Lourain of 1892. This version was taken from the English translation introduced by René Basset and published by the University of France and the Académie D'Alger, published in 1901. This is a Berber tale.

There was a sheik who gave instruction to two young talebs. One day one of them was eating a dish of couscous with meat, and the genii stole him and bore him away. When they had arrived at the place of the genii, the genii set about teaching the young taleb.

One day the child was crying. The King of the genii asked him, "Why do you cry?"

"I am crying for my father and my mother. I don't want to stay here any longer."

The King asked his sons, "Who will take him back?"

"I," said one of them, "but how shall I take him back?"

"Carry him back after you have stuffed his ears with wool so that he shall not hear the angels worshipping the Lord."

As they travelled at a certain place the child heard the angels worshipping the Lord, and did as the genii did. His guide released him and he remained three days without awaking. When he came to himself, he took up his journey and found a mother-dog which slept while her little ones barked, although yet unborn. He proceeded and met next an ass attacked by a swarm of flies. Further on he saw two trees, and on the boughs of one tree perched a blue bird. Afterward it flew upon the other tree and began to sing. He found next a fountain of which the bottom was of silver, the vault of gold and the waters white. He went on and met a man who had been standing for three days without saying a word. Finally he arrived at a village protected by God, but which no one entered.

He met a wise man and said to him, "I want to ask you some questions."

"What do you wish to ask me?"

"I found a mother-dog which was asleep while her little ones were barking, although yet unborn."

The sage answered, "It is the good of the world that the old man should keep silence because he is ashamed to speak."

"I saw an ass attacked by a swarm of flies."

"It is Pjoudj and Madjoudj of God, Gog and Magog, and the Antichrist."

"I met two trees. A blue bird perched on one, then flew upon the other and began to sing."

"It is the picture of the man who has two wives. When he speaks to one the other gets angry."

"I saw a fountain of which the bottom was of silver, the vault of gold, and the waters white."

"It is the fountain of life. He who drinks of it shall not die."

"I found a man who was praying. I stayed three days and he did not speak."

"It is he who never prayed upon the earth and is now making amends."

"Send me to my parents," concluded the child.

The old man saw a light cloud and said to it, "Take this human creature to Egypt."

And the cloud bore him to his parents.

The Seven Brothers

This story has been edited and adapted from Moorish Literature, a collection work from sources such as Adolphe Hanoteau's Poésies Populaires de la Khabylie du Jurgura of 1867, Émile Masqueray's Observations grammaticales sur la grammaire Touareg et textes de la Tourahog des Tailog, and René Basset's L'insurrection Algerienne, de 1871 dans les chansons populaires Khabyles Lourain of 1892. This version was taken from the English translation introduced by René Basset and published by the University of France and the Académie D'Alger, published in 1901. This is a Berber tale.

Here is a story that happened once upon a time. A man had seven sons who owned seven horses, seven guns, and seven pistols for hunting. Their mother was about to increase the family. They said to their father, "If we have a little sister we shall remain. If we have a little brother we shall go."

The woman had a little boy.

They asked, "Which is it?"

"A boy."

They mounted their horses and departed, taking provisions with them. They arrived at a tree, divided their bread, and ate it. The next day they started and travelled as far as a place where they found a well, from which they drew water. The older one said, "Come, let us put the youngest one in the well." They united against him, put him in, and departed, leaving him there. They came to a city.

The young man remained some time in the well where they had put him, until one day a caravan passing that way stopped to draw water. While the people were drinking they heard something moving at the bottom of the well.

"Wait a moment," they said, and they let down a rope. The young man caught it and climbed up. He was covered in black dirt and filth from the well. The people took him away and sold him to a man who conducted him to his house. He stayed there a month and with washing became white as snow. The wife of the man said, "Come, let us go away together."

"Never!" he answered.

At evening the man returned and asked, "What is the slave doing?"

"Sell him," said the woman.

He said, "You are free. Go where you please."

The young man went away and came to a city where there was a fountain inhabited by a serpent. They couldn't draw water from this fountain without his eating a woman. This day it was the turn of the King's daughter to be eaten.

The young man asked her, "Why do you weep?"

"Because it is my turn to be devoured today."

The stranger answered, "Courage, I will kill the serpent, if it please God."

The young girl entered the fountain. The serpent darted toward her, but as soon as he showed his head the young man struck it with his stick and made it fly away. He did the same to the next head until the serpent was dead. All the people of the city came to draw water.

The King asked, "Who has done this?"

"It is he," they cried, "the stranger who arrived yesterday."

The King gave him his daughter and named him his lieutenant The wedding-feast lasted seven days. My story is finished before my resources are exhausted.

Half-A-Cock

This story has been edited and adapted from Moorish Literature, a collection work from sources such as Adolphe Hanoteau's Poésies Populaires de la Khabylie du Jurgura of 1867, Émile Masqueray's Observations grammaticales sur la grammaire Touareg et textes de la Tourahog des Tailog, and René Basset's L'insurrection Algerienne, de 1871 dans les chansons populaires Khabyles Lourain of 1892. This version was taken from the English translation introduced by René Basset and published by the University of France and the Académie D'Alger, published in 1901. This is a Berber tale.

In times past there was a man who had two wives, and one was wise and one was foolish. They owned a cock in common. One day they quarrelled about the cock, cut it in two, and each took half. The foolish wife cooked her part. The wise one let her part live, and it walked on one foot and had only one wing.

Some days passed thus. Then the half-a-cock got up early, and started on his pilgrimage. At the middle of the day he was tired and went toward a brook to rest. A jackal came there to drink. Half-a-Cock jumped on his back, stole one of his hairs, which it put under its wing and resumed its journey. It proceeded until evening and stopped under a tree to pass the night there. It had not rested long when it saw a lion pass near the tree where it was lying. As soon as it perceived the lion it jumped on its back and stole one of its hairs, which it put with that of the jackal.

The next morning it got up early and took up its journey again. Arrived at the middle of a forest, it met a boar and said, "Give me a hair from your back, as the king of the animals and the trickiest of them have done - the jackal and the lion."

The boar answered, "As these two personages so important among the animals have done this, I will also give you what you request." He plucked a hair from his back and gave it to Half-a-Cock. The latter went on his way and arrived at the palace of a king.

It began to crow and to say, "Tomorrow the King will die, and I will take his wife."

Hearing these words the King gave to his soldiers the command to seize Half-a-Cock, and cast him into the middle of the sheep and goat-pen to be trampled upon and killed by them, so that the King might get rid of his crowing. The soldiers seized him and cast him into the pen to perish. When he got there Half-a-Cock took from under his wing the jackal's hair and burnt it in the fire. As soon as it was near the fire the jackal came and said, "Why are you burning my hair? As soon as I smelled it, I came running."

Half-a-Cock replied, "You see what situation I am in. Get me out of it."

"That is an easy thing," said the jackal, and immediately bellowed in order to summon his brothers. They gathered around him, and he gave them this command, "My brothers, save me from Half-a-Cock, for it has a hair from my back which it has put in the fire. I don't want to burn. Take Half-a-Cock out of the sheep-pen, and you will be able to take my hair from its hands."

At once the jackals rushed to the pen, strangled everything that was there, and rescued Half-a-Cock. The next day the King found his stables deserted and his animals killed. He sought for Half-a-Cock, but in vain. The latter, the next day at the supper hour, began to crow as it did the first time. The prince called his soldiers and said to them, "Seize Half-a-Cock and cast him into the cattle-yard so that it may be crushed under their feet."

The soldiers caught Half-a-Cock and threw him into the middle of the cow-pen. As soon as it reached there, it took the lion's hair and put it into the fire. The lion came, roaring, and said, "Why do you burn my hair? I smelled from my cave the odour of burning hair, and came running to learn the motive of your action."

Half-a-Cock answered, "You see my situation. Help me out of it."

The lion went out and roared to call his brothers. They came in great haste and said to him, "Why do you call us now?"

"Take the Half-a-Cock from the ox-yard, for it has one of my hairs, which it can put into the fire. If you don't rescue Half-a-Cock, it will burn the hair, and I don't want to smell the odour of burning hair while I am alive."

His brothers obeyed. They at once killed all the cattle in the pen. The King saw that his animals were all dead, and he fell into such a rage that he nearly strangled himself. He looked for Half-a-Cock to kill it with his own hands. He searched a long time without finding it, and finally went home to rest. At sunset Half-a-Cock came to his usual place and crowed as on the former occasions.

The King called his soldiers and said to them, "This time when you have caught Half-a-Cock, put it in a house and shut all the doors till morning. I will kill it myself."

The soldiers seized him immediately and put him in the treasure-room. When it got there, it saw money under its feet. It waited till it had nothing to fear from the masters of the house, who were all sound asleep, took from under its wing the hair of the boar, started a fire, and placed the hair in it. At once the boar came running and shaking the earth. It thrust its head against the wall. The wall shook and half of it fell down, and going to Half-a-Cock the boar said, "Why are you burning my hair at this moment?"

"Pardon me, you see the situation in which I am, without counting what awaits me in the morning, for the King is going to kill me with his own hands if you don't get me out of this prison."

The boar replied, "The thing is easy. Fear not, I will open the door so that you may go out. In fact, you have stayed here long enough. Get up, go and take money enough for you and your children."

Half-a-Cock obeyed. It rolled in the gold, took all that stuck to its wing and its foot, and swallowed as much as it could hold. It took the road it had followed the first day and when it had arrived near the house it called the mistress and said, "Strike now, be not afraid to kill me."

His mistress began to strike until Half-a-Cock called from beneath the mat, "Enough now. Roll the mat."

She obeyed and saw the earth all shining with gold.

Strange Meetings

This story has been edited and adapted from Moorish Literature, a collection work from sources such as Adolphe Hanoteau's Poésies Populaires de la Khabylie du Jurgura of 1867, Émile Masqueray's Observations grammaticales sur la grammaire Touareg et textes de la Tourahog des Tailog, and René Basset's L'insurrection Algerienne, de 1871 dans les chansons populaires Khabyles Lourain of 1892. This version was taken from the English translation introduced by René Basset and published by the University of France and the Académie D'Alger, published in 1901. This is a Berber tale.

Once upon a time a man was on a journey and he met a mare who grazed in the meadow. She was thin, lean, and had only skin and bone. He went on until he came to a place where he found a mare which was fat, although she did not eat. He went on further until he met a sheep which kicked against a rock till evening to pass the night there. Advancing he met a serpent which hung in a hole from which it could not get out. Farther on, he saw a man who played with a ball, and his children were old men.

Then he came to an old man who said to him, "I will explain all that to you. The lean mare which you saw represents the rich man whose brothers are poor. The fat mare represents the poor man whose brothers are rich. The serpent which swings unable to enter nor to leave the hole is the picture of the word which once spoken and heard can never go back. The sheep which kicks against the rock to pass the night there, is the man who has an evil house. The one whose children you saw aged while he was playing ball, what does he represent? That is the man who has taken a pretty wife and does not grow old. His children have taken bad ones."

The King And His Family

This story has been edited and adapted from Moorish Literature, a collection work from sources such as Adolphe Hanoteau's Poésies Populaires de la Khabylie du Jurgura of 1867, Émile Masqueray's Observations grammaticales sur la grammaire Touareg et textes de la Tourahog des Tailog, and René Basset's L'insurrection Algerienne, de 1871 dans les chansons populaires Khabyles Lourain of 1892. This version was taken from the English translation introduced by René Basset and published by the University of France and the Académie D'Alger, published in 1901. This is a Berber tale.

In times gone by a king reigned over Maghreb. He had four sons. He started, he, his wife, and his children, for the Orient. They set sail, but their ship sank with them. The waves bore them all in separated directions. One wave took the wife, while another bore the father alone to the middle of the sea on an island where he found a mine of silver. He dug out enough silver until he had a great quantity and he established himself in the country.

His people after heard tell of him and learned that he dwelt in the midst of the sea. They built houses until there was a great city. He was king of that country. Whoever came poor to him he gave him pieces of money. A poor man married his wife. As for his sons, they applied themselves to a study, each in a different country. They all became learned men and feared God.

The King had a search made for *tolbas* who should worship God. The first of the brothers was recommended to him. He sent for him. He sought also a *khodja*. The second brother was designated. He summoned him to the court. The prince also especially wanted an *adel*. Another brother was pointed out to him. He made him come to him as, indeed, he also did the imam, who was none other than the fourth brother. They arrived at their father's without knowing him or being known by him.

The wife and the man who had espoused her also came to the King to make complaint. When they arrived the wife went alone that night to the palace. The prince sent for the four *tolba* to pass the night with him until morning. During the night he spied upon them to see who they were.

One of them said to the others, "Since sleep comes not upon us, let each one make known who he is."

One said, "My father was a king. He had much money and four sons whose names were like yours."

Another said, "My father was a king. My case is like yours."

Another said, "My father was a king. My case is like yours."

The fourth said in his turn, "My father, too, was a king. My case is like that of your three. you are my brothers."

Their mother overheard them and took to weeping until day.

They took her to the prince, who said, "Why do you weep?"

She answered, "I was formerly the wife of a king and we had four sons. We set sail, he, our children, and I. The ship which bore us was wrecked. Each one was borne away alone, until yesterday when they spoke before me during the night and showed me what had happened to them, to their father, and to their mother."

The King said, "Let me know your adventure."

They told him all that had happened. Then the prince arose, weeping, and said, "You are my children," and to the woman, "You are my wife."

God reunited them.

Beddou

This story has been edited and adapted from Moorish Literature, a collection work from sources such as Adolphe Hanoteau's Poésies Populaires de la Khabylie du Jurgura of 1867, Émile Masqueray's Observations grammaticales sur la grammaire Touareg et textes de la Tourahog des Tailog, and René Basset's L'insurrection Algerienne, de 1871 dans les chansons populaires Khabyles Lourain of 1892. This version was taken from the English translation introduced by René Basset and published by the University of France and the Académie D'Alger, published in 1901. This is a Berber tale.

Two men, one of whom was named Beddou and the other Amkammel, went to market bearing a basket of figs. They met a man who was working, and said to him, "God assist you!"

"Amen!" he answered.

One of them wanted to wash himself, but there was no water. The labourer said, "What is your name?"

"Beddou."

"By the Lord, Beddou, watch my oxen while I go to drink."

"Go!"

When he had gone, Beddou took away one of the oxen. On his return the labourer saw that one was missing. He went to the other traveller and asked him, "By my father, what is your name?"

"Amkammel Ouennidhui", he answered.

"By the Lord, Amkammel Ouennidhui, watch this ox for me while I go look for the one that is gone."

"Go!"

Amkammel Ouennidhui stole the other ox. When the labourer returned he didn't even find the second.

The two thieves went away, taking the oxen. They killed them to roast them. One drank all the water of the sea, the other all the fresh water, to wash it down. When they had finished, one stayed there to sleep, and the other covered him with ashes. The former got up to get a drink and the ashes fell on the road. When he came back, the second covered himself with the ox-head. His brother, who had gone to get a drink, was afraid, and ran away.

They divided the other ox to eat it. The one who had drunk the sea-water now drank fresh water, and the one who had drunk fresh water now drank sea-water. When they had finished their repast they took up their journey. They found an old woman who had some money, upon which she was sitting. When they arrived they fought. She arose to separate them. One of them took her place to pass the night, and pretended that he was dead.

The old woman said to him, "Get up, my son."

He refused. In the evening one of them stole the money, and said to his brother, "Arise! Let us go!"

They went away to a place where was sleeping the one who had taken the money was sleeping. The other took away the *dirkhems* and departed, leaving the first asleep. When he awaked he found nothing. He started in pursuit of the other, and when he arrived he found him dying of illness.

The latter had said to his wife, "Bury me."

She buried him. He who had first stolen the money went away.

He said, "It is an ox."

"It is I, my friend," he cried. "Praise be to God, my friend! May your days pass in happiness!"

Beddou said to him, "Let us go for a hunt."

They went away alone.

Beddou added, "I will shave you." He shaved him, and when he came to the throat he killed him and buried his head. A pomegranate-tree sprang up at this place.

One day Beddou found a fruit, which he took to the King. When he arrived he felt that it was heavy. It was a head. The King asked him, "What is that?"

"A pomegranate."

"We know what you have been doing," said the King, and had his head cut off. My story is finished.

The Language Of The Beasts

This story has been edited and adapted from Moorish Literature, a collection work from sources such as Adolphe Hanoteau's Poésies Populaires de la Khabylie du Jurgura of 1867, Émile Masqueray's Observations grammaticales sur la grammaire Touareg et textes de la Tourahog des Tailog, and René Basset's L'insurrection Algerienne, de 1871 dans les chansons populaires Khabyles Lourain of 1892. This version was taken from the English translation introduced by René Basset and published by the University of France and the Académie D'Alger, published in 1901. This is a Berber tale.

Once upon a time there was a man who had many goods. One day he went to market. There came a greyhound, which ate some meat. The butcher gave it a blow, which made it yelp. Seeing this, the heart of the man was touched with compassion. He bought half a piece of meat and flung it to the greyhound. The dog took it and went away. It was the son of a king of the nether world.

Fortune changed with the man. He lost all his possessions, and began to wash clothes for people. One day, he had gone to wash something, and he stretched it on the sand to dry. A jerboa appeared with a ring in its ear. The man ran after it, killed it, hid the ring, made a fire, cooked the jerboa and ate it. A woman came out of the earth, seized him, and demanded, "Haven't you seen my son, with an ear-ring?"

"I haven't seen anybody," he answered, "but I saw a jerboa which had a ring in its ear."

"It is my son."

She drew him under the earth and told him, "You have eaten my son, you have separated me from him. Now I will separate you from your children, and you shall work in the place of my son."

The long forgotten greyhound saw this man that day, and said to him, "Is it you who bought some meat for a greyhound and threw it to him?"

"It is I."

"I am that greyhound. Who brought you here?"

"A woman," answered the man, and he recounted all his adventure.

"Go and make a complaint to the King," answered the other. "I am his son. I'll tell him that this man did me a good service.' When he asks you to go to the treasure and take as much money as you wish, answer him, 'I don't want any. I only want you to spit a benediction into my mouth,' If he asks you, 'Who told you that?' answer, 'Nobody.'"

The man went and found the King and complained of the woman. The King called her and asked her, "Why have you taken this man captive?"

"He ate my son."

"Why was your son changed into a jerboa? When men see one of those they kill him and eat him." Then addressing the man, he said, "Give her back the ear-ring."

He gave it to her.

"Go," said the King, "take this man to the place from which you brought him."

The son of the King then said to his father, "This man did me a favour, and you ought to reward him."

The King said to him, "Go to the treasure, take as much money as you can."

"I don't want money," he answered, "I want you to spit into my mouth a benediction."

"Who told you that?"

"Nobody."

"You will not be able to bear it."

"I will be able."

"When I have spat into your mouth, you will understand the language of beasts and birds. You will know what they say when they speak, but if you reveal it to the people you will die."

"I will not reveal it." So the King spat into his mouth and sent him away, saying to the woman, "Go and take him back where you found him."

She departed, and took him back there. He mounted his ass and came back to his house. He arranged the load and took back to the people the linen he had washed. Then he remounted the beast to go and seek some earth. He was going to dig when he heard a crow say in the air, "Dig beneath. You will sing when God has made you rich."

He understood what the crow said, dug beneath, and found a treasure. He filled a basket with it. On the top he put a little earth and went home, but often returned to the spot. On one of these occasions his ass met a mule, which said, "Are you working still?"

The ass replied, "My master has found a treasure and he is taking it away."

The mule answered, "When you are in a crowd balk and throw the basket to the ground. People will see it, all will be discovered, and your master will leave you in peace."

The man had heard every word of this. He filled his basket with earth only. When they arrived at a crowd of people the ass kicked and threw the load to the ground. Her master beat her till she had enough. He applied himself to gathering the treasure, and became a rich merchant.

He had at home some chickens and a dog. One day he went into the granary, and a hen followed him and ate the grain. A cock said to her, "Bring me a little."

She answered, "Eat for yourself."

The master began to laugh. His wife asked him, "What are you laughing at?"

"Nothing."

"You are laughing at me."

"Not at all."

"You must tell me what you are laughing at."

"If I tell you I shall die."

"You shall tell me, and you shall die."

"Tonight."

He brought out some grain and said to his wife, "Give alms." He invited the people, bade them to eat, and when they had gone he brought food to the dog, but he would not eat. The neighbour's dog came, as it did every day, to eat with his dog. Today it found the food intact.

"Come and eat," it said.

"No," the dog answered.

"Why not?"

Then the dog told the other, "My master, hearing the chickens talk, began to laugh. His wife asked him, 'Why are you laughing?' 'If I tell you, I shall die.' 'Tell me and die,' That is why," continued the dog, "he has given alms, for when he reveals his secret he will die, and I shall never find anyone to act as he has."

The other dog replied, "As he knows our language, let him take a stick and give it to his wife until she has had enough. As he beats her let him say, 'This is what I was laughing at. This is what I was laughing at. This is what I was laughing at,' until she says to him, 'Reveal to me nothing.'"

The man heard the conversation of the dogs, and went and got a stick. When his wife and he went to bed she said to him, "Tell me that now."

Then he took the stick and beat her, saying, "This is what I was laughing at. This is what I was laughing at. This is what I was laughing at," until she cried out, "Don't tell it to me. Don't tell it to me. Don't tell it to me."

He left her alone. When the dogs heard that, they rejoiced, ran out on the terrace, played, and ate their food.

From that day the wife never again said to her husband, "Tell me that!" They lived happy ever after.

If I have omitted anything, may God forgive me for it.

The Apple Of Youth

This story has been edited and adapted from Moorish Literature, a collection work from sources such as Adolphe Hanoteau's Poésies Populaires de la Khabylie du Jurgura of 1867, Émile Masqueray's Observations grammaticales sur la grammaire Touareg et textes de la Tourahog des Tailog, and René Basset's L'insurrection Algerienne, de 1871 dans les chansons populaires Khabyles Lourain of 1892. This version was taken from the English translation introduced by René Basset and published by the University of France and the Académie D'Alger, published in 1901. This is a Berber tale.

There once lived a king who had five daughters and no sons. They grew up. He wanted them to marry, but they would not have any of the young men of the city. A youth came from a far country and stood under the castle, beneath the window of the youngest daughter. She saw him, and told her father she would marry him.

"Bring him in," said the King.

"He will come tomorrow."

"God be praised," said the King, "that you are pleased with us."

The young man answered, "Give me your daughter for a wife."

"Advise me," said the King.

The stranger said, "Go and wait till tomorrow."

The next day the young man said to the King, "Make all the inhabitants of the city come out. You will stand with the clerks at the entrance to the gate. Dress your daughters and let them choose their husbands themselves."

The people began to come out. The eldest daughter struck one of them on the chest with an apple, and they said, "That daughter has chosen a husband. Bravo!"

Each one of the daughters thus selected a husband, and the youngest kept hers. A little while afterward, the King received a visit from one of his sons-in-law, who said to him, "What do you want us to give you?"

"I'll see what my daughters want," he answered. "Come back in six days."

When they went to see their wives the King said to them, "I will ask of you a thing about which they have spoken to me."

"What is it? We are anxious to know."

"It is an apple, the odour of which gives to the one who breathes it youth, no matter what his age may be."

"It is difficult," they answered. "We know not where it can be found."

"If you do not bring it to me, you cannot marry my daughter."

They kept silent, and then consulted with each other. The youngest said to them, "Seek the means to satisfy the King."

"Give us your advice."

"Father-in-law, tomorrow we shall bring you the apple."

His brothers-in-law added, "Go out. Tomorrow we will meet you outside the city."

The next day they all five met together. Four of them said to the other, "Advise us or we will kill you."

"Cut off your fingers," he said.

The first one began, and the three others did the same. The youngest one took them and put them into his game-bag, and then he added, "Wait near the city till I come back."

He went out into the desert and came to the city of an ogress. He entered, and found her ready to grind some wheat. He said to the ogress, "Show me the apple whose colour gives eternal youth to the old man who smells it."

"You are in the family of ogres," she said. "Cut a hair from the horse of their King. When you go into the garden cast this hair into the fire. You will find a tree, from which you must pick five fruits. When plucking them do not speak a word, and keep silence on your return. It is the smallest fruit that possesses the magic power."

This he did. He then took the apple and went back to the city, where he found his companions. He concealed in his breast the wonderful fruit, and gave others to his brothers-in-law, one to each. They entered the palace of the King, who was overjoyed to see them, gave them seats, and asked them, "Have you brought it or not?"

"We have brought it," they answered.

He said to the eldest, "Give me your apple first."

He took a mirror in his left hand, and the fruit in the right hand, bent down, and inhaled the odour of the apple, but without results. He threw it down upon the ground. The others gave him their apples, with no more success.

"You have deceived me," he said to them. "The apples do not produce the effect that I sought."

Addressing, then, the stranger, he said, "Give me your apple."

The other son-in-law replied, "I am not of this country. I will not give you my fruit."

"Give it to me to look at," said the King. The young man gave it to him, saying, "Take a mirror in your right hand and the apple in your left hand."

The King put the apple to his nose, and, looking at his beard, saw that it became black. His teeth became white. He grew young again.

"You are my son," he said to the young man. And he made a proclamation to his subjects, "When I am dead he shall succeed me on the throne."

His son-in-law stayed some time with him, and after the death of the King he reigned in his place, but he did not marry the other daughters of the King to his companions.

Ali And Ou Ali

This story has been edited and adapted from Moorish Literature, a collection work from sources such as Adolphe Hanoteau's Poésies Populaires de la Khabylie du Jurgura of 1867, Émile Masqueray's Observations grammaticales sur la grammaire Touareg et textes de la Tourahog des Tailog, and René Basset's L'insurrection Algerienne, de 1871 dans les chansons populaires Khabyles Lourain of 1892. This version was taken from the English translation introduced by René Basset and published by the University of France and the Académie D'Alger, published in 1901. This is a tale from the Kabyles.

Ali and Ou Ali were two friends. One day they met at the market. One of them bore ashes and the other carried dust. The first one had covered his goods with a little flour. The other had concealed his merchandise under some black figs.

"Come, I will sell you some flour," said Ali.

"Come, I will sell you some black figs," answered Ou Ali.

Each regained his own horse. Ali, who thought he was carrying flour, found, on opening his sack, that it was only ashes. Ou Ali, who thought he was bearing black figs, found on opening his sack that it was nothing but dust. Another day they again greeted each other in the market. Ali smiled. Ou Ali smiled, and said to his friend, "For the love of God, what is your name?"

"Ali. And yours?"

"Ou Ali."

Another time they were walking together, and said to each other, "Let us go and steal."

One of them stole a mule and the other stole a rug. They passed the night in the forest. Now, as the snow was falling, Ali said to Ou Ali, "Give me a little of your rug to cover me."

Ou Ali refused. "You remember," he added, "that I asked you to put my rug on your mule, and you would not do it."

An instant afterward Ali cut off a piece of the rug, for he was dying of cold. Ou Ali got up and cut the lips off the mule. The next morning, when they awakened, Ou Ali said to Ali, "O my dear friend, your mule is grinning."

"O my dear friend," replied Ali, "the rats have gnawed your rug."

And they separated.

Sometime afterward they met anew. Ali said to Ou Ali, "Let us go and steal."

They saw a peasant, who was working. One of them went to the brook to wash his cloak there, and found it dry. He laid the blade of his sabre so that it would reflect the rays of the sun, and began to beat his cloak with his hands as if to wash it. The labourer came to the brook also, and found the man who was washing his cloak without water.

"May God exterminate you," said he, "who wash without water."

"May God exterminate you," answered the washer, "who work without a single ox."

The other robber watched the labourer, and had already stolen one of his oxen. The labourer went back to his plough, and said to the washer, "Keep this ox for me while I go and hunt for the other."

As soon as he was out of sight the robber took away the ox left in his charge. The labourer returned, and seizing the goad by one end he gave a great blow on the plough-handle, crying, "Break, now. It matters little."

The robbers met in a wood and killed the oxen. As they lacked salt, they went to purchase it. They salted the meat, roasted it, and ate it. Ali discovered a spring. Ou Ali not being able to find water, was dying of thirst.

"Show me your spring," he said to Ali, "and I will drink."

"Eat some salt, my dear friend," answered Ali. What could he do?

Some days afterward Ou Ali put ashes on the shoes of Ali. The next day he followed the traces of the ashes, found the spring, and discovered the water that his friend was drinking. He took the skin of one of the oxen and carried it to the fountain. He planted two sticks above the water, hung the skin on the sticks, and placed the horns of the ox opposite the road. During the night his friend went to the spring. At the sight of the skin thus stretched out, fear seized him, and he fled.

"I am thirsty," said Ou Ali.

"Eat some salt, my dear friend," answered Ali, "for salt removes thirst."

Ali retired, and, after having eaten, ran to examine the skin that he had stretched out. Ou Ali ate the salt, and was dying of thirst.

"For the love of God," he said finally, "show me where you drink."

Ali was avenged. "Come, and I will show you the water."

He made him drink at the spring, and said to him, "See what you were afraid of." The meat being finished, they started away. Ou Ali went to the house of Ali, and said to him, "Come, we will marry you to the daughter of an old woman."

Now, the old woman had a herd of oxen. She said to Ali, "Take this drove to the fields and mount one of the animals."

Ali mounted one of the oxen. He fell to the ground, and the oxen began to run and trample on him. Ou Ali, who was at the house, said to the old woman, "O my old woman, give me your daughter in marriage."

She called her daughter. "Take a club," she said to her, "and we will give it to him until he cries for mercy."

The daughter brought a club and gave Ou Ali a good beating. Ali, who was watching the herd, came at nightfall and met his friend.

"Did the old woman accept you?" he asked him.

"She accepted me," answered Ali. "And is the herd easy to watch?"

"From morning till night I have nothing to do but to repose. Take my place tomorrow, and mount one of the oxen."

The next day Ou Ali said to the old woman, "Today I will take care of the herd." And, on starting, he recommended Ali to ask the old woman for her daughter's hand.

"It is well," answered Ali.

Ou Ali arrived in the fields, where one of the oxen seized him with his horns and tossed him into the air. All the others did the same thing. He regained the horse half dead.

Ali, who had remained at the house, asked the old woman for her daughter's hand. "You ask me again?" said she. She took a club and gave it to him till he had had enough.

Ou Ali said to Ali, "You have played me a trick."

Ali answered him, "Without doubt they gave me the stick so hard that I did not hear the last blow."

"It is well, my dear friend. Ali owes nothing to Ou Ali."

They went away. The old woman possessed a treasure. Ou Ali therefore said to Ali, "I will put you in a basket, for you know that we saw that treasure in a hole."

They returned to the old woman's house. Ali went down into the hole, took the treasure, and put it into the basket. Ou Ali drew up the basket, took the treasure, abandoned his friend, now a prisoner, and ran to hide the treasure in the forest.

Ali was in trouble, for he knew not how to get out. What could he do? He climbed up the sides of the hole. When he found himself in the house, he opened the door and fled. Arriving at the edge of the forest he began to bleat. Ou Ali, thinking it was a ewe, ran up. It was his friend.

"O my dear," cried Ali, "I have found you at last."

"God be praised. Now, let us carry our treasure."

They started on the way. Ou Ali, who had a sister, said to Ali, "Let us go to my sister's house."

They arrived at nightfall. She received them with joy. Her brother said to her, "Prepare some pancakes and some eggs for us."

She prepared the pancakes and the eggs and served them with the food.

"O my sister," cried Ou Ali, "my friend does not like eggs. Bring us some water."

She went to get the water. As soon as she had gone, Ali took an egg and put it into his mouth. When the woman returned, he made such efforts to give it up that he was all out of breath.

The repast was finished, and Ali had not eaten anything. Ou Ali said to his sister, "O my sister, my friend is ill. Bring me a skewer."

She brought him a skewer, which he put into the fire. When the skewer was red with the heat, Ou Ali seized it and applied it to the cheek of Ali. The latter uttered a cry, and spat out the egg.

"Truly," said the woman, "you do not like eggs."

The two friends started and arrived at a village. "Let us go to my sister's house," said Ali to his friend. She received them with open arms.

Ali said to her, "O my sister, prepare a good stew for us."

They placed themselves at the table at nightfall, and she served them with food.

"O my sister," cried Ali, "my friend does not like stew."

Ali ate alone. When he was satisfied, the two friends started off again, without forgetting the treasure. On the way Ali said to Ou Ali, "Give it to me today and I will deposit it in my house."

He took it and gave it to his wife. "Bury me," he said to her. "And if Ou Ali comes tell him that his old friend is dead, and receive him with tears."

Ou Ali arrived, and asked the woman in tears to see the tomb of his dead friend. He took an ox-horn and began to dig in the earth that covered the body.

"Behind! Behind!" cried the pretended dead man.

"Get up, there, you liar," answered Ali.

They went away together. "Give me the treasure," said Ou Ali, "today I will take it to my house."

He took it to his house, and said to his wife, "Take this treasure. I am going to stretch myself out as if I were dead. When Ali comes receive him weeping, and say to him, 'Your friend is dead. He is stretched out in the bedroom.'"

Ali went and said to the woman, "Get me some boiling water, for your husband told me to wash him when he should die."

When the water was ready the woman brought it. Ali seized the kettle and poured it on the stomach of Ou Ali, who sprang up with a bound.

Thus he got even for the trick of his friend. The two friends divided the treasure then, and Ali went home.

The Sheik's Head

This story has been edited and adapted from Moorish Literature, a collection work from sources such as Adolphe Hanoteau's Poésies Populaires de la Khabylie du Jurgura of 1867, Émile Masqueray's Observations grammaticales sur la grammaire Touareg et textes de la Tourahog des Tailog, and René Basset's L'insurrection Algerienne, de 1871 dans les chansons populaires Khabyles Lourain of 1892. This version was taken from the English translation introduced by René Basset and published by the University of France and the Académie D'Alger, published in 1901. This is a tale from the Kabyles.

A man died, leaving a son. The child spent day and night with his mother. The sheik chanted a prayer every morning and woke him up. The child went to find the sheik, and said, "Ali Sheik, do not sing so loudly, you wake us up every morning - my mother and me."

But the sheik kept on singing. The child went to the mosque armed with a club. At the moment when the sheik bowed to pray he struck him a blow and killed him. He ran to his mother, and said to her, "I have killed that sheik. Come, let us bury him."

They cut off his head and buried his body. The child went to the Thadjeinath, where the men of the village were assembled. In his absence his mother killed a sheep. She took the head and buried it in place of the sheik's head. The child arrived at the Thadjeinath and said to those present, "I have killed the sheik who waked us up every morning."

"It is a lie," said they.

"Come to my mother's house and we will show you where we buried his head."

They went to the house, and the mother said to them, "Ali Sidi, this child is mad. It is a sheep that we have killed. Come and see where we buried its head."

They went to the spot, dug, and found a sheep's head.

The Flute-Player

This story has been edited and adapted from Moorish Literature, a collection work from sources such as Adolphe Hanoteau's Poésies Populaires de la Khabylie du Jurgura of 1867, Émile Masqueray's Observations grammaticales sur la grammaire Touareg et textes de la Tourahog des Tailog, and René Basset's L'insurrection Algerienne, de 1871 dans les chansons populaires Khabyles Lourain of 1892. This version was taken from the English translation introduced by René Basset and published by the University of France and the Académie D'Alger, published in 1901. This is a tale from the Kabyles.

A servant tended the sheep of his master. Arrived in the meadow, he played the flute. The sheep heard him, and would not browse. One day the master perceived that his sheep did not graze. He followed the servant to the fields and hid himself in the bush. The shepherd took his flute and began to play. His master began to dance so that the bushes scratched him and brought blood upon him. He returned home.

"Who scratched you so?" asked his wife.

"The servant played on the flute, and I began to dance."

"That is a lie," said she, "people don't dance against their will."

"Well," answered the husband, "tie me to this post and make the servant play."

She tied him to the post and the servant took the flute. Our man began to dance. He struck his head against a nail in the post and died.

The son of the dead man said to the servant, "Pay me for the loss of my father."

They went before the cadi. On the way they met a labourer, who asked them where they were going.

"Before the cadi."

"Could you tell me why?"

"This man killed my father," answered the son of the dead man.

"It was not I that killed him," answered the shepherd, "I played on the flute, he danced and died."

"That is a lie!" cried the labourer. "I will not dance against my will. Take your flute and we shall see if I dance."

The shepherd took his flute. He began to play, and the labourer started dancing with such activity that his oxen left to themselves fell into the ravine.

"Pay me for my oxen," he cried to the shepherd.

"Come before the cadi," he answered. They presented themselves before the cadi, who received them on the second floor of the house. They all sat down. Then the cadi said to the servant, "Take your flute and play before me. I will see how you play."

The servant took his flute and all began to dance. The cadi danced with the others, and they all fell down to the ground floor and were killed. The servant stayed in the house of the cadi and inherited the property of all.

The Child

This story has been edited and adapted from Moorish Literature, a collection work from sources such as Adolphe Hanoteau's Poésies Populaires de la Khabylie du Jurgura of 1867, Émile Masqueray's Observations grammaticales sur la grammaire Touareg et textes de la Tourahog des Tailog, and René Basset's L'insurrection Algerienne, de 1871 dans les chansons populaires Khabyles Lourain of 1892. This version was taken from the English translation introduced by René Basset and published by the University of France and the Académie D'Alger, published in 1901. This is a tale from the Kabyles.

A child had a thorn in his foot. He went to an old woman and said to her, "Take out this thorn for me."

The old woman took out the thorn and threw it away.

"Give me my thorn," and he began to cry.

"Take an egg."

He went to another old woman, "Hide me this egg."

"Put it in the hen's nest."

In the night he took his egg and ate it. The next day he said to the old woman, "Give me my egg."

"Take the hen," she answered.

He went to another old woman, "Hide my hen for me."

"Put her on the stake to which I tie my he-goat."

At night he took away the hen. The next morning he demanded his hen.

"Look for her where you hid her."

"Give me my hen."

"Take the he-goat."

He went to another old woman, "O, old woman, hide this goat for me."

"Tie him to the sheep's crib."

During the night he took away the buck. The next day he claimed the buck.

"Take the sheep."

He went to another old woman, "O, old woman, keep my sheep for me."

"Tie him to the foot of the calf."

During the night he took away the sheep. Next morning he demanded his sheep.

"Take the calf."

He went to another old woman, "Keep my calf for me."

"Tie him to the cow's manger."

In the night he took away the calf. The next morning he asked for his calf.

"Take the cow."

He went to another old woman, "Keep my cow for me."

"Tie her to the foot of the old woman's bed."

In the night he took away the cow. The next morning he demanded his cow.

"Take the old woman."

He went to another old woman and left the old dame, whom he killed during the night. The next morning he demanded his old woman.

"There she is by the young girl."

He found her dead.

"Give me my old woman."

"Take the young girl."

He said to her, "From the thorn to the egg, from the egg to the hen, from the hen to the buck, from the buck to the sheep, from the sheep to the calf, from the calf to the cow, from the cow to the old woman, from the old woman to the young girl, and now come and marry me."

The Monkey And The Fisherman

This story has been edited and adapted from Moorish Literature, a collection work from sources such as Adolphe Hanoteau's Poésies Populaires de la Khabylie du Jurgura of 1867, Émile Masqueray's Observations grammaticales sur la grammaire Touareg et textes de la Tourahog des Tailog, and René Basset's L'insurrection Algerienne, de 1871 dans les chansons populaires Khabyles Lourain of 1892. This version was taken from the English translation introduced by René Basset and published by the University of France and the Académie D'Alger, published in 1901. This is a tale from the Kabyles.

A fisherman went one day to the sea to catch some fish. In the evening he sold his catch, and bought a little loaf of bread, on which he made his supper. The next day he returned to his fishing and found a chest. He took it to his house and opened it. Out jumped a monkey, which said to him, "Bad luck to you. I am not the only one to conquer. You may bewail your sad lot."

"My lot is already unbearable," he answered.

The next day he returned to his fishing. The monkey climbed to the roof of the house and sat there. A moment afterward he cut all the roses of the garden. The daughter of the King saw him, and said to him, "O Sidi Mahomet, what are you doing there? Come here, I need you."

He took a rose and approached.

"Where do you live?" asked the princess.

"With the son of the Sultan of India," answered the monkey.

"Tell him to buy me."

"I will tell him, provided he will accept."

The next day he stayed in the house and tore his face. The princess called him again. The monkey brought her a rose.

"Who put you in that condition?" she cried.

"It was the son of the Sultan of India," answered the monkey. "When I told him to buy you he gave me a blow."

The princess gave him 100 ecus, and he went away. The next day he scratched his face worse and climbed on the house. The daughter of the King called him, "Sidi Mahomet!"

"Well?"

"Come here. What did you say to him?"

"I told him to buy you, and he gave me another blow."

"Since this is so, come and find me tomorrow."

The next day the monkey took the fisherman to a shop and bought him some clothes. He took him to the baths and made him bathe. Then he went along the road and cried, "Flee, flee, here is the son of the Sultan of India!"

They went into a coffee-house, and Sidi Mahomet ordered two coffees. They drank their coffees, gave an ecu to the proprietor, and went out. While going toward the palace Sidi Mahomet said to-the fisherman, "Here we are at the house of your father-in-law. When he serves us to eat, eat little. When he offers us coffee, drink only a little of it. You will find silken rugs stretched on the floor, keep on your sandals."

When they arrived the fisherman took off his sandals. The King offered them something to eat, and the fisherman ate a great deal. He offered them some coffee, and the fisherman did not leave a drop of it. They went out. When they were outside the palace Sidi Mahomet said to the fisherman, "Fool of a fisherman, you are lucky that I do not scratch your face."

They returned to their house. Sidi Mahomet climbed upon the roof. The daughter of the King perceived him, and said, "Come here."

The monkey approached.

"Truly you have lied. Why did you tell me that the son of the Sultan of India was a distinguished person?"

"Is he a worthless fellow?"

"We furnished the room with silken rugs, he took off his sandals. We gave him food, and he ate like a servant. We offered him some coffee, and he licked his fingers."

The monkey answered, "We had just come out of the coffeehouse. He had taken too much wine and was drunk, and not master of himself. That is why he ate so much."

"Well," replied the princess, "come to the palace again tomorrow, but do not take him to the coffee-house first."

The next day they set out. On the way the monkey said to the fisherman, "Fool of a fisherman, if today you take off your sandals or eat too much or drink all your coffee, look out for yourself. Drink a little only, or I will scratch your eyes out."

They arrived at the palace. The fisherman walked on the silken rugs with his sandals. They gave him something to eat, and he ate little. They brought him some coffee, and he hardly tasted it. The King gave him his daughter.

Sidi Mahomet said to the King, "The son of the Sultan of India has quarrelled with his father, so he only brought one chest of silver."

In the evening the monkey and the fisherman went out for a walk. The fisherman said to Sidi Mahomet, "Is it here that we are going to find the son of the Sultan of India?"

"I can show him to you easily," answered the monkey. "Tomorrow I will find you seated. I will approach, weeping, with a paper in my hands. I will give you the paper, and you must read it and burst into tears. Your father-in-law will ask you why you weep so. Answer him, 'My father is dead. Here is the letter I have just received. If you have finally determined to give me your daughter, I will take her away and we will go to pay the last duties to my father.'"

They did this and the King said, "Take her." He gave him an escort of horsemen and soldiers. Arriving at the place, Sidi Mahomet said to the soldiers, "You may return to the palace, for our country is far from here."

The escort went back to the palace, and the travellers continued on their journey. Soon Sidi Mahomet said to the fisherman, "Stay here till I go and look at the country of your father."

He started, and arrived at the gates of an abandoned city. He mounted upon the ramparts. An ogress perceived him, "I salute you, Sidi Mahomet."

"May God curse you, sorceress! Come, I am going to your house."

"What do you want of me, Sidi Mahomet?"

"They are seeking to kill you."

"Where can I hide?" He put her in the powder-house of the city, shut the door on her, and set the powder on fire. The ogress died. He came back to the fisherman.

"Forward," he said.

They entered the city and established themselves there. One day Sidi Mahomet fell ill and died The two spouses put him in a coffin lined with silk and buried him.

My story is told.

The Two Friends

This story has been edited and adapted from Moorish Literature, a collection work from sources such as Adolphe Hanoteau's Poésies Populaires de la Khabylie du Jurgura of 1867, Émile Masqueray's Observations grammaticales sur la grammaire Touareg et textes de la Tourahog des Tailog, and René Basset's L'insurrection Algerienne, de 1871 dans les chansons populaires Khabyles Lourain of 1892. This version was taken from the English translation introduced by René Basset and published by the University of France and the Académie D'Alger, published in 1901. This is a tale from the Kabyles.

Sidi El-Marouf and Sidi Abd-el-Tadu were travelling in company. Toward evening they separated to find a resting-place. Sidi Abd-el-Tadu said to his friend, "Let us say a prayer, that God may preserve us from the evil which we have never committed."

Sidi El-Marouf answered, "Yes, may God preserve us from the evil that we have not done!"

They went toward the houses, each his own way. Sidi El-Marouf presented himself at a door. "Can you entertain a traveller?"

"You are welcome," said a woman to him. "Enter, you may remain for the night."

Night came. He took his supper. The woman spread a mat on the floor and he went to sleep. The woman and her husband slept also. When all was quiet, the woman got up, took a knife, and killed her husband. The next day at dawn she began to cry, "He has killed my husband!"

The whole village ran up to the house and seized the stranger. They bound him, and everyone brought wood to burn the guilty man.

Sidi Abd-el-Tadu came also, and saw his friend in tears. "What have you done?" he asked.

"I have done no evil," answered Sidi El-Marouf.

"Did I not tell you yesterday," said Sidi Abd-el-Tadu, "that we would say the prayer that God should preserve us from the evil we had never committed? And now you will be burned for a crime of which you are innocent!"

Sidi El-Marouf answered him, "Bring the woman here."

"Did he really kill your husband?" asked Sidi Abd-el-Tadu.

"He killed him," she replied.

There was a bird on a tree nearby. Sidi Abd-el-Tadu asked the bird. The bird answered, "It was the woman who killed her husband. Feel in her hair and you will find the knife she used."

They searched her hair and found the knife still covered with blood, which gave evidence of the crime. The truth was known and innocence was defended. God avenged the injustice.

The Robber And The Two Pilgrims

This story has been edited and adapted from Moorish Literature, a collection work from sources such as Adolphe Hanoteau's Poésies Populaires de la Khabylie du Jurgura of 1867, Émile Masqueray's Observations grammaticales sur la grammaire Touareg et textes de la Tourahog des Tailog, and René Basset's L'insurrection Algerienne, de 1871 dans les chansons populaires Khabyles Lourain of 1892. This version was taken from the English translation introduced by René Basset and published by the University of France and the Académie D'Alger, published in 1901. This is a tale from the Kabyles.

Two robbers spent their time in robbing. One of them got married, and the other continued his trade. They went a long time without seeing each other. Finally the one who was not married went to visit his friend, and said to him, "If your wife has a daughter, you must give her to me."

"I will give her to you seven days after her birth."

The daughter was born, and the robber took her to bring up in the country. He built a house, bought flocks, and tended them himself. One day some pilgrims came to the house. He killed a cow for them and entertained them. The next day he accompanied them on their pilgrimage. The pilgrims said to him, "If you come with us, two birds will remain with your wife."

The woman stayed in the country. One day the son of the Sultan came that way to hunt. One of the birds saw him and said to the woman, "Don't open the door."

The prince heard the bird speak, and returned to the palace without saying a word. An old woman was called to cast spells over him, and said to the King, "He could not see a woman he has never seen."

The prince spoke and said to her, "If you come with me, I will bring her here."

They soon arrived, and the old dame called the young woman, "Come out, that we may see you."

She said to the bird, "I am going to open the door."

The bird answered, "If you open the door you will meet the same fate as Si El-Ahcen. He was reading with many others in the mosque. One day he found an amulet. His betrothed went no longer to school, and as she was old enough he married her.

"Some days after he said to his father, 'Watch over my wife.'

"'Fear nothing,' answered the father.

"He started, and came back. 'Watch over my wife,' he said to his father again.

"'Fear nothing,' repeated his father.

"The latter went to the market. On his return he said to his daughter-in-law, 'There were very beautiful women in the market,'

"'I surpass them all in beauty,' said the woman, 'take me to the market.'

"A man offered 1,000 francs for her. The father-in-law refused, and said to her, 'Sit down on the mat. The one that covers you with silver may have you,'

"A man advanced. 'If you want to marry her,' said her father-in-law, 'cover her with silver, and she will be your wife.'

"Soon Si El-Ahcen returned from his journey and asked if his wife were still living.

"'Your wife is dead,' said his father. She fell from her mule.

"Si El-Ahcen threw himself on the ground. They tried to lift him up. It was useless trouble. He remained stretched on the earth.

"One day a merchant came to the village and said to him, 'The Sultan married your wife,' She had said to the merchant, 'The day that you leave I will give you a message,' She wrote a letter to her husband, and promised the bearer a flock of sheep if he would deliver it.

"Si El-Ahcen received the letter, read it, was cured, ran to the house, and said to his father, 'My wife has married again in my absence. She is not dead. I brought home much money. I will take it again.'

"He took his money and went to the city where his wife lived. He stopped at the gates. To the first passer-by he gave five francs, to the second five more.

"'What do you want, O stranger?' they asked. 'If you want to see the Sultan we will take you to him,' They presented him to the Sultan.

"'Render justice to this man,'

"'What does he want?'

"'My lord,' answered Sidi El-Ahcen, 'the woman you married is my wife,'

"'Kill him!' cried the Sultan.

"'No,' said the witnesses, 'let him have justice,'

"'Let him tell me if she carries an object.'

Si El-Ahcen answered, 'This woman was betrothed to me before her birth. An amulet is hidden in her hair,'

"He took away his wife, returned to the village, and gave a feast."

"If you open the door," continued the bird, "you will have the same fate as Fatima-ou-Lmelh. Hamed-ou-Lmelh married her. Fatima said to her father-in-law, 'Take me to my uncle's house.'

"Arriving there she married another husband. Hamed-ou-Lmelh was told of this, and ran to find her. At the moment he arrived he found the wedding over and the bride about to depart for the house of her new husband. Then Hamed burst into the room and cast himself out of the window. Fatima did the same, and they were both killed.

"The intended father-in-law and his family returned to their house, and were asked the cause of the misfortune. 'The woman was the cause,' they answered.

"Nevertheless, the father of Hamed-ou-Lmelh went to the parents of Fatima and said, 'Pay us for the loss of our son. Pay us for the loss of Fatima.'

"They could not agree, and went before the justice. Passing by the village where the two spouses had died they met an old man, and said, 'Settle our dispute.'

"'I cannot,' answered the old man.

Farther on they met a sheep, which was butting a rock. 'Settle our dispute,' they said to the sheep.

"'I cannot,' answered the sheep.

Farther on they met a serpent. 'Settle our dispute,' they said to him.

"'I cannot,' answered the serpent.

"They met a river. 'Settle our dispute,' they said to it.

"'I cannot,' answered the river.

"They met a jackal. 'Settle our dispute,' they said to him.

"'Go to the village where your children died,' answered the jackal.

They went back to the village, and applied to the Sultan, who had them all killed."

The bird stopped speaking, and the pilgrims returned. The old woman saw them and fled. The robber prepared a feast for the pilgrims.

The Little Child

This story has been edited and adapted from Moorish Literature, a collection work from sources such as Adolphe Hanoteau's Poésies Populaires de la Khabylie du Jurgura of 1867, Émile Masqueray's Observations grammaticales sur la grammaire Touareg et textes de la Tourahog des Tailog, and René Basset's L'insurrection Algerienne, de 1871 dans les chansons populaires Khabyles Lourain of 1892. This version was taken from the English translation introduced by René Basset and published by the University of France and the Académie D'Alger, published in 1901. This is a tale from the Kabyles.

"Come, little child, eat your dinner."

"I won't eat it."

"Come, stick, beat the child."

"I won't beat him."

"Come, fire, burn the stick."

"I won't burn it."

"Come, water, quench the fire."

"I won't quench it."

"Come, ox, drink the water."

"I won't drink it."

"Come, knife, kill the ox."

"I won't kill him."

"Come, blacksmith, break the knife."

"I won't break it."

"Come, strap, bind the blacksmith."

"I won't bind him."

"Come, rat, gnaw the strap."

"I won't gnaw it."

"Come, cat, eat the rat."

"Bring it here."

"Why eat me?" said the rat, "bring the strap and I'll gnaw it."

"Why gnaw me?" said the strap, "bring the blacksmith and I'll bind him."

"Why bind me?" said the blacksmith, "bring the knife and I'll break it."

"Why break me?" said the knife, "bring the ox and I'll kill him."

"Why kill me?" said the ox, "bring the water and I'll drink it."

"Why drink me?" said the water, "bring the fire and I'll quench it."

"Why quench me?" said the fire, "bring the stick and I'll burn it."

"Why burn me?" said the stick, "bring the child and I'll strike him."

"Why strike me?" said the child, "bring me my dinner and I'll eat it."

Thadhellala

This story has been edited and adapted from Moorish Literature, a collection work from sources such as Adolphe Hanoteau's Poésies Populaires de la Khabylie du Jurgura of 1867, Émile Masqueray's Observations grammaticales sur la grammaire Touareg et textes de la Tourahog des Tailog, and René Basset's L'insurrection Algerienne, de 1871 dans les chansons populaires Khabyles Lourain of 1892. This version was taken from the English translation introduced by René Basset and published by the University of France and the Académie D'Alger, published in 1901. This is a tale from the Kabyles.

A woman had seven daughters and no son. She went to the city, and there saw a rich shop. A little farther on she perceived at the door of a house a young girl of great beauty. She called her parents, and said, "I have my son to marry. Let me have your daughter for him."

They let her take the girl away. She came back to the shop and said to the man in charge of it, "I will gladly give you my daughter, but go first and consult your father."

The young man left a servant in his place and departed. Thadhellala, for that was her name, sent the servant to buy some bread in another part of the city. Along came a caravan of mules. Thadhellala packed all the contents of the shop on their backs and said to the muleteer, "I will go on ahead. My son will come in a moment. Wait for him - he will pay you."

She went off with the mules and the treasures which she had packed upon them. The servant came back soon.

"Where is your mother?" cried the muleteer, "hurry and, pay me."

"You tell me where she is and I will make her give me back what she has stolen." And they went before the justice.

Thadhellala pursued her way, and met seven young students. She said to one of them, "A hundred francs and I will marry you." The student gave them to her. She made the same offer to the others, and each one took her word.

Arriving at a fork in the road, the first one said, "I will take you," the second one said, "I will take you," and so on to the last.

Thadhellala answered, "You shall have a race as far as that ridge over there, and the one that gets there first shall marry me."

The young men started. Just then a horseman came passing by. "Lend me your horse," she said to him. The horseman jumped off. Thadhellala mounted the horse and said, "You see that ridge? I will re-join you there."

The scholars perceived the man. "Have you not seen a woman?" they asked him. "She has stolen 700 francs from us."

"Haven't you others seen her? She has stolen my horse?"

They went to complain to the Sultan, who gave the command to arrest Thadhellala. A man promised to seize her. He secured a comrade, and they both pursued Thadhellala, who had taken flight. Nearly overtaken by the man, she met a man who pulled teeth, and said to him, "You see my son coming down there? Pull out his teeth."

When the other passed, the man pulled out his teeth. The poor toothless one seized the man and led him before the Sultan to have him punished. The man said to the Sultan, "It was his mother that told me to pull them out for him."

"Sidi," said the accuser, "I was pursuing Thadhellala."

The Sultan then sent soldiers in pursuit of the woman, who seized her and hung her up at the gates of the city. Seeing herself arrested, she sent a messenger to her relatives.

Then there came by a man who led a mule. Seeing her he said, "How has this woman deserved to be hanged in this way?"

"Take pity on me," said Thadhellala, "give me your mule and I will show you a treasure." She sent him to a certain place where the pretended treasure was supposed to be hidden. By this time the brother-in-law of Thadhellala had arrived.

"Take away this mule," she said to him.

The searcher for treasures dug in the earth at many places and found nothing. He came back to Thadhellala and demanded his mule.

She began to weep and cry. The sentinel ran up, and Thadhellala brought complaint against this man. She was released, and he was hanged in her place.

She fled to a far city, of which the Sultan had just then died. Now, according to the custom of that country, they took as king the person who happened to be at the gates of the city when the King died. Fate took Thadhellala there at the right time. They conducted her to the palace, and she was proclaimed Queen.

The Good Man And The Bad One

This story has been edited and adapted from Moorish Literature, a collection work from sources such as Adolphe Hanoteau's Poésies Populaires de la Khabylie du Jurgura of 1867, Émile Masqueray's Observations grammaticales sur la grammaire Touareg et textes de la Tourahog des Tailog, and René Basset's L'insurrection Algerienne, de 1871 dans les chansons populaires Khabyles Lourain of 1892. This version was taken from the English translation introduced by René Basset and published by the University of France and the Académie D'Alger, published in 1901. This is a tale from the Kabyles.

Two men, one good and the other bad, started out together to do business, and took provisions with them. Soon the bad one said to the good one, "I am hungry. Give me some of your food." He gave him some, and they both ate.

They went on again till they were hungry. "Give me some of your food," said the bad one. He gave him some of it, and they ate.

They went on until they were hungry. "Give me some of your food," said the bad one. He gave him some, and they ate.

They went on until they were hungry. The good man said to his companion, "Give me some of your food."

"O, no, my dear," said the bad one.

"I beg you to give me some of your food," said the good one.

"Let me pluck out one of your eyes," answered the bad one. He consented. The bad one took his pincers and took out one of his eyes.

They went on until they came to a certain place. Hunger pressed them. "Give me some of your food," said the good man.

"Let me pluck out your other eye," answered his companion.

"O my dear," replied the good man, "leave it to me, I beg of you."

"No!" responded the bad one, "no eye, no food."

But finally the good man said, "Pluck it out."

They proceeded until they came to a certain place. When hunger pressed them anew the bad one abandoned his companion.

A bird came passing by, and said to him, "Take a leaf of this tree and apply it to your eyes."

He took a leaf of the tree, applied it to his eyes, and was healed. He arose, continued on his way, and arrived at a city where he found the one who had plucked out his eyes.

"Who cured you?"

"A bird passed near me," said the good man. "He said to me, 'Take a leaf of this tree.' I took it, applied it to my eyes, and was cured."

The good man found the King of the city blind.

"Give me back my sight and I will give you my daughter."

Using the same leaves he restored his sight to him, and the King gave him his daughter. The good man took his wife to his house. Every morning he went to present his respects to the King, and kissed his head. One day he fell ill. He met the bad one, who said to him, "Eat an onion and you will be cured, but when you kiss the King's head, turn your head aside or the King will notice your breath and will kill you."

After these words he ran to the King and said, "O King, your son-in-law disdains you."

"O my dear," answered the King, "my son-in-law does not disdain me."

"Watch him," answered the bad one, "when he comes to kiss your head he will turn away from you."

The King remarked that his son-in-law did turn away on kissing his head.

"Wait a moment," he said to him. Immediately he wrote a letter to the Sultan, and gave it to his son-in-law, commanding him to carry it to the Sultan. Going out of the house he met the bad one again, who, sensing treasure, wanted to carry the letter himself. The good man gave it to him. The Sultan read the letter, and had the bad one's head cut off. The good man returned to the King.

"What did he say?" asked the King.

"Ah, Sidi, I met a man who wanted to carry the letter. I entrusted it to him and he took it to the Sultan, who condemned him to death in the city."

The Crow And The Child

This story has been edited and adapted from Moorish Literature, a collection work from sources such as Adolphe Hanoteau's Poésies Populaires de la Khabylie du Jurgura of 1867, Émile Masqueray's Observations grammaticales sur la grammaire Touareg et textes de la Tourahog des Tailog, and René Basset's L'insurrection Algerienne, de 1871 dans les chansons populaires Khabyles Lourain of 1892. This version was taken from the English translation introduced by René Basset and published by the University of France and the Académie D'Alger, published in 1901. This is a tale from the Kabyles.

A man had two wives. He was a rich merchant. One of them had a son whose forehead was curved with a forelock. Her husband said to her, "Don't work anymore, but only take care of the child. The other wife will do all the work."

One day he went to market. The childless wife said to the other, "Go, get some water."

"No," she answered, "our husband does not want me to work."

"Go, get some water, I tell you."

And the woman went to the fountain. On the way she met a crow half dead with fatigue. A merchant who was passing took it up and carried it away. He arrived before the house of the woman who had gone to the fountain, and there found the second woman.

"Give something to this crow," demanded the merchant.

"Give it to me," she answered, "and I will make you rich."

"What will you give me?" asked the merchant.

"A child," replied the woman.

The merchant refused, and said to her, "Where did you steal it?"

"From whom did I steal it?" she cried. "It is my own son."

"Bring him."

She brought the child to him, and the merchant left her the crow and took the boy to his home and soon became very, rich. The mother came back from the fountain.

The other woman said, "Where is your son? Listen, he is crying, that son of yours."

"He is not crying," she answered.

"You don't know how to amuse him. I'll go and take him."

"Leave him alone," said the mother. "He is asleep."

They ground some wheat, and the slumbering form of the child did not appear to wake up.

At this the husband returned from the market and said to the mother, "Why don't you busy yourself looking after your son?"

Then she arose to take him, and found a crow in the cradle. The other woman cried, "This is the mother of a crow! Take it into the other house, sprinkle it with hot water."

She went to the other house and poured hot water on the crow.

Meanwhile, the child called the merchant his father and the merchant's wife his mother. One day the merchant set off on a journey. The child's mother brought some food to him in the room where he was confined.

"My son," she said, "will you promise not to betray me?"

"You are my mother," answered the child, "I will not betray you."

"Only promise me."

"I promise not to betray you."

"Well, know that I am not your mother and my husband is not your father."

The merchant came home from his journey and took the child some food, but he would not eat it.

"Why won't you eat?" asked the merchant. "Could your mother have been here?"

"No," answered the child, "she has not been here."

The merchant went to his wife and said to her, "Could you have gone up to the child's chamber?"

The woman answered, "I did not go up to the room."

The merchant carried food to the child, who said, "For the love of God, I adjure you to tell me if you are my father and if your wife is my mother."

The merchant answered, "My son, I am not your father and my wife is not your mother."

The child said to her, "Prepare us some food."

When she had prepared the food the child mounted a horse and the merchant a mule. They proceeded a long way, and arrived at the village of which the real father of the child was the chief. They entered his house. They gave food to the child, and said, "Eat."

"I will not eat until the other woman comes up here."

"Eat. She is a bad woman."

"No, let her come up."

They called her. The merchant ran to the child.

"Why do you act thus toward her?"

"O!" cried those present, "She had a child that was changed into a crow."

"No doubt," said the merchant, "but the child had a mark."

"Yes, he had one."

"Well, if we find it, we shall recognize the child. Put out the lamp."

They put it out. The child threw off its hood. They lighted the lamp again.

"Rejoice," cried the child, "I am your son!"

H'ab Sliman

This story has been edited and adapted from Moorish Literature, a collection work from sources such as Adolphe Hanoteau's Poésies Populaires de la Khabylie du Jurgura of 1867, Émile Masqueray's Observations grammaticales sur la grammaire Touareg et textes de la Tourahog des Tailog, and René Basset's L'insurrection Algerienne, de 1871 dans les chansons populaires Khabyles Lourain of 1892. This version was taken from the English translation introduced by René Basset and published by the University of France and the Académie D'Alger, published in 1901. This is a tale from the Kabyles.

A man had a boy and a girl. Their mother died and he took another wife. The little boy stayed at school until evening. The schoolmaster asked the young boys at class, "What do your sisters do?"

One answered, "She makes bread."

A second, "She goes to fetch water."

A third, "She prepares the couscous."

When he questioned H'ab Sliman, the child played deaf, and the master struck him.

One day his sister said to him, "What is the matter, O my brother? you seem to be sad."

"Our schoolmaster punishes us," answered the child.

"And why does he punish you?" inquired the young girl.

The child replied, "After we have studied until evening he asks each of us what our sisters do. They answer him, she kneads bread, she goes to get water. But when he questions me I have nothing to say, and he beats me."

"Is it nothing but for that?"

"That is all."

"Well," added the young girl, "the next time he asks you, answer him, 'This is what my sister does. When she laughs the sun shines. When she weeps it rains. When she combs her hair, legs of mutton fall. When she goes from one place to another, roses drop.'"

The child gave that answer.

"Truly," said the schoolmaster, "that is a rich match."

A few days after he bought her, and they made preparations for her departure for the house of her husband. The stepmother of the young girl made her a little loaf of salt bread. She ate it and asked for some drink from her sister, the daughter of her stepmother.

"Let me pluck out one of your eyes," said the sister.

"Pluck it out," said the promised bride, "for our people are already on the way."

The stepmother gave her water to drink and plucked out one of her eyes.

"A little more," she said.

"Let me take out your other eye," answered the cruel woman.

The young girl drank and let her pluck out the other eye. Scarcely had she drunk the water than the stepmother thrust her out on the road. She dressed her own daughter and put her in the place of the blind one. The new husband and his people arrived.

"Comb yourself," they told her, and there fell dust.

"Walk," and nothing happened.

"Laugh," and her front teeth fell out.

All cried, "Hang H'ab Sliman!"

Meanwhile some crows came flying near the young blind girl, and one said to her, "Some merchants are on the point of passing this way. Ask them for a little wool, and I will restore your sight."

The merchants came up and the blind girl asked them for a little wool, and each one of them threw her a bit. The crow descended near her and restored her sight.

"Into what shall I change you?" he asked.

"Change me into a pigeon," she answered.

The crow stuck a needle into her head and she was changed into a pigeon. She took flight to the house of the schoolmaster and perched upon a tree nearby. The people went to sow wheat.

"O master of the field," she said, "is H'ab Sliman yet hanged?"

She began to weep, and the rain fell until the end of the day's work.

One day the people of the village went to find a venerable old man and said to him, "O, old man, a bird is perched on one of our trees. When we go to work the sky is covered with clouds and it rains. When the day's work is done the sun shines."

"Go," said the old man, "put glue on the branch where it perches."

They put glue on the branch and caught the bird. The daughter of the stepmother said to her mother, "Let us kill it."

"No," said a slave, "we will amuse ourselves with it."

"No, kill it."

And they killed it. Its blood spurted upon a rose-tree. The rose-tree became so large that it overspread all the village. The people worked to cut it down until evening, and yet it remained the size of a thread.

"Tomorrow," they said, "we will finish it."

The next morning they found it as big as it was the day before. They returned to the old man and said to him, "O, old man, we caught the bird and killed it. Its blood gushed upon a rose-tree, which became so large that it overspreads the whole village. Yesterday we worked all day to cut it down. We left it the size of a thread. This morning we find it as big as ever."

"O my children," said the old man, "you are not yet punished enough. Take H'ab Sliman, perhaps he will have an idea. Make him sleep at your house."

H'ab Sliman said to them, "Give me a sickle."

Someone said to him, "We who are strong have cut all day without being able to accomplish it, so do you think you will be capable of it? Let us see if you will find a new way to do it."

At the moment when he gave the first blow a voice said to him, "Take care of me, O my brother!"

The voice wept, the child began to weep, and it rained. H'ab Sliman recognized his sister.

"Laugh," he said. She laughed and the sun shone, and the people got dried.

"Comb yourself," and legs of mutton fell. All those who were present eagerly took them home.

"Walk," and roses fell.

"But what is the matter with you, my sister?"

"It is what has happened to me."

"What revenge does your heart desire?"

"Attach the daughter of my stepmother to the tail of a horse that she may be dragged in the bushes."

When the young girl was dead, they took her to the house, cooked her, and sent her to her mother.

"O my mother," cried the girl's other sister, "this eye is that of my sister Aftelis."

"Eat, unhappy one," said the mother, "your sister Aftelis has become the slave of slaves."

"But look at it," insisted the young girl. "You have not even looked at it. I will give this piece to the one who will weep a little."

"Well," said the cat, "if you give me that piece I will weep with one eye."

The King And His Son

This story has been edited and adapted from Moorish Literature, a collection work from sources such as Adolphe Hanoteau's Poésies Populaires de la Khabylie du Jurgura of 1867, Émile Masqueray's Observations grammaticales sur la grammaire Touareg et textes de la Tourahog des Tailog, and René Basset's L'insurrection Algerienne, de 1871 dans les chansons populaires Khabyles Lourain of 1892. This version was taken from the English translation introduced by René Basset and published by the University of France and the Académie D'Alger, published in 1901. This is a tale from the Kabyles.

A King had a son whom he brought up well. The child grew and said one day to the King, "I am going out for a walk."

"It is well," answered the King.

At a certain place he found an olive-tree on fire. "O, God," he cried, "help me to put out this fire!"

Suddenly God sent the rain, the fire was extinguished, and the young man was able to pass. He came to the city and said to the governor, "Give me a chance to speak in my turn."

"It is well," said he, "speak."

"I ask the hand of your daughter," replied the young man.

"I give her to you," answered the governor, "for if you had not put out that fire the city would have been devoured by the flames."

He departed with his wife. After a long march the wife made to God this prayer, "O God, place this city here." A city appeared at the very spot.

Toward evening the Marabout of the city of which the father of the young bridegroom was King went to the mosque to say his prayers. "O marvel!" he cried, "what do I see down there?"

The King called his wife and sent her to see what this new city was. The woman departed, and, addressing the wife of the young prince, asked alms of him. He gave her alms. The messenger returned and said to the King, "It is your son who commands in that city."

The King, pricked by jealousy, said to the woman, "Go, tell him to come and find me. I must speak with him."

The woman went away and returned with the King's son. His father said to him, "If you are the son of the King, go and see your mother in the other world."

The young prince returned to his palace in tears.

"What is the matter with you," asked his wife, "you whom destiny has given me?"

He answered her, "My father told me, 'Go and see your mother in the other world.'"

"Return to your father," she replied, "and ask him for the book of the grandmother of your grandmother."

He returned to his father, who gave him the book. He brought it to his wife, who said to him, "Lay it on the grave of your mother."

He placed it there and the grave opened. He descended and found a man who was licking the earth. He saw another who was eating mildew. And he saw a third who was eating meat.

"Why do you eat meat?" he asked him.

"Because I did good on earth," responded the shade.

"Where shall I find my mother?" asked the prince.

The shade said, "She is down there."

He went to his mother, who asked him why he came to seek her.

He replied, "My father sent me."

"Return," said the mother, "and say to your father to lift up the beam which is on the hearth."

The prince went to his father. "My mother bids you take up the beam which is above the hearth."

The King raised it and found a treasure.

"If you are the son of the King," he added, "bring me someone a foot high whose beard measures two feet."

The prince began to weep.

"Why do you weep," asked his wife, "you whom destiny has given me?"

The prince answered her, "My father said to me, 'Bring me someone a foot high whose beard measures two feet."

"Return to your father," she replied, "and ask him for the book of the grandfather of your grandfather."

His father gave him the book and the prince brought it to his wife.

"Take it to him again and let him put it in the assembly place, and call a public meeting."

A man a foot high with a long beard appeared, took up the book, went around the city, and ate up all the inhabitants.

Mahomet-Ben-Soltan

This story has been edited and adapted from Moorish Literature, a collection work from sources such as Adolphe Hanoteau's Poésies Populaires de la Khabylie du Jurgura of 1867, Émile Masqueray's Observations grammaticales sur la grammaire Touareg et textes de la Tourahog des Tailog, and René Basset's L'insurrection Algerienne, de 1871 dans les chansons populaires Khabyles Lourain of 1892. This version was taken from the English translation introduced by René Basset and published by the University of France and the Académie D'Alger, published in 1901. This is a tale from the Kabyles.

A certain sultan had a son who rode his horse through the city where his father reigned, and killed everyone he met. The inhabitants united and promised a flock to any man who should make him leave the city. An old woman took it upon herself to realize the wishes of her fellow-citizens. She procured some bladders and went to the fountain to fill them with the cup of an acorn.

The young man came to water his horse and said to the old woman, "Get out of my way." She would not move. The young man rode his horse over the bladders and burst them.

"If you had married Thithbirth, cavalier," cried the old woman, "you would not have done this damage. But I predict that you will never marry her, for already seventy cavaliers have met death on her account."

The young man, pricked to the quick, reigned his horse, took provisions, and set out for the place where he should find the young girl. On the way he met a man. They journeyed together. Soon they perceived an ogress with a dead man at her side.

"Place him in the earth," said the ogress to them, "it is my son, The Sultan hanged him and cut off his foot with a sword."

They did this thing and took one of the rings of the dead man and went on their way. Soon they entered a village and offered the ring to the governor, who asked them for another like it. They went away from there, returned through the country which they had traversed, and met a pilgrim who had made a tour of the world. He had visited every place except the sea.

The travellers turned toward the sea and found a ship. At the moment of embarking, a whale barred their passage. They retraced their steps, and met the ogress, took a second ring from the dead man, and departed.

At another place they found sixty corpses. A singing bird was guarding them. The travellers stopped and heard the bird say, "He who shall speak here shall be changed into a rock and shall die. Mahomet-ben-Soltan, you shall never wed the young girl. Ninety-nine cavaliers have already met death on her account."

Mahomet stayed till morning without saying one word. Then he departed with his companion for the city where Thithbirth dwelt. When they arrived they were pressed with hunger. Mahomet's companion said to him, "Sing the song that you heard the bird sing."

He began to sing. The young girl, whom they meant to buy, heard him and asked him from whom he had got that song.

"From my head," he answered.

Mahomet's companion said, "We learned it in the fields from a singing bird."

"Bring me that bird," she said, "or I'll have your head cut off."

Mahomet took a lantern and a cage which he placed upon the branch of the tree where the bird was perching.

"Do you think to catch me?" cried the bird, but the next day it entered the cage and the young man took it away.

When they were in the presence of the young girl the bird said to her, "We have come to buy you."

The father of the young girl said to Mahomet, "If you find her you may have her. But if not, I will kill you. Ninety-nine cavaliers have already met death thus. You will be the hundredth."

The bird flew toward the woman. "Where shall I find you?" it asked her.

She answered, "You see that trapdoor under which I am sitting? It is the usual place that my father hides me. I shall be hidden underneath."

The next day Mahomet presented himself before the Sultan, "Arise," he said, "your daughter is hidden there."

The Sultan imposed this new condition, "My daughter resembles ninety-nine others of her age. She is the hundredth. If you recognize her in the group I will give her to you. But if not, I will kill you."

The young girl said to Mahomet, "I will ride a lame horse." Mahomet recognized her, and the Sultan gave her to him, with a serving-maid, a female slave, and another woman.

Mahomet and his companion departed. Arriving at a certain road they separated. Mahomet retained for himself his wife and the slave woman, and gave to his companion the two other women. He gained the desert and left his wife and the slave woman for a moment. In his absence an ogre took away his wife. He ran in search of her and met some shepherds.

"O, shepherds," he said, "can you tell me where the ogre lives?"

They pointed out the place. Arriving, he saw his wife. Soon the ogre appeared, and Mahomet asked where he should find his destiny.

"My destiny is far from here," answered the ogre. "My destiny is in an egg, the egg in a pigeon, the pigeon in a camel, the camel in the sea."

Mahomet arose and ran to dig a hole at the shore of the sea. He stretched a mat over the hole, and a camel sprang from the water and fell into the hole. He fed a pigeon to the camel and then he killed it and took out an egg, crushed the egg in his hands, and the ogre died. Mahomet took his wife and came to his father's city, where he built himself a palace. The father promised a flock to any man who should kill his wayward son. As no one offered, he sent an army of soldiers to besiege him.

He called one of them in particular and said to him, "Kill Mahomet and I will enrich you."

The soldiers managed to get near the young prince, put out his eyes, and left him in the field. An eagle passed and said to Mahomet, "Don't do any good to your parents, but since your father has made you blind take the bark of this tree, apply it to your eyes, and you will be cured."

The young man was healed.

A short time after his father said to him, "I will wed your wife."

"You cannot," he answered.

The Sultan convoked the Marabout, who refused him the dispensation he demanded. Soon Mahomet killed his father and celebrated his wedding-feast for seven days and seven nights.

Part 2 – Legends From Ancient Egypt

The Book Of Knowing The Evolutions Of Ra, And Of Overthrowing Apep

This story has been edited and adapted from Sir Ernest Alfred Thompson Wallis Budge's Legends Of The Gods, published in London in 1916.

These are the words of the god Neb-er-tcher, who said, "I am the creator of what has come into being, and I myself came into being under the form of the god Khepera, and I came into being in primeval time. I came into being in the form of Khepera, and I am the creator of what did come into being, that is to say, I formed myself out of the primeval matter, and I made and formed myself out of the substance which existed in primeval time. My name is Osiris, who is the primeval matter of primeval matter.

I have done my will in everything in this earth. I have spread myself abroad therein, and I have made strong my hand. I was one by myself, for they, the gods, had not yet been brought forth, and I had emitted from myself neither Shu nor Tefnut. I brought my own name into my mouth as a word of power, and I forthwith came into being under the form of things which are and under the form of Khepera. I came into being from out of primeval matter, and from the beginning I appeared under the form of the multitudinous things which exist. Nothing whatsoever existed at that time in this earth, and it was I who made whatsoever was made.

I was one by myself, and there was no other being who worked with me in that place. I made all the things under my forms then by means of the Soul-God which I raised into firmness at that time from out of Nu, from a state of inactivity. I found no place whatsoever there whereon I could stand, I worked by the power of a spell by means of my heart, I laid a foundation for all things before me, and whatsoever was made, I made.

I was one by myself, and I laid the foundation of things by means of my heart, and I made the other things which came into being, and the things of Khepera which were made were manifold, and their offspring came into existence from the things to which they gave birth. I it was who emitted Shu, and I it was who emitted Tefnut, and from being the one god, the only god, I became three gods. The two other gods who came into being on this earth sprang from me, and Shu and Tefnut rejoiced and were raised up from out of Nu in which they were.

Now behold, they brought my Eye to me after two hen periods since the time when they went forth from me. I gathered together my members which had appeared in my own body, and afterwards I had union with my hand, and my heart came to me from out of my hand, and the seed fell into my mouth. Shu and Tefnut covered up my Eye with the plant-like clouds which were behind them for very many hen periods. Plants and creeping things sprang up from the god Rem, through the tears which I let fall. I cried out to my Eye, and men and women came into existence.

Then I bestowed upon my Eye the uraeus of fire, and it was wroth with me when another Eye, namely the Moon, came and grew up in its place. Its vigorous power fell on the plants, on the plants which I had placed there, and it set order among them, and it took up its place in my face, and it does rule the whole earth.

Then Shu and Tefnut brought forth Osiris, and Heru-khenti-an-maa, and Set, and Isis, and Nephthys and behold, they have produced offspring, and have created multitudinous children in this earth, by means of the beings which came into existence from the creatures which they produced. They invoke my name, and they overthrow their enemies, and they make words of power for the overthrowing of Apep, over whose hands and arms Aker keeps ward. His hands and arms shall not exist, his feet and leas shall not exist, and he is chained in one place whilst Ra inflicts upon him the blows which are decreed for him. He is thrown upon his accursed back, his face is slit open by reason of the evil which he has done, and he shall remain upon his accursed back."

The Legend Of The Destruction Of Mankind

This story has been edited and adapted from Sir Ernest Alfred Thompson Wallis Budge's Legends Of The Gods, published in London in 1916.

Chapter I

Here is the story of Ra, the god who was self-begotten and self-created, after he had assumed the sovereignty over men and women, and gods, and things, the one god.

One day men and women started to speak words of complaint, saying, "Behold, his Majesty - life, strength, and health to him - has grown old, and his bones have become like silver, and his members have turned into gold and his hair is like to real lapis-lazuli."

His Majesty heard the words of complaint which men and women were uttering, and his Majesty said to those who were in his train, "Cry out, and bring to me my Eye, and Shu, and Tefnut, and Seb, and Nut, and the father-gods, and the mother-gods who were with me, even when I was in Nu side by side with my god Nu. Let there be brought along with my Eye his ministers, and let them be led to me here secretly, so that men and women may not perceive them

276

coming here, and may not therefore take to flight with their hearts. Come with them to the Great House, and let them declare their plans fully, for I will go from Nu into the place where I brought about my own existence, and let those gods be brought to me there."

The gods were drawn up on each side of Ra, and they bowed down before his Majesty until their heads touched the ground, and the maker of men and women, the king of those who have knowledge, spoke his words in the presence of the Father of the first-born gods.

And the gods spoke in the presence of his Majesty, saying, "Speak to us, for we are listening to your words."

Then Ra spoke to Nu, saying, "O, you first-born god from whom I came into being, O you gods of ancient time, my ancestors, take heed to what men and women are doing, for behold, those who were created by my Eye are uttering words of complaint against me. Tell me what you would do in the matter, and consider this thing for me, and seek out a plan for me, for I will not slay them until I have heard what you shall say to me concerning it."

Then the Majesty of Nu spoke to his son, Ra, saying, "You are the god who are greater than he who made you, you are the sovereign of those who were created with you, your throne is set, and the fear of you is great. Let your Eye go against those who have uttered blasphemies against you."

And the Majesty of Ra, said, "Behold, they are fleeing into the mountain lands, for their hearts are afraid because of the words which they have uttered."

Then the gods spoke in the presence of his Majesty, saying, "Let your Eye go forth and let it destroy those who revile you with words of evil, for there is no eye whatsoever that can go before your Eye and resist you when it journeys in the form of Hathor."

Thereupon this goddess went forth and slew the men and the women who were on the mountain and in the desert land.

And the Majesty of this god said, "Come, come in peace, O Hathor, for the work is accomplished."

Then this goddess said, "You have made me live, and when I gained mastery over men and women it was sweet to my heart."

The Majesty of Ra said, "I myself will be master over them as king, and I will destroy them."

And it came to pass that Sekhet of the offerings waded about in the night season in their blood, beginning at Suten-henen.

Then the Majesty of Ra, spoke, saying, "Cry out, and let there come to me swift and speedy messengers who shall be able to run like the wind..." and straightway messengers of this kind were brought to him. And the Majesty of this god said, "Let these messengers go to Abu and bring to me mandrakes in great numbers."

When these mandrakes were brought to him the Majesty of this god gave them to Sekhet, the goddess who dwells in Annu to crush. When the maidservants were bruising the grain for making beer, these mandrakes were placed in the vessels which were to hold the beer, along with some of the blood of the men and women who had been slain. They made seven thousand vessels of beer.

The Majesty of Ra, the King of the South and North, came with the gods to look at the vessels of beer. Daylight returned after the slaughter of men and women, made by the goddess Hathor as she sailed up the river.

The Majesty of Ra said, "It is good, it is good, nevertheless I must protect men and women against her." And Ra then said, "Let them take up the vases and carry them to the place where the men and women were slaughtered by her." Then the Majesty of the King of the South and North in the three-fold beauty of the night caused to be poured out these vases of beer and the meadows of the Four Heavens were filled with beer by reason of the Souls of the Majesty of this god.

And it came to pass that when this goddess arrived at the dawn of day, she found these Heavens flooded with beer, and she was pleased. She drank the beer and blood, and her heart rejoiced, and she became drunk, and she gave no further attention to men and women.

Then said the Majesty of Ra to this goddess, "Come in peace, come in peace, O Amit," and thereupon beautiful women came into being in the city of Amit. And the Majesty of Ra spoke about Hathor, saying, "Let there be made for her vessels of the beer which produces sleep at every holy time and season of the year, and they shall be in number according to the number of my hand-maidens." From that early time until now men have been wont to make on the occasions of the festival of Hathor vessels of the beer in number according to the number of the handmaidens of Ra.

And the Majesty of Ra spoke to this goddess again, saying, "I am smitten with the pain of the fire of sickness. Where does this pain come from? " And the Majesty of Ra said, "I live, but my heart has become exceedingly weary with the existence of men. I have slain some of them, but there is a remnant of worthless ones, for the destruction which I wrought among them was not as great as my power."

Then the gods who were in his following said to him, "Be not overcome by your inactivity, for your might is in proportion to your will."

And the Majesty of this god said to the Majesty of Nu, "My arms are weak for the first time. I will not permit this to come upon me a second time."

The Majesty of the god Nu said, "O son Shu, you be the Eye for your father. You, goddess Nut, place him."

The goddess Nut said, "How can this be then, O my father Nu?" But the goddess straightway became a cow and she set the Majesty of Ra upon back.

When these things had been done, men and women saw the god Ra, upon the back of the cow. Then these men and women said, "Remain with us, and we will overthrow your enemies who speak words of blasphemy against you, and we will destroy them."

Then his Majesty Ra set out for the Great House, while the gods who were following Ra remained with men. During that time the earth was in darkness. And when the earth became light again and the morning had dawned, men came forth with their bows and their weapons, and they set their arms in motion to shoot the enemies of Ra.

Then said the Majesty of this god, "Your transgressions of violence are now forgotten, for the slaughtering of my enemies is above the slaughter of men." Through this came the slaughter of men as a holy sacrifice.

And the Majesty of this god said to Nut, "I have placed myself upon my back in order to stretch myself out and to be one with you. I am departing from men, and anyone who wants to see me must follow my path."

Then the Majesty of this god looked forth, saying, "Gather together good men for me, and make an abode ready for me and for my for multitudes.

And his Majesty said, "Let a great field, a sekhet, be produced." Thereupon Sekhet-hetep came into being.

And the god said, "I will gather herbs here." Thereupon Sekhet-aaru came into being.

And the god said, "I will make this space contain stars of all sorts." Thereupon the akhekha came into being.

Then the goddess Nut trembled because of the height of the heavens.

And the Majesty of Ra said, "I decree that there will be columns called Heh to bear the goddess up." Thereupon the props of heaven came into being.

And the Majesty of Ra said, "O my son Shu, I pray you to stand guard under my daughter, Nut. Guard the columns of the millions which are there, and which live in darkness. Take the goddess upon your head, and act as nurse for her. " Thereupon came into being the custom of a son nursing a daughter, and the custom of a father carrying a son upon his head.

Chapter II

This Chapter shall be said over the figure of a cow.

The supporters, called Heh-enti, shall be by her shoulder. The Heh-enti shall be at her side, and one cubit and four spans of hers shall be in colours, and nine stars shall be on her belly, and Set shall be by her two thighs and shall keep watch before her two legs, and before her two legs shall be Shu, under her belly, and he shall be painted in green qenat colour. His two arms shall be under the stars, and his name shall be written in the middle of them, namely, Shu himself.

A boat with a rudder and a double shrine shall be therein, and Aten shall be above it, and Ra shall be in it, in front of Shu, near his hand. And the udders of the Cow shall be made to be between her legs, towards the left side. And on the two flanks, towards the middle of the legs, shall be the words, 'The exterior heaven', and 'I am what is in me', and 'I will not permit them to make her to turn'.

That which is written under the boat which is in front shall read, 'You shall not be motionless, my son'. and the words which are written in an opposite direction shall read, 'Your support is like life', and 'The word is as the word there', and 'Your son is with me', and 'Life, strength, and health be to your nostrils!'

And that which is behind Shu, near his shoulder, shall read, 'They keep ward', and that which is behind him, written close to his feet in an opposite direction, shall read, 'Maat', and 'They come in', and 'I protect daily'.

And that which is under the shoulder of the divine figure, which is under the left leg, and is behind it shall read, 'He who seals all things.'

That which is over his head, under the thighs of the Cow, and that which is by her legs shall read, 'Guardian of his exit'.

That which is behind the two figures which are by her two legs, that is to say, over their heads, shall read, 'The Aged One who is adored as he goes forth', and 'The Aged One to whom praise is given when he goes in'.

That which is over the head of the two figures, and is between the two thighs of the Cow, shall read, 'Listener, Hearer, Sceptre of the Upper Heaven, and Star'.

Chapter III

Then the majesty of this god spoke to Thoth, saying "Let a call go forth for me to the Majesty of the god Seb, saying, 'Come, with the utmost speed, at once.'"

And when the Majesty of Seb had come, the Majesty of this god said to him, "Let war be made against your worms and serpents, which are in you. Truly, they shall fear me as long as I have being, but you know their magical powers. Go to the place where my father Nu is, and say to him, 'Keep ward over the worms and serpents, which are in the earth and water.' And moreover, you shall make a writing for each of the nests of your serpents which are there, saying, 'Keep your guard. Do not cause injury to anything.' They shall know that I am withdrawing from them, but indeed I shall shine upon them.

Since, however, they wish for a father, you shall be a father to them in this land forever. Moreover, let good heed be taken to the men who have my words of power, and to those whose mouths have knowledge of such things. Truly my own words of power are there, truly it shall not happen that any shall participate with me in my protection, by reason of the majesty which has come into being before me. I will decree them to your son Osiris, and their children shall be watched over. The hearts of their princes shall be obedient and ready by reason of the magical powers of those who act according to their desire in all the earth through their words of power which are in their bodies."

Chapter IV

And the majesty of this god said, "Call to me the god Thoth," and Thoth was brought to him forthwith. And the Majesty of this god said to Thoth, "Let us depart to a distance from heaven, from my place, because I would make light and the god of light, Khu, in the Tuat and in the Land of Caves. you shall write down the things which are in it, and you shall punish those who are in it, that is to say, the workers who have worked iniquity and rebellion. Through you I will keep away from the servants whom this heart of mine loaths. You shall be in my place, and you shall therefore be called, O Thoth, the 'Asti of Ra.'

Moreover, I give you power and thereupon shall come into being the Ibis bird of Thoth. I moreover give you power to lift up your hand before the two Companies of the gods who are greater than you, and what you do shall be fairer than the work of the god Khen. Therefore shall the divine bird tekni of Thoth come into being.

Moreover, I give you power to embrace the two heavens with your beauties, and with your rays of light. From that shall come into being the Moon-god, Aah of Thoth.

Moreover, I give you power to drive back the Ha-nebu, the North-lords, and from that shall come into being the dog-headed Ape of Thoth, and he shall act as governor for me.

Moreover, you are now in my place in the sight of all those who see you and who present offerings to you, and every being shall ascribe praise to you, O you who are God."

Chapter V

Whosoever shall recite the words of this composition over himself shall anoint himself with olive oil and with thick unguent, and he shall have propitiatory offerings on both his hands of incense, and behind his two ears shall be pure natron, and sweet-smelling salve shall be on his lips. He shall be arrayed in a new double tunic, and his body shall be purified with the water of the Nile-flood, and he shall have upon his feet a pair of sandals made of white leather, and a figure of the goddess Maat shall be drawn upon his tongue with green- coloured ochre.

Whensoever Thoth shall wish to recite this composition on behalf of Ra, he must perform a sevenfold purification for three days, and priests and ordinary men shall do likewise. Whosoever shall recite the above words shall perform the ceremonies which are to be performed when this book is being read. And he shall stand in a circle with a reflection which is beyond, so that his two eyes shall be fixed upon himself, his arms and legs shall be composed, and his steps shall not carry him away from the place. Whosoever among men shall recite these words shall be like Ra on the day of his birth, and his possessions shall not become fewer, and his house shall never fall into decay, but shall endure for a million eternities.

Then the Ra, Aged One embraced the god Nu, and spoke to the gods who came forth in the east of the sky, "Ascribe your praise to the god, the Aged One, from whom I have come into being. I am he who made the heavens, and I set in order the earth, and created the gods, and I was with them for an exceedingly long period. But my soul is older than time. It is the Soul of Shu. It is the Soul of Khnemu. It is the Soul of Heh. It is the Soul of Kek and Kerh, of Night and Darkness. It is the Soul of Nu and of Ra. It is the Soul of

Osiris, the lord of Tettu. It is the Soul of the Sebak Crocodile-gods and of the Crocodiles. It is the Soul of every god who dwells in the divine Snakes. It is the Soul of Apep in Mount Bakhau, the Mount of Sunrise, and it is the Soul of Ra which pervades the whole world."

Whosoever says these words works his own protection by means of the words of power, "I am the god Hekau, the divine Word of power, and I am pure in my mouth, and in my belly. I am Ra from whom the gods proceeded. I am Ra, I am Khu, the Light-god."

When you say this, step forth in the evening and in the morning if you would make the enemies of Ra fall. I am his Soul, and I am Heka.

Hail, you lord of eternity, you creator of everlastingness, who brings to nought the gods who came forth from Ra, you lord of your god, you prince who did make what made you, who are beloved by the fathers of the gods, on whose head are the pure words of power, who did create the woman that stands on the south side of you, who did create the goddess who has her face on her breast, and the serpent which stands on his tail, with her eye on his belly, and with his tail on the earth, to whom Thoth gives praises, and upon whom the heavens rest, and to whom Shu stretches out his two hands, deliver me from those two great gods who sit in the east of the sky, who act as wardens of heaven and as wardens of earth, and who make firm the secret places, and who are called Aaiu-su, and Per-f-er-maa-Nu. Moreover, there shall be a purifying day of the month just as there was according to the performance of the ceremonies in the oldest time.

Whosoever shall recite this Chapter shall have life in Neter-kher , the Underworld, and the fear of him shall be much greater than it was upon earth. And they shall say, "Your names are Eternity and Everlastingness."

They are called Au-peh-nef-n-aa-em-ta-uat-apu and Rekh-kua-[tut]-en-neter- pui-en en-hra-f-Her-shefu. I am he who has strengthened the boat with the company of the gods, and his Shenit, and his Gods, by means of words of power.

The Legend Of Ra And Isis

This story has been edited and adapted from Sir Ernest Alfred Thompson Wallis Budge's Legends Of The Gods, published in London in 1916.

The Chapter of the divine and mighty god, who created himself, who made the heavens and the earth, and the breath of life, and fire, and the gods, and men, and beasts, and cattle, and reptiles, and the fowl of the air, and the fish, who is the king of men and gods, who exists in one Form, to whom periods of one hundred and twenty years wax and wane as single years, whose names by reason of their multitude are unknowable, for even the gods know them not.

The goddess Isis lived in the form of a woman, who had the knowledge of words of power. Her heart turned away in disgust from the millions of men, and she chose for herself the millions of the gods, but esteemed more highly the millions of the spirits. Was it not possible to become like Ra in heaven and upon earth, and to make herself mistress of the earth, and a mighty goddess? Thus she meditated in her heart and by the knowledge of the Name of the holy god.

Ra entered heaven each day at the head of his mariners, establishing himself upon the double throne of the two horizons. The divine one had become old, he dribbled at the mouth, and he let his emissions go forth from him upon the earth, and his spittle fell upon the ground. This Isis kneaded in her hand with some dust, and she fashioned it in the form of a sacred serpent, and made it to have the form of a dart, so that none might be able to escape alive from it, and she left it lying upon the road whereon the great god travelled, according to his desire, about the two lands.

Then the holy god rose up in the tabernacle of the gods in the great double house among those who were in his train, and as he journeyed on his way according to his daily wont, the holy serpent shot its fang into him, and the living fire was departing from the god's own body, and the reptile destroyed the dweller among the cedars. And the mighty god opened his mouth, and the cry of His Majesty reached up to the heavens, and the company of the gods said, "What is it? What is the matter?"

And the god found no words with which to answer them. His jaws shook, his lips trembled, and the poison took possession of all his flesh just as Hapi, the Nile, takes possession of the land through which he flows. Then the great god made firm his heart and he cried out to those who were in his following, "Come to me, O, you who have come into being from my body, you gods who have proceeded from me, for I would make you know what has happened. I have been smitten by some deadly thing, of which my heart has no knowledge, and which I have neither seen with my eyes nor made with my hand. I have no knowledge at all who has done this to me. I have never before felt any pain like it, and no pain can be worse than this.

"I am a Prince, the son of a Prince, and the divine emanation which was produced from a god. I am a Great One, the son of a Great One, and my father has determined for me my name. I have multitudes of names, and I have multitudes of forms, and my being exists in every god. I have been invoked and proclaimed by Temu and Heru-Hekennu. My father and my mother uttered my name, and they hid it in my body at my birth so that none of those who would use against me words of power might succeed in making their enchantments have dominion over me.

"I came forth from my tabernacle to look upon that which I had made, and was making my way through the two lands which I had made, when a blow was aimed at me, but I know not of what kind. Is it fire? Is it water? My heart is full of burning fire, my limbs are shivering, and my arms and legs have darting pains in them. Let there be brought to me my children the gods, who possess words of magic, whose mouths are cunning, and whose powers reach up to heaven."

Then his children came to him, and every god was there with his cry of lamentation, and Isis came with her words of magic, and her mouth was filled with the breath of life, for the words which she puts together destroy diseases, and her words make to live those whose throats are choked. And she said, "What is this, O divine father? What is it? Has a serpent shot his venom into you? Has a thing which you have fashioned lifted up its head against you? Truly it shall be overthrown by beneficent words of power, and I will make it retreat in the sight of your rays."

The holy god opened his mouth, saying, "I was going along the road and passing through the two lands of my country, for my heart wished to look upon what I had made, when I was bitten by a serpent which I did not see. Is it fire? Is it water? I am colder than water, I am hotter than fire, all my limbs sweat, I myself quake, my eye is unsteady. I cannot look at the heavens, and water forces itself on my face as in the time of the Inundation."

And Isis said to Ra, "O, my divine father, tell me your name, for he who is able to pronounce his name lives."

Ra said, "I am the maker of the heavens and the earth, I have knit together the mountains, and I have created everything which exists upon them. I am the maker of the Waters, and I have made Meht-ur to come into being, I have made the Bull of his Mother, and I have made the joys of love to exist. I am the maker of heaven, and I have made to be hidden the two gods of the horizon, and I have placed the souls of the gods within them. I am the Being who opens his eyes and the light comes, I am the Being who shuts his eyes and there is darkness. I am the Being who gives the command, and the waters of the Nile burst forth. I am the Being whose name the gods know not. I am the maker of the hours and the creator of the days. I am the opener of the festivals, and the maker of the floods of water. I am the creator of the fire of life whereby the works of the houses are caused to come into being. I am Khepera in the morning, and Ra at noon, and Temu in the evening."

Nevertheless the poison was not driven from its course, and the great god felt no better. Then Isis said to Ra, "Among the things which you have said to me your name has not been mentioned. O, declare it to me, and the poison shall come forth, for the person who has declared his name shall live."

Meanwhile the poison burned with blazing fire and the heat was stronger than that of a blazing flame. Then the Majesty of Ra, said,

"I will allow myself to be searched through by Isis, and my name shall come forth from my body and go into hers."

Then the divine one hid himself from the gods, and the throne in the Boat of Millions of Years was empty. And it came to pass that when it was the time for the heart to come forth from the god, she said to her son Horus, "The great god shall bind himself by an oath to give his two eyes."

Thus was the great god made to yield up his name, and Isis, the great lady of enchantments, said, "Flow on, poison, and come forth from Ra. Let the Eye of Horus come forth from the god and shine outside his mouth. I have worked, and I make the poison to fall on the ground, for the venom has been mastered. Truly, the name has been taken away from the great god. Let Ra live, and let the poison die, and if the poison live then Ra shall die. And similarly, a certain man, the son of a certain man, shall live and the poison shall die."

These were the words which Isis said, the great lady, the mistress of the gods, and she had knowledge of Ra in his own name. The above words shall be said over an image of Temu and an image of Heru-Hekennu, and over an image of Isis and an image of Horus.

The Legend Of Horus Of Behutet And The Winged Disk

This story has been edited and adapted from Sir Ernest Alfred Thompson Wallis Budge's Legends Of The Gods, published in London in 1916.

In the three hundred and sixty-third year of Ra-Heru-Khuti, who lives forever, His Majesty was in Ta-Kens, and his soldiers were with him. At that time the enemy did not conspire against their lord, and the land is called Uauatet to this day.

And Ra set out on an expedition in his boat, and his followers were with him, and he arrived at Uthes-Heru, to the west of this Nome, and to the east of the canal Pakhennu. And Heru-Behutet was in the boat of Ra, and he said to his father Ra-Heru-Khuti, "I see now that the enemies are conspiring against their lord. Let your fiery serpent gain mastery over them."

Then the Majesty of Ra-Harmachis said to your divine KA, "O Heru-Behutet, O son of Ra, you exalted one, who did proceed from me, overthrow the enemies who are before you straightway."

And Heru-Behutet flew up into the horizon in the form of the great Winged Disk, for which reason he is called 'Great god, lord of heaven' to this day. And when he saw the enemies in the heights of heaven he set out to follow after them in the form of the great Winged Disk, and he attacked with such terrific force those who opposed him, that they could neither see with their eyes nor hear with their ears, and each of them slew his fellow. In a moment of time there was not a single creature left alive.

Then Heru-Behutet, shining with very many colours, came in the form of the great Winged Disk to the Boat of Ra-Harmachis, and Thoth said to Ra, "O, Lord of the gods, Behutet has returned in the form of the great Winged Disk, shining with many colours. For this reason he is called Heru-Behutet to this day."

And Thoth said, "The city Teb shall be called the city of Heru-Behutet", and thus is it called to this day.

And Ra said to Heru-Behutet, "You put grapes into the water which comes forth from the city, and your heart rejoiced, and for this reason the water of Heru-Behutet is called Grape-Water to this day."

And Heru-Behutet said, "Advance, O Ra, and look you upon your enemies who are lying under you on this land."

The Majesty of Ra set out on the way, and the goddess Asthertet was with him, and he saw the enemies overthrown on the ground, each one of them being fettered. Then Ra said to Heru-Behutet, "There is sweet life in this place" and for this reason the abode of the palace of Heru-Behutet is called "Sweet Life" to this day.

And Ra, said to Thoth, "Here was the slaughter of my enemies, and the place is called Teb."

Thoth said to Heru-Behutet, "You are a great protector", and the Boat of Heru-Behutet is called Makaa to this day.

Then said Ra to the gods who were in his following, "Behold now, let us sail in our boat upon the water, for our hearts are glad because our enemies have been overthrown on the earth." The water where the great god sailed is called P-Khen-Ur to this day.

The enemies of Ra rushed into the water, and they took the forms of crocodiles and hippopotami, but nevertheless Ra-Heru-Khuti sailed over the waters in his boat, and when the crocodiles and the hippopotami had come near to him, they opened wide their jaws in order to destroy Ra-Heru-Khuti. And when Heru-Behutet arrived and his followers who were behind him in the forms of workers in metal, each having in his hands an iron spear and a chain, according to his name, they smote the crocodiles and the hippopotami, and there were brought in there straightway six hundred and fifty-one crocodiles, which had been slain before the city of Edfu.

Then Ra-Harmachis said to Heru-Behutet, "My Image shall be here in the land of the South, which is a house of victory and strength", and the House of Heru-Behutet is called Nekht-Het to this day.

Then the god Thoth spoke, after he had looked upon the enemies lying upon the ground, saying, "Let your hearts rejoice, O you gods of heaven! Let your hearts rejoice, O you gods who are in the earth! Horus, the Youthful One, comes in peace, and he has made manifest on his journey deeds of very great might, which he has performed according to the Book of Slaying the Hippopotamus." And from that day figures of Heru-Behutet in metal have existed.

Then Heru-Behutet took upon himself the form of the Winged Disk, and he placed himself upon the front of the Boat of Ea. And he placed by his side the goddess Nekhebet and the goddess

Uatchet, in the form of two serpents, that they might make the enemies to quake in their limbs when they were in the forms of crocodiles and hippopotami in every place where he came in the Land of the South and in the Land of the North.

Then those enemies rose up to make their escape from him, and their face was towards the Land of the South. And their hearts were stricken down through fear of him. And Heru-Behutet was at the back of them in the Boat of Ra, and there were in his hands a metal lance and a metal chain, and the metal workers who were with their lord were equipped for fighting with lances and chains. And Heru-Behutet saw them to the south-east of the city of Uast some distance away.

Then Ra said to Thoth, "Those enemies shall be smitten with blows that kill."

Thoth said to Ra, "That place is called the city Tchet-Met to this day."

And Heru-Behutet made a great overthrow among them, and Ra said, "Stand still, O Heru-Behutet," and that place is called Het-Ra to this day, and the god who dwells therein is Heru-Behutet-Ra-Amsu.

Then those enemies rose up to make their escape from him, and the face of the god was towards the Land of the North, and their hearts were stricken through fear of him. And Heru-Behutet was at the back of them in the Boat of Ra, and those who were following him had spears of metal and chains of metal in their hands, and the god himself was equipped for battle with the weapons of the metal workers which they had with them. And he passed a whole day before he saw them to the north-east of the Nome of Tentyra.

The Majesty of Ra-Harmachis said to Heru-Behutet, "You are my exalted son who did proceed from Nut. The courage of the enemies has failed in a moment."

Heru-Behutet made great slaughter among them.

And Thoth said "The Winged Disk shall be called Heru-Behutet. His name is to the South in the name of this god, and the acacia and the sycamore shall be the trees of the sanctuary."

Then the enemies turned aside to flee from him, and their faces were towards the North, and they went to the swamps of Uatch-ur, and their courage failed through fear of him. And Heru-Behutet was at the back of them in the Boat of Ra, and the metal spear was in his hands, and those who were in his following were equipped with the weapons for battle of the metal workers. And the god spent four days and four nights in the water in pursuit of them, but he did not see one of the enemies, who fled from before him in the water in the forms of crocodiles and hippopotami. At length he found them and saw them.

And Ra said to Horus of Heben, "O, Winged Disk, you great god and lord of heaven, seize them."

He hurled his lance after them, and he slew them, and worked a great overthrow of them. And he brought one hundred and forty-two enemies to the forepart of the Boat of Ra, and with them was a male hippopotamus which had been among those enemies. And he hacked them in pieces with his knife, and he gave their entrails to those who were in his following, and he gave their carcases to the gods and goddesses who were in the Boat of Ra on the river-bank of the city of Heben.

Then Ra said to Thoth, "See what mighty things Heru-Behutet has performed in his deeds against the enemies. Truly, he has smitten them! And of the male hippopotamus he has opened the mouth, and he has speared it, and he has mounted upon its back."

Then said Thoth to Ra, "Horus shall be called 'Winged Disk, Great God, Smiter of the Enemies in the town of Heben' from this day forward, and he shall be called 'He who stands on the back' and 'prophet of this god,' from this day forward."

These are the things which happened in the lands of the city of Heben, in a region which measured three hundred and forty-two measures on the south, and on the north, on the west, and on the east.

Then the enemies rose up before him by the Lake of the North, and their faces were set towards Uatch-ur which they desired to reach by sailing, but the god smote their hearts and they turned and fled in the water, and they directed their course to the water of the Nome of Mertet-Ament, and they gathered themselves together in the water of Mertet in order to join themselves with the enemies who serve Set and who are in this region. And Heru-Behutet followed them, being equipped with all his weapons of war to fight against them. And Heru-Behutet made a journey in the Boat of Ra, together with the great god who was in his boat with those who were his followers, and he pursued them on the Lake of the North twice, and passed one day and one night sailing down the river in pursuit of them before he perceived and overtook them, for he knew not the place where they were.

Then he arrived at the city of Per-Rehu. And the Majesty of Ra said to Heru-Behutet, "What has happened to the enemies? They have gathered together themselves in the water to the west of the Nome of Mertet in order to unite themselves with the enemies who serve Set, and who are in this region, at the place where we have our staff and sceptre."

And Thoth said to Ra, "Uast in the Nome of Mertet is called Uaseb because of this to this day, and the Lake which is in it is called Tempt."

Then Heru-Behutet spoke in the presence of his father Ra, saying, "I beseech you to set your boat against them, so that I may be able to perform against them that which Ra wills."

This was done and he made an attack upon them on the Lake which was at the west of this district, and he perceived them on the bank of the city, which belongs to the Lake of Mertet. Then Heru-Behutet made an expedition against them, and his followers were with him, and they were provided with weapons of all kinds for battle, and he wrought a great overthrow among them, and he brought in three hundred and eighty-one enemies, and he slaughtered them in the forepart of the Boat of Ra, and he gave one of them to each of those who were in his train.

Then Set rose up and came forth, and raged loudly with words of cursing and abuse because of the things which Heru-Behutet had done in respect of the slaughter of the enemies. And Ra said to Thoth, "This fiend Nehaha-hra utters words at the top of his voice because of the things which Heru-Behutet has done to him."

Thoth said to Ra, "Cries of this kind shall be called Nehaha-hra to this day."

Heru-Behutet did battle with the Enemy for a period of time, and he hurled his iron lance at him, and he threw him down on the ground in this region, which is called Pa-Rerehtu to this day. Then Heru-Behutet came and brought the Enemy with him, and his spear was in his neck, and his chain was round his hands and arms, and the weapon of Horus had fallen on his mouth and had closed it, and he went with him before his father Ra, who said, "O, Horus, you Winged Disk, twice great is the deed of valour which you have done, and you have cleansed the district."

And Ra said to Thoth, "The palace of Heru-Behutet shall be called, 'Lord of the district which is cleansed' because of this," and thus is it called to this day. And the name of the priest thereof is called Ur-Tenten to this day.

Then Ra said to Thoth, "Let the enemies and Set be given over to Isis and her son Horus, and let them work all their heart's desire upon them."

And she and her son Horus set themselves in position with their spears in him at the time when there was storm and disaster in the district, and the Lake of the god was called She-En-Aha from that day to this. Then Horus, the son of Isis, cut off the head of the Enemy, Set, and the heads of his fiends in the presence of Father Ra and of the great company of the gods, and he dragged him by his feet through his district with his spear driven through his head and back.

Ra said to Thoth, "Let the son of Osiris drag the being of disaster through his territory."

Thoth said, "It shall be called Ateh," and this has been the name of the region from that day to this.

And Isis, the divine lady, spoke before Ra, saying, "Let the exalted Winged Disk become the amulet of my son Horus, who has cut off the head of the Enemy and the heads of his fiends."

Thus Heru-Behutet and Horus, the son of Isis, slaughtered that evil Enemy, and his fiends, and the inert foes, and came forth with them to the water on the west side of this district. And Heru-Behutet was in the form of a man of mighty strength, and he had the face of a hawk, and his head was crowned with the White Crown and the Red Crown, and with two plumes and two uraei, and he had the back of a hawk, and his spear and his chain were in his hands. And Horus, the son of Isis, transformed himself into a similar shape, even as Heru-Behutet had done before him. And they slew the enemies all together on the west of Per-Rehu, on the edge of the stream, and this god has sailed over the water wherein the enemies had banded themselves together against him from that day to this. Now these things took place on the 7th day of the first month of the season Pert.

And Thoth said, "This region shall be called AAT-SHATET," and this has been the name of the region from that day to this, and the Lake which is close by it has been called Tempt from that day to this, and the 7th day of the first month of the season Pert has been called the Festival of Sailing from that day to this.

Then Set took upon himself the form of a hissing serpent, and he entered into the earth in this district without being seen. And Ra said, "Set has taken upon himself the form of a hissing serpent. Let Horus, the son of Isis, in the form of a hawk-headed staff, set himself over the place where he is, so that the serpent may never more appear."

And Thoth said, "Let this district be called Hemhemet by name", and thus has it been called from that day to this. And Horus, the son of Isis, in the form of a hawk-headed staff, took up his abode there with his mother Isis. In this manner did these things happen.

Then the Boat of Ra arrived at the town of Het-Aha. Its forepart was made of palm wood, and the hind part was made of acacia wood, and so the palm tree and the acacia tree have been sacred trees from that day to this.

And Ra said to Heru-Behutet, "Behold the fighting of the Smait fiend and his two-fold strength, and the Smai fiend Set, are upon the water of the North, and they will sail downstream."

Heru-Behutet said, "Whatsoever you command shall take place, O Ra, Lord of the gods. Grant you, however, that this your Boat may pursue them into every place wheresoever they shall go, and I will do to them whatsoever pleases Ra."

And everything was done according to what he had said. Then this Boat of Ra was brought by the winged Sun-disk upon the waters of the Lake of Meh, and Heru-Behutet took in his hands his weapons, his darts, and his harpoon, and all the chains which he required for the fight.

And Heru-Behutet looked and saw one of these Sebau fiends there on the spot, and he dragged them along straightway, and he slaughtered them in the presence of Ra. And he made an end of them, and there were no more of the fiends of Set in this place.

Thoth said, "This place shall be called Ast-Ab-Heru", because Heru-Behutet wrought his desire upon the enemy, and he passed six days and six nights coming into port on the waters there and did not see one of them. And he saw them fall down in the watery depths, and he made ready the place of Ast-ab-Heru there. It was situated on the bank of the water, and the direction was full-front towards the South. And all the rites and ceremonies of Heru-Behutet were performed on the first day of the first month of the season Akhet, and on the first day of the first month of the season Pert, and on the twenty-first and twenty- fourth days of the second month of the season Pert. These are the festivals in the town of

Ast-ab, by the side of the South, in An- rut-f. And he came into port and went against them, keeping watch as for a king over the Great God in An-rut-f, in this place, in order to drive away the Enemy and his Smaiu fiends at his coming by night from the region of Mertet, to the west of this place.

And Heru-Behutet was in the form of a man who possessed great strength, with the face of a hawk, and he was crowned with the White Crown, and the Red Crown, and the two plumes, and the Urerit Crown, and there were two uraei upon his head. His hand grasped firmly his harpoon to slay the hippopotamus, which was as hard as the Khenem stone in its mountain bed.

And Ra said to Thoth, "Indeed, Heru-Behutet is like a Master-fighter in the slaughter of his enemies."

Thoth said to Ra, "He shall be called Neb-Ahau, or Master-fighter", and for this reason he has been thus called by the priest of this god to this day.

And Isis made incantations of every kind in order to drive away the fiend Ra from An-rut-f, and from the Great God in this place. And Thoth said to Ra, "The priestess of this god shall be called by the name of Nebt-Heka for this reason."

And Thoth said to Ra, "Beautiful, beautiful is this place where you have taken up your seat, keeping watch, as for a king, over the Great God who is in An-rut-f in peace."

And Thoth said, "This Great House in this place shall therefore be called Ast-Nefert from this day. It is situated to the south-west of the city of Nart, and covers a space of four schoinoi."

Ra Heru-Behutet said to Thoth, "Have you not searched through this water for the enemy?"

And Thoth said, "The water of the God-house in this place shall be called by the name of Heh."

And Ra said, "Your ship, O Heru-Behutet, is great upon Ant-mer."

Thoth replied, "The name of Your ship shall be called Ur, and this stream shall be called Ant-mer. The place Ab-Bat is situated on the shore of the water. Ast-Nefert is the name of the Great house, and Neb- Aha is the name of] the priest. Heh is the name of the lake, and Am-her-net is the name of the holy acacia tree. Neter het is the name of the domain of the god, Uru is the name of the sacred boat, and the gods in that boat are Heru-Behutet, the smiter of the lands, Horus, the son of Isis and Osiris, and his blacksmiths are with him, and those who are in his following are with in his territory, with his metal lance, with his mace, with his dagger, and with all his chains, which are in the city of Heru-Behutet."

And when he had reached the land of the North with his followers, he found the enemy. The blacksmiths who were over the middle regions, they made a great slaughter of the enemy, and there were brought back one hundred and six of them. As for the blacksmiths of the West, they brought back one hundred and six of the enemy. The blacksmiths of the East, among whom was Heru-Behutet, he slew the enemy in the presence of Ra in the Middle Domains.

And Ra, said to Thoth, "My heart is satisfied with the works of these blacksmiths of Heru-Behutet who are in his bodyguard. They shall dwell in sanctuaries, and libations and purifications and offerings shall be made to their images, and there shall be appointed for them priests who shall minister by the month, and priests who shall minister by the hour, in all their God-houses whatsoever, as their reward because they have slain the enemies of the god."

And Thoth said, "The Middle Domains shall be called after the names of these blacksmiths from this day onwards, and the god who dwells among them, Heru-Behutet, shall be called the 'Lord of Mesent' from this day onwards, and the domain shall be called 'Mesent of the West' from this day onwards."

As concerning Mesent of the West, the border shall be towards the East, towards the place where Ra rises, and beyond this border the Mesent shall be called "Mesent of the East" from this day onwards. The double town of Mesent shall face towards the South, towards the city of Behutet, the hiding-place of Heru-Behutet. And there shall be performed all the rites and ceremonies of Heru- Behutet on the second day of the first month of the season of Akhet, and on the twenty-fourth day of the fourth month of the season of Akhet, and on the seventh day of the first month of the season Pert, and on the twenty-first day of the second month of the season Pert, from this day onwards. Their stream shall be called Asti, the name of their Great House shall be called Abet, the priest shall be called Qen-aha, and their domain shall be called Kau-Mesent from this day onwards.

And Ra said to Heru-Behutet, "These enemies have sailed up the river, to the country of Setet, to the end of the pillar-house of Hat, and they have sailed up the river to the east, to the country or Tchalt, which is their region of swamps."

Heru-Behutet said, "Everything which you have commanded has come to pass, Ra, Lord of the Gods. You are the lord of commands."

And they untied the Boat of Ra, and they sailed up the river to the east. Then he looked upon those enemies and some of them had fallen into the seas and rivers, and the others had fallen headlong on the mountains.

Heru-Behutet transformed himself into a lion which had the face of a man, and which was crowned with the triple crown. His paw was like to a flint knife, and he went round and round by the side of them, and brought back one hundred and forty-two of the enemy, and he rent them in pieces with his claws. He tore out their tongues, and their blood flowed on the ridges of the land in this place, and he made them the property of those who were in his following while he was upon the mountains.

Ra said to Thoth, "Behold, Heru-Behutet is like a lion in his lair when he is on the back of the enemy who have given him their tongues."

And Thoth said, "This domain shall be called Khent-abt, and it shall also be called Tchalt from this day onwards. And the bringing of the tongues from the remote places of Tchalt shall be commemorated from this day onwards. And this god shall be called 'Heru-Behutet, Lord of Mesent,' from this day onwards."

And Ra said to Heru-Behutet, "Let us sail to the south up the river, and let us smite the enemies who are in the forms of crocodiles and hippopotami in the face of Egypt."

And Heru-Behutet said, "Your divine Ka, O Ra, Lord of the gods! Let us sail up the river against the remaining third of the enemies who are in the water."

Then Thoth recited the Chapters that protect the Boat of Ra and the boats of the blacksmiths, and made tranquil the sea even when a storm was raging on it.

And Ra said to Thoth, "Have we not journeyed throughout the whole land? Shall we not journey over the whole sea in like manner?"

And Thoth said, "This water shall be called the 'Sea of journeying,' from this day onward."

And they sailed about over the water during the night, and they did not see any of those enemies at all.

Then they made a journey and arrived in the country of Ta- sti, at the town of Shas-hertet, and he found the most able of their enemies in the country of Uaua, and they were uttering treason against Horus their Lord.

Heru-Behutet changed his form into that of the Winged Disk, and took his place above the bow of the Boat of Ra. And he made the goddess Nekhebit and the goddess Uatchit come with him in the form of serpents, so that they might make the Sebau fiends quake. The boldness of the fiends subsided through their fear of him, they made no resistance whatsoever, and they died straightway.

Then the gods who were following of the Boat of Heru-khuti said, "Great, great is that which he has done among them by means of the two Serpent Goddesses, for he has overthrown the enemy by means of their fear of him."

And Ra Heru-khuti said, "The great one of the two Serpent Goddesses of Heru-Behutet shall be called 'Ur-Uatchti' from this day onwards."

Heru-khuti travelled on in his boat, and landed at the city of Thes-Heru. And Thoth said, "The being of light who has come forth from the horizon has smitten the enemy in the form which he has made, and he shall be called 'Being of light who has come forth from the horizon' from this day onwards."

Ra Heru-khuti said to Thoth, "You shall make this Winged Disk be in every place where I dwell, and in all the seats of the gods in the South, and in all the seats of the gods in the Land of the North, and in the Country of Horus, that it may drive away the evil ones from these domains."

Then Thoth made the image of the Winged Disk in every sanctuary and in every temple, where they are now, where all the gods and all the goddesses are from this day onwards. The Winged Disk is on the temple-buildings of all the gods and all the goddesses of the Land of the Lily, and the Land of the Papyrus, and these buildings have become shrines of Heru-Behutet.

Heru-Behutet, the great god, the lord of heaven, the president of the Ater of the South, he it is who is made to be on the right hand. This is Heru-Behutet on whom the goddess Nekhebit is placed in the form of a serpent. Heru-Behutet, the great god, the lord of heaven, the lord of Mesent, the president of the Ater of the North, he it is who is made to be on the left hand. This Heru-Behutet on whom the goddess Uatchit is placed is in the form of a serpent.

Ra Heru-khuti set the Winged Disk in every place to overthrow the enemies in every place where they are found. And Heru-Behutet shall be called President of the two Aterti of the South and North because of this from this day onwards.

A Hymn To Osiris And A Legend Of The Origin Of Horus

This story has been edited and adapted from Sir Ernest Alfred Thompson Wallis Budge's Legends Of The Gods, published in London in 1916.

Homage to you, Osiris, Lord of eternity, King of the gods, whose names are manifold, whose transformations are sublime, whose form is hidden in the temples, whose Ka is holy, the Governor of Tetut, the mighty one of possessions in the shrine, the Lord of praises in the name of Anetch, President of the tchefa food in Anu, Lord who are commemorated in Maati, the mysterious Soul, the Lord of Qerret, the sublime one in White Wall, the Soul of Ra and his very body, who have your dwelling in Henensu, the beneficent one, who is praised in Nart, who makes to rise up your Soul, Lord of the Great House in the city of the Eight Gods, who inspires great terror in Shas-hetep, Lord of eternity, Governor of Abydos.

Your domain reaches far into Ta-tchesert, and your name is firmly established in the mouths of men. You are the two-fold substance of the Two Lands, and the divine food of the Kau, the Governor of the Companies of the Gods, and the beneficent and perfect Spirit-soul among Spirit-souls. The god Nu draws his waters from you, and you bring forth the north wind at eventide, and wind from your nostrils to the satisfaction of your heart. Your heart flourishes, and you bring forth the splendour of food.

The height of heaven and the stars are obedient to you, and you makes to be opened the great gates of the sky. You are the lord to whom praises are sung in the southern heaven, you are he to whom thanks are given in the northern heaven. The stars which never diminish are under the place of your face, and your seats are the stars which never rest. Offerings appear before you by the command of Keb. The Companies of the Gods ascribe praise to you, the Star-gods of the Tuat smell the earth before you, the domains make bowings before you, and the ends of the earth make supplication to you when they see you.

Those who are among the holy ones are in terror of him, and the Two Lands, all of them, make acclamations to him when they meet His Majesty. You are a shining Noble at the head of the nobles, permanent in high rank, established in sovereignty, the beneficent Power of the Company of the Gods. Well-pleasing is your face, and you are beloved by him that sees you. You set the fear of you in all lands, and because of their love for you, men hold your name to be pre-eminent. Every man makes offerings to you, and you are the Lord who is commemorated in heaven and upon earth.

Manifold are the cries of acclamation to you in the Uak festival, and the Two Lands shout joyously to you with one accord. You are the eldest, the first of your brethren, the Prince of the Company of the Gods, and the establisher of Truth throughout the Two Lands. You set your son upon the great throne of his father Keb. You are the beloved one of your mother Nut, whose valour is most mighty when you overthrow the Seba Fiend. You have slaughtered your enemy, and have put the fear of you into your Adversary.

You are the bringer in of the remotest boundaries, and are stable of heart, and your two feet are lifted up. You are the heir of Keb and of the sovereignty of the Two Lands, and Keb has seen your splendid qualities, and has commanded you to guide the lands by your hand so long as times and seasons endure.

You have made this earth with your hand, the waters, the winds, the trees and herbs, the cattle of every kind, the birds of every kind, the fish of every kind, the creeping things, and the four-footed beasts. The land of the desert belongs by right to the son of Nut, and the Two Lands have contentment in making him to rise upon the throne of his father like Ra.

You roll up into the horizon, you set the light above the darkness, you illuminate the Two Lands with the light from your two plumes, you flood the Two Lands like the Disk at the beginning of the dawn. Your White Crown pierces the height of heaven saluting the stars. You are the guide of every god. You are perfect in command and word. You are the favoured one of the Great Company of the Gods, and you are the beloved one of the Little Company of the Gods.

Your sister, Isis acted as a protectress to you. She drove your enemies away. She averted seasons of calamity from you. She recited the words with the magical power of her mouth, being skilled of tongue and never halting for a word, being perfect in command and word. Isis the magician avenged her brother. She went about searching for him untiringly.

She flew round and round over this earth uttering wailing cries of grief, and she did not alight on the ground until she had found him.

She made light come forth from her feathers, she made air to come into being by means of her two wings, and she cried out the death cries for her brother. She made to rise up the helpless limbs of him whose heart was at rest, she drew from him his essence, and she made an heir from this essence.

She suckled the child in solitariness and none knew where his place was, and he grew in strength. His hand is mighty and victorious within the house of Keb, and the Company of the Gods rejoice greatly at the coming of Horus, the son of Osiris, whose heart is firmly established, the triumphant one, the son of Isis, the flesh and bone of Osiris. The Tchatcha of Truth, and the Company of the Gods, and Neb-er-tcher himself, and the Lords of Truth, gather together to him, and assemble therein. Truly those who defeat iniquity rejoice in the House of Keb to bestow the divine rank and dignity upon him to whom it belongs, and the sovereignty upon him whose it is by right.

A Legend Of Ptah Nefer-Hetep And The Princess Of Bekhten

This story has been edited and adapted from Sir Ernest Alfred Thompson Wallis Budge's Legends Of The Gods, published in London in 1916.

To Horus, Mighty Bull of risings, established in sovereignty like Tem. To the Golden Horus, Mighty one of strength, destroyer of the Nine Nations of the Bow. King of the South and North. To the Lord of the Two Lands, User-Maat-Ra-setep-en-Ra, Son of Ra, of Ra's body, Ra-meses-meri-Amen, of Amen-Ra. To the Lord of the thrones of the Two Lands, and of the Company of the Gods, the Lords of Thebes, the beloved one. To the beneficent god, the son of Amen, born of Mut, begotten of Heru-khuti, the glorious offspring of Neb-tchert, begetting as the Bull of his Mother, king of Egypt, Governor of the deserts, the Sovereign who has taken possession of the Nine Nations of the Bow, who on coming forth from the womb ordained mighty things, who gave commands whilst he was in the egg. To the Bull, stable of heart, who has sent forth his seed, the king who is a bull, and a god who comes forth on the day of battle like Menthu, the mighty one of strength like the son of Nut.

His Majesty was in the country of Neheru according to his custom every year, and the chiefs of every land, even as far as the swamps, came to pay homage, bearing offerings to the Souls of His Majesty. They brought their gifts, gold, lapis-lazuli, turquoise, bars of wood of every kind of the Land of the God, on their backs, and each one surpassed his neighbour.

And the Prince of Bekhten also caused his gifts to be brought, and he set his eldest daughter at the head of them all, and he addressed words of praise to His Majesty, and prayed to him for his life. And the maiden was beautiful, and His Majesty considered her to be the loveliest woman in the world, and he wrote down as her title, Great Royal Wife, Ra-neferu. When His Majesty arrived in Egypt, he did for her whatsoever was done for the Royal Wife.

On the twenty-second day of the second month of the season of Shemu, in the fifteenth year of his reign, His Majesty was in Thebes, the Mighty City, the Mistress of Cities, performing the praises of Father Amen, the Lord of the thrones of the Two Lands, in his beautiful Festival of the Southern Apt. Thebes was the seat of his heart from primaeval times. A servant came to say to His Majesty, "An ambassador of the Prince of Bekhten has arrived bearing many gifts for the Royal Wife."

And having been brought into the presence of His Majesty with his gifts, he spoke words of adoration to His Majesty, saying, "Praise be to you, O Sun of the Nine Nations of the Bow, permit us to live before you!" And when he had spoken, and had smelt the earth before His Majesty, he continued his speech before His Majesty, saying, "I have come to you, my King and Lord, on behalf of Bent-Resht, the younger sister of the Royal Wife Ra-neferu. Some disease has penetrated into her limbs, and I beseech your Majesty to send a man of learning to see her."

And His Majesty said, "Bring to me the magicians and scribes of the House of Life, and the nobles of the palace." And having been brought into his presence straightway, His Majesty said to them, "I summoned you here in order that you may hear this matter. Now bring to me one of your company whose heart is wise and whose fingers are deft."

And the royal scribe Tehuti-em-heb came into the presence of His Majesty, and His Majesty commanded him to depart to Bekhten with that ambassador. And when the man of learning had arrived in Bekhten, he found Bent- Resht in the condition of a woman who is possessed by a spirit, and he found this spirit to be an evil one, and to be hostile in his disposition towards him.

And the Prince of Bekhten sent a messenger a second time into the presence of His Majesty, saying, "O King, my Lord, I pray His Majesty to command that a god be brought here to contend against the spirit."

The messenger came to His Majesty in the first month of the season of Shemu, in the twenty-sixth year of his reign, on the day which coincided with that of the Festival of Amen, His Majesty was in the palace of Thebes. The messenger spoke a second time in the presence of Khensu in Thebes, called "Nefer-Hetep," saying, "O, my fair Lord, I present myself before you a second time on behalf of the daughter of the Prince of Bekhten."

Then the messenger was taken to Pa-ari-sekher, the great god who drives away the spirits which attack. And the messenger said, "O, my fair Lord, if you will turn your face to Pa-ari-sekher, the great god who drives away the spirits which attack, and allow him to depart for Bekhten?"

The god inclined his head with a deep inclination twice. And His Majesty said, "Let, I pray, your protective and magical power go with him, so that I may make Pa-ari-sekher go to Bekhten to deliver the daughter of the Prince of Bekhten from the spirit."

And Khensu in Thebes inclined his head with a deep inclination twice. And he made his protective power pass into Pa-ari-sekher in a fourfold measure. Then His Majesty commanded that Pa-ari-sekher should set out on his journey in a great boat, accompanied by five smaller boats, and chariots, and a large number of horses, which marched on the right side and on the left.

And when this god arrived in Bekhten at the end of a period of one year and five months, the Prince of Bekhten came forth with his soldiers and his chief[s] before Khensu, [called] "Pa-ari-sekher," and he cast himself down upon his belly, saying, "You have come to us, and you are welcomed by us, by the commands of the King of the South and North, User-Maat-Ra-setep-en-Ra!"

And when this god had passed over to the place where Bent-Resht was, he worked upon the daughter of the Prince of Bekhten with his magical power, and she became better straightway. And this spirit which had been with her said, in the presence of Pa-ari-sekher, "Come in peace, O great god, who does drive away the spirits which attack! Bekhten is your city, the people here, both men and women, are your servants, and I myself am your servant. I will depart and go back the place where I came from, so that I may cause your heart to be content about the matter concerning which you have come. I pray that your Majesty will command that a happy day, a festival, be made with me, and with the Prince of Bekhten."

And the god inclined his head in approval to his priest, saying, "Let the Prince of Bekhten make a great offering in the presence of this spirit."

Now whilst Pa-ari-sekher was arranging these things with the spirit, the Prince of Bekhten and his soldiers were standing there, and they feared with an exceedingly great fear. And the Prince of Bekhten made a great offering in the presence of Pa-ari-sekher and the spirit of the Prince of Bekhten, and he made a festival on their behalf, and then the spirit departed in peace, returning to the place which he loved, by the command of Pa-ari-sekher. And the Prince of Bekhten, and every person who was in the country of Bekhten, rejoiced very greatly, and he took counsel with his heart, saying, "It has happened that this god has been given as a gift to Bekhten, and I will not permit him to depart to Egypt."

When this god had tarried for three years and nine months in Bekhten, the Prince of Bekhten, who was lying down asleep on his bed, saw this god come forth outside his shrine in the form of a golden hawk, and he flew up into the heavens and departed to Egypt. When the Prince woke up he was trembling. And he said to the prophet Pa-ari-sekher, "This god who tarried with us has departed to Egypt. Let his chariot also depart to Egypt."

And the Prince of Bekhten permitted the image of the god to set out for Egypt, and he gave him many great gifts of beautiful things of all kinds, and a large number of soldiers and horses went with him. And when they had arrived in peace in Thebes, Pa-ari- sekher went into the Temple of Khensu in Thebes, and he placed the offerings which the Prince of Bekhten had given to him, beautiful things of all kinds, before Khensu in Thebes, and he gave nothing thereof whatsoever to his temple.

Thus Pa-ari-sekher arrived in his temple in peace, on the nineteenth day of the second month of the season Pert, in the thirty-third year of the reign of the King of the South and North, User-Maat-en-Ra-setep-en-Ra, the giver of life, like Ra, for ever.

A Legend Of The God Khnemu And Of A Seven Years' Famine

This story has been edited and adapted from Sir Ernest Alfred Thompson Wallis Budge's Legends Of The Gods, published in London in 1916.

In the eighteenth year of the Horus, Neter-Khat, of the King of the South and North, Neter-Khat, of the Lord of the Shrines of Uatchit and Nekhebit, Neter-Khat, of the Golden Horus Tcheser, builder of the step pyramid at Sakkarah, when Matar was Ha Prince, and Erpa, and Governor of the temple-cities in the Land of the South, and director of the Khenti folk in Abtu, there was brought to him the following royal despatch, 'This is to inform you that misery has laid hold upon me as I sit upon the great throne by reason of those who dwell in the Great House. My heart is grievously afflicted by reason of the exceedingly great evil which has happened because the Nile has not come forth in my time to the proper height for seven years. Grain is very scarce, vegetables are lacking altogether, every kind of thing which men eat for their food has ceased, and every man now plunders his neighbour. Men wish to walk, but are unable to move. The child wails, the young man drags his limbs along, and the hearts of the aged folk are crushed with despair, and their legs give way under them, and they sink down to the ground, and their hands are laid upon their bodies in pain. The shennu nobles, the high court officials, are destitute of counsel, and when the storehouses which should contain supplies are opened, there comes forth therefrom nothing but wind. Everything is in a state of ruin. My mind has remembered, going back to former time, when I had an advocate, to the time of the gods, and of the Ibis-god, and of the chief Kher-heb priest I-em-hetep, the son of Ptah of his Southern Wall.

'Where is the place of birth of Hapi, the Nile? What god, or what goddess, presides over it? What manner of form has he or she? It is the gods who establish revenue for me, and a full store of grain. I would go to the Chief of Het-Sekhet whose beneficence strengthens all men in their works. I would enter into the House of Life, the Per-ankh, I would unfold the written rolls there, and I would lay my hand upon them.'

Then Matar set out on his journey, and he returned to me straightway. He gave me instruction concerning the Nile flood and told me all things which men had written concerning it, and he revealed to me the secret doors where my ancestors had taken themselves quickly, the like of which has never been, to any king since the time of Ra. And he said to me, "There is a city in the middle of the stream where Hapi makes his appearance. Abu was its name in the beginning. It is the City of the Beginning, and it is the Nome of the City of the Beginning. It reaches to Uaua, which is the beginning of the land. There is a flight of steps, which climbs up to a great height, and is the support of Ra, when he makes his calculation to prolong life to everyone. Netchemtchem Ankh is the name of its abode. 'The two Qerti, the places where the Nile enters this world from the celestial ocean, is the name of the water, and they are the two breasts from which every good thing comes forth.

"Here is the bed of Hapi, where he renews his youth in his season, when he causes the flooding of the land. He comes and has union as he journeys, as a man has union with a woman. And again he plays the part of a husband and satisfies his desire. He rises to the height of twenty-eight cubits at Abu, and he drops at Sma-Behutet to seven cubits. The union there is that of the god Khnemu with his sandals, and Hapi's fulness becomes abundant;. He opens the bolt of the door with his hand, and he throws open the double door through which the water comes.

"Moreover, he dwells there in the form of the god Shu, as one who is lord over his own territory, and his homestead, the name of which is Aa. There he keeps an account of the products of the Land of the South and of the Land of the North, in order to give to every god his proper share, and he leads to each the metals, and the precious stones, and the four-footed beasts, and the feathered fowl, and the fish, and everything whereon they live. And the cord for the measuring of the land and the tablet whereon the register is kept are there.

"And there is an edifice of wood there, with the portals formed of reeds, where he dwells as one who rules his own territory, and he makes the foliage of the trees to serve as a roof.

"His God-house has an opening towards the south-east, and Ra, the Sun, stands immediately opposite every day. The stream which flows along the south side has danger for anyone who attacks him, and it has as a defence a wall which enters into the region of the men of Kens on the South. Huge mountains are round about its domain on the east side, and shut it in.

"There come the quarrymen with tools of every kind, when they want to build a House for any god in the Land of the South, or in the Land of the North, or shrines as abodes for sacred animals, or royal pyramids, and statues of all kinds. They stand up in front of the House of the God and in the sanctuary chamber, and their sweet smelling offerings are presented before the face of the god Khnemu during his circuit, even as they bring garden herbs and flowers of every kind.

"The fore parts are in Abu, and the hind parts are in the city of Sunt. One portion is on the east side of the river, and another portion is on the west side of the river, and another portion is in the middle of the river. The stream decks the region with its waters during a certain season of the year, and it is a place of delight for every man. And works are carried on among these quarries on the edges of the river, for the stream immediately faces this city of Abu, and there exists the granite, which is hard is hard and is called Stone of Abu.

"Here is a list of the names of the gods who dwell in the Divine House of Khnemu. The goddess of the star Sept, Sothis, the goddess Anqet, Hap, the Nile-god, Shu, Keb, Nut, Osiris, Horus, Isis, and Nephthys.

"Here are the names of the stones which lie in the heart of the mountains, some on the east side, some on the west side, and some in the midst of the stream of Abu. They exist in the heart of Abu, they exist in the country on the east bank, and in the country on the west bank, and in the midst of the stream, namely, Bekhen-stone, Meri-stone, Atbekhab-stone, Rakes-stone, and white Utshi-stone. These are found on the east bank. Per-tchani-stone is found on the west bank, and the Teshi-stone in the river.

Here are the names of the hidden precious stones, which are found in the upper side, among them being Gold, Silver, Copper, Iron, Lapis-lazuli, Emerald, Thehen Crystal, Khenem Rubies, Kai, Mennu, Betka, Temi, and Na. The following come forth from the fore part of the land to the south of Nubia. They are Mehi-stone, Hemaki-stone, Abheti-stone, iron ore, alabaster for statues, mother-of-emerald, antimony, seeds and gum of the sehi plant, seeds of the amem plant, and seeds of the incense plant"

These were the things which I learned from Matar. Now my heart was very happy when I heard these things, and I entered into the temple of Khnemu. The overseers unrolled the documents which were fastened up, the water of purification was sprinkled upon me, a progress was made through the secret places, and a great offering consisting of bread-cakes, beer, geese, oxen, and beautiful things of all kinds were offered to the gods and goddesses who dwell in Abu, whose names are proclaimed at the place which is called 'Couch of the heart in life and power.'

And I found the God standing in front of me, and I made him to be at peace with me by means of the thank-offering which I offered to him, and I made prayer and supplication before him. Then he opened his eyes, and his heart was inclined to hear me, and his words were strong when he said, "I am Khnemu, the builder of men, maker of the gods, the Father who was from the beginning, the maker of things which are, the creator of things which shall be, the source of things which exist, Father of fathers, Mother of mothers, Father of the fathers of the gods and goddesses, lord of created things, maker of heaven, earth, Tuat, water and mountains, who fashioned you.

"My two hands were about you and knitted together your body, and healed your body. It is I who gave you your heart. Yet the precious stones lie under each other, and they have done so from olden time, and no man has worked them in order to build the houses of the god, or to restore those which have fallen into ruin, or to hew out shrines for the gods of the South and of the North, or to do what he ought to do for his lord, notwithstanding that I am the Lord and the Creator.

"I am he who created himself, Nu, the Great God, who came into being at the beginning, and Hapi, who rises according to his will, in order to give health to him that labours for me. I am the Director and Guide of all men at their seasons, the Most Great, the Father of the Gods, Shu, the Great One, the Chief of the Earth. The two halves of the sky are as a habitation below me. A lake of water has been poured out for me, and it is Hapi, which embraces the field-land, and his embrace provides the means of life for everyone, according to the extent of his embrace of the field-land.

"With old age comes weakness. I will make Hapi rise for you, and in no year shall he fail, and he shall spread himself out in rest upon every land. Green plants and herbs and trees shall bow beneath the weight of their produce. The goddess Renenet, the goddess of the harvest, shall be at the head of everything, and every product shall increase by hundreds of thousands, according to the cubit of the year. The people shall be filled, truly, to their hearts' desire. Misery shall pass away, and the emptiness of their store-houses of grain shall come to an end. The land of Ta-Mert, our Egypt, shall come to be a region of cultivated land, the districts shall be yellow with grain crops, and the grain shall be goodly. And fertility shall come according to the desire of the people, more than there has ever been before."

Then I woke up at the mention of crops. My heart and courage came back, and was equal to my former despair, and I made the following decree in the temple of my father Khnemu:

"The king gives an offering to Khnemu, the Lord of the city of Qebhet, the Governor of Ta-Sti, in return for those things which you have done for me. There shall be given to you on your right hand the riverbank of Manu, and on your left hand the riverbank of Abu, together with the land about the city, for a space of twenty measures, on the east side and on the west side, with the gardens, and the river front everywhere throughout the region included in these measures. From every husbandman who tills the ground, and makes the slain live again, and places water upon the riverbanks and all the islands which are in front of the region of these measures, shall be demanded a further contribution from the growing crops and from every storehouse, as Your share.

"Whatsoever is caught in the nets by every fisherman and by every fowler, and whatsoever is taken by the catchers of fish, and by the snarers of birds, and by every hunter of wild animals, and by every man who snares lions in the mountains, when these things enter the city one tenth of them shall be demanded.

"And of all the calves which are cast throughout the regions which are included in these measures, one tenth of their number shall be set apart as animals which are sealed for all the burnt offerings which are offered up daily.

"And, moreover, the gift of one tenth shall be levied upon the gold, ivory, ebony, spices, carnelians, sa wood, seshes spice, dum palm fruit, nef wood, and upon woods and products of every kind whatsoever, which the Khentiu, and the Khentiu of Hen- Resu, and the Egyptians, and every person whatsoever shall bring in.

"And every hand shall pass them by, and no officer of the revenue whatsoever shall utter a word beyond these places to demand or levy things from them, or to take things over and above those which are intended for Your capital city.

"And I will give to you the land belonging to the city, which bears stones, and good land for cultivation. Nothing shall be withheld of all these things in order to deceive the scribes, and the revenue officers, and the inspectors of the king, on whom it shall be incumbent to certify everything.

"And further, I will cause the masons, and the miners, and the workers in metal, and the smelters of gold, and the sculptors in stone, and the ore-crushers, and the furnace-men, and handicraftsmen of every kind whatsoever, who work in hewing, and cutting, and polishing these stones, and in gold, and silver, and copper, and lead, and every worker in wood who shall cut down any tree, or carry on a trade of any kind, or work which is connected with the wood trade, to pay tithe upon all the natural products, and also upon the hard stones which are brought from their beds above, and quarried stones of all kinds.

"And there shall be an inspector over the weighing of the gold, and silver, and copper, and precious stones, and the things, which the metal-workers require for the House of Gold, and the sculptors of the images of the gods need in the making and repairing of them, and these things shall be exempted from tithing, and the workmen also. And everything shall be delivered in front of the storehouse to their children, a second time, for the protection of everything. And whatsoever is before your God-house shall be in abundance, just as it has ever been from the earliest time.

"And a copy of this decree shall be inscribed upon a stele in the holy place, according to the writing of the document which is cut upon wood, and his god and the overseers of the temple shall be carved thereon. Whosoever shall spit upon that which is on it shall be admonished by the rope. And the overseers of the priests, and every overseer of the people of the House of the God, shall ensure the perpetuation of my name in the House of the god Khnemu-Ra, the lord of Abu, forever."

The Legend Of The Death Of Horus

This story has been edited and adapted from Sir Ernest Alfred Thompson Wallis Budge's Legends Of The Gods, published in London in 1916.

Get you back, Apep, you enemy of Ra, you winding serpent in the form of an intestine, without arms, without legs. Your body cannot stand upright, and long is your tail in front of your den, you enemy - retreat before Ra.

Your head shall be cut off, and the slaughter of you shall be carried out. you shall not lift up your face, for Ra's flame is in your accursed soul. The odour which is in his chamber of slaughter is in your members, and your form shall be overthrown by the slaughtering knife of the great god. The spell of the Scorpion-goddess Serq drives back your might. Stand still, stand still, and retreat through her spell.

Be vomited, O poison, I adjure you to come forth on the earth. Horus utters a spell over you. Horus hacks you in pieces, he spits upon you, and you shall not rise up towards heaven, but shall totter downwards, O feeble one, without strength, cowardly, unable to fight, blind, without eyes, and with your head turned upside down.

Do not lift up your face. Get back quickly, and find not the way. Lie down in despair, rejoice not, retreat speedily, and show not your face because of the speech of Horus, who is perfect in words of power. The poison rejoiced, but the hearts of many were very sad. Horus has smitten it with his magical spells, and he who was in sorrow is now in joy.

Stand still then, O you who are in sorrow, for Horus has been endowed with life. He comes charged, appearing himself to overthrow the Sebiu fiends which bite. All men when they see Ra praise the son of Osiris. Get you back, Worm, and draw out your poison which is in all the members of him that is under the knife. Truly the might of the word of power of Horus is against you. Vomit you, O Enemy, get you back, O poison.

The Narrative Of Isis

This story has been edited and adapted from Sir Ernest Alfred Thompson Wallis Budge's Legends Of The Gods, published in London in 1916.

I am Isis. I have come forth from the dwelling where my brother Set placed me. The god Thoth, the great god, the Chief of Maat, both in heaven and on the earth, said to me, "Come now, O Isis, you goddess, moreover it is a good thing to listen, for there is life for one who shall be guided by the advice of another. Hide yourself with your son, and there shall come to him these things. His limbs shall grow, and two-fold strength of every kind shall spring up in him. He shall be made to take his seat upon the throne of his father, whom he shall avenge, and he shall take possession of the exalted position of Heq of the Two Lands."

I came forth at the time of evening, and there came forth the Seven Scorpions which were to accompany me and to strike for me with their stings. Two scorpions, Tefent and Befent, were behind me, two scorpions, Mestet and Mestetef, were by my side, and three scorpions, Petet, Thetet, and Maatet, were for preparing the road for me. I charged them very strictly, and my words penetrated into their ears, "Have no knowledge of anyone, make no cry to the

Tesheru beings, and pay no attention to the son of any man who belongs to a man of no account." Then I said, "Let your faces be turned towards the ground so that you may show me the way."

So the guardian of the company brought me to the boundaries of the city of Pa-Sui, the city of the goddesses of the Divine Sandals, which was situated in front of the Papyrus Swamps.

When I had arrived at the place where the people lived I came to the houses wherein dwelt the wives and husbands. And a certain woman of quality spied me as I was journeying along the road, and she shut her doors on me. Now she was sick at heart by reason of those scorpions which were with me. Then the Seven Scorpions took counsel concerning her, and they all at one time shot out their venom on the tail of the scorpion Tefen. As for me, the woman Taha opened her door, and I entered into the house of the miserable lady.

Then the scorpion Tefen entered in under the leaves of the door and stung the son of Usert, and a fire broke out in the house of Usert, and there was no water there to extinguish it. The sky rained upon the house of Usert, though it was not the season for rain.

The heart of the woman who had not opened her door to me was grievously sad, for she knew not whether her son would live, and although she went round about through her town uttering cries for help, there were none who came. My own heart was grievously sad for the sake of the child, and I wished to make him live again as, in this situation, he was free from fault. I cried out to the noble lady, "Come to me. Come to me. Truly, my mouth possesses life. I am a daughter known in her town, and I can destroy the demon of death by the spell which my father taught me. I am his daughter, the beloved offspring of his body."

Then Isis placed her two hands on the child in order to make him live, and she said, "O, poison of the scorpion Tefent, come forth and appear on the ground! You shall neither enter nor penetrate further into the body of the child. O, poison of the scorpion Befent, come forth and appear on the ground! I am Isis, the goddess, the lady and mistress of words of power, and I am the maker of words of power, and I know how to utter words with magical effect. Listen to me, O every reptile which possesses the power to bite and sting, and fall headlong to the ground! O, poison of the scorpion Mestet, make no advance. O, poison of the scorpion Mestetef, rise not up. O, poison of the scorpions Petet and Thetet, penetrate not into his body. O, poison of the scorpion Maatet, fall down on the ground."

And Isis, the goddess, the great mistress of words of power, she who is at the head of the gods, to whom the god Keb gave his own magical spells for the driving away of poison, and for making poison retreat and withdraw, spoke, saying, "Ascend not into heaven, through the command of the beloved one of Ra, the egg of the Smen goose which comes forth from the sycamore. Truly, my words are made to command the uttermost limit of the night. I speak to you, O scorpions. I am alone and in sorrow because our names will suffer disgrace throughout the lands. Do not make love, do not cry out to the Tesheru fiends, and cast no glances upon the noble ladies in their houses. Turn your faces towards the earth and the road, so that we may arrive at the hidden places in the town of Khebt. O, the child shall live and the poison die! Ra lives and the poison dies! Truly, Horus shall be in good health for his mother Isis. Truly, he who is stricken shall be in good health likewise."

And the fire was extinguished, and heaven was satisfied with the utterance of Isis, the goddess.

Then the lady Usert came, and she brought to me her possessions, and she filled the house of the woman Tah because she had not opened her door to me. Now the lady Usert suffered pain and anguish the whole night, and her mouth tasted the sting, which her son had suffered. And she brought her possessions as the penalty for not having opened the door to me. O, the child shall live and the poison die! A bread-cake made of barley meal shall drive out the poison, and natron shall make it withdraw, and the fire made of hetchet-plant shall drive out fever-heat from the limbs.

"O Isis, O Isis, come to your Horus, O you woman of the wise mouth! Come to your son." Thus cried the gods who dwelt in her quarter of the town. "For he is as one whom a scorpion has stung, like one whom the scorpion Uhat, which the animal Antesh drove away, has wounded."

Then Isis ran out like one who had a knife stuck in her body, and she opened her arms wide, saying, "Behold me, behold me, my son Horus, have no fear, have no fear, O, son my glory! No evil thing of any kind whatsoever shall happen to you, for there is in you the essence which made the things which exist. You are the son from the country of Mesqet, You have come forth from the celestial waters and you shall not die by the heat of the poison. You were the Great Bennu or the top of the balsam-trees which are in the House of the Aged One in Anu. You are the brother of the Abtu Fish, who orders what is to be, and are the nursling of the Cat who dwells in the House of Neith. The goddess Reret, the goddess Hat, and the god Bes protect your limbs. Your head shall not fall to the Tchat fiend that attacks you. Your limbs shall not receive the fire which is your poison. You shall not go backwards on the land, and you shall not be brought low on the water. No reptile which bites or, stings shall gain mastery over you, and no lion shall subdue you or have dominion over you. You are the son of the sublime god who proceeded from Keb. You are Horus, and the poison shall not gain the mastery over your limbs. You are the son of the sublime god who proceeded from Keb, and thus likewise shall it be with those who are under the knife. And the four august goddesses shall protect your body."

A Hymn Of Praise To Horus

This story has been edited and adapted from Sir Ernest Alfred Thompson Wallis Budge's Legends Of The Gods, published in London in 1916.

A hymn of praise to Horus to glorify him, which is to be said 102 over the waters and over the land.

Thoth speaks and this god recites:

"Homage to you, god, son of a god. Homage to you, heir, son of an heir. Homage to you, bull, son of a bull, who was brought forth by a holy goddess. Homage to you, Horus, who comes forth from Osiris, and was brought forth by the goddess Isis. I recite your words of power. I speak with your magical utterance. I pronounce a spell in your own words, which your heart has created, and all the spells and incantations which have come forth from your mouth, which your father Keb commanded you to recite, and your mother Nut gave to you, and the majesty of the Governor of Sekhem taught you to make use of for your protection, in order to double your protective formulae, to shut the mouth of every reptile which is in heaven, and on the earth, and in the waters, to make men and women live, to make the gods be at peace with you, and to make Ra employ his magical spells through your chants of praise.

"Come to me this day, quickly, quickly, as you work the paddle of the Boat of the god. Drive away from me every lion on the plain, and every crocodile in the waters, and all mouths which bite or sting in their holes. Make them like stone before me, like a broken pot lying about in a quarter of the town. Dig out from me the poison which rises and is in every limb of him that is under the knife. Keep your watch over him by means of your words. Truly, let your name be invoked this day. Let your power come into being in him. Exalt you your magical powers. Make me live and him whose throat is closed up. Then shall mankind give you praise, and the righteous shall give thanks to you. And all the gods likewise shall invoke you, and in truth your name shall be invoked this day. I am Horus of Shetenu.

"You who are in the cavern, you who are at the mouth of the cavern, you who are on the way, you who are at the mouth of the way. He is Urmer who approaches every man and every beast. He is like the god Sep who is in Anu. He is the Scorpion-god who is in the Great House. Bite him not, for he is Ra. Sting him not, for he is Thoth. Shoot not your poison over him, for he is Nefer-Tem. O, every male serpent, every female serpent, every scorpion, which bite with your mouths, and sting with your tails, bite him not with your mouths, and sting him not with your tails. Get away from him, for he is the son of Osiris. [Say this four times.]

"I am Thoth, I have come from heaven to make protection of Horus, and to drive away the poison of the scorpion which is in every limb of Horus. Your head is to you, Horus. It shall be stable under the Urert Crown. Your eye is to you, Horus, for you are

Horus, the son of Keb, the Lord of the Two Eyes, in the midst of the Company of the gods. Your nose is to you, Horus, for you are Horus the Elder, the son of Ra, and you shall not inhale the fiery wind. Your arm is to you, Horus, great is your strength to slaughter the enemies of your father. Your two thighs are to you, Horus. Receive the rank and dignity of your father Osiris. Ptah has balanced for you your mouth on the day of your birth. Your heart is to you, Horus, and the Disk makes your protection. Your eye is to you, Horus. Your right eye is like Shu, and your left eye like Tefnut, who are the children of Ra. Your belly is to you, Horus, and the Children are the gods who are therein, and they shall not receive the essence of the scorpion. Your strength is to you, Horus, and the strength of Set shall not exist against you. Your phallus is to you, Horus, and you are Kamutef, the protector of his father, who makes an answer for his children in the course of every day. Your thighs are to you, Horus, and your strength shall slaughter the enemies of your father. Your calves are to you, Horus, the god Khnemu has built them, and the goddess Isis has covered them with flesh. The soles of your feet are to you, Horus, and the nations who fight with the bow fall under your feet. You rule the South, North, West, and East, and you see like Ra. [Say four times.]

Beautiful god, Senetchem-ab-Ra-setep-[en]-Amen, son of Ra, Nekht-Heru-Hebit, you are protected, and the gods and goddesses are protected, and conversely. Beautiful god, Senetchem-ab-Ra-setep-[en]-Ra, son of Ra, Nekht-Heru-Hebit, you are protected, and Heru-Shetenu, the great god, is protected, and conversely.

The History Of Isis And Osiris

This story has been edited and adapted from Sir Ernest Alfred Thompson Wallis Budge's Legends Of The Gods, published in London in 1916.

Isis was the daughter of Keb, the Earth-god, and Nut, the Sky-goddess. She was the wife of Osiris, mother of Horus, and sister of Set and Nephthys.

The Egyptian Tehuti, or Thoth, who invented letters and mathematics, was the "heart of Ra," the scribe of the gods, and he uttered the words which created the world. He composed the "words of power," or magical formulae which were beneficial for the dead, and the religious works which were used by souls in their journey from this world to the next. Isis was none other, it is said, than Wisdom pointing out the knowledge of divine truths to her votaries, the true Hierophori and Hierostoli.

The goddess Rhea, having secretly made love with Kronos, was discovered by Helios, who straightway cursed her, and declared that she should not be delivered of a child in any month or year. Hermes, however, being also in love with Rhea, in return for the favours which he had received from her, went and played at dice with Selene, and won from her the seventieth part of each day. These parts he joined together and made from them five complete days, and he added them to the three hundred and sixty days of which the year formerly consisted of. These five days are to this day called the Epagomenae, and they are observed as the birthdays of their gods.

On the first of these Osiris was born, and as he came into the world a voice was heard saying, "The Lord of All is born."

Pamyles, as he was fetching water from the temple of Dios at Thebes, then heard a voice commanding him to proclaim aloud that the good and great king Osiris was born, and that Kronos committed the education of the child to him, and in memory of this event the Pamylia were afterwards instituted.

Upon the second of these days was born Aroueris, whom some call Apollo, and others the Elder Horus.

Upon the third day Typhon was born, who came into the world neither at the proper time nor by the right way, but he forced a passage through a wound which he made in his mother's side.

Upon the fourth day Isis was born, in the marshes of Egypt, and upon the fifth day Nephthys, whom some call Teleute, or Aphrodite, or Nike, was born.

As regards the fathers of these children, the first two are said to have been begotten by Helios, Isis by Hermes, and Typhon and Nephthys by Kronos. Therefore, since the third of the superadded days was the birthday of Typhon, the kings considered it to be unlucky, and in consequence they neither transacted any business in it, nor even suffered themselves to take any refreshment until the evening.

It is said that Typhon married Nephthys, and that Isis and Osiris, having a mutual affection, enjoyed each other in their mother's womb before they were born, and that from this commerce sprang Aroueris, whom the Egyptians likewise call Horus the Elder, and the Greeks Apollo.

When Osiris became king of Egypt, he applied himself to civilizing his countrymen by turning them from their former indigent and barbarous course of life. He taught them how to cultivate and improve the fruits of the earth, and he gave them a body of laws whereby to regulate their conduct, and instructed them in the reverence and worship which they were to pay to the gods.

With the same good disposition he afterwards travelled over the rest of the world, inducing the people everywhere to submit to his discipline, not indeed compelling them by force of arms, but persuading them to yield to the strength of his reasons, which were conveyed to them in the most agreeable manner, in hymns and songs, accompanied with instruments of music.

During the absence of Osiris from his kingdom, Typhon had no opportunity to make innovations or trouble in the kingdom because Isis was extremely vigilant in the government, and always upon her guard. After Osiris's return, however, having first persuaded seventy-two people to join with him in the conspiracy, together with a certain queen of Ethiopia called Aso, who chanced to be in Egypt at that time, Typhon formed a crafty plot against Osiris.

Typhon had a chest made in exactly the same size as Osiris, and it was very beautiful and highly decorated. This chest he brought into a certain banqueting room, where it was greatly admired by all who were present, and Typhon, as if in jest, promised to give it to that man whose body when tried would fit it. Thereupon the whole company, one after the other, went into it, but it did not fit any of them. Last of all Osiris himself lay down in it, and all the conspirators ran to the chest, and clapped the cover upon it, and then they fastened it down with nails on the outside, and poured molten lead over it.

They next took the chest to the river, which carried it to the sea through the Tanaitic mouth of the Nile, and for this reason this mouth of the Nile is still held in the utmost abomination by the Egyptians, and is never mentioned by them except with marks of detestation. These things, some say, took place on the seventeenth day of the month of Hathor, when the sun was in Scorpio, in the twenty-eighth year of the reign of Osiris, though others tell us that this was the year of his life and not of his reign.

The first who had knowledge of the accident which had befallen their king were the Pans and Satyrs, who inhabited the country round about Chemmis. It is from this that we have derived the term 'panic' to signify any sudden fright or amazement.

As soon as the report reached Isis, she immediately cut off one of the locks of her hair, and put on mourning apparel, and that very place where she happened to be has ever since been called 'Koptos', or the 'city of mourning'. After this she wandered round about through the country, being full of disquietude and perplexity, searching for the chest, and she inquired of every person she met, including some children whom she saw, whether they knew what was become of it.

Now, it so happened that these children had seen what Typhon's accomplices had done with the body, and they accordingly told her by what mouth of the Nile it had been conveyed to the sea. Isis meanwhile had also been informed that Osiris had been deceived by her sister Nephthys, who was in love with him, and had unwittingly enjoyed her instead of his wife. This she concluded from the melilot-garland which he had left with her. Isis made it her business to search out the child, the fruit of this unlawful commerce. Accordingly, after many pains and difficulty, by means of some dogs that conducted her to the place where it was, she found it and bred the child up, and in process of time it became her constant guard and attendant, and obtained the name of Anubis, and it is thought that it watches and guards the gods as dogs do men.

At length Isis received more particular news that the chest had been carried by the waves of the sea to the coast of Byblos, and there gently lodged in the branches of a tamarisk bush, which in a short time had grown up into a large and beautiful tree, and had grown round the chest and enclosed it on every side so completely that it was not to be seen. Moreover, the king of the country, amazed at its unusual size, had cut the tree down, and made that part of the trunk wherein the chest was concealed into a pillar to support the roof of his house.

Isis was told these things by the report of demons, and she immediately went to Byblos, where, setting herself down by the side of a fountain, she refused to speak to anybody except the queen's women who chanced to be there. These, however, she saluted and caressed in the kindest manner possible, plaiting their hair for them, and transmitting into them part of that wonderful odour which issued from her own body. This raised a great desire in the queen their mistress to see the stranger who had this admirable faculty of transfusing so fragrant a smell from herself into the hair and skin of other people. She therefore sent for her to come to court, and, after a further acquaintance with her, made her nurse to one of her sons. The name of the king who reigned at this time at Byblos was Melkander, and that of his wife was Astarte, or, according to others, Saôsis, though some call her Nemanoun, which answers to the Greek name Athenais.

Isis nursed the child by giving it her finger to suck instead of the breast. She likewise put him each night into the fire in order to consume his mortal part, whilst, having transformed herself into a swallow, she circled round the pillar and bemoaned her sad fate. This she continued to do for some time, till the queen, who stood watching her, observing the child to be all of a flame, cried out, and thereby deprived him of some of that immortality which would otherwise have been conferred upon him.

The goddess then made herself known, and asked that the pillar which supported the roof might be given to her. Having taken the pillar down, she cut it open easily, and having taken out what she wanted, she wrapped up the remainder of the trunk in fine linen, and having poured perfumed oil over it, she delivered it again into the hands of the king and queen. Now, this piece of wood is to this day preserved in the temple, and worshipped by the people of Byblos.

When this was done, Isis threw herself upon the chest, and made at the same time such loud and terrible cries of lamentation over it, that the younger of the king's sons who heard her was frightened out of his life. But the elder of them she took with her, and set sail with the chest for Egypt. While travelling, and it being morning, the river Phaedrus sent forth a keen and chill air, which h angered Isis, and she dried up its current.

At the first place where she stopped, and when she believed that she was alone, she opened the chest, and laying her face upon that of her dead husband, she embraced him and wept bitterly. Then, seeing that the little boy had silently stolen up behind her, and had found out the reason of her grief, she turned upon him suddenly, and, in her anger, gave him so fierce and terrible a look that he died of fright immediately.

When Isis finally returned to her own son, Horus, who was being raised at Buto, she deposited the chest in a remote and unfrequented place. One night, however, when Typhon was hunting by the light of the moon, he came upon it by chance, and recognizing the body which was enclosed in it, he tore it into fourteen pieces and scattered them in different places up and down the country.

When Isis found out what had been done, she set out in search of the scattered portions of her husband's body, and in order to pass more easily through the lower, marshy parts of the country, she made use of a boat made of the papyrus plant. For this reason, Egyptians say, either fearing the anger of the goddess, or else venerating the papyrus, the crocodile never injures anyone who travels in this sort of vessel.

These searches undertaken by Isis have also given rise to the report that there are very many different sepulchres of Osiris in Egypt, for wherever Isis found one of the scattered portions of her husband's body, there she buried it. This she did in order to increase the honours which would by these means be paid to his memory, and also to defeat Typhon, who was about to engage in war with Horus. Isis believed that Typhon would search for the body parts of Osiris, and being distracted by the number of sepulchres would despair of ever being able to find the true whole body.

Notwithstanding all her efforts, Isis was never able to discover the phallus of Osiris, which, having been thrown into the Nile immediately upon its separation from the rest of the body, had been devoured by the Lepidotus, the Phagrus, and the Oxyrhynchus, fish which above all others, for this reason, the Egyptians avoid. In order, however, to make some amends for the loss, Isis consecrated the phallus made in imitation of it, and instituted a solemn festival to its memory, which is even to this day observed by the Egyptians.

After these things were done, Osiris returned from the other world, and appeared to his son Horus, and encouraged him to fight, and at the same time instructed him in the exercise of arms. He then asked him what he thought was the most glorious action a man could perform, to which Horus replied, "To revenge the injuries offered to his father and mother."

Osiris then asked him what animal he thought most serviceable to a soldier, and Horus replied, "A horse."

On this Osiris wondered, and he questioned him further, asking him why he preferred a horse to a lion, and Horus replied, "Though the lion is the more serviceable creature to one who stands in need of help, yet is the horse more useful in overtaking and cutting off a flying enemy."

These replies caused Osiris to rejoice greatly, for they showed him that his son was sufficiently prepared for his enemy. A great number of people were now deserting from Typhon's party, including his concubine Thoueris, and that a serpent which pursued her as she was coming over to Horus was slain by his soldiers.

Afterwards a battle took place between Horus and Typhon, which lasted many days, but Horus was at length victorious, and Typhon was taken prisoner. He was delivered over into the custody of Isis, who, instead of putting him to death, loosed his fetters and set him free. This action of his mother incensed Horus to such a degree that he seized her, and pulled the royal crown off her head, but Hermes came forward, and set upon her head the head of an ox instead of a helmet.

After this Typhon accused Horus of illegitimacy, but, by the assistance of Hermes, his legitimacy was fully established by a decree of the gods themselves. After this two other battles were fought between Horus and Typhon, and in both Typhon was defeated. Moreover, Isis is said to have had union with Osiris after his death, and she brought forth Harpokrates, who came into the world before his time, and was lame in his lower limbs.

The Taking Of Joppa

This story has been edited and adapted from Egyptian Tales, published in 1901 on behalf of the Co-operative Publishing Society by The Colonial Press, New York and London.

There was once in the time of King Men-kheper-ra a revolt of the servants of his Majesty who were in Joppa, and his Majesty said, "Let Tahutia go with his footmen and destroy this wicked Foe in Joppa."

And he called one of his followers, and said moreover, "Hide my great cane, which works wonders, in the baggage of Tahutia that my power may go with him."

Now when Tahutia came near to Joppa, with all the footmen of Pharaoh, he sent a message to the Foe in Joppa, and said, "Behold now his Majesty, King Men-kheper-ra, has sent all this great army against you, but what is that if my heart is as your heart? Come, and let us talk in the field, and see each other face to face."

So Tahutia came with certain of his men, and the Foe in Joppa came likewise, but his charioteer was actually true of heart to the King of Egypt. And they spoke with one another in his great tent, which Tahutia had placed far off from the soldiers. But Tahutia had made ready 200 sacks, with cords and fetters, and had made a great sack of skins with bronze fetters, and many baskets, and they were in his tent. He had placed them as forage for the horses is put in baskets. For while the Foe in Joppa drank with Tahutia, the people who were with him drank with the footmen of Pharaoh, and made merry with them.

And when their bout of drinking was past, Tahutia said to the Foe in Joppa, "If it please you, while I remain with the women and children of your own city, let your people bring provisions to mine with their horses, or let one of the Apuro run to fetch them."

So they came, and hobbled their horses, and gave them provender, and one of them found the great cane of Men-kheper-ra, and came to tell of it to Tahutia. And thereupon the Foe in Joppa said to Tahutia, "My heart is set on examining the great cane of Men-kheper-ra."

And Tahutia did this, and he brought the cane of King Men-kheper-ra. He laid hold of the Foe in Joppa by his garment, and he arose and stood up, and said, "Look on me, O Foe in Joppa. Here is the great cane of King Men-kheper-ra, the terrible lion, the son of Sekhet, to whom Amen his father gives power and strength."

And he raised his hand and struck the forehead of the Foe in Joppa, and he fell helpless before him. He put him in the sack of skins and he bound with gyves the hands of the Foe in Joppa, and put on his feet the fetters with four rings. And he made them bring the 200 sacks which he had cleaned, and he made 200 soldiers climb into them. Then he filled the hollows with cords and fetters of wood, sealed them with a seal, and added to them their rope-nets and the poles to bear them. And he put every strong footman to bear them, in all 600 men, and said to them, "When you come into the town you shall open your burdens, you shall seize all the inhabitants of the town, and you shall quickly put fetters upon them."

Then one went out and said to the charioteer of the Foe in Joppa, "Your master is fallen. Go, say to your mistress, 'A pleasant message! For Sutekh has given Tahutia to us, with his wife and his children, behold the beginning of their tribute,' that she may see the two hundred sacks, which are full of men and cords and fetters."

So the charioteer went before them to please the heart of his mistress, saying, "We have laid hands on Tahutia."

Then the gates of the city were opened before the footmen, and they entered the city, they opened their burdens, they laid hands on the citizens of the city, both small and great, they put on them the cords and fetters quickly, and the power of Pharaoh seized upon that city.

After he had rested Tahutia sent a message to Egypt to the King Men-kheper-ra his lord, saying, "Be pleased, for Amen your good father has given to you the Foe in Joppa, together with all his people, likewise also his city. Send, therefore, people to take them as captives that you may fill the house of your father Amen Ra, king of the gods, with men-servants and maid-servants, and that they may be overthrown beneath your feet for ever and ever."

Anpu And Bata

This story has been edited and adapted from Egyptian Tales, published in 1901 on behalf of the Co-operative Publishing Society by The Colonial Press, New York and London.

Once there were two brethren of one mother and one father. Anpu was the name of the elder, and Bata was the name of the younger. Anpu had a house, and he had a wife. But his little brother was like a son to him, and he it was who made for him his clothes, he it was who followed behind his oxen to the fields, and he it was who did the ploughing. He harvested the corn, and did for him all the matters that were in the field. His younger brother grew to be an excellent worker, for there was not his equal in the whole land, for the spirit of a god was in him.

The younger brother followed his oxen in his daily manner, and every evening he returned again to the house, laden with all the herbs of the field, with milk and with wood, and with all things of the field. And he put them down before his elder brother, who was sitting with his wife, and he drank and ate, and he lay down in his stable with the cattle.

And at the dawn of day he took bread which he had baked, and laid it before his elder brother, and he took with him his bread to the field, and he drove his cattle to pasture in the fields. And as he walked behind his cattle, they said to him, "Good is the herbage which is in that place", and he listened to all that they said, and he took them to the good place which they desired. And the cattle which were before him became exceedingly excellent, and they multiplied greatly.

At the time of ploughing his elder brother said to him, "Let us make ready for ourselves a goodly yoke of oxen for ploughing, for the land has come out from the water, it is fit for ploughing. Moreover, come to the field with corn, for we will begin the ploughing tomorrow morning."

When the morning came, they went to the fields with their things, and their hearts were pleased exceedingly with their task at the beginning of their work. And it came to pass after this that as they were in the field they stopped for corn, and the older brother sent his younger brother, saying, "Haste, bring to us corn from the farm."

The younger brother found the wife of his elder brother, as she was sitting tying her hair. He said to her, "Get up, and give me corn, that I may run to the field, for my elder brother hastened me. Do not delay."

She said to him, "Go, open the bin, and take what you need according to your will, that I may not drop my locks of hair while I dress them."

The youth went into the stable and found a large measure, for he desired to take much corn. He loaded it with wheat and barley, and he went out carrying it.

She said to him, "How much of the corn that you need is on your shoulder?"

He said to her, "Three bushels of barley, and two of wheat, in all five. These are what are upon my shoulder."

She conversed with him, saying, "There is great strength in you, for I see your might every day." And her heart knew him with the knowledge of youth. And she arose and came to him, and conversed with him, saying, "Come, stay with me, and it shall be well for you, and I will make for you beautiful garments."

Then the youth became like a panther of the south with fury at the evil speech which she had made, and she feared greatly. And he spoke to her, saying, "You are like a mother to me, and your husband is like a father to me, for he has brought me up. What is this wickedness that you have said to me? Say it not again. I will not tell it to any man, for I will not let it be uttered by the mouth of any man."

He lifted up his burden, and he went to the field and came to his elder brother, and they took up their work, to labour at their task.

Now afterward, at evening time, his elder brother was returning to his house, and the younger brother was following after his oxen, and he loaded himself with all the things of the field, and he brought his oxen before him, to make them lie down in their stable which was in the farm. The wife of the elder brother was afraid because of the words which she had said.

She took a parcel of fat, and made herself up to look like she had been evilly beaten, desiring to say to her husband, "It is your younger brother who has done this wrong."

Her husband returned in the evening, as was his wont of every day. He came to his house where he found his wife ill of violence. She did not give him water upon his hands as he used to have, she did not make a light for him, his house was in darkness, and she was lying very sick.

Her husband said to her, "Who has spoken, with you?"

She said, "No one has spoken with me except your younger brother. When he came to take the corn he found me sitting alone. He said to me, 'Come, let us stay together, tie up your hair.' That was how he spoke to me. I did not listen to him, but I said, Am I not your mother, is not your elder brother to you as a father?' And he feared, and he beat me to stop me from making report to you, and if you let him live I shall die. Look, he is coming, and I complain of these wicked words, for he would have done this even in daylight."

The elder brother became as a panther of the south. He sharpened his knife, took it in his hand, and he stood behind the door of his stable to slay his younger brother as he came in the evening to bring his cattle into the stable.

As the sun went down, the younger brother loaded himself with herbs in his daily manner. He came, and his foremost cow entered the stable, and she said to her keeper, "Beware. Your elder brother stands before you with his knife to slay you. Flee from him."

He heard what his first cow had said, and the next entering, she also said likewise. He looked beneath the door of the stable, where he saw the feet of his elder brother. He was standing behind the door, and his knife was in his hand.

The younger brother cast down his load and started to flee swiftly, but his elder brother pursued him with his knife.

Then the younger brother cried out unto

Ra Harakhti, saying, "My good Lord! You are he who divides the evil from the good."

And Ra stood and heard all his cry, and Ra made a wide water between him and his elder brother, and it was full of crocodiles, and the one brother was on one bank, and the other on the other bank, and the elder brother smote twice on his hands at not slaying him.

The younger brother called to the elder on the bank, saying, "Stand still until the dawn of day, and when Ra arises, I shall judge with you before him, and he will discern between the good and the evil. For I shall not be with you any more forever. I will not stay in the same place as you. I shall go to the valley of the acacia."

When the land was lightened, and the next day appeared, Ra Harakhti arose, and one looked to the other. And the youth spoke with his elder brother, saying, "Why did you chase after me to slay me in craftiness, when you had not heard the words of my mouth? For I am your brother in truth, and you are to me as a father, and your wife even as a mother. Is it not so?

"Truly, when I was sent to bring for us corn, your wife said to me, 'Come, stay with me'. This story has been turned around."

So speaking he caused his older brother to understand all that happened with him and his wife. He swore an oath by Ra Harakhti, saying, "Your coming to slay me by deceit with your knife was an abomination."

Then the youth took a knife, and cut off of his flesh, and cast it into the water, and the fish swallowed it. He fell ill and he became faint, and his elder brother cursed his own heart greatly. He stood weeping for him afar off, for he did not know how to pass over to where his younger brother was, because of the crocodiles.

The younger brother called to him, saying, "Where once you planned an evil thing, will you not also devise a good thing, just like I have done for you? When you go to your house you must look to your cattle, for I shall not stay in the place where you are. I am going to the valley of the acacia.

"As to what you shall do for me, it is this. You shall come to seek after me, if you understand that there are things happening to me. And this is what shall come to pass, that I shall draw out my soul, and I shall put it upon the top of the flowers of the acacia, and when the acacia is cut down, and the flower falls to the ground, and even if you search for it for seven years, do not let your heart be wearied. You will find it, and you must put it in a cup of cold water, and you should expect that I shall live again, and that I may make answer to what has been done wrong. You shall know that things are happening to me, because someone will give you a cup of beer and it shall be troubled. Stay not then for it shall come to pass with you."

The youth went to the valley of the acacia, while his elder brother went to his house. He laid his hand on his head, and he cast dust on his head. He came to his house, where he slew his wife, cast her to the dogs, and he sat in mourning for his younger brother.

Many days after these things had happened, the younger brother was alone in the valley of the acacia. He spent his time in hunting the beasts of the desert, and he came back in the evening to lie down under the acacia, which bore his soul upon the topmost flower. After this he built himself a tower with his own hands, in the valley of the acacia, and it was full of all good things, that he might provide for himself a home.

One day he went out from his tower, and he met the Nine Gods, who were walking forth to look upon the whole land. The Nine Gods talked one with another, and they said to him, "Ho! Bata, bull of the Nine Gods, are you remaining alone? You have left your village because of the wife of Anpu, your elder brother. "Know that his wife is slain. You have given him an answer to all that was transgressed against you."

And their hearts were vexed for him exceedingly. And Ra Harakhti said to Khnemu, "Make a woman for Bata, that he may not remain alive alone."

Khnemu made a mate to dwell with him. She was more beautiful in her limbs than any woman who is in the whole land. The essence of every god was in her. The seven Hathors came to see her, and they said with one mouth, "She will die a sharp death."

Bata loved her very much, and she dwelt in his house. He passed his time in hunting the beasts of the desert, and brought and laid them before her. He said, "Do not go outside, lest the sea seize you, for I cannot rescue you from it, for I am a woman like you. My soul is placed on the head of the flower of the acacia, and if another finds it, I must fight with him." And he opened to her his heart in all its nature.

The next day Bata went to hunt in his daily manner. And the young girl went to walk under the acacia which was by the side of her house. Then the sea saw her, and cast its waves up after her. She fled from it, and she entered her house.

The sea called to the acacia, saying, "Oh, would that I could seize her!"

The acacia brought a lock from her hair, and the sea carried it to Egypt, and dropped it in the place of the fullers of Pharaoh's linen. The smell of the lock of hair entered into the clothes of Pharaoh, and he was angry with the fullers of Pharaoh, saying, "The smell of ointment is in the clothes of Pharaoh."

The people were rebuked every day, they knew not what they should do. And the chief fuller of Pharaoh walked by the bank, and his heart was very evil after the quarrel with Pharaoh. He stood still upon the sand opposite to the lock of hair, which was in the water, and he made a servant enter into the water and bring it to him, and there was found in it a smell, exceeding sweet.

He took it to Pharaoh, and they brought the scribes and the wise men, and they said to Pharaoh, "This lock of hair belongs to a daughter of Ra Harakhti. The essence of every god is in her, and it is a tribute to you from another land. Let messengers go to every strange land to seek her, and as for the messenger who shall go to the valley of the acacia, let many men go with him to bring her."

Then said his Majesty, "Excellent. That is good advice.".

After many days the people who were sent to strange lands came to give report to the King, but none bar one returned from the valley of the acacia, for Bata had slain almost all of them. This survivor gave a report to the King, and his Majesty sent many men and soldiers, as well as horsemen, to bring the woman back.

Among them there was a woman, and to her had been many beautiful ornaments. And swayed by these gifts, the girl came back with her, and they rejoiced over her in the whole land.

His Majesty loved her exceedingly, and raised her to high estate, and he spoke to her, asking her to tell him about her husband. She said, "Cut down the acacia, and have someone chop it up."

They sent men and soldiers with their weapons to cut down the acacia, and they came to the acacia, and they cut the flower upon which lay the soul of Bata, and he fell dead suddenly.

When the next day came, and the earth was lightened, the acacia was cut down. And Anpu, the elder brother of Bata, entered his house, and washed his hands, and someone gave him a cup of beer, and it became troubled. Another person gave him a cup of wine, and the smell of it was evil. Then he took his staff, and his sandals, and likewise his clothes, with his weapons of war, and he went forth to the valley of the acacia.

He entered his younger brother's tower, and he found him lying upon his mat. He was dead. He wept when he saw his younger brother truly lying dead. And he went out to seek the soul of his younger brother under the acacia tree, under which his younger brother used to lay in the evening. He spent three years in seeking for it, but found it not. And when he began the fourth year, he desired in his heart to return into Egypt.

He said in his heart, "I will go tomorrow morning."

When the land lightened, and the next day appeared, Anpu was walking under the acacia, spending his time looking for the Bata's flower. And he returned in the evening, and laboured to find it again. He found a seed, and he returned with it, and this was truly the soul of his younger brother. He brought a cup of cold water, and he cast the seed into it, and he sat down, as he liked to do.

When the night came Bata's soul sucked up the water. Bata shuddered in all his limbs, and he looked on his elder brother, for his soul was in the cup. Then Anpu took the cup of cold water and drank it. Bata's his soul returned to its rightful place, and he became as he had been. They embraced each other, and they conversed together.

Bata said to his elder brother, "I am to become a great bull, which bears every good mark. No one will know its history, and you must sit upon my back. When the sun arises I shall return to where my wife is, that I may answer her. Then you must take me to the place where the King is, for all good things shall be done for you. You will be laden with silver and gold because you bring me to Pharaoh, for I will become a great marvel, and they shall rejoice for me in all the land. And you shall go to your village."

The land was lightened, and the next day appeared, and Bata turned into the form of a great bull, as he had told his elder brother. And Anpu sat upon his back until the dawn. He came to the place where the King was, and they made his Majesty know him.

Pharaoh saw him, and he was exceeding joyful. He made great offerings, saying, "This is a great wonder which has come to pass," and there were rejoicings over the whole land. They presented him with silver and gold for his elder brother, who went and stayed in his village. They gave to the bull many men and many things, and Pharaoh loved him exceedingly above all that is in this land.

After many days, the bull entered the purified place, where he stood with the princess. He began to speak with her, saying, "Behold, I am alive indeed."

And she said to him, "And, pray, who are you?"

He said to her, "I am Bata. I knew when you caused the soldiers to come and destroy Pharaoh's acacia, which was my abode. I knew that I might not be suffered to live. But I am alive indeed, I am as an ox."

Then the princess feared exceedingly for the words that her husband had spoken to her. And he went out from the purified place.

Later, his Majesty was sitting talking to the princess. They were at table, and the King was exceedingly pleased with her. And she said to his Majesty, "Swear to me by God, saying, 'What you shall say, I will obey it for your sake.'"

He listened to all that she said, even this. "Let me eat of the liver of the ox, because he is fit for naught."

The King was very sad at her words, and the heart of Pharaoh grieved him greatly. And after the land was lightened once again, and the next day appeared, they proclaimed a great feast with offerings to the ox. And the King sent one of the chief butchers of his Majesty, to cause the ox to be sacrificed. And when he was sacrificed, as he was carried upon the shoulders of the people, and he shook his neck, and he threw two drops of blood over against the two doors of his Majesty's palace. One drop fell upon the one side, on the great door of Pharaoh, and the other upon the other door. The doors then grew as two great Persea trees, and each of them was excellent.

Someone went to tell his Majesty, "Two great Persea trees have grown, as a great marvel of his Majesty, in the night by the side of the great gate." And there was rejoicing for them in all the land, and there were offerings made to them.

Many days after all of this happened, his Majesty was adorned with the blue crown, with garlands of flowers on his neck, and he rode upon the chariot of pale gold, and he went out from the palace to behold the Persea trees. The princess also went out with horses behind his Majesty.

His Majesty sat beneath one of the Persea trees, and it spoke with his wife, "Oh you deceitful one, I am Bata, I am alive, though I have been evilly entreated. I knew who caused the acacia to be cut down by Pharaoh at my dwelling. I then became an ox, and you are the cause of my being killed."

After these things happened the princess stood at the table of Pharaoh, and the King was pleased with her. And she said to his Majesty, "Swear to me by God, saying, 'That which the princess shall say to me I will obey it for her.'"

He listened to all she said. And he commanded, "Let these two Persea trees be cut down, and let them be made into goodly planks."

After this his Majesty sent skilful craftsmen, and they cut down the Persea trees of Pharaoh, and the princess, the royal wife, was standing looking on, and they did all that was in her heart to the trees. But a chip flew up, and it entered into the mouth of the princess. She swallowed it, and after many days she bore a son.

A courtier went to tell his Majesty, "There is born to you a son."

They brought him, and gave to him a nurse and servants, and there were rejoicings in the whole land. And the King sat making a merry day, as they were about the naming of him, and his Majesty loved him exceedingly at that moment, and the King raised him to be the royal son of Kush.

After much time had passed his Majesty made him heir of all the land. And many days after that, when he had fulfilled many years as heir, his Majesty flew up to heaven, and the heir said, "Let my great nobles be brought before me, that I may Let them know all that has happened to me."

They also brought before him his wife, and he judged her, and they agreed with him. They brought to him his elder brother, and he made him hereditary prince in all his land. He was thirty years King of Egypt, and he died, and his elder brother stood in his place on the day of burial.

This tale is excellently finished in peace, for the ka of the scribe of the treasury Kagabu, of the treasury of Pharaoh, and for the scribe Hora, and the scribe Meremapt. Written by the scribe Anena, the owner of this roll. He who speaks against this roll, may Tehuti smite him.

Setna And The Magic Book

This story has been edited and adapted from Egyptian Tales, published in 1901 on behalf of the Co-operative Publishing Society by The Colonial Press, New York and London.

The mighty King User-maat-ra (Rameses the Great) had a son named Setna Kha-em-uast who was a great scribe, and very learned in all the ancient writings. And he heard that the magic book of Thoth, by which a man may enchant heaven and earth, and know the language of all birds and beasts, was buried in the cemetery of Memphis. He went to search for it with his brother An-he-hor-eru, and when they found the tomb of the King's son, Na-nefer-ka-ptah, son of the King of Upper and Lower Egypt, Mer-neb-ptah, Setna opened it and went in.

Now in the tomb was Na-nefer-ka-ptah, and with him was the ka of his wife Ahura, for though she was buried at Koptos, her ka dwelt at Memphis with her husband, whom she loved. And Setna saw them seated before their offerings, and the book lay between them.

Na-nefer-ka-ptah said to Setna, "Who are you that break into my tomb in this way?"

Setna said, "I am Setna, son of the great King User-maat-ra, living forever, and I come for that book which I see between you."

Na-nefer-ka-ptah said, "It cannot be given to you."

Then Setna said, "But I will carry it away by force."

Then Ahura said to Setna, "Do not take this book, for it will bring trouble on you, as it has upon us. Listen to what we have suffered for it."

Ahura's Tale

We were the two children of the King Mer-neb-ptah, and he loved us very much, for he had no others, and Na-nefer-ka-ptah was in his palace as heir over all the land. And when we were grown, the King said to the Queen, "I will marry Na-nefer-ka-ptah to the daughter of a general, and Ahura to the son of another general."

The Queen said, "No, he is the heir, let him marry his sister, like the heir of a king, for none other is fit for him."

The King said, "That is not fair. They had better be married to the children of the general."

And the Queen said, "It is you who are not dealing rightly with me."

The King answered, "If I have no more than these two children, is it right that they should marry one another? I will marry Na-nefer-ka-ptah to the daughter of an officer, and Ahura to the son of another officer. It has often been done so in our family."

And at a time when there was a great feast before the King, they came to fetch me to the feast. And I was very troubled, and did not behave as I used to do.

The King said to me, "Ahura, have you sent someone to me about this sorry matter, saying, 'Let me be married to my elder brother?'"

I said to him, "Well, let me marry the son of an officer, and he marry the daughter of another officer, as it often happens so in our family."

I laughed, and the King laughed. And the King told the steward of the palace, "Let them take Ahura to the house of Na-nefer-ka-ptah to-night, and all kinds of good things with her."

So they brought me as a wife to the house of Na-nefer-ka-ptah, and the King ordered them to give me presents of silver and gold, and things from the palace.

Na-nefer-ka-ptah passed a happy time with me, and received all the presents from the palace, and we loved one another. And when I expected a child, they told the King, and he was most heartily glad, and he sent me many things, and a present of the best silver and gold and linen.

When the time came, I bore this little child that is before you. And they gave him the name of Mer-ab, and registered him in the book of the *House of life*.

When my brother Na-nefer-ka-ptah went to the cemetery of Memphis, he did nothing on earth but read the writings that are in the catacombs of the kings, and the tablets of the *House of life*, and the inscriptions that are seen on the monuments, and he worked hard on the writings. There was a priest there called Nesi-ptah, and as Na-nefer-ka-ptah went into a temple to pray, and it happened that he went behind this priest, and was reading the inscriptions that were on the chapels of the gods. The priest mocked him and laughed.

So Na-nefer-ka-ptah said to him, "Why are you laughing at me?"

The priest replied, "I was not laughing at you, or if I happened to do so, it was at your reading writings that are worthless. If you wish so much to read writings, come to me, and I will bring you to the place where the book is which Thoth himself wrote with his own hand, and which will bring you to the gods. When you read but two pages in this you will enchant the heaven, the earth, the abyss, the mountains, and the sea. You shall know what the birds of the sky and the crawling things are saying. You shall see the fishes of the deep, for a divine power is there to bring them up out of the depth.

"And when you read the second page, if you are in the world of ghosts, you will become again in the shape you were in on earth. You will see the sun shining in the sky, with all the gods, and the full moon."

Na-nefer-ka-ptah said, "By the life of the King! Tell me of anything you want done and I'll do it for you, if you will only send me where this book is."

The priest answered Na-nefer-ka-ptah, "If you want to go to the place where the book is, you must give me 100 pieces of silver for my funeral, and provide that they shall bury me as a rich priest." So Na-nefer-ka-ptah called his lad and told him to give the priest 100 pieces of silver, and he made them do as he wished, giving everything that he asked for.

Then the priest said to Na-nefer-ka-ptah, "This book is in the middle of the river at Koptos, in an iron box. In the iron box is a bronze box, and in the bronze box is a sycamore box. In the sycamore box is an ivory and ebony box, and in the ivory and ebony box is a silver box. In the silver box is a golden box, and in that is the book. It is twisted all round with snakes and scorpions and all the other crawling things around the box, and there is a deathless snake by the box."

When the priest finished his tale he was very, very pleased with himself for striking such a bargain.

When Na-nefer-ka-ptah came from the temple he told me all that had happened to him. He said, "I shall go to Koptos, for I must fetch this book. I will not stay any longer in the north."

I said, "Let me dissuade you, for you prepare sorrow and you will bring me into trouble in the Thebaid."

I laid my hand on Na-nefer-ka-ptah, to keep him from going to Koptos, but he would not listen to me, and he went to the King, and told the King all that the priest had said.

The King asked him, "What is it that you want?"

He replied, "Let them give me the royal boat with its belongings, for I will go to the south with Ahura and her little boy Mer-ab, and fetch this book without delay."

So they gave him the royal boat with its belongings, and we went with him to the haven, and sailed from there up to Koptos.

The priests of Isis of Koptos, and the high-priest of Isis, came down to us without waiting, to meet Na-nefer-ka-ptah, and their wives also came to me. We went into the temple of Isis and Harpokrates, and Na-nefer-ka-ptah brought an ox, a goose, and some wine, and made a burnt-offering and a drink-offering before Isis of Koptos and Harpokrates.

Then they brought us to a very fine house, with all good things, and Na-nefer-ka-ptah spent four days there and feasted with the priests of Isis of Koptos, and the wives of the priests of Isis also made holiday with me.

On the morning of the fifth day Na-nefer-ka-ptah called a priest to him, and made a magic cabin that was full of men and tackle. He put the spell upon it, and put life in it, and gave them breath, and sank it in the water. He filled the royal boat with sand, and took leave of me, and sailed from the haven, while I sat by the river at Koptos that I might see what would become of him.

He said, "Workmen, work for me, even at the place where the book is."

They toiled by night and by day, and when they had reached it in three days, he threw the sand out, and made a shoal in the river. And then he found on it entwined serpents and scorpions and all kinds of crawling things around the box in which the book was, and by it he found a deathless snake around the box. And he laid the spell upon the entwined serpents and scorpions and all kinds of crawling things which were around the box, so that they should not come out.

Then he went to the deathless snake, and fought with him, and killed him, but the snake came to life again, and took a new form. He then fought again with him a second time, but he came to life again, and took a third form. He then cut him in two parts, and put sand between the parts, so that he should not appear again.

Na-nefer-ka-ptah then went to the place where he found the box. He uncovered a box of iron, and opened it. He found then a box of bronze and opened that. Then he found a box of sycamore wood and opened that. Again, he found a box of ivory and ebony and opened that. Yet, he found a box of silver, and opened that, and then he found a box of gold. He opened that, and found the book in it.

He took the book from the golden box, and read a page of spells from it. He enchanted the heaven and the earth, the abyss, the mountains, and the sea. He knew what the birds of the sky, the fish of the deep, and the beasts of the hills all said. He read another page of the spells, and saw the sun shining in the sky, with all the gods, the full moon, and the stars in their shapes. He saw the fishes of the deep, for a divine power was present that brought them up from the water.

He then read the spell upon the workmen that he had made, and taken from the haven, and said to them, "Work for me, back to the place from which I came." They toiled night and day, and so he came back to the place where I sat by the river of Koptos. I had not drunk nor eaten anything, and had done nothing on earth, but sit like one who is gone to the grave.

I then told Na-nefer-ka-ptah that I wished to see this book, for which we had taken so much trouble. He gave the book into my hands, and when I read a page of the spells in it I also enchanted heaven and earth, the abyss, the mountains, and the sea. I also knew what the birds of the sky, the fishes of the deep, and the beasts of the hills all said. I read another page of the spells, and I saw the sun shining in the sky with all the gods, the full moon, and the stars in their shapes. I saw the fishes of the deep, for a divine power was present that brought them up from the water.

As I could not write, I asked Na-nefer-ka-ptah, who was a good writer, and a very learned one. He called for a new piece of papyrus, and wrote on it all that was in the book before him. He dipped it in beer, and washed it off in the liquid, for he knew that if it were washed off, and he drank it, he would know all that there was in the writing.

We returned back to Koptos the same day, and made a feast before Isis of Koptos and Harpokrates. We then went to the haven and sailed, and went northward of Koptos. And as we went on Thoth discovered all that Na-nefer-ka-ptah had done with the book, and Thoth hastened to tell Ra, and said, "Now know that my book and my revelation are with Na-nefer-ka-ptah, son of the King Mer-neb-ptah. He has forced himself into my place, and robbed it, and seized my box with the writings, and killed my guards who protected it."

Ra replied to him, "He is before you, take him and all his kin." He sent a power from heaven with the command, "Do not let Na-nefer-ka-ptah return safe to Memphis with all his kin."

And after this hour, the little boy Mer-ab, going out from the awning of the royal boat, fell into the river. He called on Ra, and everybody who was on the bank raised a cry. Na-nefer-ka-ptah went out of the cabin, and read the spell over him. He brought his body up because a divine power brought him to the surface. He read another spell over him, and made him tell of all that happened to him, and of what Thoth had said before Ra.

We turned back with him to Koptos. We brought him to the Good House, we fetched the people to him, and made one embalm him, and we buried him in his coffin in the cemetery of Koptos like a great and noble person.

And Na-nefer-ka-ptah, my brother, said, "Let us go down, let us not delay, for the King has not yet heard of what has happened to him, and his heart will be sad about it."

So we went to the haven, we sailed, and did not stay to the north of Koptos. When we were come to the place where the little boy Mer-ab had fallen into the water, I went out from the awning of the royal boat, and I fell into the river. They called Na-nefer-ka-ptah, and he came out from the cabin of the royal boat. He read a spell over me, and brought my body up, because a divine power brought me to the surface. He drew me out, and read the spell over me, and made me tell him of all that had happened to me, and of what Thoth had said before Ra.

Then he turned back with me to Koptos. He brought me to the Good House, he fetched the people to me, and made one embalm me, as great and noble people are buried, and laid me in the tomb where Mer-ab my young child was.

He turned to the haven, and sailed down, and delayed not in the north of Koptos. When he was come to the place where we fell into the river, he said to his heart, "Shall I not better turn back again to Koptos, that I may lie by them? For, if not, when I go down to Memphis, and the King asks after his children, what shall I say to him? Can I tell him, 'I have taken your children to the Thebaid, and killed them, while I remained alive, and I have come to Memphis still alive?'"

Then he made them bring him a linen cloth of striped byssus. He made a band, and bound the book firmly, and tied it upon him. Na-nefer-ka-ptah then went out of the awning of the royal boat and fell into the river. He cried on Ra, and all those who were on the bank made an outcry, saying, "Great woe! Sad woe! Is he lost, that good scribe and able man that has no equal?"

The royal boat went on, without anyone on earth knowing where Na-nefer-ka-ptah was. It went on to Memphis, and they told all this to the King. Then the King went down to the royal boat in mourning, and all the soldiers and high-priests of Ptah were in mourning, and all the officials and courtiers. And when he saw Na-nefer-ka-ptah, who was in the inner cabin of the royal boat he lifted him up.

They saw the book by him, and the King said, "Let one hide this book that is with him."

And the officers of the King, the priests of Ptah, and the high-priest of Ptah, said to the King, "Our Lord, may the King live as long as the sun! Na-nefer-ka-ptah was a good scribe, and a very skilful man."

And the King had him laid in his Good House to the sixteenth day, and then had him wrapped to the thirty-fifth day, and laid him out to the seventieth day, and then had him put in his grave in his resting-place.

I have now told you the sorrow which has come upon us because of this book for which you ask, saying, "Let it be given to me."

You have no claim to it, and, indeed, for the sake of it, we have given up our life on earth.

Setna's Tale

And Setna said to Ahura, "Give me the book which I see between you and Na-nefer-ka-ptah, for if you do not I will take it by force."

Na-nefer-ka-ptah rose from his seat and said, "Are you Setna, to whom my wife has told of all these blows of fate, which you have not suffered? Can you take this book by your skill as a good scribe? If, indeed, you can play games with me, let us play a game, then, of 52 points."

And Setna said, "I am ready," and the board and its pieces were put before him. And Na-nefer-ka-ptah won a game from Setna, and he put the spell upon him, and defended himself with the game board that was before him, and sunk him into the ground above his feet.

He did the same at the second game, and won it from Setna, and sunk him into the ground to his waist. He did the same at the third game, and made him sink into the ground up to his ears. Then Setna struck Na-nefer-ka-ptah a great blow with his hand. And Setna called his brother An-he-hor-eru and said to him, "Make haste and go up upon earth, and tell the King all that has happened to me, and bring me the talisman of my father Ptah, and my magic books."

An-he-hor-eru hurried up upon earth, and told the King all that had happened to Setna. The King said, "Bring him the talisman of his father Ptah, and his magic books."

An-he-hor-eru hurried down into the tomb, where he laid the talisman on Setna, and he sprang up again immediately. And then Setna reached out his hand for the book, and took it. Then, as Setna went out from the tomb, there went a Light before him, and Darkness behind him. Ahura wept at him, and she said, "Glory to the King of Darkness! Hail to the King of Light! All power is gone from the tomb."

But Na-nefer-ka-ptah said to Ahura, "Do not let your heart be sad. I will make him bring back this book, with a forked stick in his hand, and a fire-pan on his head."

And Setna went out from the tomb, and it closed behind him as it was before. Then Setna went to the King, and told him everything that had happened to him with the book.

The King said to Setna, "Take back the book to the grave of Na-nefer-ka-ptah, like a prudent man, or else he will make you bring it with a forked stick in your hand, and a fire-pan on your head," but Setna would not listen to him, and when Setna had unrolled the book he did nothing on earth but read it to everybody.

That night Setna dreamed that he was walking in the court of the temple of Ptah, where he met Tabubua, a fascinating girl, daughter of a priest of Bast, of Ankhtaui. He made advances towards her but she repelled his advances, all the while flirting with him to beguile him into giving up all his possessions. He dreamed that she slayed his children, until, at last, she gave a fearful cry and vanished, leaving Setna bereft of even his clothes.

So, Setna immediately went to Memphis, and embraced his children for they were alive. And the King said to him, "Were you not drunk so?"

Then Setna told all things that had happened with Tabubua and Na-nefer-ka-ptah. And the King said, "Setna, I have already lifted up my hand against you, and said, 'He will kill you if you do not take back the book to the place you took it from.' But you have never listened to me till this hour. Now, then, take the book to Na-nefer-ka-ptah, with a forked stick in your hand, and a fire-pan on your head."

So Setna went from the King, with a forked stick in his hand, and a fire-pan on his head. He went down to the tomb in which was Na-nefer-ka-ptah. Ahura said to him, "It is Ptah, the great god, that has brought you back safe."

Na-nefer-ka-ptah laughed, and he said, "This is the business that I told you before."

And when Setna had praised Na-nefer-ka-ptah, he found it as the proverb says, 'The sun was in the whole tomb.'

Then Ahura and Na-nefer-ka-ptah begged a favour of Setna. Setna said, "Na-nefer-ka-ptah, is it anything disgraceful that you ask of me?"

Na-nefer-ka-ptah said, "Setna, you know this, that Ahura and Mer-ab, her child, are in Koptos. Bring them here into this tomb, by the skill of a good scribe. Let it be impressed upon you to take pains, and to go to Koptos to bring them here."

Setna then went out from the tomb to the King, and told the King all that Na-nefer-ka-ptah had told him. The King said, "Setna, go to Koptos and bring back Ahura and Mer-ab."

He answered the King, "Let one give me the royal boat and its belongings." And they gave him the royal boat and its belongings, and he left the haven, and sailed without stopping till he came to Koptos. And they made this known to the priests of Isis at Koptos and to the high-priest of Isis, and behold they came down to him, and gave him their hand to the shore. He went up with them and entered into the temple of Isis of Koptos and of Harpokrates.

He offered an ox, a goose, and some wine, and he made a burnt-offering and a drink-offering before Isis of Koptos and Harpokrates. He went to the cemetery of Koptos with the priests of Isis and the high-priest of Isis. They dug about for three days and three nights, for they searched even in all the catacombs which were in the cemetery of Koptos. They turned over the steles of the scribes of the *Double House of Life*, and read the inscriptions that they found on them. But they could not find the resting-place of Ahura and Mer-ab.

Na-nefer-ka-ptah perceived that they could not find the resting-place of Ahura and her child Mer-ab. So he raised himself up as a venerable ancient, and came before Setna. And Setna saw him, and Setna said to the ancient, "You look like a very old man. Do you know where the resting-place of Ahura and her child Mer-ab might be?"

The ancient said to Setna, "It was told by the father of the father of my father to the father of my father, and the father of my father has told it to my father. The resting-place of Ahura and of her child Mer-ab is in a mound south of the town of Pehemato."

Setna said to the ancient, "Perhaps we may do damage to Pehemato, and you are ready to lead us to the town for the sake of that."

The ancient replied to Setna, "If you listen to me, shall you therefore destroy the town of Pehemato! If they do not find Ahura and her child Mer-ab under the south corner of their town may I be disgraced."

They attended to the ancient, and found the resting-place of Ahura and her child Mer-ab under the south corner of the town of Pehemato. Setna laid them in the royal boat to bring them as honoured persons, and restored the town of Pehemato as it originally was.

Na-nefer-ka-ptah let Setna know that it was he who had come to Koptos, to enable them to find out where the resting-place was of Ahura and her child Mer-ab. So Setna left the haven in the royal boat, and sailed without stopping, and reached Memphis with all the soldiers who were with him. And when they told the King he came down to the royal boat. He took them as honoured persons escorted to the catacombs, where Na-nefer-ka-ptah lay, and smoothed down the ground over them.

This is the completed writing of the tale of Setna Kha-em-uast, and Na-nefer-ka-ptah, and his wife Ahura, and their child Mer-ab. It was written in the 35th year, the month Tybi.

Tales Of The Magicians

This story has been edited and adapted from Egyptian Tales, published in 1901 on behalf of the Co-operative Publishing Society by The Colonial Press, New York and London.

One day, when King Khufu reigned over all the land, he said to his chancellor, who stood before him, "Go call me my sons and my councillors, that I may ask of them a thing." And his sons and his councillors came and stood before him, and he said to them, "Do you know of a man who can tell me tales of the deeds of the magicians?"

Then the royal son Khafra stood forth and said, "I will tell your Majesty a tale of the days of your forefather Nebka, the blessed, of what came to pass when he went into the temple of Ptah of Ankhtaui..."

Khafra's Tale

His Majesty was walking to the temple of Ptah, and went to the house of the chief reciter Uba-aner, with his train. When the wife of Uba-aner saw a page, among those who stood behind the King, her heart longed after him, and she sent her servant to him, with a present of a box full of garments.

He soon came with the servant. There was a lodge in the garden of Uba-aner, and one day the page said to the wife of Uba-aner, "In the garden of Uba-aner there is now a lodge. Let us therein take our pleasure."

So the wife of Uba-aner sent to the steward who had charge over the garden, saying, "Let the lodge which is in the garden be made ready." And she remained there, and rested and drank with the page until the sun went down.

When the evening was now come, the page went forth to bathe. The steward said, "I must go and tell Uba-aner of this matter."

When this day was past, and another day came, the steward went to Uba-aner, and told him of all these things.

Then said Uba-aner, "Bring me my casket of ebony and electrum."

They brought it, and he fashioned a crocodile of wax, seven fingers long, and he enchanted it, and said, "When the page comes and bathes in my lake, be ready for him."

And he gave it to the steward, and said to him, "When the page goes down into the lake to bathe, as he is daily wont to do, then throw in this crocodile behind him."

The steward went forth bearing the crocodile.

The wife of Uba-aner sent to the steward who had charge over the garden, saying, "Let the lodge, which is in the garden be made ready, for I come to tarry there."

The lodge was prepared with all good things, and she came and made merry therein with the page. And when the evening was now come, the page went forth to bathe as he was wont to do. And the steward cast in the wax crocodile after him into the water, and, it became a great crocodile seven cubits in length, and it seized the page.

Uba-aner stayed yet seven days with the King of Upper and Lower Egypt, Nebka, the blessed, while the page was stifled in the crocodile. After the seven days were passed, the King of Upper and Lower Egypt, Nebka, the blessed, went forth, and Uba-aner went before him.

Uba-aner said to his Majesty, "Will your Majesty come and see this wonder that has come to pass to a lowly page?"

The King went with Uba-aner. And Uba-aner called to the crocodile and said, "Bring forth the page." And the crocodile came forth from the lake with the page.

Uba-aner said to the King, "Behold, whatever I command this crocodile he will do it."

And his Majesty said, "I pray you send back this crocodile."

Uba-aner stooped and took up the crocodile, and it became in his hand a crocodile of wax. And then Uba-aner told the King that which had passed in his house with the page and his wife.

His Majesty said to the crocodile, "Take to you your prey," and the crocodile plunged into the lake with his prey, and no man knew where he went.

His Majesty the King of Upper and Lower Egypt, Nebka, the blessed, commanded, and they brought forth the wife of Uba-aner to the north side of the harem, and burned her with fire, and cast her ashes in the river.

This is a wonder that came to pass in the days of your forefather the King of Upper and Lower Egypt, Nebka, of the acts of the chief reciter Uba-aner."

His Majesty the King of Upper and Lower Egypt, Khufu, then said, "Let there be presented to the King Nebka, the blessed, 1,000 loaves, 100 draughts of beer, an ox, two jars of incense, and let there be presented a loaf, a jar of beer, a jar of incense and a piece of meat to the chief reciter Uba-aner, for I have seen the token of his learning."

And they did all things as his Majesty commanded.

Bau-F-Ra's Tale

The royal son Bau-f-ra then stood forth and spoke. He said, "I will tell your Majesty of a wonder which came to pass in the days of your father Seneferu, the blessed, of the deeds of the chief reciter Zazamankh…"

One day King Seneferu, being weary, went throughout his palace seeking for a pleasure to lighten his heart, but he found none. And he said, "Haste, and bring before me the chief reciter and scribe of the rolls Zazamankh."

They straightway brought him. And the King said, "I have sought in my palace for some delight, but I have found none."

Then said Zazamankh to him, "Let your Majesty go upon the lake of the palace, and let there be made ready a boat, with all the fair maidens of the harem of your palace, and the heart of your Majesty shall be refreshed with the sight, in seeing their rowing up and down the water, and seeing the goodly pools of the birds upon the lake, and beholding its sweet fields and grassy shores. Thus will your heart be lightened. And I also will go with you. Bring me twenty oars of ebony inlaid with gold, with blades of light wood inlaid with electrum, and bring me twenty maidens, fair in their limbs, their bosoms, and their hair, all virgins, and bring me twenty nets, and give these nets to the maidens for their garments."

They did according to all the commands of his Majesty.

They rowed down the stream and up the stream, and the heart of his Majesty was glad with the sight of their rowing. But one of them at the steering struck her hair, and her jewel of new malachite fell into the water. She ceased her song, and stopped rowing, and her companions ceased singing and rowing.

His Majesty said, "Why do you not row further?"

They replied, "Our little steerer stays here and rows not."

His Majesty then said to her, "Why do you not row?"

She replied, "It is for my jewel of new malachite which is fallen in the water."

But he said to her, "Row on, for I will replace it."

She answered, "But I want my own piece back in its setting."

His Majesty said, "Haste, bring me the chief reciter Zazamankh," and they brought him. And his Majesty said, "Zazamankh, my brother, I have done as you said, and the heart of his Majesty is refreshed with the sight of their rowing. But now a jewel of new malachite owned by one of the little ones is fallen in the water, and she ceases and rows not, and she has spoiled the rowing of her side. And I asked her, 'Why do you not row?' and she answered, 'It is for my jewel of new malachite which is fallen in the water.' I replied to her, 'Row on, for behold I will replace it,' and she answered, 'But I want my own piece again back in its setting.'"

Then the chief reciter Zazamankh spoke his magic speech. And he placed one part of the waters of the lake upon the other, and discovered the jewel lying upon a shard, and he took it up and gave it to its mistress. And the water, which was twelve cubits deep in the middle, reached now to twenty-four cubits after he turned it.

And he spoke again, and used his magic speech, and he brought the water of the lake back to its proper place.

His Majesty spent a joyful day with the whole of the royal house. Then rewarded he the chief reciter Zazamankh with all good things. This is a wonder that came to pass in the days of your father, the King of Upper and Lower Egypt, Seneferu, of the deeds of the chief reciter, the scribe of the rolls, Zazamankh.

Then said the majesty of the King of Upper and Lower Egypt, Khufu, the blessed, "Let there be presented an offering of 1,000 cakes, 100 draughts of beer, an ox, and two jars of incense to the King of Upper and Lower Egypt, Seneferu, the blessed, and let there be given a loaf, a jar of beer, and a jar of incense to the chief reciter, the scribe of the rolls, Zazamankh, for I have seen the token of his learning."

And they did all things as his Majesty commanded.

Hordedef's Tale

The royal son Hordedef then stood forth and spoke. He said, "Hitherto you have only heard tokens of those who have gone before, and about which no man knows their truth. But I will show your Majesty a man of your own days."

His Majesty said, "Who is he, Hordedef?"

The royal son Hordedef answered, "It is a certain man named Dedi, who dwells at Dedsneferu. He is a man of 110 years old, and he eats 500 loaves of bread and a side of beef, and drinks 100 draughts of beer, to this day. He knows how to restore the head that is smitten off. He knows how to cause the lion to follow him trailing his halter on the ground. He knows the designs of the dwelling of Tehuti. The majesty of the King of Upper and Lower Egypt, Khufu, the blessed, has long sought for the designs of the dwelling of Tehuti, that he may make the like of them in his pyramid."

And his Majesty said, "Hordedef, my son, bring him to me."

Then ships were made ready for the King's son Hordedef, and he went up the stream to Dedsneferu. And when the ships had moored at the haven, he landed, and sat in a litter of ebony, the poles of which were of cedar wood overlaid with gold.

When he drew near to Dedi, they set down the litter. He arose to greet Dedi, and found him lying on a palmstick couch at the door of his house. One servant held his head and rubbed him, and another rubbed his feet.

The King's son Hordedef said, "Your state is that of one who lives to good old age, for old age is the end of our voyage, the time of embalming, the time of burial. Lie, then, in the sun, free of infirmities, without the babble of dotage. This is the salutation to worthy age.

"I come from afar to call you, with a message from my father Khufu, the blessed, for you shall eat of the best which the King gives and his followers can offer you. He wishes to bring you in good estate to your fathers who are in the tomb."

And Dedi replied to him, "Peace to you! Peace to you, Hordedef, son of the King, beloved of his father. May your father Khufu, the blessed, praise you, may he advance you among the elders, may your ka prevail against the enemy, may your soul know the right road to the gate of he who clothes the afflicted. This is the salutation to the King's son."

Then the King's son, Hordedef, stretched forth his hands to him, and raised him up, and went with him to the haven, giving to him his arm.

Dedi then said, "Let there be given me a boat, to bring me my youths and my books."

They made ready for him two boats with their rowers, and Dedi went down the river in the barge with Hordedef. When he had reached the palace, the King's son, Hordedef, entered in to give account to his Majesty the King of Upper and Lower Egypt, Khufu, the blessed.

Hordedef said, "O King, life, wealth, and health! My lord, I have brought Dedi."

His Majesty replied, "Bring him to me speedily." And his Majesty went into the hall of columns of Pharaoh, and Dedi was led before him. His Majesty said, "Why, Dedi, have I not yet seen you?"

Dedi answered, "You have not called me. Now the King calls me, and behold I come."

His Majesty said, "Is it true that you can restore a head which is smitten off?"

Dedi replied, "Truly, I know that, O King, my lord."

And his Majesty said, "Bring me a prisoner, so that his punishment may be fulfilled."

Dedi then said, "Let it not be a man, O King, my lord. We do not do such a thing even to our cattle."

A duck was brought to him, and its head was cut off. And the duck was laid on the west side of the hall, and its head on the east side of the hall. Dedi spoke his magic speech. And the duck fluttered along the ground, and its head came likewise, and when it had come part to part, the duck stood and quacked.

They brought likewise a goose before him, and he did the same magic to it. His Majesty caused an ox to be brought, and its head cast on the ground. And Dedi spoke his magic speech, and the ox stood upright behind him, and followed him with his halter trailing on the ground.

King Khufu asked, "Is it true what is said, that you know the number of the designs of the dwelling of Tehuti?"

Dedi replied, "Pardon me, I know not their number, O King, but I know where they are."

And his Majesty said, "Where is that?"

Dedi replied, "There is a chest of whetstone in a chamber named the plan-room, in Heliopolis. They are in this chest. O King, my lord, it is not I that is to bring them to you."

And his Majesty said, "Who, then, is it that shall bring them to me?"

Dedi answered, "It is the eldest of the three children who are in the body of Rud-didet who shall bring them to you."

His Majesty said, "Would that it may be as you say! But who is this Rud-didet?"

And Dedi replied, "She is the wife of a priest of Ra, lord of Sakhebu. She has conceived these three sons by Ra, lord of Sakhebu, and the god has promised her that they shall fulfil this noble office of reigning over all this land, and that the eldest of them shall be high-priest in Heliopolis."

His Majesty's heart became troubled for this, but Dedi spoke to him again, "What is this that you think, O King, my lord? Is it because of these three children? I tell you your son shall reign, and your son's son, and then one of them."

His Majesty said, "And when shall Rud-didet bear these?"

Dedi replied, "She shall bear them on the twenty-fifth of the month Tybi."

And his Majesty said, "When the banks of the canal of Letopolis are cut, I will walk there so that I may see the temple of Ra, lord of Sakhebu."

Dedi replied, "Then I will ensure that there be four cubits of water by the banks of the canal of Letopolis."

When his Majesty returned to his palace, his Majesty said, "Let them place Dedi in the house of the royal son Hordedef, that he may dwell with him, and let them give him a daily portion of 1,000 loaves, 100 draughts of beer, an ox, and 100 bunches of onions." The councillors did everything as his Majesty commanded.

One day it came to pass that Rud-didet felt the pains of birth. And the majesty of Ra, Lord of Sakhebu, said to Isis, to Nebhat, to Meskhent, to Hakt, and to Khnemu, "Go and deliver Rud-didet of these three children that she shall bear, who are to fulfil this noble office over all this land, and that they may build up your temples, furnish your altars with offerings, supply your tables of libation, and increase your endowments."

Then these deities went in the form of dancing-girls, and Khnemu was with them as a porter. They drew near to the house of Ra-user, and found him standing, with his girdle fallen. And they played before him with their musical instruments.

But he said to them, "My ladies, behold, here is a woman who feels the pains of birth."

They said to him, "Let us see her, for we know how to help her."

And he replied, "Come, then."

They entered in straightway to Rud-didet, and they closed the door on her and on themselves. Then Isis stood before her, and Nebhat stood behind her, and Hakt helped her.

And Isis said, "O child, by your name of User-ref, do not do violence." And the child came upon her hands, as a child of a cubit, for its bones were strong, the beauty of its limbs was like gold, and its hair was like true lapis-lazuli. They washed him, and prepared him, and placed him on a carpet on the brickwork.

Then Meskhent approached him and said, "This is a king who shall reign over all the land." And Khnemu gave strength to his limbs.

Then Isis stood before her, and Nebhat stood behind her, and Hakt helped her. And Isis said, "O child, by your name of Sah-ra, stay not in her."

Then the child came upon her hands, a child of a cubit, its bones were strong, the beauty of its limbs was like gold, and its hair was like true lapis-lazuli. They washed him, and prepared him, and laid him on a carpet on the brickwork.

Then Meskhent approached him and said, "This is a king who shall reign over all the land." And Khnemu gave strength to his limbs.

Then Isis stood before her, and Nebhat stood behind her, and Hakt helped her. And Isis said, "O child, by your name of Kaku, remain not in darkness in her."

And the child came upon her hands, a child of a cubit its bones were strong, the beauty of its limbs was like gold, and its hair was like true lapis-lazuli.

And Meskhent approached him and said, "This is a king who shall reign over all the land." And Khnemu gave strength to his limbs.

They washed him, and prepared him, and laid him on a carpet on the brickwork. And the deities went out, having delivered Rud-didet of the three children. And they said, "Rejoice! O Ra-user, for behold three children are born to you."

He said to them, "My ladies, and what shall I give to you? Give this bushel of barley here to your porter, that you may take it as your reward to the brew-house."

Khnemu loaded himself with the bushel of barley. And they went away toward the place from which they came. And Isis spoke to these goddesses, and said, "Why have we not blessed these children with a marvel, something that we may tell their father who has sent us?"

Then made they the divine diadems of the King, and laid them in the bushel of barley. And they caused the clouds to come with wind and rain, and they turned back again to the house.

They said, "Let us put this barley in a closed chamber, sealed up, until we return northward, dancing." They placed the barley in a close chamber.

Rud-didet purified herself, with a purification of fourteen days. And she said to her handmaid, "Is the house made ready?"

And she replied, "All things are made ready, but the brewing barley is not yet brought."

Rud-didet said, "Why is the brewing barley not yet brought?"

The servant answered, "It would have been long since ready if the barley had not been given to the dancing-girls, who then laid it in the chamber under their seal."

Rud-didet said, "Go down, and bring it, and Ra-user shall give them something else in its stead when he comes."

The handmaid went, and opened the chamber, where she heard talking and singing, music and dancing, quavering, and all things which are performed for a king in his chamber. She returned and told to Rud-didet all that she had heard. Rud-didet went to the chamber, but she could not find the source of the sounds. When she laid her temple to the sack, she found that the sounds were in it.

She placed the sack of barley in a chest, and put that in another locker, and tied it fast with leather, and laid it in the storeroom. and sealed it. And Ra-user came from the field, and Rud-didet repeated to him these things, and his heart was glad above all things, and they sat down and made a joyful day.

It came to pass that Rud-didet was angry with her servant, and beat her with stripes. And the servant said to those that were in the house, "Shall this hurt be be done to me? She has borne three kings, and I will go and tell this to his Majesty King Khufu the blessed."

She went, and found the eldest brother of her mother, who was binding his flax on the floor. And he said to her, "Where are you going, my little maid?" She told him of all these things. And her brother said to her, "Why do you come to me? Shall I agree to treachery?"

He took a bunch of the flax to her, and laid on her a violent blow. The servant then went to fetch a handful of water, and a crocodile carried her away. Her uncle went to tell of this to Rud-didet, and he found Rud-didet sitting, her head on her knees, and her heart sad beyond measure. And he said to her, "My lady, why do you grieve so?"

She answered, "It is because of this little wretch that was in the house. She went out saying, 'I will go and tell it.'"

And he bowed his head to the ground, and said, "My lady, she came and told me of these things, and made her complaint to me, and I laid on her a violent blow. And she went forth to draw water, and a crocodile carried her away."

Sadly, the rest of this tale is lost...

The Peasant And The Workwoman

*This story has been edited and adapted from Egyptian Tales,
published in 1901 on behalf of the Co-operative Publishing Society
by The Colonial Press, New York and London.*

There dwelt in the Sekhet Hemat, or Salt Country, a peasant called
the Sekhti, with his wife and children, his asses and his dogs, and
he trafficked in all good things of the Sekhet Hemat to Henenseten.
He went with rushes, natron, and salt, with wood and pods, with
stones and seeds, and all good products of the Sekhet Hemat.

This Sekhti journeyed to the south to Henenseten, and when he
came to the lands of the house of Fefa, north of Denat, he found a
man there standing on the bank, a man called Hemti, the workman,
son of a man called Asri, who was a serf of the high-steward
Meruitensa.

When he saw Sekhti's fine asses, Hemti said, , "O that some good
god would grant me the skill to steal the goods of Sekhti from
him!"

The Hemti's house was by the dike of the tow-path, which was
straightened, and no wider than the width of a waistcloth. On one
side of it was water, and on the other side of it grew corn. Hemti

said then to his servant, "Hasten! Bring me a shawl from the house," and it was brought instantly.

Then spread he out this shawl on the face of the dike, and it lay with its fastening on the water and its fringe on the corn. Sekhti approached along the path used by all men.

Hemti said, "Have a care, Sekhti! You are not going to trample on my clothes!"

Sekhti said, "I will do as you like. I will pass carefully." He then went up on the higher side.

But Hemti said, "Would you trample my corn, instead of using the path?"

Sekhti replied, "I am going carefully. This high field of corn is not my choice, for you have stopped the path with your clothes, but you will not let us pass by the side of the path?"

Just then one of the asses filled its mouth with a cluster of corn, and Hemti cried, "Look! I shall take away your ass, Sekhti, for eating my corn. It will have to pay according to the amount of the injury."

Said Sekhti, "I am going carefully. The one way is stopped, so took I my ass by the higher ground, but you seize it for filling its mouth with a cluster of corn? Moreover, I know to whom this domain belongs, even to the lord steward Meruitensa. He it is who smites every robber in this whole land, so shall I then be robbed in his domain?"

Hemti replied, "This is the proverb which men speak: 'A poor man's name is only his own matter.' I am he of whom you spoke, even the lord steward of whom you think."

Thereon he took branches of green tamarisk and scourged all his limbs, took the asses, and drove them into the pasture. Sekhti wept very greatly.

Hemti said, "Do not lift up your voice, Sekhti, or you shall go to the demon of silence."

Sekhti answered, "You beat me, you steal my goods, and now would take away even my voice, O demon of silence! If you will restore my goods, then will I cease to cry out at your violence."

Sekhti stayed the whole day petitioning Hemti, but he would not give ear to him. Sekhti went his way to Khenensuten to complain to the lord steward Meruitensa. He found him coming out from the door of his house to embark on his boat, that he might go to the judgment-hall.

Sekhti said, "Ho! Turn, that I may please your heart with this discourse. Please, send one of your followers to me so that I can tell him of all that has happened so that he can repeat the tale to you."

The lord steward Meruitensa made his follower, whom he chose, go straight to him, and Sekhti sent him back with an account of all these matters. Then the lord steward Meruitensa accused Hemti in front of the nobles who sat with him, and they said to him, "By your leave. As to this Sekhti of yours, let him bring a witness. It is our custom with our people. Witnesses come with them, and that is our custom. Then it will be fitting to beat this Hemti for a trifle of natron and a trifle of salt, for if he is commanded to pay for it, he will pay for it."

But the high steward Meruitensa held his peace, for he would not reply to these nobles, but would reply to the Sekhti. Sekhti came to appeal to the lord steward Meruitensa, and said:

"O my lord steward, greatest of the great, guide of the needy.

Let us embark on the lake of truth.

May you sail upon it with a fair wind,

May your mainsail not fly loose.

May there not be lamentation in your cabin,

May not misfortune come after you.

May not your mainstays be snapped,

May you not run aground.

May not the wave seize you,

May you not taste the impurities of the river,

May you not see the face of fear.

May the fish come to you without escape,

May you reach to plump water-fowl.

For you are the orphan's father, the widow's husband,

The desolate woman's brother, the garment of the motherless.

Let me celebrate your name in this land for every virtue,

A guide without greediness of heart,

A great one without any meanness.

Destroying deceit, encouraging justice,

Coming to the cry, and allowing utterance.

Let me speak, do you hear and do justice,

O praised! whom the praised ones praise.

Abolish oppression, I am overladen,

Reckon with me, behold me defrauded."

Now the Sekhti made this speech in the time of the majesty of the blessed King Neb-ka-n-ra. The lord steward Meruitensa went away straight to the King and said, "My lord, I have found one of these Sekhti, excellent of speech. In very truth, stolen are his goods, and he has come to complain to me of the matter."

His Majesty said, "As you wish that I may see health, lengthen out his complaint, without replying to any of his speeches. He who desires to continue speaking should be silent. Bring us his words in writing, that we may listen to them. But provide for his wife and his children, and let the Sekhti himself also have a living. You must give him his portion without letting him know that you are the one who is giving it to him."

There were given to the Sekhti four loaves and two draughts of beer each day, which the lord steward Meruitensa provided for him, giving it to a friend of his, who furnished it to him. Then the lord steward Meruitensa sent the governor of the Sekhet Hemat to make provision for the wife of the Sekhti, that being three rations of corn each day.

Then the Sekhti came a second time, and even a third time, to the lord steward Meruitensa, but he told two of his followers to go to the Sekhti, and seize him, and beat him with staves. But he came again, even to six times, and said, "My Lord Steward…

"Destroying deceit, and encouraging justice,

Raising up every good thing, and crushing every evil,

As plenty comes removing famine,

As clothing covers nakedness,

As clear sky after storm warms the shivering,

As fire cooks that which is raw,

As water quenches the thirst,

Look with your face upon my lot,

do not covet, but content me without fail,

do the right and do not evil, "

But yet Meruitensa would not listen to his complaint, and the Sekhti came yet, and yet again, even to the ninth time. Then the lord steward told two of his followers to go to the Sekhti, and the Sekhti feared that he should be beaten again. But the lord steward Meruitensa then said to him, "Fear not, Sekhti, for what you have done. The Sekhti has made many speeches, delightful to the heart of his Majesty, and I take an oath, as I eat bread, and as I drink water, that you shall be remembered to eternity. Moreover, you shall be satisfied when you shall hear of your complaints."

He then had a scribe write on a clean roll of papyrus each petition to the end, and the lord steward Meruitensa sent it to the majesty of the King Neb-ka-n-ra, blessed, and it was good to him more than anything that is in the whole land.

His Majesty said to Meruitensa, "Judge it yourself. I do not desire it."

The lord steward Meruitensa made two of his followers to go to the Sekhet Hemat, and bring a list of the household of the Sekhti, and its amount was six persons, beside his oxen and his goats, his wheat and his barley, his asses and his dogs, and moreover he gave all that which belonged to the Hemti to the Sekhti, including all of his property and his officers, and the Sekhti was beloved of the King more than all his overseers, and ate of all the good things of the King, with all his household.

The Shipwrecked Sailor

This story has been edited and adapted from Egyptian Tales, published in 1901 on behalf of the Co-operative Publishing Society by The Colonial Press, New York and London.

The wise servant said, "Let your heart be satisfied, O my lord, for we have come back to the country. After we have long been on board, and rowed much, the prow has at last touched land. All the people rejoice, and embrace us one after another. Moreover, we have come back in good health, and not a man is lost, although we have been to the ends of Wawat, and gone through the land of Senmut. We have returned in peace, and our land is safe. Hear me, my lord, for I have no other refuge. Wash now, and turn the water over your fingers, then go and tell the tale to the Majesty."

His lord replied, "Your heart continues still its wandering words! But although the mouth of a man may save him, his words may also cover his face with confusion. Will you do then as your heart moves you? Tell your tale quietly."

The sailor then answered, "Now I shall tell my tale…"

I was going to the mines of Pharaoh, and I went down on the sea on a ship of 150 cubits long and forty cubits wide, with 150 of the best Egyptian sailors, who had seen heaven and earth, and whose hearts were stronger than lions. They had said that the wind would not be contrary, or that there would be none. But as we approached the land the wind arose, and threw up waves eight cubits high. As for me, I seized a piece of wood, but those who were in the vessel perished, without one remaining alive.

A wave threw me on an island and for three days I was alone, without a companion beside my own heart. I laid myself down in a thicket, and the shadow covered me. Then stretched I my limbs to try to find something to eat. I found figs and grapes, all manner of good herbs, berries and grain, melons of all kinds, fishes and birds. Nothing was lacking. And I satisfied myself, and left on the ground the things I couldn't carry. I dug a pit, I lighted a fire, and I made a burnt-offering to the gods.

Suddenly I heard a noise like thunder, which I thought to be that of a wave of the sea. The trees shook, and the earth was moved. I uncovered my face, and I saw that a serpent drew near. He was thirty cubits long, and his beard was longer than two cubits. His body was as overlaid with gold, and his colour was that of true lazuli. He coiled himself before me.

Then he opened his mouth, while I lay on my face before him, and he said to me, "What has brought you, what has brought you, little one, what has brought you? If you do not answer speedily I will make you know yourself! As a flame you shall vanish, if you do not tell me something I have not already heard, or which I knew not, before you came here."

Then he took me in his mouth and carried me to his resting-place, and laid me down without any hurt. I was whole and sound, and nothing was gone from me. Then he opened his mouth again, while I lay on my face before him, and he said, "What has brought you, what has brought you, little one, what has brought you to this isle which is in the sea, and of which the shores are in the midst of the waves?"

Then I replied to him, and holding my arms low before him, I said to him, "I was embarked for the mines by the order of the majesty, in a ship. 150 cubits was its length, and the width of it forty cubits. It had 150 sailors, who had seen heaven and earth, and the hearts of whom were stronger than lions. They said that the wind would not be contrary, or that there would be none. Each of them exceeded his companion in the prudence of his heart and the strength of his arm, and I was not beneath any of them. A storm came upon us while we were on the sea. We could not make the shore before the wind waxed yet greater, and the waves rose even eight cubits. As for me, I seized a piece of wood, while those who were in the boat perished, and I was left alone here for three days. I was brought to this isle by a wave of the sea."

Then said he to me, "Fear not, fear not, little one, and don't be sad. If you have come to me, it is God who has let you live. For it is he who has brought you to this isle of the blessed, where nothing is lacking, and which is filled with all good things. See now, you shall pass one month after another, until you shall be four months in this isle. Then a ship shall come from your land with sailors, and you shall leave with them and go to your country, and you shall die in your town.

"This conversation is pleasing to me, and he who tastes of it passes over his misery. I will tell you about this isle. I am here with my brethren and my children around me. We are seventy-five serpents, children and kindred. There is also a young girl who was brought to me by chance, and on whom the fire of heaven fell, and burnt her to ashes.

"As for you if you are strong, and if your heart waits patiently, you shall press your infants to your bosom and embrace your wife. You shall return to your house, which is full of all good things. You shall see your land, where you shall dwell in the midst of your kindred."

Then I bowed, in my obeisance, and I touched the ground before him. I spoke quietly, "I shall tell of your presence to Pharaoh. I shall make him know of your greatness, and I will bring to you the sacred oils and perfumes, and incense of the temples with which all gods are honoured. I shall tell of all that I now see, and there shall be rendered to you praises before the fulness of all the land. I shall slay asses for you in sacrifice, I shall pluck birds for you, and I shall bring for you ships full of all kinds of the treasures of Egypt, as is comely to do unto a god, a friend of men in a far and unknown country"

Then he smiled at my speech, because of what was in his heart, for he said to me, "You art not rich in perfumes, for all that you have is common incense. As for me I am Prince of the land of Punt, and I have perfumes. Only the oil which you describe is not common in this isle. But, when you depart from this place, you shall never see this isle again, for it shall be changed into waves.'

Later, when the ship drew near, according to all that he had told me before, I got up into a high tree, to strive to see those who were within the ship. Then I came and told to him, but he already knew all about this matter.

Then he said to me, "Farewell, farewell. Go home, little one. See again your children, and let your name be good in your town. These are my wishes for you."

Then I bowed before him, and held my arms low, and he gave me gifts of precious perfumes, of cassia, of sweet woods, of kohl, of cypress, an abundance of incense, of ivory tusks, of baboons, of apes, and all kinds of precious things. I embarked all in the ship, which was come, and, bowing myself, I prayed God for him.

Then he said to me, "You shall come to your country in two months. You shall press to your bosom your children, and you shall rest in your tomb."

After this I went down to the shore to the ship, and I called to the sailors who were there. Then on the shore I rendered adoration to the master of this isle and to those who dwelt therein.

The sailor finished his tale and said, "Now, we return to the house of Pharaoh in the second month, according to all that the serpent has said. We shall approach the palace, and I shall go in before Pharaoh, and I shall bring the gifts which I have brought from this isle into the country. Then he shall thank me before the fulness of all the land. He will grant me a follower, and lead me to the courtiers of the King. Cast your eye upon me, now that I am come to land again, after all that I have seen and heard. Hear my prayer, for it is good to listen to people. It was said to me, 'Become a wise man, and you shall come to honour,' and behold I have become such."

This is finished from its beginning to its end, even as it was found in a writing. It is written by the scribe of cunning fingers, Ameni-amen-aa. May he live in life, wealth, and health!

The Adventures Of Sanehat

This story has been edited and adapted from Egyptian Tales, published in 1901 on behalf of the Co-operative Publishing Society by The Colonial Press, New York and London.

The hereditary prince, royal seal-bearer, confidential friend, judge, keeper of the gate of the foreigners, true and beloved royal acquaintance, the royal follower Sanehat says:

I attended my lord as a follower of the King, of the house of the hereditary princess, the greatly favoured, the royal wife, Ankhet-Usertesen, who shares the dwelling of the royal son Amenemhat in Kanefer.

In the thirtieth year, the month Paophi, the seventh day, the god entered his horizon, for the King Sehotepabra flew up to heaven and joined the sun's disk, and the follower of the god met his maker. The palace was silenced, and in mourning, the great gates were closed, the courtiers crouching on the ground, the people in hushed mourning.

His Majesty had sent a great army with the nobles to the land of the Temehu (now Libya), with his son and heir, the good god King Usertesen as their leader. Now he was returning, and had brought away living captives and all kinds of cattle without end. The councillors of the palace had sent to the West to let the King know the matter that had come to pass in the inner hall. The messenger was to meet him on the road, and reach him at the time of evening, for the matter was urgent.

The king said, "A hawk had soared with his followers," but he did not let the army know of these events. Even if the royal sons who commanded in that army were to send a message, he was not to speak to a single one of them.

But I was standing near, and heard his voice while he was speaking. I fled far away, my heart beating, my arms failing, for a trembling had fallen on all my limbs. I turned about in running to seek a place to hide, and I threw myself between two bushes, to wait while all should pass by. Then I turned toward the south, not from wishing to come into this place, for I knew not if war was declared, nor even thinking to live here. I turned my back to the sycamore, I reached Shi-Seneferu, and rested on the open field.

In the morning I went on and overtook a man, who passed by the edge of the road. He asked of me mercy, for he feared me. By the evening I drew near to Kher-ahau, and I crossed the river on a raft without a rudder. Carried over by the west wind, I passed over to the east to the quarries of Aku and the land of the goddess Herit, mistress of the red mountain, Gebel Ahmar.

Then I fled on foot, northward, and reached the walls of the prince, built to repel the Sati. I crouched in a bush for fear of being seen by the guards, changed each day, who watch on the top of the fortress. I took my way by night, and at the lighting of the day I reached Peten, and turned toward the valley of Kemur.

Then thirst hastened me on. I dried up, and my throat narrowed, and I said, "This is the taste of death." When I lifted up my heart and gathered strength, I heard a voice and the lowing of cattle. I saw men of the Sati, and one of them, a friend to Egypt, knew me. He gave me water and boiled me milk, and I went with him to his camp. They did me good turns, and one tribe passed me on to another. I passed on to Sun, and reached the land of Adim.

When I had dwelt there half a year Amu-an-shi, who is the Prince of the Upper Tenu, sent for me and said, "Dwell with me so that you may hear the speech of Egypt."

He said this for that he knew of my excellence, and had heard tell of my worth, for men of Egypt who were there with him bore witness of me. He said to me, "Why have you come here? Has a matter come to pass in the palace? Has the King of the two lands, Sehotepabra, gone to heaven? We have not heard any such news."

But I answered with concealment, and said, "When I came from the land of the Temehu, and my desires changed, I did not flee by reason of remorse. I am not a fugitive. I have not failed in my duty, my mouth has not said any bitter words, I have not heard any evil counsel, nor has my name come into the mouth of a magistrate. I know not by what I have been led into this land."

And Amu-an-shi said, "This is by the will of the god, the King of Egypt, for what is a land like if it know not that excellent god, of whom the dread is upon the lands of strangers, as they dread Sekhet in a year of pestilence?"

I spoke to him, and replied, "Forgive me. His son now enters the palace, and has received the heritage of his father. He is a god who has none like him, and there is none before him. He is a master of wisdom, prudent in his designs, excellent in his decrees, with good-will to any man who goes or who comes. He subdued the land of strangers while his father yet lived in his palace, and he rendered account of that which his father destined him to perform. He is a brave man, who strikes with his sword, a valiant one, who has no equal. He springs upon the barbarians, and throws himself on the spoilers. He breaks the horns and weakens the hands, and those whom he smites cannot raise the buckler. He is fearless, and dashes the heads, and none can stand before him. He is swift of foot, to destroy those who flee, and none who flees from him reaches his home.

"His heart is strong in his time. He is a lion who strikes with the claw, and never has he turned his back. His heart is closed to pity, and when he sees multitudes, he leaves none to live behind him. He is a valiant one who springs in front when he sees resistance, he is a warrior who rejoices when he flies on the barbarians. He seizes the buckler, he rushes forward, he never needs to strike again, he slays and none can turn his lance, and when he takes the bow the barbarians flee from his arms like dogs. The great goddess has given him the power to strike those who know her not, and if he reaches forth he spares none, and leaves naught behind.

"He is a friend of great sweetness, who knows how to gain love. His land loves him more than itself, and rejoices in him more than in its own god, for men and women run to his call. A king, he has ruled from his birth. He, from his birth, has increased births, a sole being, a divine essence, by whom this land rejoices to be governed. He enlarges the borders of the South, but he covets not the lands of the North. He does not smite the Sati, nor crush the Nemau-shau. If he descends here, let him know your name, by the homage which you will pay to his majesty. For he refuses not to bless the land which obeys him."

And he replied to me, "Egypt is indeed happy and well settled. You are far from it, but whilst you are with me I will do good to you."

He placed me before his children, he married his eldest daughter to me, and gave me the choice of all his land, even the best of his lands on the border of the next land. It is a goodly land. Iaa is its name. There are figs and grapes. There is wine commoner than water, and abundant is the honey. Many are its olives, and all fruits are upon its trees. There are barley and wheat, and cattle of kinds without end. This was truly a great thing that he granted me, when the prince came to invest me, and establish me as prince of a tribe in the best of his land.

I had my continual portion of bread and of wine each day, of cooked meat, of roasted fowl, as well as the wild game which I took, or which was brought to me, beside what my dogs captured. They made me much butter, and prepared milk of all kinds. I passed many years, and the children that I had became great, each ruling his tribe.

When a messenger went or came to the palace, he turned aside from the way to come to me, for I helped every man. I gave water to the thirsty, I set on his way him who went astray, and I rescued the robbed. The Prince of the Tenu appointed me to be general of his soldiers and I commanded the Sati who went to strike and turn back the princes of other lands. In every land which I attacked I played the champion, I took the cattle, I led away the vassals, I carried off the slaves, and I slew the people, by my sword, my bow, my marches and my good devices. I was excellent to the heart of my prince, and he loved me when he knew my power, and set me over his children when he saw the strength of my arms.

One day a champion of the Tenu came to defy me in my tent. He was a bold man without equal, for he had vanquished the whole country. He said, "Let Sanehat fight with me", for he desired to overthrow me. He thought to take my cattle for his tribe.

The prince counselled with me. I said, "I do not know him. I certainly am not of his degree, as I live far from his place. Have I ever opened his door, or leaped over his fence? It is some envious jealousy from seeing me. Does he think that I am like some steer among the cows, whom the bull overthrows? If this is a wretch who thinks to enrich himself at my cost, not a Bedawi and a Bedawi fit for fight, then let us put the matter to judgment. Truly, a bull loves battle, but a vainglorious bull turns his back for fear of contest. If he has a heart for combat, let him speak what he pleases. Will God forget what he has ordained, and how that shall be known?"

I lay down, and when I had rested I strung my bow, I made ready my arrows, I loosened my poniard, and I furbished my arms. At dawn the land of the Tenu came together. It had gathered its tribes and called all the neighbouring people, and spoke of nothing but the fight. Each heart burnt for me, with men and women crying out, for each heart was troubled for me, and they said, "Is there another strong one who would fight with him? His adversary has a buckler, a battle-axe, and an armful of javelins."

Then I drew him to the attack. I turned aside his arrows, and they struck the ground in vain. One drew near to the other, and he fell on me, and then I shot him. My arrow fastened in his neck. He cried out, and fell on his face. I drove his lance into him, and raised my shout of victory on his back. While all the men of the land rejoiced, I, and his vassals whom he had oppressed, gave thanks unto Mentu. This prince, Amu-an-shi, embraced me. Then I carried off his goods and took his cattle, just as he had wished to do to me. I seized what was in his tent, and I spoiled his dwelling. As time went on I increased the richness of my treasures and the number of my cattle.

Petition To The King Of Egypt

Having fled away as a fugitive, now all in the palace give me a good name. After I had been dying of hunger, now I give bread to those around me. I had left my land naked, and now I am clothed in fine linen. After having been a wanderer without followers, now I possess many serfs. My house is fine, my land wide, and my memory is established in the temple of all the gods.

And let this flight obtain your forgiveness, that I may be appointed in the palace, and that I may see the place where my heart dwells. How great a thing is it that my body should be embalmed in the land where I was born! To return there is happiness. I have made offering to God to grant me this thing. His heart suffers who has run away to a strange land. Let the gods hear the prayer of he who is far off, that he may revisit the place of his birth, and the place from which he fled.

May the King of Egypt be gracious to me that I may live through his favour. I render my homage to the mistress of the land, who is in his palace. May I hear the news of her children, and thus will my limbs grow young again. Now old age comes, feebleness seizes me, my eyes are heavy, my arms are feeble, my legs will not move, and my heart is slow. Death draws near to me, and soon shall they lead me to the city of eternity. Let me follow the mistress of all.

Let her tell me the excellencies of her children. May she bring eternity to me.

Then the majesty of King Kheper-ka-ra, the blessed, spoke upon my desire that I had made known to him. His Majesty sent presents to me from the King, that he might enlarge the heart of his servant, like to the province of any strange land, and the royal sons who are in the palace addressed themselves to me.

Copy of the Decree, Which Was Brought, To Me Who Speak To You, To Lead Me Back Into Egypt

The Horus, life of births, lord of the crowns, life of births, King of Upper and Lower Egypt, Kheper-ka-ra, son of the Sun, Amen-em-hat, ever living to eternity. Order for the follower Sanehat. Behold this order of the King is sent to you to instruct you of his will.

Now, although you have gone through strange lands from Adim to Tenu, and passed from one country to another at the wish of your heart, understand what you have done, or what has been done against you, and what is amiss? Moreover, you are not reviled, but you have not spoken in the assembly of the nobles, even if you wished to, and we know not your word. Now that you have thought on this matter, let your heart not change again. On this matter your Heaven, your queen, who is in the palace, is fixed, for she is flourishing, she is enjoying the best in the kingdom and the land, and her children are in the chambers of the palace.

Leave all the riches that you have, and that are with you. When you come into Egypt come to the palace, and when you enter the palace, bow your face to the ground before the Great House. You shall be chief among the companions. And day by day understand that you grow old, that your vigour is lost, and think about the day of your burial. You shall see yourself come to the blessed state. They will give you the bandages from the hand of Tait, the night of applying the oil of embalming. They shall follow your funeral, and visit the tomb on the day of burial, which shall be in a gilded case, the head painted with blue, a canopy of cypress wood above you, and oxen shall draw you, the singers going before you, and they shall dance the funeral dance. The weepers crouching at the door of your tomb shall cry aloud the prayers for offerings. They shall slay victims for you at the door of your pit, and your pyramid shall be carved in white stone, in the company of the royal children. Thus you shall not die in a strange land, nor be buried by the Amu. You shall not be laid in a sheepskin when you are buried. All people shall beat the earth, and lament on your body when you go to the tomb."

When this order came to me, I was in the midst of my tribe. When it was read to me, I threw myself down into the dust. I threw dust in my hair, and I went around my tent rejoicing and saying, "How may it be that such a thing is done to the servant, who with a rebellious heart has fled to strange lands? Now with an excellent deliverance, and mercy delivering me from death, you shall cause me to end my days in the palace."

Copy Of The Answer To This Order

The follower Sanehat says, "In excellent peace above everything consider of that he made this flight in his ignorance. You, the Good God, Lord of both Lands, Loved of Ra, Favourite of Mentu, the Lord of Thebes, and of Amen, lord of thrones of the lands, of Sebek, Ra, Horus, Hathor, Atmu, and of his fellow-gods, of Sopdu, Neferbiu, Samsetu, Horus, lord of the east, and of the royal uræus which rules on your head, of the chief gods of the waters, of Min, Horus of the desert, Urrit, mistress of Punt, Nut, Harnekht, Ra, all the gods of the land of Egypt, and of the isles of the sea. May they give life and peace to your nostril, may they load you with their gifts, may they give to you eternity without end, everlastingness without bound. May the fear of you be doubled in the lands of the deserts. May you subdue the circuit of the sun's disk. This is the prayer to his master of the humble servant who is saved from a foreign land.

"O wise King, the wise words which are pronounced in the wisdom of the majesty of the sovereign, your humble servant fears to tell. It is a great thing to repeat. O great God, like to Rā in fulfilling that to which he has set his hand, what am I that he should take thought for me? Am I among those whom he regards, and for whom he arranges? Your majesty is as Horus, and the strength of your arms extends to all lands.

"Then let his Majesty bring Maki of Adma, Kenti-au-ush of Khenti-keshu, and Tenus from the two lands of the Fen-khu. These are the princes who bear witness of me as to all that has passed, out of love for you. Does not Tenu believe that it belongs to you like your dogs? Behold this flight that I have made. I did not have it in my heart, for it was like the leading of a dream, as a man of Adehi sees himself in Abu, as a man of the plain of Egypt who sees himself in the deserts. There was no fear, there was no hastening after me, I did not listen to an evil plot, my name was not heard in the mouth of the magistrate, but my limbs went, my feet wandered, my heart drew me. My god commanded this flight, and drew me on, but I am not stiff-necked. Does a man fear when he sees his own land? Ra spread your fear over the land, your terrors in every strange land. See me now in the palace, see me in this place, and you who is over all the horizon, the sun rises at your pleasure, the water in the rivers is drunk at your will, and the wind in heaven is breathed at your speaking.

"I who speak to you shall leave my goods to the generations to follow in this land. And as to this messenger who is come, let your majesty do as it pleases him, for one lives by the breath that you give. O you who art beloved of Ra, of Horus, and of Hathor, Mentu, lord of Thebes, desires that your august nostril should live forever."

I made a feast in Iaa, to pass over my goods to my children. My eldest son was leading my tribe, so all my goods passed to him, and I gave him my corn and all my cattle, my fruit, and all my pleasant trees. When I had taken my road to the south, and arrived at the roads of Horus, the officer who was over the garrison sent a messenger to the palace to give notice. His Majesty sent the good overseer of the peasants of the King's domains, and boats laden with presents from the King for the Sati who had come to conduct me to the roads of Horus. I spoke to each one by his name, and I gave the presents to each as was intended. I received and I returned the salutation, and I continued thus until I reached the city of Thetu.

When the land was brightened, and the new day began, four men came with a summons for me, and the four men went to lead me to the palace. I saluted with both my hands on the ground. The royal children stood at the courtyard to conduct me, and the courtiers who were to lead me to the hall brought me on the way to the royal chamber.

I found his Majesty on the great throne in the hall of pale gold. Then I threw myself on my belly, for this god, in whose presence I was, knew me not. He questioned me graciously, but I was as one seized with blindness. My spirit fainted, my limbs failed, my heart was no longer in my bosom, and I knew the difference between life and death.

His Majesty said to one of the companions, "Lift him up, let him speak to me." And his Majesty said, "Behold, you have come, you have trodden the deserts, you have played the wanderer. Decay falls on you, old age has reached you. It is no small thing that your body should be embalmed, that the Pedtiu shall not bury you. Do not be silent and speechless. Tell me your name. Is it fear that prevents you?"

I answered in reply, "I fear, what my lord has said and how I should answer it? I have not called on me the hand of God, but it is terror in my body, like that which brings sudden death. Now I am before you, and you are life. Let your Majesty do what pleases him."

The royal children were brought in, and his Majesty said to the Queen, "Behold, Sanehat has come as an Amu, whom the Sati have produced."

She cried aloud, and the royal children spoke with one voice, saying, before his Majesty, "Truly, it is not so, O King, my lord."

His Majesty said, "It is truly he."

Then they brought their collars, and their wands, and their sistra in their hands, and displayed them before his Majesty, and they sang:

"May your hands prosper, O King,

May the ornaments of the Lady of Heaven continue.

May the Goddess Nub give life to your nostril,

May the mistress of the stars favour you when you sail south

and north.

All wisdom is in the mouth of your Majesty,

Your uræus is on your forehead, you drive away the miserable.

You art pacified, O Ra, lord of the lands,

They call on you as on the mistress of all.

Strong is your horn,

You let fly thine arrow.

Grant the breath to him who is without it,

Grant good things to this traveller, Sanehat the Pedti, born in

the land of Egypt,

Who fled away from fear of you,

And fled this land from your terrors.

Does not the face grow pale, of him who beholds your
countenance,

Does not the eye fear, which looks upon you."

His Majesty then said, "Let him not fear, let him be freed from terror. He shall be a Royal Friend amongst the nobles. He shall be put within the circle of the courtiers. Go to the chamber of praise to seek wealth for him."

When I went out from the palace, the royal children offered their hands to me, and we walked afterward to the Great Gates. I was placed in a house of a king's son, in which were delicate things, a place of coolness, fruits of the granary, treasures of the White House, clothes of the King's garderobe, frankincense, the finest perfumes of the King and the nobles whom he loves, in every chamber. All the servitors were in their several offices.

Years were removed from my limbs. I was shaved, and polled my locks of hair. The foulness was cast to the desert with the garments of the Nemau-sha. I was clothed in fine linen, and anointed myself with the fine oil of Egypt. I laid on a bed. I gave up the sand to those who lie on it, and the oil of wood to him who would anoint himself therewith. There was given to me the mansion of a lord of serfs, which had belonged to a royal friend. Many excellent things were in its buildings, and all its wood was renewed. There were brought to me portions from the palace, thrice and four times each day, beside the gifts of the royal children, always without ceasing.

There was built for me a pyramid of stone among the pyramids. The overseer of the architects measured its ground, the chief treasurer wrote it, the sacred masons cut the well, the chief of the laborers on the tombs brought the bricks, and all good things used to make a strong building were used. I was given peasants, and a garden was made, and there were ripe fields before my mansion, as is done for the chief royal friend. My statue was inlaid with gold, its girdle of pale gold. His majesty caused it to be made. Such is not done to a man of low degree.

May I be in the favour of the King until the day shall come of my death!

Historical Notes

This section contains some brief biographical notes about the original collectors and their books featured in this collection. These notes have been adapted from those primarily on Wikipedia along with other supporting sources and notes.

Sir Ernest Alfred Thompson Wallis Budge

Sir Ernest Alfred Thompson Wallis Budge was born in 1857 in Bodmin, Cornwall. Budge left Cornwall as a boy, and eventually came to live with his maternal aunt and grandmother in London.

Budge became interested in languages before he was ten years old, but left school at the age of twelve in 1869 to work as a clerk at the retail firm of W.H. Smith, which sold books, stationery and related products. In his spare time, he studied Biblical Hebrew and Syriac with the aid of a volunteer tutor named Charles Seeger. Budge became interested in learning the ancient Assyrian language in 1872, when he also began to spend time in the British Museum. Budge's tutor introduced him to the Keeper of Oriental Antiquities, the pioneer Egyptologist Samuel Birch, and Birch's assistant, the Assyriologist George Smith. Smith helped Budge occasionally with his Assyrian. Birch allowed the youth to study cuneiform tablets in his office and obtained books for him from the British Library of Middle Eastern travel and adventure, such as Austen Henry Layard's Nineveh and Its Remains.

From 1869 to 1878, Budge spent his free time studying Assyrian, and during these years, often spent his lunch break studying at St. Paul's Cathedral. John Stainer, the organist of St. Paul's, noticed Budge's hard work, and met the youth. He wanted to help the working-class boy realise his dream of becoming a scholar. Stainer contacted W.H. Smith, a Conservative Member of Parliament, and the former Liberal Prime Minister William Ewart Gladstone, and asked them to help his young friend. Both Smith and Gladstone agreed to help Stainer to raise money for Budge to attend the University of Cambridge.

Budge studied at Cambridge from 1878 to 1883. His subjects included Semitic languages: Hebrew, Syriac, Ge'ez and Arabic, he continued to study Assyrian independently. Budge worked closely during these years with William Wright, a noted scholar of Semitic languages, among others.

In 1883 he married Dora Helen Emerson, who died in 1926.

Budge entered the British Museum in 1883 in the recently renamed Department of Egyptian and Assyrian Antiquities. Initially appointed to the Assyrian section, he soon transferred to the Egyptian section. He studied the Egyptian language with Samuel Birch until the latter's death in 1885. Budge continued to study ancient Egyptian with the new Keeper, Peter le Page Renouf, until the latter's retirement in 1891.

Between 1886 and 1891, Budge was assigned by the British Museum to investigate why cuneiform tablets from British Museum sites in Iraq, which were to be guarded by local agents of the Museum, were showing up in the collections of London antiquities dealers. The British Museum was purchasing these collections of what were their "own" tablets at inflated London market rates. Edward Bond, the Principal Librarian of the Museum, wanted Budge to find the source of the leaks and to seal it. Bond also wanted Budge to establish ties to Iraqi antiquities dealers in order to buy available materials at the reduced local prices, in comparison to those in London. Budge also travelled to Istanbul during these years to obtain a permit from the Ottoman Empire government to reopen the Museum's excavations at these Iraqi sites. The Museum archaeologists believed that excavations would reveal more tablets.

During his years in the British Museum, Budge also sought to establish ties with local antiquities dealers in Egypt and Iraq so that the Museum could buy antiquities from them, and avoid the uncertainty and cost of excavating. This was a 19th-century approach to building a museum collection, and it was changed markedly by more rigorous archaeological practices, technology and cumulative knowledge about assessing artefacts in place. Budge returned from his many missions to Egypt and Iraq with large collections of cuneiform tablets; Syriac, Coptic and Greek manuscripts, as well as significant collections of hieroglyphic papyri. Perhaps his most famous acquisitions from this time were the *Papyrus of Ani, a Book of the Dead*, a copy of Aristotle's lost *Constitution of Athens*, and the *Amarna* letters. Budge's prolific and well-planned acquisitions gave the British Museum arguably the best Ancient Near East collections in the world, at a time when European museums were competing to build such collections. In 1900 the Assyriologist Archibald Sayce said to Budge, "What a revolution you have effected in the Oriental Department of the

Museum! It is now a veritable history of civilisation in a series of object lessons."

Budge became Assistant Keeper in his department after Renouf retired in 1891, and was confirmed as Keeper in 1894. He held this position until 1924, specialising in Egyptology. Budge and collectors for other museums of Europe regarded having the best collection of Egyptian and Assyrian antiquities in the world as a matter of national pride, and there was tremendous competition for such antiquities among them. Museum officials and their local agents smuggled antiquities in diplomatic pouches, bribed customs officials, or simply went to friends or countrymen in the Egyptian Service of Antiquities to ask them to pass their cases of antiquities unopened. During his tenure as Keeper, Budge was noted for his kindness and patience in teaching young visitors to the British Museum.

Budge's tenure was not without controversy. In 1893 he was sued in the high court by Hormuzd Rassam for both slander and libel. Budge had written that Rassam had used his relatives to smuggle antiquities out of Nineveh and had sent only "rubbish" to the British Museum. The elderly Rassam was upset by these accusations, and when he challenged Budge, he received a partial apology that a later court considered "ungentlemanly". Rassam was supported by the judge but not the jury. After Rassam's death, it was alleged that, while Rassam had made most of the discoveries of antiquities, credit was taken by the staff of the British Museum, notably Austen Henry Layard.

Budge was also a prolific author, and he is especially remembered today for his works on ancient Egyptian religion and his hieroglyphic primers. Budge argued that the religion of Osiris had emerged from an indigenous African people:

"There is no doubt", he said of Egyptian religions in *Osiris and the Egyptian Resurrection* (1911), "that the beliefs examined herein are of indigenous origin, Nilotic or Sûdânî in the broadest signification of the word, and I have endeavoured to explain those which cannot be elucidated in any other way, by the evidence which is afforded by the Religions of the modern peoples who live on the great rivers of East, West, and Central Africa ... Now, if we examine the Religions of modern African peoples, we find that the beliefs underlying them are almost identical with those Ancient Egyptian ones described above. As they are not derived from the Egyptians, it follows that they are the natural product of the religious mind of the natives of certain parts of Africa, which is the same in all periods."

Budge's contention that the religion of the Egyptians was derived from similar religions of the people of north-eastern and central Africa was regarded as impossible by his colleagues. At the time, all but a few scholars followed Flinders Petrie in his theory that the culture of Ancient Egypt was derived from an invading "Dynastic Race," which had conquered Egypt in late prehistory.

Budge's works were widely read by the educated public and among those seeking comparative ethnological data, including James Frazer. He incorporated some of Budge's ideas on Osiris into his ever-growing work on comparative religion, *The Golden Bough*. Though Budge's books remain widely available, since his day both translation and dating accuracy have improved, leading to significant revisions. The common writing style of his era - a lack of clear distinction between opinion and incontrovertible fact - is no longer acceptable in scholarly works. According to Egyptologist James Peter Allen, Budge's books "were not too reliable when they first appeared and are now woefully outdated."

Budge was also interested in the paranormal, and believed in spirits and hauntings. Budge had a number of friends in the Ghost Club, a group in London committed to the study of alternative religions and the spirit world. He told his many friends stories of hauntings and other uncanny experiences. Many people in his day who were involved with the occult and spiritualism after losing their faith in Christianity were dedicated to Budge's works, particularly his translation of the *Egyptian Book of the Dead*. Such writers as the poet William Butler Yeats and James Joyce studied and were influenced by this work of ancient religion. Budge's works on Egyptian religion have remained consistently in print since they entered the public domain.

Budge was a member of the literary and open-minded Savile Club in London, proposed by his friend H. Rider Haggard in 1889, and accepted in 1891. He was a much sought-after dinner guest in London, his humorous stories and anecdotes being famous in his circle. He enjoyed the company of the well-born, many of whom he met when they brought to the British Museum the scarabs and statuettes they had purchased while on holiday in Egypt. Budge never lacked for an invitation to a country house in the summer or to a fashionable townhouse during the London season.

Budge was knighted in the 1920 New Year Honours for his distinguished contributions to Colonial Egyptology and the British Museum. In the same year he published his sprawling autobiography, *By Nile and Tigris*.

He retired from the British Museum in 1924, and lived until 1934. He continued to write and published several books, his last work was *From Fetish to God in Ancient Egypt* (1934).

Andrew Lang

Andrew Lang FBA was a Scottish poet, novelist, literary critic, and contributor to the field of anthropology. He is best known as a collector of folk and fairy tales. The Andrew Lang lectures at the University of St Andrews are named after him.

Lang was born on 31st March 1844 in Selkirk. He was the eldest of the eight children born to John Lang, the town clerk, and his wife Jane Plenderleath Sellar, who was the daughter of Patrick Sellar, factor to the first duke of Sutherland. On 17th April 1875, he married Leonora Blanche Alleyne, youngest daughter of C. T. Alleyne of Clifton and Barbados. She was (or should have been) variously credited as author, collaborator, or translator of Lang's Colour / Rainbow Fairy Books, which he edited.

He was educated at Selkirk Grammar School, Loretto School, and the Edinburgh Academy, as well as the University of St Andrews and Balliol College, Oxford, where he took a first class in the final classical schools in 1868, becoming a fellow and subsequently honorary fellow of Merton College. He soon made a reputation as one of the most able and versatile writers of the day as a journalist, poet, critic, and historian. In 1906, he was elected FBA.

He died of angina pectoris on 20th July 1912 at the Tor-na-Coille Hotel in Banchory, survived by his wife. He was buried in the cathedral precincts at St Andrews, where a monument can be visited in the south-east corner of the 19th century section.

Lang is now chiefly known for his publications on folklore, mythology, and religion. The earliest of his publications is *Custom and Myth* (1884). In *Myth, Ritual and Religion* (1887) he explained the "irrational" elements of mythology as survivals from more primitive forms. Lang's *Making of Religion* was heavily influenced by the 18th century idea of the "noble savage", in it, he maintained the existence of high spiritual ideas among so-called 'savage" races, drawing parallels with the contemporary interest in occult phenomena in England.

His *Blue Fairy Book* (1889) was a beautifully produced and illustrated edition of fairy tales that has become a classic. This was followed by many other collections of fairy tales, collectively known as *Andrew Lang's Fairy Books*. In the preface of the *Lilac Fairy Book* he credits his wife with translating and transcribing most of the stories in the collections.

Lang was one of the founders of "psychical research" and his other writings on anthropology include *The Book of Dreams and Ghosts* (1897), *Magic and Religion* (1901) and *The Secret of the Totem* (1905). He served as President of the Society for Psychical Research in 1911.

He collaborated with S. H. Butcher in a prose translation (1879) of Homer's *Odyssey*, and with E. Myers and Walter Leaf in a prose version (1883) of the *Iliad*, both still noted for their archaic but attractive style.

Lang's writings on Scottish history are characterised by a scholarly care for detail, a piquant literary style, and a gift for disentangling complicated questions. *The Mystery of Mary Stuart* (1901) was a consideration of the fresh light thrown on Mary, Queen of Scots, by the Lennox manuscripts in the University Library, Cambridge, approving of her and criticising her accusers.

Lang was active as a journalist in various ways, ranging from sparkling "leaders" for the Daily News to miscellaneous articles for the Morning Post, and for many years he was literary editor of Longman's Magazine.

Kate Douglas Wiggin

Kate Douglas Smith Wiggin was born in Philadelphia, the daughter of lawyer Robert N. Smith, and of Welsh descent. Kate experienced a happy childhood, even though it was coloured by the American Civil War and her father's death. Kate and her sister Nora were still quite young when their widowed mother moved her little family from Philadelphia to Portland, Maine, then, three years later, upon her remarriage, to the little village of Hollis. There Kate matured in rural surroundings, with her sister and her new baby brother Philip.

Notably, she once met the novelist Charles Dickens. Her mother and another relative had gone to hear Dickens read in Portland, but Wiggin, aged 11, was thought to be too young to warrant an expensive ticket. The following day, she found herself on the same train as Dickens and engaged him in a lively conversation for the course of the journey, an experience which she later detailed in a short memoir titled *A Child's Journey with Dickens* (1912).

Her education was spotty, consisting of a short stint at a dame school, some home schooling under the "capable, slightly impatient, somewhat sporadic" instruction of Albion Bradbury (her stepfather), a brief spell at the district school, a year as a boarder at the Gorham Female Seminary, a winter term at Morison Academy in Baltimore, Maryland, and a few months' stay at Abbot Academy in Andover, Massachusetts, where she graduated with the class of 1873. Although rather casual, this was more education than most women received at the time.

Wiggin met dry goods (specifically, linen) importer George Christopher Riggs on her way to England in 1894. The pair are said to have hit it off and had agreed to marry even before the ship docked in England. In the Ellis Island logs from Wiggin's 1894 trip back to New York City from Liverpool, the two sign their names next to each other, indicating their closeness. The pair married in New York City on March 30, 1895, at All Souls Church. George Riggs soon became one of Wiggin's biggest advocates as she became more successful.

After the marriage she continued to write under the name of Wiggin. Her literary output included popular books for adults, and with her sister, Nora A. Smith, she published scholarly work on the educational principles of Friedrich Fröbel: *Froebel's Gifts* (1895), *Froebel's Occupations* (1896), and *Kindergarten Principles and Practice* (1896), and she wrote the classic children's novel *Rebecca of Sunnybrook Farm* (1903), as well as the 1905 best-seller *Rose o' the River*. *Rebecca of Sunnybrook Farm* became an immediate bestseller, both it and *Mother Carey's Chickens* (1911) were adapted to the stage. Houghton Mifflin collected her writings in 10 volumes in 1917.

For a time, she lived at Quillcote, her summer home in Hollis, Maine. Quillcote is around the corner from the town's library, the Salmon Falls Library, which Wiggin founded in 1911. Wiggin founded the Dorcas Society of Hollis & Buxton, Maine in 1897. The Tory Hill Meeting House in the adjacent town of Buxton, Maine inspired her book, and later play, *The Old Peabody Pew* (1907).

Wiggin was an active and popular hostess in New York and in the community of Upper Largo, Scotland, where she had a summer home and where she organized plays for many years, as detailed in her memoir *My Garden of Memory*.

In 1921, Wiggin and her sister Nora Archibald Smith edited an edition of Jane Porter's *The Scottish Chiefs*, an 1809 novel of William Wallace, for the Scribner's Illustrated Classics series, illustrated by N.C. Wyeth. During the spring of 1923, Kate Wiggin travelled to England as a New York delegate to the Dickens Fellowship. There she became ill and died, at age 66, of bronchial pneumonia. At her request, her ashes were brought home to Maine and scattered over the Saco River. Her autobiography *My Garden of Memory* was published after her death. In sorting through material for her autobiography, she put many items in a box she and her sister labelled "Posthumous." Her sister Nora A. Smith later published her own reminiscences, titled *Kate Douglas Wiggin as her Sister Knew Her*, from these materials.

Wiggin was also a songwriter and composer. For *Kindergarten Chime*s (1885) and other collections for children, she wrote some of the lyrics, music, and arrangements. For *Nine Love Songs and a Carol* (1896), she composed all of the music.

Many of Kate Douglas Wiggin's novels were made into movies. Perhaps the most famous film adaptation of her books is the *Rebecca of Sunnybrook Farm* (1938 film), which stars Shirley Temple.

Nora Archibald Smith

Nora Archibald Smith was the sister of Kate Douglas Wiggin, known best for her novel *Rebecca of Sunnybrook Farm*. Both girls were born in Philadelphia to Robert Noah Smith and Helen Elizabeth (Dyer) Smith. Their father died shortly after Nora's birth and their mother then moved the family to Portland, Maine. She soon remarried and the family moved into Nora and Kate's stepfather's (Dr. Albion Bradbury) house in Hollis, Maine. It was in the farmhouse called "Quillcote" that both Nora and Kate grew up and to which they would later retire.

In 1873, while Kate attended finishing school in Andover, Massachusetts, Dr. Bradbury moved the family to California. Kate opened the first free kindergarten west of the Rocky Mountains on Silver Street in San Francisco, California while Nora was teaching in the public schools of Tucson, Arizona. In 1877 Nora was awarded an A.B. from Santa Barbara College. In 1880 Nora and Kate founded the California Kindergarten Training School together and Nora received a certificate from the school in 1881.

Nora then went on to become the superintendent of the free kindergarten on Silver Street and later to take over the running of the California Kindergarten Training School in 1889. Ms. Smith was president of the California Froebel Society, an executive member of the committee of the International Kindergarten Association, and the vice-president (1891-1892) of the kindergarten department of the National Education Association.

Nora Archibald Smith collaborated with her sister to write or edit fifteen books. Nora, a writer in her own right, also published many serial stories and academic journal articles on early childhood education. Two of Nora's poems *Doll's Calendar* and *Feast of the Doll* were set to music by composer Grace Chadbourne.

René Basset

René Basset was born in July 1855 and died in January 1924. He was a French orientalist, specialising in the Berber and Arabic languages.

René Basset was the first director of the École des lettres d'Alger, created in 1879 during the French colonisation of Algeria.

He was a member of the Société Asiatique of Paris as well as those of Leipzig and Florence. He collaborated with the *Journal Asiatique* and studied Chinese Islam.

René Basset's publications included *Étude sur la zenatia du Mzab, Notes de lexicographie berbère* (1887), *La Religion des Berbères de l'antiquité jusqu'à l'islam, Prières des musulmans chinois, Recherches sur la religion des Berbères* (1910) and *Anthologie Mille*.

During his lifetime he received many honours, including Commandeur of the Légion d'honneur, Officiere of the Ordre des Palmes Académiques, Grand-officier of the Nichan Iftikhar, Commandeur of the Order of Menelik II, and Chevalier of the Order of St. Sylvester

Hans Stumme

Hans Stumme, November 1864 to December 1936, was a German linguist, known for his research of Semitic and other Afroasiatic languages.

He studied at the universities of Tübingen, Halle, Leipzig and Strasbourg, obtaining his habilitation in 1895. While a student at Leipzig, his teachers were Ludolf Krehl, Albert Socin and Friedrich Delitzsch. In 1900 he became an associate professor of Oriental philology at Leipzig, where in 1909 he was named an honorary professor of Neo-Arabic and Hamitic languages.

He taught classes on Arabic literature and dialects of the Maghreb; and also gave lectures on Persian, Turkish, Maltese, Ge'ez, Hausa and Berber languages. He was an editor of the *Zeitschrift der Deutschen Morgenländischen Gesellschaft (Journal of the German Oriental Society)*.

Charles Monteil

Charles Monteil was born in Paris in February 1871. He was the brother of Parfait-Louis Monteil, a French colonial military officer and explorer. He was admitted to Saint-Cyr in 1892.

Monteil's brother Louis-Parfait took him to French West Africa in 1893, where he began work as a native affairs clerk, and later rose through several administrative levels and held many positions. At one time he was the deputy of Maurice Delafosse in the Ivory Coast. In 1898 Monteil was the first to have collected a soninké version of the legend of Wagadu on the founding of the Mandingo Empire. He wrote the answer to the Questionnaire concerning the legal customs of the natives of Africa issued by the Berlin-based International Union of Law and Political Economy and transmitted by the French Colonial Union. He was promoted to head of the Djenné cercle in May 1901. Between then and December 1902 he recorded 800 interviews with the educated people of the city.

Monteil was head of the French Sudan economy and trade office at the Colonial Office in Paris for two years. He was senior writer at the Caisse des dépôts et consignations in Paris from 1904 to 1911. He also lectured in Sudanese languages at the École nationale des langues orientales vivantes from 1904 to 1909. He graduated with a degree in law in 1911. He was a receiver of finance until 1936. He worked with the Comité des études historiques et scientifiques de l'AOF and the Institut d'Afrique Noire in Dakar, Senegal.

Monteil died in Tulle on 20 April 1949.

Monteil received awards from the National Agricultural Society of France in 1903, the Geographical Society of Paris in 1916 and 1924 (Gold Medal), the Institute of France (Academy of Moral and Political Sciences) in 1917 and 1925. He was made a Chevalier of the Legion of Honour and Officer of the Academy. He was a holder of the Colonial Medal (Ivory Coast). He was elected a corresponding member of the Academy of Colonial Sciences from its foundation in 1923.

About The Editor

I was born in 1962 into a predominantly sporting household – Dad being a good footballer, playing senior amateur and lower league professional football in England, as well as running a series of private businesses in partnership with mum, herself an accomplished and medal winning dancer.

I obtained a degree in History from Leeds University before wandering rather haphazardly into the emerging world of business computing in the late nineteen-eighties.

I followed a succession of amateur writing paths alongside my career in technology, including working as a freelance journalist and book reviewer, my one claim to fame being a by-line in a national newspaper in the UK, The Sunday people.

I also spent 10 years treading the boards, appearing all over the south of the UK in pantos and plays, in village halls and occasionally on the stage of a professional theatre or two.

Following the sporting theme I worked on live TV broadcasts for the BBC, ITV, TVNZ, EuroSport and others as a rugby "Stato", covering Heineken Cups, Six Nations, IRB World Sevens and IRB World Cups in the late '90's and early '00's.

You can find out more at: www.clivegilson.com